The WITCHES *of* CHISWICK

Also by Robert Rankin:

The Antipope
The Brentford Triangle
East of Ealing
The Sprouts of Wrath
Armageddon the Musical
The Came and Ate Us
The Suburban Book of the Dead
Nostradamus Ate My Hamster
The Dance of the Voodoo Handbag
The Garden of Unearthly Delights
The Greatest Show Off Earth
The Most Amazing Man Who Ever Lived
Snuff Fiction
Sex and Drugs and Sausage Rolls
Web Site Story
Waiting For Godalming
The Fandom of The Operator
The Brentford Chainstore Massacre
The Raiders of the Lost Car Park
Apocalypso
A Dog Called Demolition
Sprout Mask Replica
The Book of Ultimate Truths
The Hollow Chocolate Bunnies of
the Apocalypse

The WITCHES *of* CHISWICK

ROBERT RANKIN

GOLLANCZ
LONDON

First published in Great Britain in 2003 by
Gollancz
An imprint of the Orion Publishing Group
Orion House, 5 Upper St Martin's Lane, London WC2H 9EA

A CIP catalogue record for this book is available from the British Library

ISBN 0 575 07314 4 (hardback)
ISBN 0 575 07547 3 (export trade paperback)

Typeset by Deltatype Ltd,
Birkenhead, Merseyside

Printed in Great Britain by
Clays Ltd, St Ives plc

This book is dedicated to SPROUTLORE on the occasion of its tenth anniversary.

To those who began it, Anna Casey, Eimer Ni Mhealoid, Robert Elliot and, of course, the now legendary Pádraig Ó Méalóid a special thanks.

For contributing to the *Mercury*, among other nefarious tasks: Tom Mathews, Peter McCanney, Darren Sant, Stephen 'Wok Boy' Malone, Kaz Rathgar, Matthew Vernon, M.J. 'Simo' Simpson, Chip Livingstone, C. elsewhere, Martin Gooch, Alan Holloway, Rachel Turkington, Katie Atkinson, Stephen Gillis, Mark J. Howard, Alf Fairweather, Paul Tonks, Simon C. Owen, Mark Howard, Neil Hind, Gordon McLean, Karl Macnaughton, Leanne Whelan, Laura Haslam, Mark Bertenshaw, Mark Paris, John Cross, Richard Allinson, Diana Hesse, Neil Gardener, John Flynn, Steve Baker, Daev Walsh, George and Chelle Bell, Kryten Krytennicus, Mark Stay, Nicholas Avenell, J. Oost, Alan Sullivan, J. Hagger, Ian 'Red' Brown, James 'Elite' Grime, Lee Peglar, Joe Nolan, Emma Jones, David Hill, Sarah Laslett, Andrew 'P.A.L.F.' Bacon, Tim Keith, Stuart Lemon, Alec Sillifant, Bob Harrison, Tim McGregor, Keith Lawlor and the great Cardinal Cox, you wordy, hard-working people.

For making events what they are, and for being there since the earliest of days: Emma King, Lorraine Loveridge, Toby 'Tobes' Valois, Robert and Hazel Newman. Dr Pete and Flick, Neil Johnson, Jason Joiner, Andrea Swinsco, Hillary Simpson, Dave Elder, Anne Stokes, Matt Langley, Rev. Jim de Liscard, Meike Benzler, Nolly, Rory Lennon, Sam and Greg Elkin, Liam Proven and Kjersti, John Waggott, Liat Cohen, Jonathon Baddeley, Trond Miatyeit Hansen, Anders Holmstrom, Mike 'Sparks' Rennie, James Brophy, Leonia Carroll, Helena and Heidi, Ben Dessau and Heather Petty, Julie Rigby and Alex McLintock, Paul Atton, Mick Champion, Isabel and Debbie

Cordwell, Lizanne Davies, David Jones, Joe Ritchie, Silas Potts, Stephen Shirras, Luke Shaw, Karl Scrammell, Nicholas Avenell, Clive Duberly, Andi Evans, Sarah Laslett, Bob Tiley, James Walker, Alan Westbury, Tony Wearing, Steven Dean and Mick and Phil O'Connor.

To those who have left this mortal coil, we bid you adieu, and toast your names: John Joseph O'Dowd and the great Gerry Conlon.

To the main movers and shakers, writers of great skill and wondrous workers: Lee Justice, Dave Baker, Billy Stirling, Alix Langridge, James Shields, Stef Lancaster, and Michael Carroll.

And finally to the guy who runs it all, surprises me with ingenious ideas, and insane capers, has a strange glint in his eye, a smile and a gift of the gab that could charm the knickers off a nun. He has made Sproutlore what it is, and what it continues to be, a wonderful fanclub. The best, to James Bacon; my sincerest thanks, my good friend.

Acknowledgements also to Sean Gallagher, who thought up the title of this book.

1

It was the day after the day after tomorrow and it was raining.

Upon this particular day, the rain was bilious green, which signified a fair to middling toxicity and so was only hazardous to health if you actually went out in it.

Will Starling would have to go out in it. He was presently employed and wished to remain so.

'Winsome Wendy Wainscot, Channel Twenty's wonderful weather woman, says it will clear by Wednesday,' ventured Will's mum, a moon-faced loon with a vermilion hairpiece and hips that were a hymn to the hamburger. 'I could call you in sick, Will, and you could apply yourself to doing a few odd jobs about the home.'

'No, thanks,' said Will.

'But some of the jobs are *really* odd. They would appeal to you.'

'No, thanks,' said Will, once again.

Will's portly father, a man who never said no to a native and took his coffee as it came, raised a quizzical eyebrow to his lady wife's banter. 'The lad has work to go to, woman,' said he, forking a sausage from the mountainous pile upon his breakfasting plate, popping it into his mouth and munching upon it. 'He is now the winner of the cakes in this household, and for this much thanks, my sweet Lord of the Laminates.'

The area in which these words were exchanged was the breakfasting area of the Starling household, the household itself being housed in a housing unit in a housing tower in the housing district of the Utility Conurbation of Brentford, which was itself to be found to the west of The Great London High Rise. The housing tower was three hundred and three storeys high. The Starling household occupied a corner of the two hundred and twenty-second floor. The windows of the breakfasting area, triple-glazed in polarised polythene, faced east, which was always a blessing on Tuesdays.

(Today, this particular day, this day after the day after tomorrow, was, however, Monday.)

Regarding the breakfasting area itself, what might be said? Well, the furnishings, at least, were not entirely without interest. Will sat at the breakfasting table, upon a chair of his own design and construction, a narrow chair of wood, of antique wood, of two-by-one.

Much, of course, has been written of the wonders of two-by-one, hailed, as it was, by twentieth-century DIY enthusiasts the world over as 'The Timber of the Gods', 'The Carpenter's Friend', 'The Wood That Won The West', and many other such appellations.

You didn't see a lot of it about on this day beyond tomorrow, what with there being so few trees left to cut down and hew. Two-by-one was hard to find, although, in truth there were very few now who actually went searching.

Will's father, William Starling senior, occupied a more orthodox sit-upon: it was Post Christian Orthodox, of the IKEA persuasion. Will's father was a part-time lay preacher to the Church of IKEA (IKEA having brought out the Christian franchise some fifty years before).

Will's mother did not share her husband's faith; she remained true to the church she had grown up with. She was a Sister of Sainsbury's. Her seating was a family heirloom: a white plastic garden sofa, dating from the age of private gardens, and a collector's item in itself, should the age of the collector, or indeed the private garden, ever return. The sofa's sidearms had been cut away to afford admittance to her broad posterior. Will's mum was a very substantial woman.

But for these items of seatery, the breakfasting area was, as all other breakfasting areas in the housing tower were, *bright* and *orange*. Just the way that the future had been promised to be, in a time before it was.

'You'll need to put on your chem-proofs, Will,' said Will's mum, swallowing a fried eggette (a synthetic egg, packed with goodness and minerals) and scooping up another with her spoon. 'And your weather dome. Coffee, husband?' She proffered the plastic pot.

'As it comes,' replied her spouse, urging another sausage into his mouth, 'that's the way I like it.' He smiled winningly towards his son. 'Take heed of what your mother says,' said he, as he chewed. 'Upon this occasion she isn't talking twaddle.'

'I certainly will,' said the son of Starling. 'I never, ever take risks.' This, however, was a lie. Will *did* take risks. Will thrived upon risks. Sadly for Will, the opportunities to take risks rarely arose, but when they did, he was always ready and willing.

Will's father reached across the breakfasting area and placed a mighty hand upon the forearm of his son. 'You are a good lad, Will,' he said. 'You make your mother and me proud of you. We care about you, you know that, don't you?'

'I've never had cause to doubt it,' Will eased his arm from beneath the pressure of his pater's portly palm, 'except upon one or two occasions, such as the time that you tried to sell me to Count Otto Black's Circus Fantastique because you needed money to buy Mum a new wig.'

'A God-feeling woman can never have too many wigs,' said Will's mum, downing another fried eggette.

'It's God-*fearing*,' said her husband, helping himself to yet another sausage. 'But your mother's right, Will. Do you recall the time that your Aunt May was caught wigless at the wedding of a tribal chieftain? That reflected very poorly on the family.'

'Yes, but trying to sell me to a freak show . . .'

'A Carnival of Curiosities,' said Will's mum, downing yet another eggette. 'An Odyssey of Oddities. A Burlesque of the Bizarre. A—'

'Get out while you're winning,' said Will's dad. 'Your mother and I felt that it was the right thing to do, Will. So you could, you know, be amongst your own people, as it were.'

'But you're my own people, you're my family.'

'You know what I mean,' said Will's dad, chasing baked beanettes with his fork. 'I don't have to say the word, do I?'

'*Slim?*' said Will. 'Is that the word?'

Will's mum traced a sacred S (for Sainsbury's, not for slim) across the vastness of her breasts. Newly proffered coffee spilled over Will's dad's waistcoat.

'Now look what you've done.' Will's dad struggled to his feet, plucking at his steaming front.

'I'm slim,' said Will. 'It's not a disease. It's not something to be ashamed of.'

Sadly, however, this was *not* the case. In these days after the days after tomorrow, being slim no longer held sway when it came to looking good. These were now the days of the weighty. That mankind should grow, not only in mental but in physical stature too, was probably an inevitability (although not one that had ever been accurately predicted). But then, the science of prediction had never been noted for its accuracy – not even when the course of future events seemed obvious.

For instance: in the year of Elvis Presley's death, nineteen seventy-seven, there were, at most, several dozen Elvis impersonators in the world. By the year two thousand and two, however, there were more than thirty-five thousand. Given this expanding growth rate, it was acurately predicted that by the year two thousand and twelve, one in four people on the planet would be an Elvis impersonator.

This, of course, proved not to be the case.

The figure was actually a mere one in six.

But those days were now long in the past, and in these days, after the days after tomorrow, things were not as might have been expected. They appeared to have escaped all attempts at prediction. That the future lay in fatness had certainly slipped right past Nostradamus.

By the days after tomorrow, the average weight of the Western human was fifteen stone. By the days after the days after tomorrow, the scales were being tipped and strained at the twenty-stone mark, and rising.

But Will was a slim 'un. And although his parents were proud of him, in the way that parents always are, the social stigma of slimness was always there.

And Will was *very* slim.

The features were fine enough – noble, almost: a good strong nose and bright blue eyes and a mop of blondy hair. But his neck was of a longness, and his fingers too. And there was also an awkwardness about him. And there was an other-worldliness about him too, although this was nothing to do with his slimness. It was more to do with the fact that Will dwelt for most of his waking hours in a world of his own making: a world of romance and adventure, a world where he could *really* take some risks.

For the world that Will inhabited was not very kind to Will. Folk pointed at him in the streets, laughed as they pointed, called him 'skeleton boy' and 'you slim bastard!' They gave him a very hard time. Will ate as much as he could manage, but it didn't help.

It was no fun being different.

But different Will was, in more ways than one.

'I'm sorry, Dad,' said Will. 'I'm sorry, Mum, too.'

The coffee was cooling on Will's dad. Will's mum mopped at his waistcoast with a proprietary-brand dishcloth. 'It's all right,' she said, without conviction. 'It doesn't matter, Will. You are what you is, as Frank Zappa once said, and so long as you're happy, we're happy for you.'

'I *am* happy, Mum. I love you and Dad and I love my job too.'

'Tell me about this job of yours.' Will's dad shooed away his wife's fussing fingers. 'Is it at IKEA? Does it involve any two-by-one?'

'No,' said Will, 'It isn't and it doesn't. Have you ever heard of the Tate Gallery?'

'Is that a trick question?' Will's mum lowered her prodigious bulk once more onto her modified lounger and returned to her consumption of fried eggettes. There were still eight left on her plate and she meant to finish them before she began on her baconettes. 'I mean, will there be a forfeit if we get it wrong? Like there is at the supermarket?'

'It's not a trick question, Mum. The Tate Gallery is an ancient building in London Central. It houses paintings from the past. You remember art, surely?'

Will's mum made a face of considerable perplexity. 'Was he a presenter on daytime TV?'

'Of course your mother remembers art,' said Will's dad, resuming the demolition of his sausage mountain. 'It's when pictures were produced by hand, using coloured pigments applied with a bundle of animal hair secured at the end of a stick.'

'There's no need to be obscene,' said Will's mum. 'Honestly, putting ungodly ideas like that into the boy's head.'

'It's true,' said Will. 'The bundles of animal hair were called brushes.'

'The boy is a regular hysteric,' said Will's mum.

'Historian,' said Will's dad. 'And you have actually seen these pictures, Will?'

'Not up close.' Will, sipped at his coffee, which came as it came, but which was not altogether to his liking. 'They are housed in the vaults deep beneath the original gallery. They are far too precious and fragile to be put on display any more. They are presently being re-photographed, so that accurate reproductions can be made and displayed in the gallery. You'll be able to see the official reopening of the Tate on the home screen soon. And all the reproductions of the paintings too.'

'Why?' asked Will's mum. 'What are these *paintings* for? What do they do?'

'They don't do anything. They are art. They are beautiful works of human achievement. You simply look at them and appreciate them for what they are.'

Will's mum spooned in further eggettes. 'Do they sing?' she asked.

'No. They don't even move about.'

Will's mum shrugged her ample shoulders. 'Well, if you're happy and employed, I suppose that's all that matters.'

'I *am* happy,' said Will. 'There's something about the past that has always fascinated me. Something about the Victorian era.'

'The *what*?' asked Will's mum.

'Be silent, woman,' said Will's dad, sending another sausage stomachwards.

'The years of Queen Victoria,' said Will. 'She ruled this country, and much of the world besides, for sixty years. She died in 1901.'

'King Charles ruled for seventy-five years,' said Will's mum. 'And so did Queen Camilla.'

'I don't think you could really call that ruling,' said Will's dad, 'although I'm impressed that you should know even that. I recall as a child learning about the last of the Royal Household of England. They didn't actually rule that long – they didn't actually rule at all. They were both assassinated at their coronation. It was a virtual reality programme that did all the subsequent ruling – until it crashed in the late twenty-first century.'

'Same thing,' said Will's mum. 'The present World leader is a programme: President Adidas the 42nd. "Corporate wisdom for a better world".'

'Hmm,' went Will. 'Well, that may be as may be, but there was a time when the world was run by human beings. And in the days of Queen Victoria, there were many wonderful things. Wonderful art and wonderful architecture. And books that were written by people.'

'I once had a book,' said Will's mum, finally beginning work on her baconettes. 'I liked the pictures in that.'

'That was *not* a book,' her husband told her. 'That was a manual, for the home screen's remote control.'

'*I've* seen books,' said Will. 'And I've read them too. I've been to the British Library.'

'The boy is just full of surprises.' Will's dad held out his cup for further coffee. 'But you can call up books on the home screen.'

'Not like these Victorian books. I've read *The Adventures of Sherlock Holmes*. The works of Oscar Wilde. And amazing books by H. G. Wells, Jules Verne and Edgar Allen Poe. I go every lunchtime. I have a special pass because I work at the Tate. I can't touch the actual books, but they're all on digital.'

'I'm amazed,' said Will's dad. 'But surely you should be on your way to work now?'

'Indeed, yes.' Will finished his coffee and rose from his special chair. 'Off to work. Off to the art and the literature of the past.'

'He's a weirdo,' said Will's mum.

'He's not,' said Will's dad. 'He's simply Will.'

Will togged up in sufficient protective outerwear to ensure the prolongation of his existence and bade his farewells to his mother and father. He would have taken the lift to the ground floor, had it been working. But it wasn't working. It was broken yet again, and so Will was forced to trudge down the many, many stairs, no easy feat in a chem-proof suit that was many, many sizes too large, before braving the acid rain and plodding through it to the tram station.

Once inside he passed through decontamination – a hose-down, followed by a big blow-dry – then he raised his weather dome to admit an iris scan of his eyeballs, which confirmed his identity and present credit status, and allowed him access to the covered platform.

The never-ending shuttle train of trams, thirty-two miles of linked carriages, followed a circular route through London Central, The Great High Rise and surrounding conurbation areas. It moved with painful slowness and was dreary to behold. Will awaited the arrival of a carriage that did not look altogether full, pressed a large entry button and, as the door slid aside, stepped aboard the moving carriage.

Large folk sat upon large seats, heavily and sombrely. None raised their eyes towards young Will, nor offered him a 'good morning'. Their heads were down, their masssive shoulders slumped; all were going off to work and few were going gladly. The morning tram had never been a transport of delight.

The in-car entertainment was, upon this particular day, of the corporate morale-boosting persuasion: plump, jolly holograms, fresh-faced guys and gals, cavorted up and down the carriage, extolling the virtues of a job well done for an employer who more than just cared. At intervals they flickered and slurred, ran into reverse, or stopped altogether. The system was long overdue for an overhaul – as was most everything else.

Will settled himself into a seat and ignored the colourful chaos. He took off his rubberised mittens, fished into the pocket of his grossly oversized chem-proof and brought out his personal palm-top.

This item was something of a treasure to Will, and would be another collectible should that bygone age of collecting ever return. In this particular time there should have been marvels of technology to be had, like plasma gel eye-screens, hardwired to cranial implants, which, when worn behind the eyelids, would offer three-dimensional virtual reality with all-around-sensasound and things of that futuristic nature generally. And there were, to a degree, but they just didn't work very well. Technology had got itself just so far before it ground to a halt and started falling to pieces. Will's palm-top was almost fifty years old, built in a time when folk really knew how to build palm-tops. It was indeed his treasure.

But what Will really wanted, of course, was a book, a real book, a book of his very own. But as books no longer existed, what with there no longer being any rainforests to denude for their manufacture, he had settled for second best. Will had been downloading the contents of the British Library into his ancient palm-top. He did not consider this to be a crime, although crime indeed it was. He considered it to be an educational supplement. Certainly he had been taught things at learning classes, when a child, all those things that the state considered it necessary for him – or any other child of the citizenry – to know. But Will craved knowledge, more knowledge, more knowledge of the past.

Somewhere in him, somewhere deep, was A Need to Know, about what the past really was, about the folk who had inhabited it, about things that they had done, the adventures they'd had. What they'd known, what they'd seen, what they'd achieved. There was excitement in the past, and romance, and adventure.

Exactly why these yearnings were inside him, Will didn't know. Nor did he understand why he was so driven by them. But he did understand that it mattered (for some reason that he did not fully understand, so to speak).

But he *would* understand. He felt certain that he would.

Will had recently downloaded a number of restricted files from the British Library's mainframe, part of the British Library's collection of Victorian erotica, and installed them into his palm-top. Will was currently reading Aubrey Beardsley's novel, *Under the Hill.**

Although Will did not understand much of what Beardsley had written, the words and phraseology being of such antiquity, he was aware that he was onto something rather special. Will had researched Mr Beardsley, the 1890s being Will's favourite period: the gay nineties, they'd been called, a time of exuberance, of decadence, a time of enormous creativity.

Will almost missed his station, London Central Three. He had been engrossed in the chapter where Venus masturbates the Unicorn, and had got a bit of a stiffy on.

(Well, it is an extremely good chapter.)

* One of the most wonderful works of Victorian erotica ever written. Buy a copy.

Will switched off the palm-top, slipped it back into his chem-proof, redonned his mittens, rose, tapped the door button and departed from the eternally moving tram. He took the belowground to the Tate Terminal, passed through the retinal scan, checked in his weather wear and made his way via lifts and walkways to his place of employment.

The workroom was circular, about half an old mile in diameter and many new metres in height, with row upon row of huge, somewhat outdated and unreliable computer workstations, mounted upon IKEA terminal tops, and manned and womanned by many, many folk, all of whom exceeded Will in both years and girth.

'Morning, stick-boy,' said Jarvis Santos, a fine hunk of flesh in a triple-breasted morning suit. Jarvis was Will's superior.

'Good morning, Mr Santos,' said Will, seating himself in the big chair before his big workstation. 'Rotten old weather, eh?'

'The weather is hardly your concern. You're here to do a job. Do you think your frail little fingers can deal with it?'

'Undoubtedly,' said Will, smiling broadly.

'And get that grin off your scrawny face. Your tasking for the day is on the screen; see to it.'

'Yes, sir,' said Will.

Jarvis Santos shook his head, rippling considerable jowls. He turned and waddled away, leaving Will smiling broadly at his terminal screen. Will read the words upon it: *The works of Richard Dadd*, and there followed a brief history of this Victorian artist.

Will read these words, and then he whistled. This really couldn't be much better: Richard Dadd was one of Will's all-time favourites; a genuine Victorian genius (although, it had to be said, a complete stone-bonker too). Like many rich Victorians, Dadd had taken the Grand Tour. He had travelled through distant lands, visited and painted Egypt, moved through Africa and India and at the end of it all, had returned to England, quite mad. His father, worrying for the mental health of his son had taken Richard under his wing and was escorting him to hospital when a singular tragedy occurred. They had booked into a hotel in Cobham, in Surrey, for the night. Richard and his father had gone out for an evening walk. But Richard returned alone and hastily made away from the hotel. He had murdered his father in the woods and, according to legend, feasted on his brain.

Dadd had murdered his dad. He made it as far as France before he'd been arrested. At his trial it became apparent to all that he was hopelessly insane. He was committed to St Mary of Bethlehem's asylum, where he spent twenty years before being transferred to Broadmoor for the final twenty-two years of his life. It was at Broadmoor that he painted his acclaimed masterwork, *The Fairy Feller's Masterstroke*.*

Although the picture is only fifty-four centimetres by thirty-nine, it took Dadd nine years to paint, and it remains incomplete. It is a remarkably complex piece of work which has been interpreted in many ways. Some scholars believe it to be allegorical, a satire on the times. Others consider it to be metaphysical, embodying some great and undiscovered truth.

Its composition is this. In the foreground stands the fairy feller of the title. He holds aloft an axe and is awaiting the precise moment to swing it and cleave a large nut, which will then be fashioned into a new coach for Queen Mab. Behind the feller, the fairies look on in expectation: many fairies, beaux and ladies, strange dwarves and satyr-like creatures. And nursery-book characters too: tinker, tailor, soldier, sailor, rich man, poor man, beggar man, thief.

There is no perspective to the painting; the numerous figures, set amidst swaying grasses and voluptuous daisies, peer from the canvas as if vying for attention.

It is a very, very strange painting.

Will knew his job well enough by now. He had to visually check the digital photoscan of the painting, to ensure that the colours and textures were all in focus. It was tedious work, or certainly would have been to anyone other than Will, but Will revelled in the hugely magnified images upon the screen, viewing every brushstroke, and brushstrokes there were aplenty upon *The Fairy Feller's Masterstroke*. Dadd had obsessively repainted the faces of the characters again and again and again in his insane desperation to 'get them right'. Some stood out from the canvas by almost half a centimetre.

For the Tate to print accurate reproductions for public display, all had to be exact and correct. Will would have to check not only every centimetre, but every millimetre also. He had many automatic checking systems to aid him, of course, but as these regularly broke down, the human touch was still required.

And Will, it had to be said, possessed the human touch.

'Oh bliss,' said Will Starling. 'This is going to be very enjoyable.'

* You really should see this painting; it's in the Tate Gallery.

A big flippery-floppery sound caused Will some momentary distraction. Gladys Nanken lowered her prodigious bulk into the terminal chair next to Will. 'Morning, lovely boy,' she said, breathlessly and breathily.

'Ah.' Will turned his gaze on Gladys. It was one of those rabbit-caught-in-car-headlights kind of gazes.

'And how's my little boy, this morning?' Gladys asked.

'Intent upon a day of dedicated labour,' said Will. 'Up against a deadline. Fearing any distraction that might result in a loss of concentration and lead inevitably to an employment termination situation. As it were.'

'You're all words,' said Gladys, winking lewdly at Will. 'And such pretty words too. I wonder what they all mean.'

'They mean that I must work hard or get sacked,' said Will, applying himself to the keyboard. (It was a *big* keyboard, with *big* keypads, designed for fingers that were far *bigger* than Will's slender digits.)

'But you'll join me for lunch?' asked Gladys, making what she considered to be a comely face. 'I have extra vouchers, just for you. My job is to build you up, you know.'

'I do know.' Will sank low over his keyboard and wondered, as he had done upon many previous, similar, occasions, what exactly life was all about.

The fat men in Will's world held him in nothing but contempt, but the fat women loved him. They couldn't get enough of him. If only he could love *them*, he would be enjoying the sex life of the gods.

But he didn't love them. He didn't, on the whole, even like them. Which was a bummer, because Will would have dearly loved some sex.

'You press on then, dearest,' said Gladys. 'Lunchtime, then?'

'Lunchtime, then,' said Will, applying himself to his keypads. Charles Fort, the twentieth-century phenomenologist (of whom Will knew nothing at all) had once written words to the effect that *when drawing a circle, one can begin at any point.* Exactly what this means is anyone's guess, but it's probably something deep and meaningful.

Will went about his work in this self-same manner: he began *anywhere*, at random, examining the image of the artwork on the screen, beginning anywhere at all. Will flipped his computer rat (a larger version of a mouse), brought a tiny portion of the overall image to the screen and perused it.

He found himself perusing the Tinker. He wore a red cap and a waistcoat, a puff-sleeved shirt and a pair of woollen breeches. Will peered at the face of the Tinker. The detail was remarkable. Will expanded the image until it all but filled his terminal screen. The detail was more than remarkable, even at this scale; you couldn't actually see the brushstrokes. Mr Dadd must have had the most amazing eyesight. Will shook his head and whistled in admiration. It was almost photographic. It was incredible.

Will twitched the rat backwards and forwards and scrolled up and down. There was certainly nothing faulty about the digitalisation of this portion of the image. You could see every button on the Tinker's shirt, every fibre of the cloth.

Will sat back in his chair and did a bit more whistling. They really knew their trade, those Victorian lads. Even the mad ones. They really knew how to paint a picture. No one could do stuff like this any more; it was a dead art. Art was a dead art. It was all computers these days, and computers that didn't even work very well.

Will twitched the rat once more, down to the Tinker's hand. Look at that: the fingernails, the veins; the detail. The sheer, amazing, wonderful detail. The fingernails, the veins, the tiny hairs, the skin of the wrist. The maker's name on the wristwatch. Will twiddled the mouse and moved on towards the Tailor. The detail of the hat, the texture of the fabric. The—

Hold on.

Will flicked back to the Tinker.

The wristwatch?

Will twiddled some more, tapped the keypads, enlarged the image.

The wristwatch?

This was a Victorian painting. They didn't have wristwatches in those days. And certainly not . . . *digital* wristwatches.

Will's jaw dropped hugely open. There was no doubt about it at all. The Tinker in the painting, the Victorian painting, painted between eighteen fifty-five and eighteen sixty-four, was wearing a digital wristwatch. Will could clearly read the maker's name engraved upon it, painted in minute detail: *Charles Babbage and Company. Digital watchmakers to Her Majesty Queen Victoria.*

'Mr Santos,' called Will, in a strangled kind of a voice. 'Mr Santos, I think we have a problem here.'

2

Mr Santos huffed and puffed and wobbled as he waddled. 'What is all this fuss and the raising of your voice?' he enquired of Will as he reached the lad's desk and leaned heavily upon it.

'Something's very wrong here,' said the lad.

'A focusing problem? You know the procedures, you've passed your grades.'

'Not a focusing problem.' Will beckoned his corpulent superior to view the screen. 'I fear the painting has been tampered with. Or possibly that it is a twentieth-century forgery.'

'Hush and hush, such nonsense.' Mr Santos leaned low and loomed over Will. 'Show me,' said he.

'It's here.' Will enlarged the area of the Tinker's wrist. The digital watch was displayed in all its wondrous detail.

'Is this some kind of joke?' Mr Santos's breath was hot upon Will's neck. The smell of his breakfast entered Will's nostrils.

'A joke?' Will shook his blondy head. 'Not on my part, I assure you. To tamper with such a work of genius would be nothing less than iconoclasm, in my humble opinion.'

'Quite so.' Mr Santos peered at the image again. Will knew well enough that Mr Santos was possessed of considerable knowledge regarding the art of the Victorian age. Will wasted a great deal of Mr Santos's time each day asking him questions. He also exerted such a degree of flattery during the asking of these questions that Mr Santos was never aware of quite how much time was being wasted.

'What sort of brush could produce such fine detail?' Will asked. 'Would it have been specially made for the artist by *Winsor and Newton's*? I recall you telling me a fascinating story about—'

'Be silent, lad; give me a minute.' Mr Santos gestured Will up from his chair and seated himself. He scanned the painting up and down, this way and that. Mr Santos made a puzzled face, and then a worried one, and then he said, 'We'll get you onto something else. I'll call up another artist for you.'

'But I want Dadd,' Will said, his voice raised in protest. 'I've been really looking forward to doing Dadd. He's one of my favourites.'

'There's no room for favourites. I'll fetch you a new disc from my office. Remove this one and bring it to me there.'

'But,' said Will, 'I want Dadd. I want Dadd.'

'Oh, isn't that sweet,' said Gladys. 'Will wants his dad.'

'Silence, Ms Nanken,' bawled Mr Santos. 'But me no buts, Starling. You just do what you're told.'

'Yes, but—'

'No buts at all, if you want to keep your job.'

Will looked down into the face of Mr Santos. The fat man's forehead was beaded with perspiration. 'As you say, sir,' said Will.

'Good lad.' Mr Santos eased his bulk from Will's chair and took to waddling away. Will watched him go, and Will noted well those beads of perspiration: although a fat and wobbling waddler, Will had never before seen Mr Santos raise a sweat.

Will tapped keypads, closed the programme, pushed buttons on the drive unit and withdrew the disc that contained the works of Richard Dadd. Will turned it upon his palm. There was a mystery here, and clearly one that was beyond his remit to investigate. Will considered the disc. Once it left his possession, he was unlikely ever to see it again. He glanced furtively about. How long would it take to make himself a copy of the disc? There were one hundred and eighty-four paintings encrypted upon it, so a few minutes at most. But if he only copied *The Fairy Feller's Masterstroke*, it would be a matter of seconds.

Of course, if he were caught doing it, he could lose his job. There was a risk here.

Will weighed up the pros and cons and then decided upon his course of action.

Mr Santos took the disc from Will. He was replacing a telephone receiver as Will entered his office.

'Thank you,' said Mr Santos. 'The situation is being dealt with.'

'So is the painting a forgery?' Will asked.

'That is for the experts to decide. I suspect later tampering. The painting was on public display for more than a hundred years. Someone with a perverse sense of humour and total lack of respect must have added the watch. Such things have happened before.'

'Have they?' Will asked. 'When and to which paintings?'

'I'm moving you on to twentieth-century art,' said Mr Santos, ignoring Will's question. 'The works of Mark Rothko.'

'Oh no,' said Will. 'Please, the twentieth century is of no interest to me.'

'Then perhaps you'll wish to tender your resignation. I have a form here; would you care to fill it out now?'

'No,' said Will. 'I'm the only winner of the cakes in my household. I have no wish to be unemployed.'

'Then just do as you are told.' Mr Santos handed Will the Mark Rothko disc. 'And Starling, for your own sake, do not speak of this to anyone. Do you understand?'

'No,' said Will. 'I don't. Why?'

'The integrity of the collection. It must not be compromised.'

'Oh I see. So what will happen to the painting? Will it be cleaned and the offending wristwatch removed?'

'The painting will probably be destroyed.'

'*What?*' went Will. 'But that's outrageous!'

'These matters are not for us to question.'

'But sir, destroying such a work of genius because someone vandalised a tiny part of it – a tiny part that is not even visible to the naked eye – it's ridiculous. It's obscene.'

Mr Santos smiled ruefully. 'You really care about these things, don't you, Starling?' he said.

'So do you, sir,' said Will. 'I know you do. When you talk to me about art, I can see how much you care.'

'Well, it's out of our hands now. Perhaps it won't be destroyed. Let's both hope for that, eh?'

'Yes,' said Will. 'All right. But Rothko? Do I really have to do *Rothko*?'

'Not my decision.' Mr Santos raised his eyebrows. 'Instructions from those on high. I'll see what I can do to get you back on the Victorians. Just go to your desk and press on. Do you understand me?'

'I understand you, sir,' said Will. 'And thanks.'

'Off you go now.'

And off Will went.

Will did Rothko all the morning, and Will really hated it. Whatever had been going on in the heads of twentieth-century folk. Admiring this kind of rubbish? A few splashes of colour on a colossal canvas: that was art, was it? No, in Will's opinion, it was not. But Will was Will, and Will was young, and the young have very definite opinions about what they like and what they do not. Age blurs boundaries, broadens horizons, alters fixed opinions, but whether this is a good thing is anybody's guess.

By lunchtime Will had had his fill of 1960s abstract art and had made a momentous decision. Thoughts had been whirling about in his head all morning, dangerous thoughts, risky thoughts. The sort of thoughts that could get him into a great deal of trouble, should those thoughts be actualised into actions.

'Come on then my lovely boy,' cooed Gladys. 'Canteen time. Big pies on offer.' And she thrust out her abounding mammaries and winked coquettishly.

'I'll be up in a minute,' said Will. 'I just have to finish this.'

'I'll wait for you, then,' said Gladys.

'You'll miss your place in the queue.'

'I'll see you up there then.'

'Save me a seat,' called Will.

Gladys departed and Will was left alone in the vast subterranean dome.

Will did furtive glancings. He really was all alone. And he was troubled, yet excited. The dangerous thoughts of the morning which had brought him to his momentous decision were causing his hands to tremble. Will made fists of them, and then he removed the Rothko disc from the drive and subtituted another, one which he took from his pocket.

The Fairy Feller's Masterstroke once more filled Will's screen. He tapped at keypads. Reference numbers appeared: the painting's location in the art gallery's archive. Will noted down these reference numbers onto the back of his left hand, below certain other reference numbers. He called up the building plan. The archive was housed on a sub-level almost directly beneath his feet. The first question was, how exactly to get there? Will traced the route, the staircases and corridors. It could be done. But then, getting to the archive was only a small part of the problem. Once he had reached and somehow entered it, would the painting still be there? Or would it have already been removed for destruction? And if it was still there, what then? Once he had got to it, if he *could* get to it, the big question was how to steal it. Because Will had become absolutely certain that this was the course of action he must take. And if he did manage to steal this painting, to *save* this painting, how was he going to get away with it?

He would certainly be the Number One suspect. And he would certainly be caught. There was very little crime in the days after the days after tomorrow. This was not because there was nothing worth stealing any more: there always *is*, and always *will be*, things worth stealing. And if there are things worth stealing, they *will* be stolen.

Will knew that the painting had to be worth millions. This would be the crime of the century.

But it isn't a crime, Will told himself. Destroying the painting was a crime, saving it was praiseworthy.

And he did have a plan, and not just *a* plan, but one, if he could pull it off, that would allow him to escape undetected with the painting.

Three security doors lay between Will and his goal, security doors to which he did not possess the access codes. Mr Santos possessed the access codes; he regularly visited the archive, although Will's pleas that he might join him had so far met with refusal. Mr Santos had the codes on a card that he kept in the top pocket of his white work coat, the white work coat that he donned when visiting the archive, the white work coat that presently hung upon the back of the door in his office.

Will removed the disc from his drive, popped it into his pocket and then removed himself to Mr Santos's office. And so it came to pass that ten minutes later Will found himself standing in the archive of the Tate Gallery.

The archive was a vast and brightly lit subterranean gallery that dwindled into hazy perspective. Will breathed in the air and sighed. The air smelled of art: of canvas and paint and varnish and veneer, smells all new to Will, smells all flavoured with the magic of a bygone age.

To the left and the right of him, and for many, many metres beyond, stood tall metal racks, upon which hung . . .

Art.

High Art. The Art of the Victorians.

Will took a deep breath. It was all a little too much for him to really be in the presence of all this. His knees were trembling, his mouth was dry. Will was scared. But for all this, he felt something, something that perhaps he'd never really felt before. He felt alive. He felt that he was on a mission. And it thrilled him greatly.

The racks moved upon casters and Will slid one out at random, exposing the work of Dante Gabriel Rossetti, one of the great Pre-Raphaelites.

Will found himself confronting *Proserpine*.

He felt almost impelled to kneel.

Will took another deep breath. He should so not be here. This was so bad.

Will had the reference number of Mr Dadd's painting penned on the back of his hand. And he also had a plan, which was a good plan – or would be, if it worked. Which it could only do if the iconoclasts who wanted to destroy the painting had not got to it first.

Will slid the rack containing Rossetti's *Proserpine* back into place and checked the writing on his hand.

Aisle 33, rack 409, painting number five.

Will went about his business.

And he was all but on the point of completing his business when he heard the noise of a door being opened. And not just any door, but the very door that Will had entered by.

'Oh damn,' said Will to himself. 'But perhaps I should have expected it.' He edged quietly away and hid himself amongst the racks.

'This way,' he heard a voice say.

'Are you sure?' he heard another.

'Well of course I'm sure.'

'So you've been here before?'

'Well, not here, but I've been to other places. I do know how to read a plan.'

'Oh yes, of course you do.'

These voices were young voices. And, to Will's surprise, they were also female voices.

'It's aisle 33, rack 409, painting number five,' said the first female voice. Will slipped a little further away.

'And what are we to do with this painting?' asked the second female voice.

'Burn it,' said the first voice. 'Like we've done with the others.'

'We should burn them all,' said the second voice. 'Just to be sure. There are too many loose ends.'

'They get fewer every day. All traces of the other past are being eradicated. There's not much left. The Sisterhood is safe. The Sisterhood will remain in control.'

Will cocked his head to one side. The Sisterhood? Would that be the Sisterhood of Sainsbury's? It was the only Sisterhood Will had ever heard of. The voices were close now; Will pressed himself into the shadows. He could see the tops of their heads: a violet wig, decorated with plastic flowers, and a pink wig. Big wigs on big heads. Will ducked his own head and held his breath.

'Here we are,' said the first voice. 'Rack 409, slide it out.' Sounds of racks sliding reached Will.

'Painting number five, fish it down.'

'It's a big one, we can't burn it here. Where's the anomaly, do you think?'

'Who cares. Fish it down; we'll smash it up here and bag it.'

'Fair enough.'

Will heard further sounds, of stampings and tearings and breakings, and then of baggings-up, all accompanied by gleeful cries of triumph.

'Job done,' said the first voice. 'Let's go and get lunch in the canteen.'

The sounds of footfalls diminished. The sounds of the door opening and closing followed.

Will emerged from the shadows. He took himself over to rack 409 and viewed the space where painting number five had hung.

'A job well done,' said Will. 'A job *very* well done.'

Which might have appeared a rather odd thing for him to say, had it not been for the fact that Will held in his hands *The Fairy Feller's Masterstroke*.

And it did have to be said that he had rather enjoyed the sounds of the Rothko that he had substituted for Dadd's masterpiece being stomped to smithereens and then bagged up.

A large smile now appeared upon the face of Will Starling. And a sigh of relief escaped from his lips.

'I no longer need to steal this painting,' said Will to himself. 'All I have to do is hide it somewhere here, recatalogue it under a different name, and tell no one. Job done, I think.'

And that was that really. Except of course that it wasn't. For Will was now greatly intrigued: hugely, greatly intrigued. Why did the painting have to be destroyed? And what was this Sisterhood, that had the authority to come into the Tate's archive and do the destroying? What kind of power did this Sisterhood have? And what was this business of 'the other past', all traces of which were being eradicated? Will was very hugely greatly intrigued. And as he had seemingly got away with saving the Dadd, well, why not try to find out what all this was really about?

Will rehung the Dadd amongst some French Impressionists that he had previously checked on his screen. Assured that it would be safe there for the time being, he took himself off to the staff canteen.

It was Will's intention to get himself very close to the two female iconoclasts and listen in to their conversation, but sadly, this was not to be.

Will joined the food queue, and Tim McGregor joined Will.

'Hi, Will,' said Tim in a jovial fashion. 'How are you doing?'

'Very well, Tim,' said Will, taking up his tray and preparing to load it.

'You look a bit hyper,' said Tim. 'Not been up to anything naughty, I trust?'

Will grinned at Tim. Tim was all of Will's height, big of hair and beard and of a medium build that was neither fat nor thin. Tim was Will's bestest friend. They'd been to corporate school together and remained close ever since. Tim, a gifted computer programmer, was presently in Forward Planning at the Tate; his influence had got Will his job.

Tim was a practising Pagan – possibly, for all Will knew, the very last practising Pagan there was. Paganism had never really made it to the big time when it came to religions, and now even the big-time religions were nothing more than memory. Those that had not been absorbed and altered by corporate sponsorship had been consigned to the web pages of history: Hinduism, Buddhism, Islam, all had vanished from the Earth, along with The Church of Branson, The Church of Elvis, The Church of England, Knotee (a string-worshipping cult) and, most recently, Roman Catholicism.

That the Church of Rome should have been dropped by its corporate sponsor had come as a bit of a shock to its millions of followers, and also to Will, who had been considering giving it a go because he'd heard that a lot of nice-looking girls of an easy-going disposition frequented its youth clubs.

Tim had explained to Will that he, Tim, had been made privy to 'certain sensitive information' regarding the Church of Rome losing its sponsorship, information, which came to him via 'certain contacts in the know'.

According to Tim's contacts, a serious scandal centring upon St Peter's of Rome had caused the sponsors to pull out.

Will had listened wide-eyed and open-mouthed while Tim explained the situation. Apparently it was down to the many incorruptible bodies of the saints housed in the catacombs beneath St Peter's, which were not altogether what they appeared. It had always been accepted by the Church of Rome that a would-be saint must have three attestable miracles to his (or her) account before his (or her) death. And upon later exhumation, the body must not have decayed: that is, it should remain inviolate and incorruptible.

The problem was that there is another order of dead person that does not rot in the grave. The vampire.

And thus it was that many of the so-called saints interred beneath St Peter's were in fact vampires. And these had, over the years, upon their many night-time forays in search of sustaining blood, managed to infect most of the clergy. And the infection had finally reached the Pope.

'Hasn't it ever occurred to you as suspicious,' Tim had said to Will, 'how over the years Popes have lasted for so long and grown so very, very old? And how when they go out in public they are always inside Pope-mobiles with polarised glass windows or heavily shielded from sunlight beneath great big awnings and suchlike?'

Will had scratched at his blondy head. 'Not really,' he replied

'Well it's true,' said Tim. 'A team of Fearless Vampire Killers, a special division of the SAS trained for such action, abseiled down into St Peter's and the Vatican and exterminated the lot of them: the Pope, the cardinals, monks and nuns and choirboys. Of course it wasn't on the newscasts, but these things never are. Stuff like this happens all the time; it's just that we never hear about it.'

Will had shaken his head and shrugged. It sounded as good an explanation as any. Will wondered whether he might apply to join the SAS Vampire Division. It sounded like an exciting kind of job.

'What are you doing at the weekend?' Tim asked.

'Nothing much,' said Will, anxiously looking towards the now distant topknots of the female iconoclasts.

'Fancy something a bit different?' Tim asked.

'Not really bothered,' said Will, scooping random foodstuffs onto his tray.

'You'll love this, a dose of the old time travel.'

'A dose of *what*?' Will ceased his foodstuff scoopings.

'I've got some Retro,' whispered Tim. 'Half a dozen tabs.'

'That stuff's illegal and it doesn't really work, does it?'

'Keep it down.' Tim fluttered his fingers. 'It does work, you can really go back into the past with it. In your head.' Tim tapped at his temple. 'It allows you to access ancestral memories. They are inside your head, you see. The memories of your father before you were conceived. And your grandfather too. Depends on how much Retro you take.'

'And you really can access your father's memories?'

'They're inside your head, cellular, part of your genetic code. You don't just inherit your father's looks and hair colour, you get his memories too. But you can't access them without chemical assistance.'

'I have my doubts about this,' said Will, helping himself to further foodstuffs. 'Do you know anyone who's actually taken Retro?'

'Well, no,' said Tim.

'And anyway, if my dad's memories are in my head, I'd prefer that they stay somewhere hidden. I don't want to know, thank you very much.'

'But you'd find out about all his dirty doings. Imagine, you could remember how he shagged your mum and conceived you.'

'What a hideous thought. No, thank you very much indeed.'

'Please yourself,' said Tim. 'But I've got six tabs. That's three each. You could go back to your precious Victorian era.'

'What?' said Will.

'It's all inside your head,' said Tim. 'Or at least that's the theory. I'm going to take the drug on Saturday night. If you're not interested, I'll let you know how I get on. But you're missing out on something special, I'm telling you.'

'I'll give it some thought,' said Will. 'But listen, can we talk later? There's someone I have to see.'

'Don't go near them,' said Tim. 'If they even suspect that you're listening in to their conversation, you'll be in real trouble.'

'What?' said Will, all but dropping his tray. 'What are you saying?'

'I saw you,' whispered Tim. 'Those corridors down to the archive are constantly scanned. My department takes care of that. I received a memo this morning that two dignitaries were coming to inspect the archive. I was to monitor them as far as the archive security door and then erase their images from the scanning program. And I did, but guess who I caught sneaking down the corridors before they did?'

'Oh no,' said Will. 'So I'm in big trouble?'

'No trouble at all,' said Tim. 'I erased you too. But don't go near them. They're *big* trouble.'

'So who are they?'

'So what were *you* doing in the archive?'

'I can't tell you that,' said Will.

'Well I can tell you this. *Don't* go down there again. And *don't* go near those women. Do we understand each other?'

'We do,' said Will. 'Can I buy you lunch?'

'You can,' said Tim. 'And I'll expect you at my housing unit at eight o'clock sharp on Saturday night. Try not to get yourself into any trouble before then, okay?'

'I'll try,' said Will. 'I'll try.'

3

Tuesday and Wednesday and Thursday came and went and these days were very dull indeed for Will. Dull they were, and worrying too. Will worried for the painting. Would someone uncover his hiding place? A cleaner, or a restorer, perhaps? Or would the iconoclastic women return? Might they have found out that they'd destroyed the wrong painting? Would investigations ensue? His fingerprints and DNA would be upon the Dadd. He should have worn gloves. He should never have got involved at all. Perhaps it hadn't been a risk worth taking. Will perched on the edge of his seat in a permanent state of tension. Will worried and fretted and worried some more. Gladys worried for Will.

'You're not yourself, little manny,' she told him, reaching forth a podgy hand to stroke at his arm. 'Come out with me this evening, I'll cheer you up.'

'Thanks,' said Will. 'But no thanks.'

'But Friday night is Rock Night at the Shrunken Head. Your kind of thing, Will, Retro Rock, twentieth-century stuff. The Apes Of Wrath are playing and Violent Macaroni and Foetus Eater, and Lawnmower Death, and The Slaughterhouse Five.'

'Not my cup of coffee,' said Will. 'But Tim McGregor in Forward Planning loves that kind of business. And between you and me, I think he's somewhat enraptured by you. He keeps mentioning your name in the canteen.'

'Really?' Gladys primped at her lemonly-tinted toupee. 'Do you really think so?'

'Absolutely,' said Will. 'But don't tell him that I told you.'

'No, I won't.'

Will twiddled his computer rat and viewed more boring Rothko. Dull dull dull it was, and Will remained as worried.

He worried until it was time to go home. Then he went off home, still worrying.

And he did have good cause to worry. Crime was hardly commonplace in these days after the day after tomorrow. And the reason for this was the almost superhuman efficiency of the Department of Correctional Science.

A one hundred per cent clean-up rate.

In former unenlightened days there had been a 'police force', armed officers of the law who pursued and arrested malcontents. These were 'brought to justice' and then housed in prisons. This had proven to be a most inefficient system. Many malcontents managed to evade capture. Others, although captured, evaded prison, through the intercession of barristers working on their behalf. Others, who had actually ended up in prison, had their sentences cut for 'good behaviour' and returned once more to a life of crime.

In the year 2050, however, a visionary appeared on the scene in the shape of a certain Mr Darius Doveston. Mr Doveston was a geneticist. In fact it was Mr Doveston who had first formulated the Retro drug. Mr Doveston's theory was that criminality was inherited. Dishonest parents passed on their dishonesty to their offspring, who inherited it through their genes and through 'learning by example'. Mr Doveston proposed a cure for crime. It would take fifty years, he said, but when the fifty years were up, there would be no more crime – because there would be no more criminals.

Mr Doveston's solution to the crime problem was simplicity itself. And history does record that the simple solution (dramatic as it sometimes must be) is often the most effective.

His solution was the compulsory sterilisation of all first-time offenders. If villains couldn't breed, reasoned Mr Doveston, then they couldn't breed more villains.

It was, of course, a stroke of pure genius.

But there are always those with motives of their own who will find something to complain about, even with such a stroke of genius as this. There was a vast public outcry. Sterilisation was some kind of punishment, went this outcry, but not much of one. Those sterilised villains would inevitably continue with their villainy. In fact, embittered as they might well be by their sterilisation, they might even broaden the scope of their villainy. And having to wait fifty years for a crime-free society? That was far too long!

Mr Doveston gave the matter some further thought.

Perhaps he had been a trifle hasty. He reconsidered and then drew up a plan, which pleased everyone, with the possible exception of the criminal classes.

Mandatory death penalty for first-time offenders.

Mr Doveston submitted his proposal in the form of a Private Member's Bill to the House of Commons. Within two weeks of it being passed and put into the statute books, the crime figures virtually halved. Within two years, crime was all but non-existent in the British Isles.

Which is why Will had good cause to worry.

And had Will known what was presently on the go at the Department of Correctional Science, he would have had even more cause to worry. But for quite another reason.

The DOCS was housed only a short tram ride from the Tate, just across the long poisoned Thames, in a magnificent black structure of obsidian and tinted glass, rising a mere three hundred storeys, fashioned to resemble an old time policeman's helmet. Most of its floors were now given over to recreational areas, casinos, corporate whorehouses and shopping malls. The actual DOCS occupied the three hundredth floor. It was run by a team of five men, one of whom was a token woman.

The head of the department, the Chief, was a black man by the name of Trubshaw. The tradition that a black man should always fill the role of police chief, was a long one, dating back to 1970s America, where, although in real life an impossibility, in the movies it was inevitably the case. It was a 'Hollywood' thing.

Beneath the Chief was the Chief Inspector, a white man named Sam Maggott, and beneath Sam, four policemen, one of whom was a token woman. The role was taken on a rota basis. This week Officer John Higgins was the token woman, and Officer John Higgins was on the telephone.

'What?' she was saying. 'What? What? What?'

Words poured into the ear of Officer John, words of a distressing nature. At length the stream of words ceased and Officer John replaced the telephone receiver. 'Damn,' she said, and 'damn and blast.'

Chief Inspector Maggott looked up from his doings, which were of the crossword persuasion and examined the young Officer, a vision in blue serge damask and dainty high heels. 'Did I hear you say "damn"?' he enquired.

'You did, sir,' said Officer John, adjusting her wig.

'And what would be the cause of this damning?' Sam Maggott jiggled his girth about and rippled a jowl or two.

'It would seem, sir, that we have a crime on our hands.'

'A crime?' said Maggott. 'A *crime*?'

'A crime, sir. The first of the year and a big one too. A murder by the sound of it.'

'*A murder*?' Sam's flesh rippled in many directions. 'We haven't had a murder since—'

'Third of Apple,* twenty-two o-seven,' said Officer Denton Colby, who was good at that kind of thing.

'Fifteen years ago,' said Sam. 'This is most upsetting. Are you certain that it wasn't just an accident, or something?'

'Multiple gunshots,' said Officer John, straightening a seam in her stocking.

'A gun!' Sam made clutchings at his heart. 'Which one of you lent this murderer your gun?'

Officers patted their weapons.

'None of us,' they all agreed.

'Then how could a murderer have a gun? Only we have guns, and even ours don't work properly most of the time.'

'Perhaps he constructed one,' said Officer Denton. 'If you recall the case of Digby Charlton, "The Cheltenham Chopper", he constructed his chopper from cheese.'

'Somewhat before my time,' said Sam.

'And mine also,' said Denton. 'But the essence of good DOCS work is always to be well informed. I, for instance, have studied—'

'What did your informant tell you?' Sam asked Officer John.

'The informant is a performance artist, sponsored by an investment corporation. He is employed to play the part of a derelict and lie in alleyways, looking wretched and saying things such as "if only I'd invested my capital with such and such a corporation, I wouldn't be in the mess I am now." He says it to passers-by, you see.'

'Nice work if you can get it,' said Officer Doggart Tenpole Tudor. 'I wonder if there are any vacancies?'

'You've never really been committed to this work, have you, Tudor?' asked Sam.

'Oh it's not that, sir. I just like to get out and about once in a while. Get a bit of fresh air when there's any going.'

'There hasn't been lately,' said Sam. 'But go on, Higgins, what did this performance artist have to say for himself?'

'He said he was lying in an alleyway in Chiswick last night, when he saw what he described as "a real bright light". Then, out of the light,

* Corporate sponsorship of months had been all the rage in 2207, but had since been discontinued, because it was stupid.

right out of nowhere, this big naked man appeared. The performance artist said that the naked man's eyes were completely black and that he "smelled something rotten!" And he stole the performance artist's trousers.'

'Another crime,' said Sam. 'No, hang about, who got murdered?'

'The owner of an antique weapons shop across the road from the alleyway. The performance artist saw it happen. The big, smelly, black-eyed, naked man, well, naked but for the trousers, shot the proprietor with one of his own antique weapons.'

'I think we've solved the mystery of the murder weapon,' said Officer Denton. 'One up to the DOCS I think.'

'Buffoon,' said Sam. 'So, is that it? Is that all your informant had to say?'

'No, sir, apparently then the half-naked, big, smelly, black-eyed man, now hung all about with antique weaponry, came out of the antique weapons shop, crossed the street, turned around and tossed a hand grenade into the shop, blowing it all to pieces.'

'There goes the crime-scene evidence,' said Officer Denton.

'Shut it!' shouted Chief Inspector Sam. 'What else did he say, Higgins?'

'He said that the murderer returned to the alleyway and shook my informant about and demanded information.'

'Asked the right chap then,' said Officer Denton, giggling foolishly. 'Information from an informant.'

'Shut it!' shouted Sam once more. 'What information?'

'He wanted to know the year,' said Officer Higgins.'

'The year?'

'That's what he wanted to know. My informant told him and the big man flung him to the ground. Knocking him unconscious, he's only just come to.'

'That's assault, probably GBH,' said Officer Denton. 'That brings the crime tally up to three. This big, near-naked, smelly, black-eyed fellow is a regular one-man crime wave.'

'Officer Higgins,' said Sam Maggott. 'Exchange clothes with Officer Denton. He can be the token woman for the next month. Perhaps that will shut him up.'

'I'll bet it won't,' said Officer Denton.

'It damn well better,' said Chief Inspector Maggott. 'Or I will be forced to—'

But his words were cut short by the ringing of Officer John Higgins's telephone.

The hand of Officer John took to hovering just above the receiver.

'Well, answer it, man,' cried Maggott.

'But it might be more bad news. Wouldn't it be better if we just pretend to be out?'

'What, with a maniac on the loose?'

'I'm really not keen,' said Officer John.

'Denton, you do it,' ordered Sam. 'This needs a woman's touch. Go to it. Hurry up.'

Officer Denton took up the receiver. 'DOCS. Policewoman Denton speaking,' she said.

Words tumbled into Denton's large-and-unshell-like.

And presently she too replaced the receiver.

'So, what is it, Officer?' Sam demanded to be told.

'It's another murder, sir. A body has just been found in a Brentford housing unit. Chap by the name of Will Starling has just been shot to death.'

4

The headquarters of the DOCS had plenty of high-tech state-of-the-art equipment. There were heaps of holographic how's-your-fathers and digital directory doodahs. There were even some inter-rositors, which were powered by a complicated process involving the trans-perambulation of pseudo-cosmic anti-matter. Most of it however had long since ceased to work, and that which still did so, did so at irregular intervals.

Officer Denton was au-fait with the running of all the equipment that still worked. She possessed the necessary operational skills and had certificates to prove it. Not that any of her comrades had ever expressed a desire to see them. Officer Denton set to the task of tracking down the killer.

'This should be a challenge,' she told Chief Inspector Sam, 'but not much of one. We'll soon have him.'

'I fear not for this,' said her superior. 'Would you care to take us through the method *you* will be employing?'

Officer Denton put aside her nail varnish and blew on her fingertips. 'As you are well aware,' said she, 'at any given time it is possible for us to locate any given person. No one can travel without being iris-scanned. Folk are constantly scanned in their housing units by iris-scanning systems installed within their home screens.'

'Which is not something known to the general public,' said Sam, tapping his nose in a significant fashion.

'Naturally not, sir. But if the scanners actually happen to be working, then they do give us the edge. We know where people are and we know where they should be. Whether they are in employment. And if not, where else they are. There are iris-scanners on the corners of every street. In every shop, store and supermarket. We shall tune in our instruments to the unit of this William Starling and see who paid him a visit.'

'It's all too easy these days,' said Officer John. 'Sometimes I hanker for the good old days, when police officers had to use their wits to apprehend villains.'

Chief Inspector Sam made shudderings. 'Stuff all that,' said he. 'Far too many margins for error. See if you can get any life out of the instruments, Denton. And if you can, we'll identify the malcontent and despatch an execution squad. And then we'll all have a nice cup of coffee.'

'Ten four, sir,' said Denton, in the time-honoured fashion.

The officers of the law gathered about their token female counterpart as she twiddled dials, pressed key-pads and made enigmatic finger-wavings over sensors and scanners and the Lord-of-the-Laminates knows what else.

And when nothing happened, she took to hammering the equipment with her shoe.

Presently she said, 'Oh.'

'Oh?' said Sam. 'I like not the sound of this "Oh".'

'It's a bit of a tricky "Oh",' said Officer Denton, applying lipstick in the general area of her mouth. 'There's nothing recorded on the iris-scanner in the home screen at William Starling's unit, other than for William Starling.'

'So the malcontent somehow shielded his eyes from the scanner?'

'Possibly so, sir. Remember the performance artist said that his eyes were completely black. Perhaps he was wearing opaque contact lenses to avoid recognition. But there's something more. The thermascan didn't register anything either.'

'For the benefit of those who might not know about the workings of the thermascan,' said Sam, carefully, 'perhaps you would care to elaborate.'

'Well, as *you* obviously know, sir,' said Officer Denton, with more than equal care, 'thermascans are incorporated into all home screens; on the off chance that crimes might be committed in the dark. The heat signatures of human beings are as distinctive as their iris patterns. According to the thermascan in the home screen of Mr Starling, which, I am impressed to see is actually working, he was all alone when he was shot to death.'

'So it was suicide.'

'No, sir, not suicide. The thermascan registered the heat from the gun as it was fired. It was several metres away from Mr Starling.'

'So what exactly are you saying, young woman?'

'I'm saying that I don't know what shot Mr Starling, sir, but it wasn't a human being.'

*

The mortal remains of William Starling, known to his friends and family as Will, were bagged up by paramedics, their uniforms made gay with holographic logos, which flashed fetchingly and falteringly all around and about them.

Chief Inspector Sam Maggott, now at the crime scene, viewed the bagging up with a sad and jaundiced eye. 'This just won't do,' he told his team. 'No thermascan, no iris identification, no murder weapon. Any physical traces, Denton?'

Token woman Denton was scanning the bright orange walls of the breakfasting area, with something that resembled an electronic frying pan. 'Let you know in just a minute, sir,' she replied.

'And what, *exactly* are you doing now?' asked Sam.

'Checking auditory residuals, sir. It's a very technical business.' Policewoman Denton gave the electronic-frying-pan affair a hearty whack with her fist. 'It's working now,' she said.

'I'll leave you to it then.'

Officer Denton went on with her very technical business. Sam glanced around and about his surroundings. The surroundings were not in tiptop condition. They presented a scene of utter destruction. The rooms of the housing unit had been thoroughly trashed, furniture smashed to laminated splinters, pictures torn from the walls and shredded. The polysynthetic carpeting had even been ripped from the floor.

'These places depress me,' Sam said.

'Why so, sir?' asked Officer John.

'Because I grew up in one of these. Crowborough Tower, Tooting sector. Five hundred and nineteenth floor. South-facing, which was fine on Thursdays, of course. But they're all the same. On the rare occasion that there is a crime and I have to visit the crime scene, it's always like going home to the unit I was brought up in. It's almost as if every crime is committed in my own front room, against one of my own family. Do you understand what I'm saying?'

'I certainly do, sir,' said Officer John. 'But I like that. It makes it personal. And after all, society is one big family really. We're all inter-related, after all.'

'I'm not related to *you*!' said Sam.

'You are, sir. I looked you up. You're a distant cousin.'

Sam shuddered. 'How's it going, Denton?' he called.

'All done, sir. Shall we wait until the paramedics have removed the body?'

Sam waved to the paramedics. 'Haul him down to the morgue,' he said. The paramedics lifted the bagged-up body onto a kind of high-tech sleigh arrangement and tapped buttons on a remote control. The high-tech sleigh arrangement rose into the air and the paramedics guided it from the breakfasting area. No sooner had it reached the hall, however, than its high-techness failed and it crashed to the floor. The paramedics, cursing and complaining, dragged body and sleigh away. Sam closed the front door upon them and returned to his team. 'So what have you got, Denton?' he asked.

'Residual auditory record, sir. The sounds that have been absorbed into the walls of this area during the last two hours. I've downloaded them.' Officer Denton displayed the electronic-frying-pan affair. 'Shall I play them back?'

'Please do,' said Sam.

And the officer did so.

There was a lot of static, crackles and poppings. Then the sound of daytime home screen entertainment.

'What is that?' Sam asked.

'It's the UK classic channel,' said Officer John. 'They play historic TV shows, some of them nearly two hundred years old. I know this one; it's *The Sweeney*.'

'The who?'

'No, sir. The Who were a classical musical ensemble in the early 1960s. This is a TV series, about policemen.'

'Fascinating,' said Sam, making the face of one who was far from fascinated. 'But what use is this to us?'

'Keep listening, sir,' said Officer Denton. 'Here it comes.'

Chief Inspector Sam listened to the playback. The sound of a corporate theme tune reached his ears.

'The door chime,' said Denton. 'Keep listening.'

The sound of the door chime was followed by the sound of footsteps.

'He got out of his chair to answer the door,' said Denton.

Then came the sound of the door opening.

'He opened the door.'

'Shut up!' said Sam.

And Officer Denton shut up.

Amidst further poppings and crackles of static and the voice of the now legendary Dennis Waterman saying, 'We'll have to turn over his drum, guv', a deep-timbred voice with a rich Germanic accent said, 'William Starling?' Another voice said, 'Yes, that's me.' The first voice said, 'Give me the painting.' William Starling said, 'What painting?' The first voice said, '*The Fairy Feller's Masterstroke.*'

'I don't know what you're talking about,' said the voice of William Starling. 'I've never heard of such a painting.'

And then there were sounds of a struggle.

And then there were sounds of gunshots.

And then.

'Switch it off,' said Sam.

And Officer Denton switched it off.

Sam glanced once more about the devastation. 'This doesn't make any sense,' said he. 'The murderer was here. His voice left an audio trace. He entered this room. What do you make of it, Denton?'

'Don't know, sir. But the voice of the murderer doesn't sound right to me; it sounds like a recording.'

'It is a recording, you buffoon.'

'No, sir. It sounds like a recording of a recording, or a synthetic voice. It doesn't sound human.'

'A robot?' said Sam. 'Is that possible?'

'What I love about this day and age,' said Will Starling's mum, as she ladled foodstuffs onto plates, 'is that anything is possible.

Will Starling's dad looked up from the breakfasting table that was now about to prove its worth as a suppering table. 'More old toot heading our way,' he warned his only son.

Will grinned up at his ample mother. 'What do you have in mind, Mum?' he asked.

'Well take today for instance,' said Will's mum. 'I went upstairs to visit your Uncle William. And you'll never guess what.'

'I know *I* won't,' said Will's dad. 'Because I'm not even going to try.'

'Shot dead. Full up with holes. Blood and guts all over the place,' said Will's mum. 'What a surprise that, eh?'

'*Eh?*' said Will.

And '*Eh?*' said Will's dad too.

'Bang bang bang,' went Will's mum, miming gun-firings with her ladle and getting foodstuffs all down her front. 'Dead as dog plop in his breakfasting area. I called it in to the DOCS.'

'*What?*' went Will.

And '*What?*' went Will's dad too.

'Well, it was the right thing to do. I'm an honest citizen and it's an honest citizen's duty to report a crime.'

'Uncle Will?' said Will. 'This is terrible.'

'I never cared for him much,' said Will's dad. 'Big thighs, he had on him. Not that mine are small, but his were far too big for my liking.'

'But murdered.'

'I didn't go in,' said Will's mum. 'The front door was open, I could see his body clearly enough and the place was a right mess.'

'Always was,' said Will's dad. 'Those big thighs bumping into furniture.'

'So I went along the corridor to your other Uncle Will's to call the DOCS.'

'How many Uncle Wills do I have?' Will asked.

'Loads,' said Will's dad. 'It's a family name. Most of them live here in this tower. Can't be having with them, myself. All those big thighs and everything.'

'But I didn't go in there either,' said Will's mum, 'because guess what, his door was open too and he was lying dead on his floor, all full up with holes. Blood and guts splattered all over the place.'

'Your Uncle Wills are getting fewer by the minute,' said Will's dad.

'What?' said Will.

'Same enema,' said Will's mum.

'It's not enema,' said Will's dad. 'It's M O. Modus Operandi. An enema is something completely different.'

'I know exactly what an enema is,' said Will's mum. 'I used to do ballroom dancing.'

'Eh?' said Will.

'Don't ask,' said Will's dad.

'But my other Uncle Will,' said Will, 'was shot dead too?'

'That's what I'm saying,' said Will's mum. 'And what are the chances of that happening, eh? It seems that anything is possible in this day and age. Which is why I love it so much.'

'So *did* you phone the DOCS from that Uncle Will's?' Will asked.

'Well no, because I didn't want to walk on any vital evidence or anything, so I went further along the corridor to another of your Uncle Wills to make the call and guess what.'

'Do you see a pattern beginning to emerge here?' Will's dad asked his son.

'He was out,' said Will's mum. 'But your other Uncle Will who lives next door was in.'

'So you made the call from there?' Will asked.

'No, because his door was open and he was—'

Will made strangled gagging noises in his throat.

'Are you all right, son?' Will's dad asked.

'How many of my Uncle Wills have been murdered?' Will managed to ask.

'Oh, I don't think we should jump to any conclusions,' said Will's mum. 'They might have committed suicide. It might be a religious thing. A millennial cult, or something.'

'Suicide?' Will spluttered. 'But you said they were full up with holes. So they must have been shot more than once.'

'Well there were four of them.'

'Four?'

'I gave up,' said Will's mum. 'I came home and made the phone call from here. I only notified the DOCS about the first Uncle Will, or perhaps it was the second one, I forget. I didn't want to go bothering them with too many deaths all in the one day.'

'This is terrible,' said Will. 'My uncles.'

'I'm getting confused here,' said Will's dad. 'Was it big-thighed Uncle Will, or the one with the pointy head, or . . .'

'Both of those,' said Will's mum. 'And the one with the funny thing on the end of his nose.'

'Oh he's not one of ours,' said Will's dad. 'He's another Will Starling, different clan altogether.'

'He didn't have the thing on his nose when I saw him,' said Will's mum. 'Mind you, he didn't have the nose either. Shot right off it was.'

'Stop!' shouted Will, rising from the soon-to-be-suppering table. 'You must call the DOCS at once. Notify them of these other murders.'

'I'll do it later,' said Will's mum. 'The supper's getting cold.'

The front door chime of the Starling household chanted a corporate ditty.

'Now I wonder who that might be,' Will's dad wondered. 'Go and answer it, son.'

5

Will looked at his dad.

And Will's dad looked at Will.

'Go on then,' said Will's dad. 'See who it is.'

'No,' Will gave his head vigorous shakings. 'It might be a man with a gun.'

'I didn't order a gun,' said Will's mum, addressing her considerable husband. 'Did *you* order a gun?'

'Of course I didn't order a gun, woman. Why would I order a gun?'

'I mean,' said Will, now getting a bit of a shake on, 'that it might be *the murderer* with a gun.'

'Good point.' Will's dad nodded chins towards his spouse. 'The lad has a good point. You answer the door, woman.'

'No,' said Will. 'Don't anyone answer the door. Perhaps they'll just go away.'

The door chime chanted its corporate ditty once again.

'I'd best go,' said Will's mum. 'Whoever it is will wear out the battery.'

'No, Mum, please.' Will rose from the soon-to-be-suppering table and flapped his slender hands about. 'Don't answer the door. I have a very bad feeling about this.'

'You're just being silly.' Will's mum laid aside her ladle and smoothed down the besmutted frontispiece of her gorgeous gingham housecoat. 'I will answer the door.'

'No!' Will did leapings. He leapt from the table and he leapt in front of his mum. 'I can't let you do that.' Will turned to face the front door. 'Who's there?' he shouted.

'It's me, Will,' came the voice of Tim McGregor. 'Let me in, you silly sod.'

'Phew,' went Will, in the way that one does. 'Hold on Tim, I'm coming.'

Will's mum shrugged her sizeable shoulders. Will's dad said, 'Serve up the vitals, woman.'

Will opened the front door. 'Tim,' he said. 'It's really good to see you.'

'Good to see you too, Will. Why the delay? Were you having—?' Tim made certain gestures about his trouser regions.

'Don't be crude,' said Will. 'Come in.'

'Thanks.' Tim took a step into the Starling household. 'Oh, I've brought this chap with me,' he said. 'Met him in the lift. He was asking for you.' And then Tim didn't say any more, as he was suddenly buffeted from his feet and hurtled forward, barging into Will and bringing him to the floor.

A terrific figure now stood framed in the doorway. Well above six feet in the height of him and broad across the naked shoulders. The cropped hair on his head was black and so too were his hooded eyes. All black these were, and horrible to look upon. His face was a mask of bitter hatred, bushy brows drawn towards a nose of the aquiline persuasion, improbable cheekbones and a mouth that was a bitter, corded line.

The torso of this being fairly heaved with muscle and all around and about the gargantuan frame hung bullet belts and a fearsome collection of antique weaponry.

In his right hand he held a twenty-first-century phase plasma rifle (with a forty-watt range, naturally).

A hideous smell accompanied this monstrous personage. A rotten-eggy smell, the smell of sulphur, of brimstone, of that now legendary biblical pit that lacks for a bottom.

The terrific, black-eyed, evil-smelling figure glared down at the two young men struggling upon the floor, and then across to Will's mum and dad.

'William Starling?' he asked in a deeply-timbred voice of the Germanic persuasion. 'Which one of you is William Starling?'

'Now just you see here,' said Will's mum, taking up her ladle once more. 'You can't come bursting into people's accommodation, in a state of half undress, tainting the air and waving your fearsome weaponry about.'

'You?' asked the terrific figure, levelling his weapon at Will's mum, a red laser dot from its sight making a caste mark on her forehead. 'Are you William Starling?'

'Don't be absurd,' said Will's mum. 'Have you been drinking?'

'You?' the weapon swung in the direction of Will's dad.

The laser dot appeared upon *his* forehead.

'Err . . .' went Will's dad. 'Well, actually . . .'

'No,' Will scrambled to his feet and fluttered his hands about. 'He isn't William Starling. There isn't any William Starling here.'

'Where is the painting?' asked the terrific figure. 'Tell me now, or all die.'

'Painting?' said Will's dad. 'What painting?'

'*The Fairy Feller's Masterstroke.*'

'Ah,' said Will. 'That painting.'

'That.' The weapon now swung towards Will. The little red dot marked his forehead.

'I'll tell you,' said Will, his hands fluttering again. 'I know where it is. Just don't harm my family. Please don't shoot anyone.'

'Give me the painting, *now*.'

'I don't have it here. It's hidden. I can take you to it.'

'What is this all about?' asked Will's mum, fanning at her nose with her ladle. 'What have you been up to, Will? Something naughty, I'll bet.'

The weapon was once more pointing at Will's mum.

'Please stay out of this,' Will told her. 'Be quiet.'

'That's no way to speak to your mother.' Will's mum waggled her ladle.

'Silence,' ordered the terrific figure, fixing Will with a horrible black-eyed stare. 'The painting must be destroyed. Take me to it, now.'

'I can't.' Will now made pleading gestures. 'The place where it's hidden is closed until Monday.'

'Now, or I shoot the woman.'

'No.' Will flung himself to his knees. 'Please don't do that.'

'Now,' the figure ordered once again.

'Can I just go?' asked Tim. 'I'm nothing to do with this.'

'*He* can get us in.' Will rose slowly and pointed at Tim.

'You bastard!' said Tim.

'He's going to shoot my mum.'

'Well, I suppose I *could* get you in. It's hidden in the archive, I suppose.'

'It is.'

'*Now!*'

'He's lying to you,' said Will's dad, heaving himself out of his chair. 'He doesn't know about any painting. I'm the real Will Starling and I know where it is.'

'No,' shouted Will, fingers a-flutter. 'No, Dad, no.'

'The boy doesn't know anything,' said Will's dad. 'The painting's hidden right here, in this housing unit.'

Will's eyes widened. '*What?*' he managed to say.

'It's inside the air-conditioning system. You can see for yourself.'

'Where?' asked the terrific figure.

'Up there.' Will's dad pointed to the grille in the ceiling above the home screen. 'I'll get it for you, if you want.'

'What are you doing, Dad?'

'Let me deal with this, Will. It's all my fault. I'll get the painting.'

'But . . .'

'Leave this to me.' Will's dad struggled to manhandle his chair towards the home screen and the air-conditioning duct above it.

'What is he doing?' whispered Tim.

'I haven't the faintest idea,' whispered Will.

Will's dad huffed and puffed.

'Out of the way.' The terrific figure, slung his weapon across his broad left shoulder, strode to the chair and snatched it from Will's dad. He flung it down in front of the home screen, climbed onto it, reached up and took hold of the ceiling grille that covered the air-conditioning duct.

With a speed, quite remarkable for one of his corpulence, Will's dad swung a foot and kicked the chair out from beneath him.

The terrific figure tumbled to the floor, bringing down the grille and a section of ceiling. Will's dad flung himself on top of the fallen figure.

'Sit on his legs woman,' he shouted. 'Squash the smelly blighter. Hurry!'

Will's mum hurried and did as she was bid.

'Phone for the DOCS, lad,' Will's dad told Will. 'Tell them we've captured a murderer.'

Will's mouth hung open.

'I'll do it,' said Tim, and he did.

'Come in here, polluting the air and menacing my family,' cried Will's dad, his beefy buttocks pressing down upon the back of the fallen figure. 'I'll teach you to mess with the Starlings.'

The fallen figure struggled, but was quite unable to rise.

'My dad,' whispered Will. 'My dad did that.'

'They're on their way,' said Tim, replacing the receiver. 'They're just up two floors. They're coming right down.'

The fallen figure lurched, all but up-ending Will's dad.

'More weight needed,' called that man. 'Tim, Will, help us keep this stinker down.'

Will climbed onto his father's shoulders. Tim sat down in Will's mum's lap.

'Well, isn't this cosy?' said Will's mum. 'Like one big happy family. That's another thing I like about living in these times. Although the supper is growing cold and I'm—'

And through the doorway came the gallant lads and token ladette of the DOCS, weapons at the ready and looks of some surprise upon their faces, faces which they now took to fanning.

'The smell is him.' Will's dad bounced up and down, eliciting moans from the foul-smelling figure beneath. 'The murderer, we have him here.'

'Let him up,' said Chief Inspector Sam Maggott. 'We'll take him in for questioning.'

'Better just to pass sentence here,' said Officer John.

'Rather too many unanswered questions,' said Sam. 'I'd like to find out more about this unfragrant character before we remove him permanently from society.'

'He's still frisky.' Will's dad came near to another upending. 'Shooting him in the head while we're still sitting on him would probably be for the best.'

'I'll do things my way, if you don't mind,' said Sam. 'I *am* the law, you know.'

'Quite so, sir,' said Will's dad. 'So we should let him up, should we? He's all covered in guns. One or two quite uncomfortable beneath my behind, as it happens.'

'Let him up,' said Sam. 'We have him covered.'

And Sam's team most definitely did. They all had their guns out and were pointing them mostly in the right direction.

'As you wish,' said Will's dad. 'Everybody up.'

And he did try. And so did Will's mum.

'I'm a bit stuck,' she said. 'Could someone give me a hand?'

'I'm at a bit of a disadvantage too,' said Will's dad. 'Can't seem to ease myself up from this position.'

'Help them up,' Sam told his team.

Sam's team holstered their weapons and set to the task of dragging Will's parents into the vertical plane.

'Thanks very much,' said Will's dad. 'This has all been most exciting.'

'Aaaagh!' went the foul-smelling fallen figure, leaping now to his feet.

'That's quite enough of that, chummy,' said Sam. 'Up with your hands and come along quietly.'

'And drop your weapons,' added Officer Denton. 'And do that before you put up your hands.'

'Good idea,' said Sam. 'Do as the nice lady tells you. Or there will be trouble.'

It must be noted that it had now become very crowded in the Starling breakfasting-cum-suppering area which, although spacious enough to accommodate at least four well-fed adults, now found itself playing host to rather more than that. There were the mountainous Maggot, Officers Denton, Higgins, and Tudor; there was Tim McGregor, Will's mum, Will's dad, and Will. And there was also the terrific figure which was now towering over all of them and snatching up one of his weapons.

'Fire upon the murderer,' Sam ordered. 'And try not to kill too many civilians.'

'Hit the deck,' shouted Will's dad.

'Aaaagh!' went you-know-who once again.

And then the carnage began.

The DOCS weaponry was, in its manner, awesome. It *was* the state of the art, and this *was* the twenty-third century. And although it did take Sam's team a moment or two to get their guns out of their holsters, and a few moments more to get them actually working, they were soon blasting away with a vengeance, spraying chunks of the murderer to the four cardinal points of the compass and all those in between.

There was so much flesh and gore – and all those other pieces.

And when the smoke had finally cleared, which took a bit of a while as the air-conditioning system was now broken, there was very little of the murderer left to be seen, other than a great deal of metal cogwheels and a lot of broken springs.

'Damn me,' said Chief Inspector Sam Maggott. 'It was a robot.'

Officer Denton shook her head. 'It *was*,' she agreed, 'but I don't see how it could have been, sir. I mean, we don't actually have any robots like that, yet. There's no such thing as robots like that. They only exist in science fiction.'

'The exception that proves the rule?' Sam suggested.

'No sir, I don't think so.'

'Well, bag up the bits; we'll take them back to the department.'

Sam glanced about at the cowering civilians. The cowering civilians were covered in all sorts of vilely-smelling guts and gore. The outer covering of the impossible robot.

'Thank you very much for your cooperation, citizens,' said Sam.

With his mouth still open, and his mind somewhat numb, Will watched as Sam's team did what they could to scoop all the bits and bobs into pink plastic bin liners.*

'I'll help you,' he said when he could find his voice.

'We'll send in a clean-up team to wipe away all the splatterings,' said Sam, once the bagging up had been completed. 'And so, farewell. And thank you once again for your cooperation.'

And he took his leave, the words 'one hundred per cent clean-up rate', being the last the Starling family heard from him as he and his team departed.

'Well,' said Will's dad. 'That *was* exciting, wasn't it?'

'The supper's stone cold,' said Will's mum. 'I'll have to reheat it.'

'I think I'll leave you to it,' said Tim. 'I think I'll go home now and take a shower.'

'Yes,' said Will. 'Okay, yes.'

'Robot, eh?' said Tim. 'Reminds you of that old movie, doesn't it? You know the one I mean?'

'Of course I do,' said Will. 'Everyone knows *that* movie.'

'Sent from the future,' said Tim. 'Amazing. Whatever next?' And walking upon wobbly legs, Tim too took his leave.

Which left just Will and his mum and dad: just Will and his mum and dad and all the terrible smelly splatterings.

And there was one thing more than this: one thing that Will held tightly in his hand; one thing that he had picked up from the floor when he'd helped the team from the Department of Correctional Science to bag the pieces of the impossible robot.

Will opened his hand and gazed down upon it. It was a small brass nameplate, a maker's nameplate, with certain words printed upon it.

They were:

* Pink being the new black this particular year.

BABBAGE & CO.
MAKERS OF
AUTOMATA TO
HER MAJESTY
QUEEN VICTORIA
PATENT NO. – 3610592
MADE IN ENGLAND, 1895.

6

Supper in the Starling household was a somewhat sombre affair. It lacked the usual cheery banter. The intended supper had been discarded due to its adulteration by splatterings of gore, and although the replacement was toothsome, it could do little to raise the spirits of the Starlings.

Will turned food with his fork and remained alone with his thoughts. His parents viewed him suspiciously. What had happened was down to Will and they knew it.

After supper Will said, 'I'm going out,' and took himself off to Tim's.

Tim McGregor lived thirteen floors up from Will, in an all-but-identical unit, the only difference being that Tim's breakfasting area was not bespattered with gore.

Will knocked at the door and Tim let him in.

'You never ring the chimes,' said Tim.

'I don't like the tunes,' said Will.

'Come inside then.'

And Will came inside.

'That was all pretty savage,' said Tim, steering Will towards his bedroom. 'I had to have a shower. I'm still shaking.'

'There's something I have to tell you, Tim, something very important.'

'I'll show you my shoe collection,' Tim said. 'I picked up a pair of antique brogues the other week. Well, they're not actually a pair, but they should interest you.'

'I'm not really interested in—'

'Come and see.' Tim opened the door to his clothes cupboard and propelled Will into it.

'Hang about,' Will protested. 'What are you doing?'

But Tim had followed Will into the cupboard and closed the door upon them both.

'What are you doing, Tim? Let me out.'

'Be silent for a moment, and I'll explain.' Tim switched on a light and put his finger to his lips.

'What are you up to?'

'Just be quiet.'

'Okay,' Will shrugged. 'What's going on?'

'I don't want us to be seen or heard. I'm going to tell you some stuff. It's very sensitive stuff. You must promise you won't mention anything I tell you to another soul.'

'Does your mum still listen at your bedroom door?'

'Not my mum. The surveillance system.'

'You've a surveillance system in your housing unit?'

'More than one, and so have you.'

'I certainly haven't,' said Will.

'You certainly have. They're all over the place. I only found out a week ago. Came across the program when I was running through the Tate's security systems. There's an iris-scanner and a thermascan inside every home screen. And how many home screens do you have in your unit?'

'One in every room,' whispered Will. 'But this is outrageous.'

'Yes, isn't it? And I'd bet there'd be a revolution if it were made common knowledge. But it's not very likely to be, is it? I don't know whether we can be picked up on audio, or not, so I'm not taking any chances. We'll conduct our conversation in this cupboard.'

Will shrugged. 'This *is* a bit of a shock,' said he.

'But not as much of a shock as being attacked by a robot.'

'That was a considerable shock. And it's what I want to talk to you about.'

'Because you've discovered that it was Babbage.'

Will's jaw dropped. 'How did you know *that*?' he asked.

'The robot was sent to kill you, because of what you discovered about the painting. And because you stopped the painting from being destroyed.'

'What?' went Will. 'What?'

'You are in very big trouble. And I just don't know what I can do to help you. Which is why I don't want to be seen or heard talking to you about it. I could have simply refused to answer the door.'

'But you didn't.'

'You're my best friend, Will. You're a bit of a weirdo, but I like you. I don't want to see you get into trouble, let alone get killed.'

'But I don't understand any of it. The business with the picture. And how do you know about *that*?'

'There are surveillance cameras in the archive too. I saw what you got up to. It did make me laugh, I've never cared too much for Rothko myself. I erased your image. But I thought I'd check on what it was all about. So I accessed your workstation and had a flip through your morning's work. I saw the digital wristwatch. Things fell into place. It's not the first time it's happened. There have been other historical artefacts that don't fit into our accepted view of history. There's a website dedicated to them: anachronisms. Or there was; it was recently closed down.'

'But what does it mean? What does *this* mean?'

Will took out the little brass plaque and handed it to Tim. Tim examined it at length and grinned broadly.

'Incredible,' he said. 'And I'm really holding it in my hand. Incredible.'

'But what does it mean?'

'It means we've been lied to,' said Tim. 'About history. What do you know about Charles Babbage?'

'A little,' said Will. 'He was the father of computer science. Born in London in 1791, he had a natural genius for mathematics and when he entered Trinity College, Cambridge in 1811, he discovered that he knew more about the subject than his tutors. In 1821 he began work on his Difference Engine, the first computer, which he completed in 1832. He designed it to work out mathematical tables and he went on to build his Analytic Engine in 1856, which was capable of advanced calculus. He should have been hailed alongside Brunel as one of the great geniuses of the Victorian age, but he was not. The British government showed no interest in funding his work and his inventions were never truly realised until the twentieth century. He was a man ahead of his time.'

'That's somewhat more than *a little*,' said Tim. 'That's a whole lot. How come you know all that?'

'I looked him up in the library archives on Wednesday lunchtime. After seeing the digital watch in the painting I wanted to know whether there really had been a Babbage in Victorian times, who had anything to do with computers. There was, but he didn't invent digital watches.'

'I think he did,' said Tim. 'And robots too. But not in the version of history that we've been brought up on.'

'What other things?' asked Will. 'On the website you saw. What other historical artefacts did you read about that don't fit in?'

'Ever heard of Jules Verne?' Tim asked.

'I've read his books, on my palm-top, I downloaded them from the British Library files; they're wonderful.'

Tim shook his head. 'What is it with you and the Victorian era?'

'I don't know. I've always felt a part of it somehow; I can't explain.'

'So you've probably read *Twenty Thousand leagues Under The Sea.*'

'Brilliant,' said Will.

'Then you'll probably be pleased to hear that according to the information on the website, the wreckage of Captain Nemo's *Nautilus* was recently discovered in the Antarctic.'

Will managed one more '*What?* '

'It's true,' said Tim. 'I know it's true. I can't prove it. But this—' he displayed the little brass plaque '– is all the proof I need. You'll have to run, Will. Get away. They know you're onto them. The painting didn't get destroyed. They'll send another robot after you.'

'Who will? The authorities?'

'The Victorians. The robot was sent through time to destroy the painting and destroy you. That robot was sent from the past.'

'Yeah, right,' said Will. 'In a time machine, I suppose. Like the one that H.G. Wells wrote about.'

'I've never heard of H.G. Wells,' said Tim. 'Was he another scientist?'

'Another novelist, like Jules Verne. This is absurd, Tim.'

'Not according to the website. According to the website the Victorians made incredible advances in technology. The wireless transmission of electricity, laser technology, even a space programme. Bits and pieces *have* been found. I'm holding such a piece in my hand.'

'So why has this been written out of history?'

'I don't know. I'm trying to piece it together. I can only conclude that it is something to do with the witches.'

There was a bit of a pause and then Will said, 'Did I hear you say "witches"?'

'You did,' said Tim. 'That's what I said.'

'You are saying that this has something to do with witches?'

Tim nodded.

'But Tim,' said Will, 'and please don't take this the wrong way, 'there are no such thing as witches.'

'Oh, there are.' Tim's head nodded and his big hair went every which way. 'Those two women who came to the Tate were witches. I recognised them. They have a triple A security clearance. All the higher echelons are in the Craft.'

'Witchcraft? Are you serious, Tim?'

'Why do you think I'm a Pagan, Will?'

Will shrugged. 'Because it's your choice. You can believe in anything you want to believe in. It's still legal.'

'No,' said Tim. 'It's because I want to get on. By declaring on my employment application that I was a Pagan, I got a head start. I've had three promotions this year. How many have you had?'

'None,' said Will. 'But how—'

'Websites, Will. Conspiracy theory websites. I've grown up on them. I love them. There was this really good one that said that witches are running the world.'

'But it got closed down?' Will said.

'It did. But by that time I had, how shall I put this, digested the intelligence. The website suggested that a cabal of witches run the planet. It all sounded terribly exciting, so I thought I'd put "Pagan" on my application and see if it helped. It did. I hear a word here and a word there, and those two women *were* witches. I know it.'

'This is all too much,' Will shook his blondy head. 'It's all too much to believe. And if real witches wanted me dead, surely they'd just cast a spell on me, or something.'

'Did you watch the newscast earlier on the home screen?'

'No,' said Will. 'Dad tuned it to the relaxation channel. We watched waves breaking on a beach throughout supper.'

'Shame. You'd have been interested in the newscast. It showed the serial killer who had butchered an undisclosed number of William Starlings being led away and later executed.'

'*What?*' went Will. 'But that's not what happened.'

'Are you telling me that you don't believe what you see on the newscasts? Are you suggesting that there might be some big conspiracy?'

'Ah,' said Will.

'I don't know what's going on,' said Tim, 'or what really went on in Victorian times, but we're not being told the truth. There is a big conspiracy. It could be something to do with witchcraft, or it couldn't, but you're in big trouble, Will. Whoever it is that wants you dead, wants you dead. They want to destroy the painting, which has the evidence of the truth in it and they want to kill you, because you know.'

'Then they'll want to kill you too,' said Will.

'I'm sure,' said Tim. 'Which is why we are talking in a cupboard. I am telling you everything I know, in confidence.'

'So what am I going to do? Run? To where?'

'I don't know. But I think you should try and find out the truth.'

'And how am I going to do that?'

'Go back into the past.'

'Oh right,' said Will. 'Like, find the time machine that this robot came in? Get real, Tim, please.'

'Take the drug,' said Tim. 'The Retro. Take all the tablets. If they really work then you'll get glimpses of the real past. You'll see what your Victorian ancestors saw, smell what they smelled, feel what they felt. It's all there inside your head, in your genetic coding, if it's true and the drug really works.'

'I'm scared,' Will said. 'I'm really scared.'

'I don't know what to say,' Tim said.

'I wish I'd never hidden that painting.'

'You did it because you cared, because you didn't want to see a thing of beauty being destroyed.'

'But if I take the drug and I do find out the truth, or some of it, where does that get me? If I'm still on some death list, what am I going to do?'

'Don't know. But perhaps an idea will come to you. Perhaps something will come to you.'

Will let out his breath.

'Pooh,' said Tim. 'Garlic.'

'I'm sorry. Give me the drug.'

'You're not going to take it here.'

'Where then?'

'I don't know, but anywhere other than here.'

'Why?'

'Well, I don't want you ODing in my cupboard.'

'What?'

'Well, it *might* happen. I'm not saying it will. Go home and take it.'

'And what if another robot turns up at my door?'

'Take it on the tram, or something.'

'No,' said Will. 'I know just the place to take it, but you're coming with me. I don't want to be on my own when I do it.

The Shrunken Head was still Brentford's premier rock pub. For more than two hundred and fifty years it had played host to countless up-and-coming rock bands that had later gone on to find fame. In their early days the Beatles had played there, and so had the Stones, and so too had Gandhi's Hairdryer, Soliloquy, The Lost T-Shirts of Atlantis, and Sonic Energy Authority.

Tonight it was the Apes of Wrath, Foetus Eater and the others, with the Slaughterhouse Five topping the bill.

The Slaughterhouse Five were a 'suit band', which is to say they were a three-piece. There was Dantalion's Chariot, lead vocals, political awareness and whistling; the Soldier of Misfortune, who impersonated weather, and Musgrave Ritual, whose strummings on the old banjo brought pleasure to literally dozens. The Slaughterhouse Five were in line to be the 'Next Big Thing', but the line was very long and with only fifteen minutes of fame allotted for any Next Big Thing, there was always the chance of being out or asleep when the moment came.

The interior of the Shrunken Head was rough: it was dire, it was ill-kempt and wretched. The management was surly, the bouncers were brutal. The beer, a pallid lager called Little, was overpriced and underpowered. It was everything that a great live-music pub should be.

The clientèle was big, fat, young and colourful, and whilst they drank, they dined upon rice muffins and an extensive variety of soft and easily chewable crisps called Soggies.

Will found a vacant table and seated himself. Tim went off to the bar and returned with two cups of Little and a large pack of rice muffins that he tucked into with gusto.

Will turned the phial of capsules on his palm. 'Tell me everything you know about this drug,' he said to Tim. 'What exactly are its effects?'

'Mind-expanding.' Tim mimed expandings of the mind. A mime-ster from the Apes of Wrath caught sight of this miming and mimed admiring applause.

'But you've never actually taken it, have you?' Will fixed Tim with a very hard stare.

'Not as such.' Tim shook his head sadly, showering Will with rice muffins.

'So you don't really know *what* will happen.'

'I know this,' said Tim. 'The drug was designed as a memory restorative for patients who'd suffered amnesia due to some accident or trauma situation or whatever, and it enjoyed a very high success rate. But then the doctors began to notice that the patients they were treating with it seemed to be remembering things they shouldn't be able to remember: very early childhood experiences, their own births, and more. They could remember things their parents had done before they themselves were born. That had the doctors scratching at their skullcaps, I can tell you. But they worked it out, what was happening. The drug was allowing patients not only to access their own lost memories, but other memories, imprinted into the very cells of their brains, memories inherited from their forefathers. Pretty incredible stuff, eh? But you won't get it on prescription through your health-care plan. As soon as its properties were confirmed it was put on the restricted list. "For High Echelon use only." Ask yourself why.'

Will asked himself why.

'Get an answer?' Tim asked.

Will shook his head.

'Secrets,' Tim gave his nose a tap. 'Too many secrets in the past that the High Echelons don't want the likes of us to know about.'

'The secret-history business,' Will said.

'Exactly. It was really tricky getting hold of it. This is powerful stuff.'

'It's not exactly a *recreational* drug, is it? Like Bawlers or Wind-ghast, or sherbet lemon.'

'It doesn't blow the snits out of your gab-trammel, if that's what you mean.'

'That's exactly what I mean.' Will sighed and gazed about the crowded bar of the Shrunken Head. It was another Friday night; young folk had come here to enjoy themselves, all dolled up in their finery. Those who had employment had finished with it for the week and were preparing to indulge in whatever excesses the weekend and their financial status allowed them. These were folk, everyday folk. *They* weren't being chased by robots from the past. They didn't have the imminent threat of arrest and probable execution hanging over their brightly-toned heads.

'This is so unfair,' said Will, taking another sup of Little. And then another swig and then another gulp. 'My cup runneth empty,' he observed.

'I'll get another.' Tim rose and took himself off to the bar.

'So unfair,' muttered Will. 'I mean, I've always been up for taking risks, but this is all frankly ridiculous.'

'Hello, my lovely boy,' came a voice Will knew only too well.

'Gladys,' said Will, as Gladys now filled most of his vision.

'And you told me you couldn't make it,' Gladys was a vision in scarlet – but a vision from the Book of Revelation.

'Tim persuaded me.' Will smiled warmly up at the acres of womanhood. 'He's at the bar. He's been hoping you'd come. He'll want to buy you a drink.'

'Oh goody.' Gladys turned and heaved herself into the swelling crowd.

Will once more considered the phial of capsules. What *would* happen if he took them? Would he be transported into some hallucinogenic vision of the past? Would his head fill up with a chaos of jumbled memories? Would he have some terrible, terrible revelation? Would he go mad? Or would the capsules turn out to be nothing more than laxatives, sold to Tim by some prankster?

'Too many questions,' whispered Will to himself. 'And I really could do with some answers. But of course, it's all such a terrible risk.'

At length, and at some length too, Tim returned to Will's table. Tim did not return in the company of Gladys. Neither did Tim return smiling.

'Thanks a lot,' said Tim, placing two cups of Little and a packet of fruitcake-flavoured Soggies on the table. 'Tuning up that scarlet harpy and setting her on me; very not funny at all. Call yourself my bestest friend?'

Will said nothing.

And Tim stared down at Will.

The plastic phial lay on the tabletop.

The plastic phial was empty.

Will sat rigidly, staring into space. His eyes were glazed, the pupils dilated. His face was an eerie grey and his lips an unnatural blue.

Tim reached cautiously forward and touched his hand to Will's neck, feeling for the pulse of the jugular.

There was no pulse.

Will Starling was dead.

7

It was the day before the day before yesterday and it was raining.

It was raining and the 8.02 morning train to Paddington was thirty seconds late.

Captain Ernest Starling of The Queen's Own Electric Fusiliers sat in the first class waiting room of Brentford Central station, knees together, shoulders back and a look of impatience tightening the corners of a mouth that lurked in the shadow of his resplendent mustachios.

Captain Starling had little patience. He liked things done at the hurry up and by the rule book, which stated unequivocally that all things *must* be done on time. His wife, the fragrant Mary, always did things on time and by the numbers. Breakfast at 7.30am, dinner at 8.30pm, sex at 10.30pm, brandy and cigar for her husband at 10.32pm.

Not that the Captain didn't feel the need for patience. He prayed nightly for it at 10.45pm. 'God give me patience,' he prayed, 'and give it to me *now*!'

But so far God had failed to heed the Captain's requests. And so the Captain sat and stewed in the first class waiting room.

He cut a magnificent figure did the Captain. He wore his finest dress uniform, a tightly-fitting tunic of patterned blue velvet, trimmed with gold brocade and decked with the many medals he had won for gallantry. A blue silk cape was slung about his shoulders, and a bearskin helmet with a high cockade was on his head. His pantaloons were of purple damask, his high top boots polished patent leather.

The waiting room was elegantly furnished with quilted Chesterfield sofas, upholstered in rich red fabric embroidered in the style of Sir William Morris. Porcelain jardinières of oriental design, embossed with dragon motifs, held orchids, which released heady fragrances into an atmosphere already enriched by the smoke of expensive cigars.

Upon the marble flooring lay a throw rug of the Afghani persuasion. The Captain's highly polished boot heels began to rap briskly upon this rug, tapping to a regimental drumbeat that only he heard, that was quite out of time with the Strauss waltz that issued melodically through the brass speaker system.

The single other occupant of the waiting room was a fellow traveller, a gentleman of considerable girth and more than a little presence. He had entered but minutes before and, much to the Captain's disgust, had chosen to sit right next to him, rather than to occupy one of the other vacant Chesterfields. This gentleman wore a stylish Amberly topcoat of grey moleskin with matching top hat and gloves. His face was broad, with hooded eyes and heavy jowls, and now he suddenly struck the marble flooring with the tip of his silver skull-topped swordstick.

'Sir,' said he. 'Might I humbly beg that you desist from that infernal rapping?'

'You might, sir,' the Captain replied, turning his head to face his inquisitor. 'But by God I will not, the train is late.' The Captain took from the breast pocket of his braided tunic a gold hunter which had been the gift of a grateful monarch, flipped open the lid of its case and perused its face. 'A minute and five seconds late! I shall fax a letter of complaint to the director of the railway.'

'Chill out,' said the fellow traveller. 'Don't get your knickers in a twist.'

'What, sir? What did you say?'

'Relax,' said the gentleman. 'Let yourself be soothed by the sounds of Strauss.'

'Damned foreigner.' the Captain rapped his heels once more. 'Give me a good British regimental band any day. I cannot be having with this foreign folderol.'

'It's technically British,' the traveller replied. 'The British Empire now encompasses most of the globe, as well you know.'

'Of course I know, sir. I am an officer in the service of Her Majesty Queen Victoria (God bless her), in one of her most noble regiments. I've put the fear up Johnny Foreigner in many distant parts.'

'I too have travelled widely,' said the gentleman. 'I have visited the Potala in Tibet and studied beneath the High Lama. I have wandered alone across the Kalahari Desert, where I met with the Bushmen, who made me their tribal chief. I have—'

'All very interesting,' said the Captain. 'But the train is late.'

'Delayed a mile up the line,' said the gentleman. 'A brewer's dray broke a wheel upon the crossing. The train will be indefinitely delayed.'

'I've heard nothing of this on the tannoy, sir. How do you know of such matters?'

'I know,' said the gentlemen, 'I know all.' And, opening his topcoat, he took from a pocket in his triple-breasted waistcoat of golden brocade a star-shaped calling card, which he passed in a gloved hand to the Captain.

The Captain took this card and read it aloud. 'Hugo Rune, philanthropist, philosopher and genius,' he read.

'At your service,' said Hugo Rune.

'I have no need for your services, sir.'

'I feel perhaps that you do.'

'Hah.' The Captain resumed his impatient heel-tapping.

Rune tapped his swordstick in time to the Strauss. 'I perceive that you are going to the launching,' said he.

'You *what*? Sir? You *what*?'

'To the launching at Greenwich. Of Her Majesty's Electric Airship *Dreadnaught*. You are bound for that, I believe.'

'I am sir, as it happens. And at this rate I will be late.' The Captain sought his cigar case.

'Left-hand pantaloon pocket,' said Rune.

The Captain located his case in his left-hand pantaloon pocket. 'Damn me, sir,' said he.

'Never,' said Rune. 'It is not in my nature.'

The Captain fumbled a cigar from his case.

'You lack for a Lucifer,' said Rune.

'I have fire,' said the Captain, patting at his pocket.

'I believe not,' said Rune.

The Captain ceased his pattings. 'Left the damned match case on my dresser,' said he.

'Allow me,' said Hugo Rune and reaching forward he plucked the cigar from the Captain's fingers and popped it into the Captain's mouth. And then Rune removed his gloves, waved his right hand before the Captain's face, snapped his thumb and forefinger, and brought fire from nowhere to the Captain's cigar.

'Taught to me by a fakir in Bombay,' said Hugo Rune.

The Captain seemed unable to suck.

'Draw breath,' said Rune.

And the Captain did so.

'There,' said Rune, blowing onto his thumb and forefinger to extinguish the flames. 'A fine cigar,' and he sniffed at the smoke. 'A Havana half-corona from Balbereth's Tobacco Emporium in the

Burlington Arcade. I have my cigarettes manufactured there, to my own personal blend.'

The Captain had ceased his puffing and his cigar hung perilously from his slack lower lip.

Rune reached forward once more and flipped up the Captain's chin. 'You'll drop your cigar,' said he. 'And that would be a waste.'

The Captain snatched the cigar from his mouth and hurled it to the floor. 'Who are you, sir?' he demanded to be told.

'Hugo Rune,' said Hugo Rune. 'You have my card. I am he.'

'Then *what* are you? Some kind of Music-Hall magician?'

'A magician,' said Rune. 'But not one from the halls. My magic is of a higher calling.'

'More likely the work of the devil.'

'Your cigar is burning the rug,' observed Rune.

'Damn my cigar,' said the Captain, growing crimson at the cheeks.

'Waste not, want not,' said Rune, taking up the cigar, dusting it down and sticking it into his mouth.

'Damn me, sir. Enough of your impudence,' Captain Starling rose from the sofa and put his hand to the hilt of his sabre.

'Draw it not,' advised Rune. 'For if you draw it, I might feel compelled to injure you.'

The Captain drew his sabre and brandished it bravely. 'Up sir,' cried he.

'Sit down, you foolish man.'

'Up sir, or I slay you where you sit.'

Rune sighed and raised himself upon his stick. He faced the Captain eye to eye, then laid his stick aside. 'I am unarmed,' said Rune. 'Would you, an officer and a gentleman, slay an unarmed man?'

The Captain sheathed his sabre and raised his fists. 'Marquis of Queensbury rules,' said he. 'And I must warn you, I am the regimental champion. Defend yourself as best you can, for I mean to smite you for your impertience.

'I think not,' said Hugo Rune. 'Sit yourself down, there are matters I must discuss with you.'

'Have at you, sir.' The Captain swung a fist at Rune, but Rune, for all the considerable bulk of him, ducked nimbly out of range.

'Raise your fists, defend yourself,' called the Captain.

'I must warn you,' said Rune, 'that I am a Grand High Master in the art of Dimac, the most deadly of all the martial arts, and that I can instantly disable and disfigure you with little more than a fingertip's pressure.'

The Captain swung another fist; this too failed to connect with Hugo Rune, philanthropist, philosopher, genius and Grand High Master in the art of Dimac.

'I inform you of my skills,' said Rune, 'because it is my duty to do so. My hands and feet are registered with the Metropolitan constabulary as deadly weapons. I am compelled to keep them in a locked cupboard when they are not in use.'

'What?' The Captain swung another fist, which similarly missed its mark.

'That was a humorous aside,' said Rune. 'A little humour to lighten an otherwise tragic occasion.'

'Tragic?' the Captain squared up for further fist-swinging.

Rune reached forward and tapped him lightly on the shoulder.

The Captain collapsed in an untidy heap on the floor. Hugo Rune sighed and hauled the Captain onto another of the Chesterfields. He applied a smelling bottle to the Captain's nostrils and returned him to consciousness.

'What?' went the Captain, floundering about. 'What, what, what?'

'You were taken poorly,' said Rune. 'But you're all right now.'

'I feel altogether odd.'

'Now listen to me,' said Hugo Rune. His face pressed close to the Captain's left ear. 'You are bound for the launching at Greenwich. Of Her Majesty's Electric Airship *Dreadnaught*. Thousands will be attending. It is to be *the* event of this year, 1885. But you must listen very carefully to me.' And Rune spoke further words into the ear of Captain Ernest Starling of the Queen's Own Electric Fusiliers.

At 8.37am, the 8.02 morning train to Paddington drew into Brentford Central station. Captain Starling, somewhat shaky about the knee regions, but otherwise with his dignity intact, climbed into the first class carriage and sat down heavily.

The carriage was unoccupied but for a single figure, who appeared to be sleeping. He was a large gentleman in an Amberly topcoat of grey moleskin with a matching top hat and gloves. A swordstick with a silver skull-shaped mount rested across his knees. Captain Starling grunted impatiently and tapped his polished heels upon the carriage floor.

At length the train left the station and proceeded to Paddington.

The launching of the Electric Airship *Dreadnaught* was indeed *the* event of 1885.

The Times newspaper recorded the details upon its front page:

'We live in an age of marvels and we, the British people, are privileged that so many of these marvels should be the products of our own sovereign nation. The triumphs of modern engineering, brought to wondrous fruition by Mr Isambard Kingdom Brunel, are well known to all, and The Electric Airship *Dreadnaught* must rank as his single greatest achievement. The sheer scale and magnificence of this aerial warship are awesome to behold. Over fifteen hundred feet in length and capable of transporting entire regiments equipped with the very latest ordinance and armoured flying carriages, the airship is powered through the sky by two great electric turbine engines. These are the creation of Mr Nikola Tesla, whose mighty power towers ornament the skyline of the capital and are daily being erected the length and breadth of the country, to supply electrical energy, broadcast on a radio frequency without the need for cables, to every home and place of industry throughout our fair land. Mr Tesla's electronic marvels could not, of course, have been made possible without the aid of the recently knighted Sir Charles Babbage, inventor of the calculating machine and many other invaluable and innovative inventions, which have advanced the nation and the British Empire.

'It seemed as if all of London had turned out to witness the launching of the *Dreadnaught*. In the great stands that had been erected for the occasion were to be seen renowned Music-Hall entertainers such as Little Tich, performer of the ever-popular Big Boot Dance, and Count Otto Black, proprietor of The Circus Fantastique. The playwright Oscar Wilde was in attendance and also the fashionable artist Mr Richard Dadd, whose latest portrait of Her Majesty the Queen (God bless Her) is to be seen on display at the Tate Gallery. Lords and ladies beyond the scope of counting were to be viewed in their finery, but it was the crowds of commoners waving their Union Jacks and singing in raucous tones that presented the most colourful cavalcade of characters. Every working type seemed to have been represented and it is only to be supposed that virtually all trade must have ceased in the great metropolis for this most special of days. Costermongers were much in evidence, as were crossing sweepers, street piemen, coffee-stall keepers, sellers of dolls and sponges, fly-papers and beetle wafers, snuff and tobacco boxes, wash leathers and rat poisons. There were draymen and ragmen, tallymen and mudlarks, coal-heavers, lightermen and big bargees. A lady in a straw hat hawked copies of *The War Cry* and all rejoiced as Her Majesty Queen Victoria (God bless Her) christened the mighty sky vessel.

'But here a grim incident brought an unwelcome discord to the otherwise harmonious proceedings. An anarchist arose from the crowd, fought his way through the Metropolitan Police cordon and rushed at Her Majesty.

'His evil intent was however thwarted by the heroic actions of one Captain Ernest Starling of the Queen's Own Electric Fusiliers, who, as if sensing the imminent attack, had positioned himself to receive it. Captain Starling cut down the assassin with his sabre, but was mortally wounded in the process.

'He has been posthumously awarded the Victoria Cross for his supreme gallantry.'

8

Will Starling awoke from the dead.

He awoke with a terrible scream and clutched at his heart.

'Easy,' called the voice of Tim, and firm hands pressed upon Will's shoulders. 'Easy now.' These hands raised Will into the vertical plane.

'You passed out,' said Tim. 'You're all right now, I think.'

'I'm not. I'm dead. 'I'm—' Will clutched some more at himself and slowly opened his eyes. 'Tim?' he said. 'It's you. It's Tim.'

'It's Tim,' said Tim. 'You don't look altogether perky.'

'Nor would you if you'd been stabbed in the chest by an anarchist.'

'Oh dear,' said Tim. 'I knew you shouldn't have had that third drink.'

'Drink?' Will blinked his eyes and stared all around and about. 'Where am I?' he asked.

'Chiswick Central,' said Tim. 'You said you were feeling ill, then you went to the onboard toilet. You were in there for ages, then you staggered out and fell down in the carriage. We missed our stop. I hauled you off the tram here.'

'The tram? I'm here. It wasn't me.'

'It certainly *was* you. You made a right exhibition of yourself.'

'Getting stabbed. That wasn't me.'

'I've no idea what you're talking about.'

'The Retro. It worked, Tim. I can remember everything. Generations and generations of Starlings. It's all in my head.'

'You took Retro?' Tim looked genuinely alarmed. 'You took Retro? When did you take Retro?'

Will stared hard at Tim, which wasn't easy as the world was now going in and out of focus. 'You gave it to me. In the Shrunken Head.'

'We haven't been to the Shrunken Head for weeks.'

'We were there tonight. The Slaughterhouse Five were on.'

'They're on next week. Next Friday night.' Tim peered into the eyes of Will. 'You really are on something aren't you?'

'We need a drink,' said Will. 'A big drink.'

'You've had enough, come on.'

'Tim,' said Will. 'It's all right. I'm all right. I'm not going to turn you in to the DOCS or anything for giving me the Retro.'

'*I didn't give you any Retro!* Will you please stop this, Will.'

'You stop it,' said Will. 'I've told you it's all right.'

'And you've told me it's next Friday night, which it's not.'

'So much stuff,' said Will. 'So much stuff.'

'Stuff?' Tim asked.

'In my head. All those memories. You were right, about the things on that website. The *Nautilus*. The digital watches. There was a spaceship too.'

'I really do have no idea what you're talking about.'

'Yeah, right,' said Will. 'And it's Thursday, not Friday.'

'Thursday, a week before the Friday you're talking about,' Tim held out his wristwatch towards Will. 'Check the day,' he said. 'Check the date.'

Will checked the day and the date. 'Your watch could be wrong,' he said.

'Now you're being absurd,' Tim laughed. Heartily. 'My watch, like yours, like everybody else's, is linked to the world timepiece in Greenwich. It can't be wrong.'

'Well, yours *is*.' Will flashed his own wristwatch. 'Observe.'

Tim observed. 'I observe,' said Tim. 'Thursday.'

'It's Friday.' Will took to observing. 'It's *Thursday*,' he said, and he said it in a voice of considerable surprise – and a great deal of shock too.

'No,' said Will. 'Oh no no no. Then everything *really* happened. It wasn't the drug. I really did go back into the past.'

'Calm down,' Tim clamped his hand over Will's mouth. 'There are people about.'

Will's eyes flashed to the left and the right. The station was all but deserted, all but for himself and Tim and a large noble looking gentleman who sat at the end of the platform. Tramcars slowly dragged themselves by, but no one got off and the gentleman didn't get on.

'Listen to me,' Tim whispered close at Will's ear. 'I have got a connection who said he could get me some Retro. But not until next week.'

Will tore Tim's hand away. 'But you did give it to me. At the Shrunken Head. We were there. The Slaughterhouse Five were playing.'

'That's next week, Will. Next Friday night.'

'Then all of it is true. I really did go back physically.'

Tim laughed once again. But this time it was a humourless laugh. 'Drugs don't do that,' he said. 'Drugs can't do that. But . . .'

'But?' Will was very wobbly now and he leaned upon Tim for support.

'But if you *did* take Retro, what *can* you remember?'

'All of it, everything. About the things we talked about. They're all true.'

'You've got me again. We didn't talk about anything.'

'About the digital watch in the painting.'

'I'm shrugging,' said Tim. 'Feel me shrug.'

'*The Fairy Feller's Masterstroke*.'

'Still shrugging,' said Tim. 'Never heard of such a painting.'

'But you saw me on the security scan, hiding it.'

'Perhaps we *should* go and have a drink,' said Tim. 'And you can tell me all about it. Not that I believe a word, you understand, but because, well, you know in movies and stuff, when something really weird happens to someone and no one believes them. I've always wondered what that would be like in real life. You know, if your best friend turned out to be an alien from outer space or something. What would you *really* feel, if it were *really* real? And I don't have the faintest idea what is going on in your head now, and you might just be a stone-bonker. But, and this is the big but, what if it's not? I'd hate to be the one you confided the truth to, and the one who didn't believe you. So, what say we give it a go? Have a drink and you tell me the lot and then we try to figure out whether it's real and if it is, what we should do about it.'

'Have you quite finished?' Will asked.

'Not sure,' said Tim. 'Did you get the general gist of what I meant?'

'Vaguely,' said Will. 'It's a kind of, you-might-believe-me-if-you-fancy-the-sound-of-it, kind of jobbie, right?'

'Something along those lines. A drink?'

'A drink,' said Will. 'And I'll tell you a story that you really won't believe is really real, but will really want to believe is really real, if you get my general gist.'

'Not really,' said Tim. 'But let's go for it.'

And so they went for it.

The pub they went for it in was known as the Flying Swan. It was a pub that Tim had never been to before. They reached it after a long and tedious walk from Chiswick. A walk necessitated by the fact that the never-ending tramcar system ran only in a clockwise direction. Which meant that had they taken it, they would have to have travelled throughout the entirety of London Central before reaching Brentford. Which was only one stop *up* the line.

Of the Flying Swan itself, what can be said?

Well, much actually.

The Flying Swan was a late Victorian public house which stood upon what had once been the Ealing road, but was now a paved walkway to the rear of the housing tower where Tim and Will both lived.

The Flying Swan had survived not only the 'sensitive' interior decorations that twentieth-century brewery owners had meted out to it, but the seemingly inevitable destruction that awaited it in the twenty-first century, when Brentford was all but levelled for redevelopment and the great housing towers erected. The Flying Swan had survived because of an old charter lodged with the Crown Estate and given the Royal seal of approval by Queen Victoria. This charter gave the Swan a thousand years of protection against demolition. Only one other building in Brentford had similarly survived and this was a late Georgian house on what had once been Brentford's elegant Butts Estate which belonged to a gentleman by the name of Professor Slocombe, who dwelt in it during the twentieth century, with his elderly retainer, Gammon.

As to the interior of the Swan, what can be said?

Well, much, but perhaps a little at a time.

It was now a most elderly pub, sedate, having age to its credit rather than its detriment. It retained the features that make a pub a pub, rather than a theme bar, which give it dignity: a mahogany saloon bar counter, eight hand-drawn ales upon tap, a row of Britannia pub tables, a darts board, a long-disabled jukebox.

Its windows, of etched glass, were tinted by a million smoke-filled breaths. Its carpet, somewhat bare of thread, had known the footfalls of a thousand heroes. And its walls wore faded paper, patterned in the past.

A yard of ale glass hung upon the wall behind the bar and below it, upon shelves, were Spanish souvenirs, bottles of rare vintage, and ancient postcards showing rooftop views of Brentford in a past now distant.

And between these and the counter stood a barman of the part-time persuasion.

And this part time barman's name was Neville.

'Good evening gents,' said this fellow as Tim and Will entered the saloon bar. 'And how may I serve you?'

Will looked at Tim.

And Tim looked at Will.

'Well,' said Will, perusing the row of antique beer engines.

'I have eight hand-drawn ales on pump,' said Neville, with much pride in his voice. 'A selection which now exceeds any other pub in the locality by . . .' Neville paused. 'Eight,' he continued.

Will smiled towards the lord of the bar. 'And what would you recommend to a weary traveller?' he asked.

'A pint of Large,' said Neville. 'And for your companion?'

'Same for me,' said Tim.

Neville did the business, drawing with the practised hand of the true professional. At length, when he was satisfied that all was, as ever was, and ever should be, he presented his new patrons with their pints.

Will viewed the pints upon the polished countertop.

'Supreme,' was what he had to say.

'Take a taste,' said Neville.

And Will took a taste.

'Beyond supreme,' he said, when he had tasted it.

'Then all is indeed as it should be,' said Neville.

Tim too took to tasting. 'On me,' he said. 'Where's the monitor?'

'Monitor?' said Neville.

'The iris-scanner,' said Tim. 'So I can credit you for the drinks.'

'We don't have one of those, I'm afraid,' said Neville. 'This is a cash-only establishment.'

'What?' went Tim. 'But no one's used cash for the last fifty years.'

'I had noticed that trade's been dropping off,' said Neville.

Tim shook his head and his features vanished beneath his hair.

'Here,' said Will, delving into his trouser pocket and bringing out a handful of change. 'Try this.'

Tim made a clearing in his hair and peered through it. 'Antique money,' he said. 'Where did you get that?'

'It's a long story; just pay the man.'

Tim took the coins and handed some to Neville.

Neville rang up No Sale on the ancient cash register and presented Tim with his change. 'I think you must have undercharged me,' said Tim.

'On the contrary,' said Neville. 'Correct to the penny.'

'Then thank you very much.'

Tim followed Will towards a corner table, where they seated themselves upon comfy chairs and took further sup from their pints.

'Unbelievable,' said Tim. 'Perfect ale. I never even knew this place existed.'

Will smiled a knowing smile.

'You've been here before?' Tim asked.

'Oh yes,' said Will.

'You never told me about it.'

'It wasn't during your lifetime.'

Tim took a further sup. 'This sounds promising,' he said. 'I feel wackiness coming on. How come we're the only people drinking in this wonderful bar?'

'All will be explained,' said Will, taking further sup. 'This really is *the best*, isn't it?'

'Spot on,' Tim raised his pint to Will. 'So, just to recap, if I may. You've been into the future, to next Friday, where I gave you Retro, which enabled you to recall generations of your past. Then you travelled back into the past physically. And now you've brought me to a pub on my very block-step, which I've never seen before, to drink the finest beer I have ever tasted, that you apparently have tasted before, but not in my lifetime. Have I got all this right?'

'There's a lot more,' said Will. 'A whole lot more.'

'Oh good,' said Tim. 'I'm really loving this.'

'There's a lot that you're not going to love.'

'Well don't tell me any of that.'

'I have to tell you all of it. It's not finished yet. It's far from finished. In fact it's only just begun and you have to help me, which is why I'm here.'

'But you were never away.'

'I was in the toilet,' said Will. 'On the tramcar.'

'You were,' said Tim, supping more ale. 'I remember that.'

'I went into the toilet, but the me who went into the toilet was not the same me that came out again. The original me, that went in, is still on the tram. I told him to carry on all the way around London Central before going home. I had to be very careful not to touch him. It's a time-paradox thing. To do with David Warner in the old *Time Cop* movie. But we won't go into that yet.'

'Still loving it,' said Tim. 'But already starting to get a tad confused. Do you think you might explain?'

'It's a long story,' said Will. 'And I do mean a *long* story. It lasts for about three hundred years.'

'I'd better get some more beer in then.'

'It's my round,' said Will.

'It's your money I'll be paying with,' said Tim. 'You tell the tale, I'll get in the beers.'

'Fair enough,' said Will.

And so Tim got in the beers.

And so Will told the tale.

Will told Tim about what was going to happen next week. About *The Fairy Feller's Masterstroke* and the digital watch on the Tinker's wrist. And the witch women who had come to the Tate to destroy the painting and about how he had hidden it from them and substituted a Rothko.

And then Will told Tim about the foul-smelling Victorian robot with the horrible black eyes that had killed the other William Starlings and had tried to kill the one who was presently sitting talking to Tim, who was a different Will to the Will that had gone into the toilet on the tram, but was really the same one.

Which confused Tim somewhat. Although Tim did say that he was reminded of a certain classic twentieth-century Hollywood movie, where the robot was from the future.

'But this one came from the past,' Will explained. 'To stop me from altering the future, which would have, in turn, altered the past. Which, in fact, it did.'

Which got Tim confused once again.

And then Will told him about exactly what had happened after Tim had given him the Retro on the Friday of the following week. Which really got Tim confused.

But the beer was *so* good.

And Will told his tale well.

And as with all well-told tales, this one was not told in the first person.

And it went something, in fact altogether, like this.

9

The plastic phial lay on the tabletop, empty.

Will sat rigidly, staring into space. His eyes were glazed, the pupils dilated. His face was an eerie grey and his lips an unnatural blue.

Tim reached cautiously forward and touched his hand to Will's neck, feeling for the pulse of the jugular.

There was no pulse.

Will Starling was dead.

Will's eyes suddenly opened and so too did his mouth.

'Through a veil of cucumber I viewed the errant bicycle,' said Will.

'Pardon me?' said Tim, in some surprise.

'The spotty youth of time dwells upon the doorknob of pasta,' said Will.

'Again I confess to bafflement,' said Tim. 'But rejoice, nevertheless, that you have not popped your clogs.'

Will said nothing more for a moment, but then his opened eyes grew wide.

And then Will said, 'Run for your life.'

'My what?' asked Tim. 'My life?'

'Run,' cried Will and he leapt from his seat, overturning the table and wastefully spilling the drinks that Tim had purchased.

'You have spilled the drinks,' said Tim, stepping back to avoid the falling table and the glasses. 'By Our Lady of the Flatpack, you have taken the Retro, haven't you, Will?'

'I know all.' Will was up and about and now on the move. 'I know the past and the near future too. We must run quickly, and now.'

A crowd was beginning to form. Detached from the general crowd, it encircled Will and Tim and the now fallen table. It was a crowd of onlookers, as crowds so often are, a crowd which had 'become interested'.

'Everybody run!' bawled Will. 'Big trouble coming. Everybody run.' And he made to push into the crowd, to reinforce his words, as it were, with appropriate and demonstrative actions.

The crowd, however, yielded not.

A lady in a straw hat said. 'There you have it, the youth of today, brains broiled on seedy substances. It was never so in my day.'

'Yes it was, too,' said a chap in a J-cloth bandana. 'In your day it was all eating frogs up flagpoles and savouring the smells of Sarah.'

'Let me through,' cried Will, buffeting against the burly belly of an interested onlooker. 'It's on its way. It will kill you all.'

'Please make way,' said Tim. 'My friend is somewhat drunk; he's liable to project his supper onto a number of you, simultaneously.'

At this, the owner of the burly belly that Will was presently drumming upon made an attempt to step back, but this attempt was without success as further ranks of interested onlookers now penned him in.

'Run!' shouted Will. 'And those who can't run, waddle.'

'And there,' declared the lady straw hat, 'you bear witness to the perils of under-eating. Delirium. Under-eaters are so ungross, aren't they?'

'I'll agree with *that*,' said the chap in the J-cloth bandana, a chap of considerable girth. 'You may be a dotty old loon, but your finger is on the return key of truth upon this occasion.'

'That's no way to speak to your mother.'

'You're not my mother.'

'If I was your mother, I'd give you poison.'

'If *you* were my mother, I'd take it.

There was some applause at this, for even in the future, the old ones are still the best.

'Prepare to receive vomit,' Will opened his mouth and began to push a finger down his throat.

'Back up!' cried he of the burly belly.

'Don't push me,' said a burlier-bellied fellow behind him.

'But this chap's about to hurl spew.'

'That's no excuse for rudeness.' The burlier-bellied fellow smote the burly-bellied fellow on the back of his broad-necked bonce.

'Fight!' shouted Tim. 'In *that* direction. Relocate yourselves, or you'll miss it.'

'You can see a fight any day,' said the lady in the straw hat. 'You can even order one via your home screen. Have a professional pugilist come round and give you a sound thrashing.'

'Can you?' asked J-cloth man.

'Indeed,' said the lady. 'Give me your mail code and I'll have one sent around to you later.'

'Well . . . I . . .'

'My point is this,' said the lady, standing her ground, although others were now giving theirs. 'You can always see a fight, but vomiting is another matter altogether. It's years since I've seen anyone actually vomit. Oi! Careful there.' And the lady swung her handbag to smite a relocating crowd member who was brushing up against her. 'My point,' she continued, to the J-cloth wearer who was now being similarly jostled, 'is that vomiting is a rarity nowadays. Like, say, a one-legged fish, or a very small pony that you might carry in your pocket rather than ride upon, or perhaps—'

'A chocolate chair,' said J-cloth.

'Don't be absurd,' said the lady and she swung her handbag once more, bringing down her jostler, who collapsed onto the fallen table, breaking two of its legs and one of his own.

As fists began to fly, or at least to swing in heavy arcs, Tim pulled Will through a gap in the crowd.

'Run?' he asked.

'Believe me,' said Will. 'I do mean "run".'

And then, amidst the to-ing and fro-ing and the barging and the fists that swung in heavy arcs and the grunts from those whom these fists struck, and the oaths that were sworn and the insults exchanged, came a voice, louder than the rest, the voice of one who had now entered the Shrunken Head.

It was a voice of deep timbre and rich Germanic accent.

It cried, 'William Starling. Where is William Starling?'

'Baal and Sons, Inc,' swore Tim, sighting a head that was higher than the rest, with a face upon it that Tim knew and feared. 'It's the robot thing again.'

'It's another one.' Will was now making speed towards the rear of the bar where stood the stage and the fire exit. 'I really do mean "run".'

'I'm running,' said Tim. 'I'm running.'

And he was.

The terrific black-eyed and foully-smelling figure, alike unto the previous terrific black-eyed and foully-smelling figure, to a point which argued in favour of cloning, but in fact was mass production, would have stormed through the bar to fall upon his prey, had his way not been barred by the mêlée, which now appeared to involve all those present, with the notable exception of Tim and Will.

And the Slaughterhouse Five, who lounged upon the stage, sipping virus cocktails and offering verbal encouragement to the struggling crowd.

Will climbed onto the stage. Tim struggled to follow him.

'Hoopla,' cried Dantalion's Chariot. 'You can't come up here, you're not an entertainer.'

Will threw a fist, a lean fist albeit, in consideration of its prospective target, but a hard fist none the less and one thrown with considerable force, and accuracy.

It caught Dantalion's Chariot on the highest of his many chins.

'Outrage!' cried the Soldier of Misfortune, as the Chariot toppled and fell to the stage. 'Breach of contract. We will sue the management of this establishment.'

'Out of the way,' shouted Will, shaking his fist at the Soldier. 'In fact, run too, if you have it in you.'

'Actually I'm a bit puffed,' said the Soldier, raising calming palms. 'Impersonating weather can really take it out of you.'

'There's a big storm coming,' said Will. 'Through the fire exit, Tim.'

'I'd be ahead of you,' said Tim, 'if I wasn't following.'

And almost together they reached the fire exit – which was locked.

'Locked!' Tim rattled at the door. 'That's illegal. I may well sue the management also.'

'Only if you live to do so.' Will now too took to rattling the door.

And then the shooting started.

Exactly where this latest terrific blackly-eyed and fetid figure had acquired its firepower was a matter that Chief Inspector Sam Maggott, who would later arrive at the crime scene to view the carnage and count the dead, would muse ruefully upon, before concluding that he just didn't know, the firepower in question being of a type that he had only viewed in a certain classic twentieth-century Hollywood movie, the now legendary 7.62 M134 General Electric Minigun which, as we all know by now, or at least should, is armed with six rotating barrels capable of despatching six thousand rounds per minute.

The six rotating barrels span and the rounds left these at the rate of precisely six thousand per minute.

And through the cacophony and chaos, the blood and the gore, the dead and the dying, and the protests of a lady whose straw hat had been shot to smithereens, the figure of terror, the Mechanical Murderer, the Automated Assassin, the Clockwork Cain, the Synthetic

Sanguinarian, the alliterative emptier of the thesaurus, marched forward.

'Duck!' cried Will.

But Tim was ahead of him.

And now somewhat below.

Gunfire strafed the stage, bringing an end, not only to the career of the Soldier of Misfortune, who would never again impersonate weather, but also Musgrave Ritual, who had brought joy to literally dozens with his strumming on the old banjo.

'We're all going to die.' Tim cowered in the foetal position.

Will had nothing to add to this statement, possibly because he didn't hear it, what with his hands being clapped over his ears and his face pressed as close to the floor as it might be humanly pressed without actually passing through, and the noise of all that gunfire. 'Think,' Will told himself. 'What happens next? You *know* what happens next. You *know*. I'm not sure how you know, but I know that you do.'

Which no doubt made some kind of sense to himself at least.

'I do know,' said Will. And he leapt up. 'I'm here,' he shouted, and the brutal weapon turned in his direction.

'Here!' shouted Will. 'I'm here. It's me. Come on, I'm here, shoot me.'

The Engineered Exterminator pressed once more upon the blood-red *fire* button.

Will dropped to his knees.

Two hundred and fifty-seven rounds shot the fire exit door from its hinges.

Will tugged at Tim.

'It's "run" again,' he told him.

'An alleyway is an alleyway,' as the twentieth century's greatest living fictional detective, Lazlo Woodbine, once said. 'But a broad with a moustache is an abomination unto the Lord.' And added, 'But what the hell, if you're desperate and your wife's on vacation in Penge.'

The now legendary Laz knew his stuff when it came to alleyways, although his taste in women was at times somewhat questionable. But be that as it may, and well may it be, an alleyway *is* an alleyway and an ideal escape route too when it becomes available.

'Run,' bawled Will once more.

But Tim was already running.

They ran down the alleyway with a will, or in Will's case with a

Tim.[*] Will's long lean legs carried him at considerable speed, and Tim's legs, although shorter and somewhat stockier, managed, (through the adrenaline rush that fear for one's life inevitably brings), to keep pace.

They ran up another alleyway. Along another. Across a junction between alleyways, ran further to be on the safe side. And then just a bit more to be absolutely sure that they had outrun their erstwhile Ersatz Executioner.

Then a tad more for safety's sake.

And then . . .

'Enough,' gasped Tim, face all red and glazed with sweat. 'We've lost him. I can't run any more.'

'Perhaps just a bit further.' Will still had much running left in him.

'Not one step.' And Tim collapsed onto his bottom, breathing heavily.

Will sank down beside him. 'Do you know where we are?' he asked.

'You blackguard,' croaked Tim. 'You're not even puffed.'

'I think my heart rate's up a bit,' said Will. 'But I do a lot of running. I've got an antique home jogging machine in my bedroom.'

'A *what*?' Tim felt his own heart. It appeared to be reaching critical mass.

'A physical training machine,' said Will, glancing warily back along the way they had come. 'Keeps me fit and keeps my weight down.'

'*Down?*' Tim asked. 'Why would anyone *want* to keep their weight down?'

'Well . . .' said Will.

'No,' Tim flapped an exhausted hand about, 'I don't want to know. I've just witnessed slaughter and had to run for my very life. This is hardly the time, or the place.'

'Right on both counts,' said Will. 'Time is all important and this isn't the place where we should be.'

'I have an uncle,' puffed Tim. 'He lives in Kew Quadrant. We could hide out in his place.'

'We have to get to Chiswick.'

'Why? Who do you know in Chiswick?' Tim took to coughing.

'Not so loud,' said Will. 'I don't know anyone in Chiswick. But that's where it is, I know it is.'

'Chiswick's always where it is,' Tim took deep breaths. 'And where it should stay, dull place that it remains.'

[*] Unforgivable, I know. I should never have left it in. Sorry.

'Not Chiswick. I'm talking about the time machine.'

Tim managed a '*What?*'

'The time machine,' said Will. 'The one that brought the first automaton here. It returned on automatic pilot to pick up the second one, when the first one was destroyed.'

'*What?*' went Tim once again, followed by, 'You know where there's a time machine?'

'I know it,' said Will. 'It's all in here,' and he tapped at his temple. 'The Retro you gave me opened up all those synapses you spoke about, allowed me to access my ancestral memory. All of it, back through generations to Victorian times. I know exactly when the time machine was sent. From which year and from which location. I met the man who built it.'

Tim couldn't manage another *what?* So, open-mouthed, he just shook his head and vanished under his hair.

'I can remember being there,' said Will, 'because it happened in *my* past. Because I stole the time machine and travelled back in it. Or *will* steal the time machine, which I intend to do very shortly.' Will checked his watch. It said Friday. 'About half an hour from now,' Will said.

'Stop, stop.' Tim managed that. '*You* travelled back in time. I mean, you're *going* to travel back in time? Or—'

'To the Victorian era,' said Will. 'And it isn't at all how you'd expect it to be. Although it was exactly how I expected it to be, because I now have all the ancestral memories of what it was really like inside my head. Although, when I got there I lost them. It's very complicated.'

'Stop!' Tim waved his hand some more. 'Here madness dwells. I want no part of this.'

'Oh God of Good Housekeeping,' went Will. 'I remember *that* too, what happens to you. You *don't* want to come with me, Tim. You mustn't have any part in this. You go straight to your uncle's. I'll go to Chiswick alone.'

'No no no,' said Tim. 'If there's really a time machine, I want to see it. There, I've got most of my breath back.'

'You *don't* want to see it,' said Will.

'I do. I really do.'

'Believe me, you don't.' Will climbed to his feet. 'I have to be off. Where *are* we?'

'We're in Chiswick,' said Tim.

'We never are? We didn't run that far, surely?'

'Believe me, we did. I can recall every aching metre of it.'

'Then this isn't good. I should have remembered this. I'm not getting all of this right. It's because I'm trying to change it. Perhaps it can't be changed.'

'I have to see it,' said Tim, in a forceful tone. 'A *real* time machine. I *have* to see it.'

'You don't want to see it. Trust me on this.'

'Trust *me* on this. I do.'

'Well, you're *not*,' said Will. 'And I do remember where I am now. And I'm off. Go to your uncle's, Tim. Stay there for a couple of days. No, actually, it doesn't matter, you can go home. I'll sort this out and I'll see you again, *a week yesterday*. I'll meet you on the tram, a week yesterday.'

'A week yesterday?'

'Time travel,' said Will. 'You know the old joke.'

'I don't,' said Tim.

'You do. Bloke walks into a newspaper office and says to the editor, "I have the scoop of a lifetime for you, I've invented a time machine." And the editor, a rather jaded fellow says, "Well, I'm rather busy today, could you come back and show it to me—" '

'Yesterday,' said Tim. 'Yes, I have heard it and it isn't very good.'

Will scratched at his blondy head. 'Strange,' he said. 'I was certain that the old ones *were* the best. Don't know what put that into my mind. But I have to be off and I will see you a week yesterday. On the tram home. You won't remember any of this because it won't have happened yet. But as it will happen *now*, up until I leave in the time machine, I'm advising you to go home, *now*. It will be for the best. You really must trust me.'

Tim looked hard at Will.

'Something happens, doesn't it?' he said.

'A lot happens,' said Will.

'I mean, to *me*.'

Will nodded. 'And I don't want it to, so go home.'

Tim climbed to his feet. 'This is deep,' said he.

'Oh yes,' Will agreed. 'And very, very complicated.'

'So I'd better just go home.'

'Trust me, you should.'

'And you'll see me *a week yesterday*?'

'I remember doing so.'

'And I'll be all right when you do?'

Will nodded.

'Then fair enough.' Tim stuck his hand out for a shake. 'Go with my blessings, friend,' said he. 'Blessed be.'

'I'll do my best,' said Will. 'Farewell.'

And so Will walked away.

He turned a corner or two and found himself in yet another alleyway. This was a substantial alleyway. There were many dustbins in it. And a fire escape with one of those retractable bottom sections. Light streamed into this alleyway from the street it led to. Across this street was a burnt-out antique gun store.

Will didn't have to search the alleyway; he knew exactly where the time machine was hidden. He knew exactly what it looked like. He flung aside bins and rubbish bags and gazed upon it.

And there it stood in all its Victorian glory, a padded leather-armchair jobbie surrounded by all manner of intricate polished brass. Valves twinkled and rivets shone. Well, we all know what a Victorian time machine looks like.

Will climbed into the padded leather seat, strapped himself into the harness and put his hands to the control panel.

And then a certain thought struck him. How, *exactly*, did he know the location of the time machine? Certainly, the Retro had allowed him access to his ancestral memories, which had also allowed him access to his own when he was in the past, which he had travelled to in this very machine. And he had met the man who had built this machine that had been sent into the future bearing the black eyed monster that sought to destroy him. But that didn't explain how he knew where the time machine was *now*, before he'd located it and travelled into the past.

'There'll be a logical explanation,' Will told himself. 'One that is so simple, that I'll kick myself for not figuring it out now. So, if I recall correctly, and I do, all I have to do is pull this lever.'

'Hold on there. Don't do it yet.'

Will turned his head.

'Tim,' he said in a voice of considerable alarm. 'Oh no, you shouldn't be here.'

'Don't worry,' said Tim. 'It's not a problem. If you're going to see me a week yesterday. I figured that—'

But Tim didn't say any more.

Because Tim was cut down by the rapid fire of a General Electric Minigun.

'Oh Tim. I'm so sorry.'

And Will threw the lever.

And back.

With all that you might expect. Or at least hope for.

The whirling tunnel of oblivion. Galaxies twisting and turning. Psychedelic special effects. The full Stanley Kubrick. Although that bit in *2001* wasn't time-travelling. *Or was it?* But it was damn good anyway.

And through whirlings and shiftings and bendings and collapsings of time and space and most of reality, a pinpoint of special light appeared and grew and grew.

Until into a burst of brilliant sunshine, the time machine, with Will onboard, materialised upon solid ground, upon a cobbled street, in the year of 1898.

And was promptly run over by a horse-drawn brewer's dray.

10

The bottom of Tim's now empty glass struck the polished surface of the Britannia pub table. The Britannia pub table was in the saloon bar of the Flying Swan, as were Tim and Will. It was Thursday night in the saloon bar of the Flying Swan, and in all the rest of Brentford.

'But that's terrible,' quoth Tim.

'I know,' said Will. 'I barely escaped in one piece. And the time machine was mangled. And I was trapped in 1898, which actually, I didn't mind at all. I mean, I've always been fascinated, you might say obsessed, with the Victorian era.'

'I *would* say obsessed,' said Tim. 'And I do, but—'

'But I didn't really care about the machine getting smashed, it didn't seem to matter. I mean, I was actually *there*, Tim. In the past. Can you imagine?'

'No I can't, but—'

Will finished his pint of Large. 'The same again would be nice,' he said.

'But this is terrible!'

'No, it's not. It's wonderful beer. The most wonderful beer in this day and age.'

'Terrible,' said Tim once again.

'It's not, it's wonderful.'

'I don't mean the beer,' Tim's glass struck the table for a second time, causing Neville to raise an eyebrow.

'I mean *me*,' said Tim in the whisper known as hoarse.* 'I mean, me getting killed. That's terrible.'

'That was your own fault,' said Will. 'I warned you, in so many words. I told you to go home.'

'Killed,' said Tim. 'I'm going to die.'

* As opposed to the Cartwright known as Hoss. Or even a man called Horse, played by Richard Harris. Who never even owned a horse. (Or Robert Redford who whispered to horses.)

'We're all going to die. That's an inevitability, it's quite impersonal reality.'

'But I'm going to die *next Friday*. *Me!* That makes it quite personal.'

'You're not going to die next Friday. Which is why I returned from the past *today*. I had to get you to this pub and tell you everything.'

'So I'm *not* going to die next Friday?'

'No,' said Will, 'you're not.'

'Oh good,' said Tim and he breathed a sigh of relief. 'That's fine then. So I'm loving this again. Go on, tell me more.'

'Go and get more drinks first.'

'Oh yes, right.' Tim went and got more drinks.

'So what happens next?' he asked, upon his return.

'Lots,' said Will, supping away at his latest pint. 'Lots and lots and lots.' And he continued with the telling of his tale.

Will's head was full of memories that were not his own. They *were* his to a degree, because he had inherited them. They had been bequeathed to him, but they were not *the thoughts* of Will; and they were not born through the experiences of Will, which made the fact that he was now actually in the nineteenth century something of a sensory shock.

If having nearly been ground into the cobbles by the enormous hooves of onrushing dray horses was not, in itself, an assault upon the senses, then his sudden awareness of his situation and surroundings, when the danger had passed and he sat, bruised to some extent, but otherwise unharmed, became momentarily overpowering – mostly because of the smell.

Will's hands clamped about his nose. His head swam and tears rose to his eyes. The nineteenth century didn't smell at all good.

The twenty-second century was all but odour-free. Personal bodily pongs had long since ceased to be problematic. There were just so many super-efficient proprietary-brand deodorants, several of which had their own church franchises. Preservatives kept foodstuffs fresh and as foodstuffs were generally consumed with swiftness, there was little left for the waste disposal and recycling systems. And although toxic rains were frequent, citizens wore protective garments when braving them, or simply stayed indoors, so it was anyone's guess what the rains smelt like.

Things were not so in the nineteenth century.

Will sat in a pile of horse manure. Will jumped up from the pile of horse manure, right hand fixed across his face, left hand flapping wildly. It took him quite some little time to truly get his bearings. But when he did. But when he did.

'Oh,' went Will. And, 'Oh.'

He was in a Victorian street. The Whitechapel Road. And if the smell of horse manure was not sufficient to have him from his feet, then the thousand other unknown and unwholesome smells and the noise and the clamour and the colours and the all over everything should have. Done. So to speak.

Will blinked his eyes and stared. There was just so much. So much stench and so much noise and so much busyness. There was hurly-burly here. And speed too. A speed that was hitherto unknown to Will. People rushed about in their busyness. Pedestrians fairly jogged and high-wheeled vehicles drawn by horses clattered by at a most alarming rate. Folk walked slowly in Will's day and age, the public tram moved slowly, everything moved slowly. But not here.

Will flattened himself against a wall of brick, made gay by many colourful posters. Here, one advertised the Electric Alhambra Music Hall in the Strand, where Little Tich peformed his ever-popular Big Boot Dance, 'to the great appreciation of all classes'. And here was another for Count Otto Black's Circus Fantastique, 'A Carnival of Curiosities, An Odyssey of Oddities, A Burlesque of the Bizarre'. And there were posters which extolled the virtues of tobaccos and toothpowders, spats and spyglasses, patent medicines and public foot spas. And also for automata, 'the perfect gentleman's gentleman'.

Will took small and careful breaths to steady himself, and viewed the busy folk coming and going. They were slim folk, these. Slim as Will himself, and some far more so. These were achingly thin, their faces pinched, their cheekbones sharp, their bright eyes peeping from dark cadaverous sockets. They were wretchedly clad in rags of the Victorian persuasion and yet they were trading folk, who all had something to sell.

Will watched them and listened, and heard for the first time the now legendary Cries of Old London.

'Two-by-one, two-by-one, that's the stuff for you, old son.'

'Soleless shoes and toeless socks, by the bag and by the box.'

'Cardboard offcuts, take your pick. Rusty nails and bits of stick.'

'Mud for sale, penny a pail.'

'Bags of air, bags of air. Get 'em while there's some to spare.'

Will shook his shaky head in some surprise at these now legendary Cries of Old London. And although there was a great deal of busyness, a great deal of hurly-burly, and a great deal of shouting, no one seemed to be doing a great deal of trade. Except for the peddler who sold used earwax. He was going great guns. But then this was a Tuesday, although Will was not to know that yet.

Will viewed the street sellers and the comers and goers and shook his head some more and smiled unto himself. He was here in the past. He was really truly here.

'Guv'nor?'

Will looked down. A small and ragged lad looked up at him.

'Guv'nor?' said this lad once more.

Will's fingers still attended to his nose. 'Wad is dis?' he asked in a nasal tone. And then he said, 'Magic.'

'Magic?' said the lad.

'Magic,' said Will. 'I'm talking to a Victorian.'

The lad offered Will a quizzical glance, which set itself into a quizzical stare. His face was disgustingly filthy. A crust of bogies lodged between his nose and upper lip.* He wore a ragged blue cloth coat and a pair of ragged corduroy trousers, secured about the waist by knotted string. Around his scrawny neck he sported a colourful 'kerchief.

'Magic?' said the lad once more. 'I seen you come, guv'nor. Gawd pickle my plonker if I ain't. You fell right out of the sky. Are you with the aerial cavalry?'

The lad's accent fascinated Will. This would be Cockney. Will had heard the accent before, in movies on the Movie Classics Channel. Spoken by the greatest exponent of the urban dialect that had ever lived, the now and ever legendary Dick Van Dyke.

'I . . .' Will paused. The enormity of all this was now pressing in upon him from all sides. He would do well to keep his calm, although he felt like leaping up and down and shouting at the top of his voice. He was here! Really truly here! In the past he loved so dearly! Trapped perhaps, for the time machine was splintered wreckage. But alive, perhaps truly alive for the first time ever. And upon an adventure beyond any he could ever have dreamed of.

It was very difficult not to shout.

But Will, with effort, maintained his calm.

'Not the aerial cavalry,' said Will. 'I'm, er, just a traveller.'

'I seen you,' said the lad once more. 'Seen you come down from the sky.'

'I was crossing the street,' said Will. 'Carrying a chair.'

'You is a flyer. I seen you, guv'nor. Take us on. I's a willing

* On the area that we now all know is your philtrum.

apprentice. Good wiv me Alices.* Gawd tan my todger if I ain't. I'll polish yer rhythms† and buff up yer patent‡ and—'

'Please go away,' said Will. 'Go away and have a wash, or something.' He shooed at the ragged lad with his non-nose-holding hand. 'I'm a traveller, nothing more.'

'Where you from, guv'nor? India is it, or Americey? You got a weirdy whistle§ on you, and no mistake.' The lad fingered the fabric of Will's trousers.

'Whistle and flute,' said Will. 'Pair of trousers. That's Cockney rhyming slang. I know that one.'

'G'us a penny, guv'nor,' the lad tugged at Will's trousers. 'You talk like a toff, so you must be a toff, Gawd jump on my John Thomas if you ain't. G'us a penny for a bun. I ain't eaten today and me belly thinks me throat's been cut.'‖

'I have no money.' Will detached himself from the ragged rascal's grip. 'We don't have money where I come from.'

'If it's foreign currency you hold, I can work out the exchange rate on me Babbage.'

'Your Babbage?' Will spoke the words slowly and with care.

'In me Davy.'¶ The lad delved into his pocket and whisked out a small brass contrivance; a pocket calculator.

'Whoa!' went Will. 'Let me see that.'

He reached down but the lad removed himself a pace.

'I only want to look at it,' said Will.

'As if you ain't seen one before.'

'I've never seen one,' said Will.

The lad whistled. 'You *must* be from distant parts,' said he. 'Is it pink on the map where you come from?'

'Pink on the map? The British Empire, I see.'

'Ah, stuff you,' said the lad. 'If you won't make free with some bangers,** would you mind if I just picked your Davys? I've a living to earn, Gawd scramble my scrotes if I ain't. A silk handkerchief will do me, or a gold fob watch if you have one about yourself.'

'Enough now,' said Will. 'Kindly go away.'

'You can touch me willy for sixpence,' said the lad.

* Alice Bands: Hands.
† Rhythm and Blues: Shoes.
‡ Patent Pelmet: Helmet.
§ Whistle and flute: Pair of trousers.
‖ This was not an old one then; it was a new one.
¶ Davy Crockett: Pocket.
** Bangers and Mash: Cash.

'Now *that is* enough,' said Will. 'Go away at once.'

'Hm,' went the lad, cupping his filthy chin between an equally filthy finger and thumb. 'You're a rum 'n, guv'nor. I can't make you out. I think I'll just whistle for me gang and have 'em bludgeon you to death. Then we can split whatever spoils you carry.'

Will looked down at the lad and sighed deeply. 'What is your name?' he asked.

'Winston,' said the lad, saluting Will.

'Well, Winston, have you quite finished?'

The lad grinned up at Will. 'I've a thought or two left in me as it 'appens,' he said. 'Gawd knacker me 'nads if I ain't. And there's always the chance that you might marvel at the audacity of at least one of me thoughts and compensate me 'andsomely. For instance, I don't feel that I pleaded 'unger with sufficient conviction, this perhaps being because I've just eaten. I might—'

'Stop, please stop!' Will held up his nose-holding hand (a mistake). 'Your sudden loquacity surprises me.'

'It's another ploy,' said the lad. 'A psychological tactic designed to win favour through empathy. On first impression you observe a ragged street urchin. But now you perceive an intelligent youth, fallen upon tragic circumstance. 'Ence you respond with a generous donation of alms, in the thought that there, but for the grace of Gawd, goes you. As it were. Gawd coddle me cods if you don't.'

'I don't,' said Will. 'Which isn't to say that I'm not impressed. But I must be going. Farewell. It was a pleasure to meet you, Winston.' Will turned to march away. And then did so.

'No, 'ang about, guv'nor.' The lad made to follow. 'Oh me leg,' wailed he, breaking into a limp. 'Me poor ulcerated leg.'

Will stopped and turned. 'Your poor ulcerated leg?' he asked.

'And me 'ip,' said the lad. 'Chronic arthritis brought on through cruel treatment in the workhouse.'

'I see,' said Will.

'Not to mention canker of the groin.'

'Canker of the groin?'

'I told you not to mention that.'

'The old ones really are the best,' said Will. 'But listen, I *am* impressed. 'I'm *really* impressed, but I have no money to offer you. I'm sorry.'

'Fair enough,' said the lad. ''Ey look up there, it's 'Er Majesty's *Dreadnaught*.' And he pointed heavenward with a grubby mitt. 'Gawd nobble me knob if it ain't.'

Will glanced in the direction of the urchin's pointings.

The sky above was clear and blue and Will could view no *Dreadnaught* there. Will smiled and mused a moment, upon the implausibility that somewhere high above that clear sky of blue, lurked an almighty Gawd who harboured an obsession with Winston's privy parts.

Will's momentary musings were, however, brought to premature and inconclusive conclusion by the sounds of a sudden smack and an equally sudden squeal.

Will looked down to see the lad, with one hand deep in Will's trouser pocket and the other clutching a reddening ear. And Will looked up once more, but this time not towards the sky. This time he looked towards the large gentleman who had just struck the erstwhile picker of Will's trouser pocket.

'Away upon your toes, small boy,' said the gentleman.

The lad withdrew his hand from Will's trouser pocket and made to take his leave at speed. The gentleman, however, grabbed him by the collar of his ragged coat and hauled him into the air.

'Steady on,' said Will. 'Don't hurt him.'

'Return it,' said the gentleman.

The lad opened his pocket-picking hand to reveal a small plastic disc, the computer disc onto which Will had copied *The Fairy Feller's Masterstroke.*

'It's of no value here,' said Will. 'Let him keep it.'

'Absolutely not,' said the gentleman. 'The repercussions could be enormous. Take back your possession, Mr Starling.'

'Mr Starling?' Will held out his hand and the dangling lad returned the disc. 'You know my name?'

'And you know mine,' said the gentleman.

Will took in the figure that stood before him.

It was a mighty figure, impressive, a full and girthsome figure. A figure which, but for its apparel, would not have looked at all out of place in the twenty-third century.

The mighty figure's apparel was of the most striking and elaborate confection. A six-piece suit of lime green Boleskine tweed, with matching shirt and trousers, jacket and waistcoat and topcoat and top hat too. Affixed to the band of the tweedy topper was a large golden brooch in the shape of a five-pointed star and inlaid with many precious stones. Upon the waistcoat hung numerous watch-chains, similarly of gold, from which depended fobs of the Masonic persuasion. Upon the third finger of the great right hand, which presently held young Winston aloft, was a ring of power, set with a star sapphire and engraved all about with enigmatic symbols. In the left hand was a swordstick topped by a silver skull.

The gentleman set free the lad, who fell to his feet and fled away.

'Farewell, Winston,' said Will.

'Speak *my* name,' said the gentleman.

'Your name is Hugo Rune,' said Will.

Hugo Rune removed his top hat and bowed. Will was amazed by the great shaven head and the pentagram tattooed upon its crown.

The gentleman straightened, replaced his top hat and patted Will upon the shoulder. 'I must offer my apologies to you,' he said. 'It would appear that my calculations were incorrect to a nine hundredth of a degree. An unforgivable and costly mistake.' Rune stooped, plucked up a broken fragment of the time machine, tut-tutted to himself, shook his head in grave sadness and let the fragment fall from his hand.

'I am confused,' said Will, who was.

'All will be made clear. If you would be so inclined as to accompany me to my lodgings.'

'Well,' said Will. 'I . . .' and he stared up into the great broad face of Hugo Rune. It was an impressive face. The hooded eyes, the noble nose, the fleshy mouth, the heavy jowls.

'I don't know,' said Will. 'I don't feel altogether right.'

'You have just travelled through time,' said Hugo Rune. 'That you should feel altogether right is unlikely. Follow me please.'

'It isn't that, I think.' A feeling of foreboding now entered Will. It was a feeling new to him and one that he didn't care for. It wasn't fear as such, it was something more. But Will didn't know just what. Which somehow made it worse. Rune knew his name. And Will knew Rune's. But Will could not now remember how he knew it. In fact Will could not now remember a whole lot of things that he felt certain he could have remembered a moment before. Or was it a moment before, or a lifetime before? And were the memories Will's?

'All will be explained,' said Rune. 'Follow me.'

The mighty figure turned upon a mighty heel and plunged into the market crowd, which parted before him, much in the manner of the Red Sea before the touch of Moses' staff. If, of course, you believed in such things, which Will, of course, did not.

Will dithered for a moment, but having no better plan in mind, in fact having no plan whatsoever in mind, followed Hugo Rune at the hurry up.

11

Rune wasn't difficult to follow, what with the crowd just parting before him. And as Will followed on, the feeling of foreboding grew. Will shook his head, but it didn't help.

Across the street Rune passed through a brick archway into a narrow tunnel between tall buildings. Will followed with some reluctance. It smelled bad here, even worse than the market street. Will fanned at his nose. The tunnel debouched at length into a yard. Tenement buildings rose to every side. Will peered up at them. There was a feeling of terrible desolation about this place, of desperate poverty and excruciating sadness. The walls were green with slime and mould. The sun but peeped in and there was a horrible chill. Will shivered and followed Hugo Rune.

A paint-flaked sign upon a greasy wall announced this ghastly place to be Miller's Court. In one corner a rusting iron staircase led up to a darkened doorway. Rune paced up this staircase.

'Follow on,' he called to Will.

And Will followed on.

Rune took a great key from his pocket, thrust it into a keyhole that seemed far too small for it, turned the key and pushed open a door, which made suitably hideous groaning sounds. 'Go through,' he said.

Will peered doubtfully into the darkness beyond.

'Go through,' commanded Rune.

And Will went through.

Rune followed him, closed the door, locked it.

The two of them stood in absolute darkness.

'What now?' asked Will in a tremulous tone.

'Creep,' whispered Rune. 'Upon stealthy toes.'

And he struck a Lucifer and applied it to a knubby candle. The meagre light revealed a loathsome corridor and Will, who had now had quite enough and wished to be returned to daylight, voiced some words to this effect.

'Hush,' said Rune. 'My lodgings are, I will agree, insalubrious, but there is a purpose behind everything that I do. You really must hush.'

'Why?' asked Will.

'Because otherwise my landlady, Mrs Gunton, will hear us. She is probably far gone with gin at this hour of the day, but nevertheless, she lacks for a month's rent and will make loud her concerns regarding this, if we grant her the wherewithal so to do.'

'Ah,' said Will.

'So kindly hush and follow me once more.' And Rune pushed past Will and led him by the faltering light of the knubby candle up a flight of rickety stairs, and eventually to the lodgings of Hugo Rune.

These lodgings were not well appointed. They were meagre. They were sparse. They were wretched. They were a bit of a shambles. A wan light fell through unwashed windowpanes and illuminated a small and charmless room. Or hovel. A straw pallet served as a narrow bed, too narrow indeed for the bulk that was Hugo Rune. This straw pallet was somewhat rucked about. A chair, far gone with the woodworm, served no purpose at all and sprawled on its side in the centre of the hovel. Many papers, most of which were unpaid bills, lay scattered all around and about. A steamer trunk stood undisturbed in a corner, a large and glorious steamer trunk, too large, it seemed, to have ever been brought in through the doorway. And too glorious to have found its way into such a hell hole as this.

'Violation!' cried Rune, peering all around and about and throwing up his mighty hands. 'Foul violation. Someone has been here. Several someones in fact.' Rune sniffed at the fetid air. '*They* have been here,' he said.

'They?' asked Will.

'All in good time.' Rune perused the steamer trunk and nodded his great head. 'All is as it should be regarding my trunk,' said he.

The steamer trunk, all brass bosses and hasps and red leather paddings, was a thing of great beauty and evident expense.

'My life's possessions dwell within' said Rune. 'I am at present a ship without a port.'

'You appear to have fallen upon unfortunate circumstances,' said Will.

'Well observed,' replied Rune. 'But this is not in fact the case. I am independently wealthy. My father was in the brewery trade. Hardly a gentleman's profession, I grant you, but his demise benefited me to the extent that I have been able to experience things that most people can only dream about.'

'Indeed?' said Will.

'Sit down,' said Rune, kicking the straw pallet back into shape. 'Would you care for a glass of champagne?'

'Champagne?' Will almost managed a smile. 'I've read of champagne, but I've never tasted it.'

'A world without champagne?' Rune shook his head, removed his top hat from it, and placed the stylish item upon the steamer trunk. 'For that crime alone we should act, if for no more.'

Will sat himself down upon the straw pallet. 'Who are you?' he asked. 'I remember you, and your name, somehow, although I don't know how I do.'

Rune shed his topcoat and removed from a large inner pocket a bottle of champagne and two glasses. 'I acquired this to toast your arrival,' said he. 'But you should have arrived here, in this room. I cannot conceive how my calculations could have been at fault.'

Rune uncorked the champagne, poured two glasses, handed one to Will.

'Thank you very much,' said Will and he took a tiny sip.

'To your liking?' asked Mr Rune.

'Indeed,' said Will. 'Very much so.'

'Then that at least is as it should be.' Rune lowered his ample posterior onto the steamer trunk and cupped his glass between his hands. Hugo Rune stared down upon Will. And Will stared up at Rune.

Will considered the man who sat before him. He was an enigma. Will found him most disturbing.

Hugo Rune said, 'What do you remember, Mr Starling?'

'About what?' Will asked.

'About how you made your arrival here, *for an instance*.'

'Ah,' said Will and he wondered that to say; what, in fact, he *should* say. He knew nothing about this giant of a man. Whether he might be trusted, *for an instance*.

'What do *you* know?' Will asked.

'I know all,' said Hugo Rune.

'Then why are you asking me?'

Rune sighed. 'It is of the greatest importance,' he explained. 'What you do remember and what you do not. If you remember too much, you will be of no use to me. If you are aware of all that lies ahead for you here in this time, you would not be able to function.'

Will shook his head. 'I have no idea what you're talking about,' he said.

'Naturally not. Then allow me to explain. You were brought here from the twenty-third century.'

'I came of my own accord,' said Will.

'You had no choice,' said Rune, 'considering the circumstances. I arranged these circumstances.'

'You sent the robots to attack me? To kill people?'

'Not that,' Rune held up a mighty hand. 'But the wherewithal that you should be able to make your escape. After all, I worked upon the construction of that machine with my good friend Mr Wells.'

'H.G. Wells?' asked Will.

'The very same. He was hopelessly lost on the project, he called upon me to explain the concept of time to him. How time actually functions. It does not function as you might believe it to. Events in the future can affect the past. Not a lot of people are aware of this ultimate truth.'

'I wasn't aware of it,' said Will.

'Naturally not. But I set Wells upon the right course.'

Will sipped further champagne and found it greatly to his liking. 'I really don't understand any of this,' he said.

'Which is how it must be. Of your ancestors, what do you remember?' Rune tapped at his temple with a pudgy finger. 'What is in here, inside your head?'

'Let me think.' Will thought. 'Actually, not too much,' he said, when he had done with his thinking. 'But I'm sure I could remember a great deal, two full centuries at least. I can remember everything up until about . . .'

'The year of eighteen ninety-eight,' said Rune.

'Yes,' said Will. 'But nothing more.'

Rune nodded his head and offered Will a very broad smile. 'Exactly as it should be. Because you are now in eighteen ninety-eight and those other memories of your ancestors that you held in your head have yet to exist. The events that will become these memories have yet to occur. You cannot have memories of things that are yet to happen.'

'But they *had* happened,' said Will. 'Where I come from. The future. They *had* happened in the past.'

'You are now in a portion of the past. This is the time that is real for you now. The only memories of your ancestors you have now, are those that exist up until the present moment. The future has yet to occur. You will achieve great things in the future. Under my tutelage, of course.'

'Oh of course,' said Will.

'Irony?' asked Rune. 'Or sarcasm? I have little time for either.'

'And you knowing about everything,' said Will.

'*That* was sarcasm,' said Rune. 'Make that the last time you use it in my presence.'

'Listen,' said Will, 'I don't know who you are, or what you want from me. I have got myself involved in something incredible, and I feel, well, I don't know, privileged I suppose, to actually be here. But how am I ever going to get home again to my own time?'

'When your work here is done, you will return home. I promise that to you.' Rune now delved into a waistcoat pocket and brought out his cigarette case. 'Care for an oily?' he asked.

'Oily rag,' said Will. 'Fag. Cockney rhyming slang. I've never actually smoked a cigarette. We don't have them any more in my time. They're deadly poison, you see. I learned in history class how the cigarette companies all went bust in the latter part of the twenty-first century, when thousands of dying smokers successfully sued them.'

'Happily, *that* is in the future,' said Rune, withdrawing a cigarette, striking a Lucifer and lighting it up. 'In this day and age cigarettes are very good for your health.'

'Then I'd love to try one,' said Will.

'It will make you sick,' said Hugo Rune.

'Then I think I'll not bother.'

'Then let us press on with the business in hand. To whit, how you will play an active role in defeating the forces of darkness.'

'Forces of darkness?' Will shook his head once more. 'All lost on me,' he said. 'Could I have some more champagne, please?'

'It will make you drunk,' said Rune.

'I've been drunk before,' said Will. 'Happily, we still have alcohol where I come from.'

Rune poured Will another glass.

'The forces of darkness,' said Rune once more. 'To whit, the witches.'

Will coughed into his glass, sending champagne up his nose. 'Witches?' he managed to say, when he had finished with coughing.

'Witches,' said Rune. 'Witchcraft is the scourge of this enlightened age.'

'Don't be silly,' said Will. 'Witchcraft is superstition. Medieval stuff. No one believes in witchcraft. Except perhaps my best friend Tim. He's convinced that the world is run by witches.'

Rune's eyes grew wide. These wide eyes fixed upon Will. 'Your best friend *Tim*?' said Rune, in a cold, dead voice. 'Not yourself?'

'Certainly not!' said Will. 'I don't believe in rubbish like that.'

'But *you* are Will Starling? Second-born son of William Edward Starling, born on the second of February, in the year two thousand, two hundred and two.'

'I'm the *only* son of William Edward Starling,' said Will.

'No you're not,' said Rune.

'Oh yes I *am*,' said Will.

'Not,' said Rune.

'Am too,' said Will

Rune shook his head once more. 'Born on the second of February, two thousand, two hundred and two.'

Will now shook his head once more. 'That's not *my* birthday. I was born on the first of January. But . . .'

'But what?'

'The second of the second, two thousand, two hundred and two, that's Tim's birthday.'

'Calamity,' cried Rune, throwing up his great hands, one of which spilled champagne while the other dropped his cigarette. 'This is all your father's doing.'

'My *father*?' Will asked. 'What has my father got to do with this?'

'Everything.' Rune waved his hands about above his head. 'From father to son the lore has passed. From second son to second son.'

'I'm an only child,' said Will.

'I've brought back the wrong brother,' Rune's hands now covered his face. 'This is disastrous.'

'Tim isn't my brother.'

'Oh yes he is.'

'Oh no he isn't.'

'Is.'

'Isn't.'

'Is,' said Hugo Rune once more.

'Isn't,' said Will. 'Although . . .'

'Although what?'

'Well, actually, he does look a bit like me, I suppose. He's heavier and darker, but there's a slight resemblance. And we've been best friends since childhood; he's very much like a brother to me. Or *was*.' For now Will recalled that terrible something. The terrible death of Tim.

'Was?' Rune peeped through his fingers.

'Something awful happened,' said Will. 'I don't want to talk about it.'

'He was killed,' said Rune. 'By the demonic automaton. I know what happened, what *will* happen. I was able to predict it. But not to predict that your father's second son would not be born within wedlock. This Tim *is* your brother, but by a different mother.'

'Bravo, Dad,' said Will. 'You dirty blighter. I remember you've always spent a lot of time round at Mrs McGregor's. So that's what you were up to, eh?'

'Ruination,' cried Rune and he jumped to his feet. 'All my calculations, all my planning, ruined by your profligate father sowing the seeds of his loins in some harlot.'

'Easy,' said Will. 'Mrs McGregor is a very nice woman.'

'Ruination,' cried Rune once more. 'Woe unto the house of Rune and to the future generations thereof. All my work in bringing my magical heir to me.'

'Your magical heir?' Will asked.

'I am one of *your* ancestors,' said Hugo Rune. 'The most important of all your ancestors. I sought to recall the last member of the True Craft back here to aid me. But instead of him, I have you.'

'*You* are one of *my* ancestors?' said Will. 'Amazing.'

'We are all doomed.' Rune's great voice rattled the windowpanes. 'And it is all the fault of your father.'

'I've had enough of this,' said Will, rising from the straw pallet. 'I'm leaving. I'll go and find Mr Wells. Maybe he can get me back home.'

'You are going nowhere, young man.' Rune glared down upon Will.

'I am too,' said Will, adding, 'you don't frighten me.'

Which was not entirely true.

'Sit down!' shouted Rune. 'If you are all that I have, then I will have to make do with you.'

'*You* will do no such thing. I'm leaving.'

Rune made certain complicated passes with his large hands and Will found his legs going weak at the knees. He sank back down onto the pallet.

'I will speak and you will listen,' said the giant.

'What have you done to my knees?' croaked Will, feeling at these now unfeeling articles.

'A spell of temporary disablement. Curb your tongue, lest I strike it from your mouth.'

Will kerbed his tongue and squeezed some more at his knees. He was scared now. Truly scared.

'It has taken me years to work out the calculations,' said Rune. 'To bring back the last in my line. Seemingly I am to be thwarted. But I will *not* be thwarted. If it is fate that you should be the one returned to me, rather than the one I called for, then so be it. I bow to fate. But I bow also to purpose. That it should be you, must have purpose. I will tutor you, boy. You will learn and you will play your part in defeating mankind's greatest enemy.'

'Please,' Will made pleading hand-wringings. 'I'm sorry that I'm not what you expected. But it's not my fault. Please just let me go. I'm no use to you. I don't believe in magic.'

'And your legs?' Rune asked.

'The champagne?' Will suggested.

Rune shook his head.

'Then I don't know. But what I do honestly know is that I don't want to play any more. I want to go home. I want my mum.' And Will began to cry.

Hugo Rune placed a great hand upon his shoulder. 'My apologies,' said he. 'I have frightened you. I understand that this is none of your doing. You are a victim of circumstance. But you *are* my heir. Not the heir I had hoped for, but my heir none the less. My blood is your blood and likeways about. You will not survive long in this time without my help. I will help you and you in turn will help me. What say you to this?'

Will looked up at Hugo Rune. 'I just want to go home,' he said.

'And you will. I have promised you this.'

'I want to go home *now*,' said Will, sniffing away.

'That, I regret, is impossible.'

Will took to sniffing some more.

'It will all be made well,' said Hugo Rune. 'I will make it well with your help. Trust me. I'm a magician.'

Will groaned, dismally.

'Come,' said Rune. 'Follow me and I will show you something marvellous.'

Will did sighings, but Will's legs suddenly worked once more and Will rose and followed Hugo Rune.

Rune led Will up further stairs, through a doorway and onto the flat roof of the tenement. Pigeons roosted, chimneys smoked, and London lay all around and about.

'Impressive, isn't it?' said Rune.

Will nodded dismally, then Will stared and then Will beheld and went, 'Wow.'

The sight was at once beautiful, awesome and terrific. It was of such a scale as to be dizzying. Acre upon grey acre of slate rooftops led away and away to wonder upon wonder upon wonder.

The dome of St Paul's glittering in the sunlight. The spires of St Pancras and St Martin in the Fields and Westminster Abbey and the Houses of Parliament. It was a panoramic view.

It was Victorian London, as Will had imagined it to be, as he had seen it pictured in engravings and lithographs. It was all there but there was more.

Will gazed up. 'What are those?' he asked.

'Airships,' said Rune. 'Electric airships. The very latest in transport for the upper classes.'

'Of course.' Will nodded thoughtfully. Memories were there, in his head. Memories of the launching of the *Dreadnaught* and the death of his ancestor, Captain Ernest Starling of the Queen's Own Electric Fusiliers. A death that Hugo Rune had somehow been involved in.

'And what are *those*?' Will pointed once again.

They rose, dozens and dozens of them, higher than the spires of the churches, diminishing into the distance on every side, slender metal towers, surmounted by great steel balls, which flickered and sparkled with electrical energy.

'Tesla towers,' said Hugo Rune. 'The brainchild of Mr Nikola Tesla, who created them through the aid of computer systems invented by Lord Babbage. Power stations generate electricity, which is broadcast from these towers on a radio frequency. Wireless transmission of energy. No cables. It has totally revolutionised technology. There will be no internal combustion engine. Automobiles will be fitted with electric motors, which receive the broadcast electricity. No heavy batteries required, hence electrically driven flying craft and soon, we are promised, a ship that will voyage into space.'

'Electricity without wires?' Will shook his blondy head. 'Incredible. We have nothing like that where I come from.'

'And there would be nothing like it now if I had not persuaded Mr Babbage to exhibit his Analytical Engine at The Great Exhibition in eighteen fifty-one. It was I who introduced him to Her Majesty, God bless Her, and suggested that she grant him Royal Patronage to develop his inventions for the glory of the British Empire.'

'But he didn't,' said Will. 'I read all about Mr Babbage; he was ignored, his genius never received recognition. He was never given Royal patronage, he never met Mr Tesla and Mr Tesla never perfected his wireless transmission of energy.'

'Not in the version of history that you were taught, which is not the version of history that you now personally inhabit. Tell me, young man, which version do you now choose to believe?'

Will shrugged and shook his head once more.

'I will teach you all that you need to know,' said Rune. 'And together we will defeat the evil that seeks to deprive the future of these wonders.'

'Evil?' Will shook his head once again. 'You can't *defeat* evil. Evil isn't a something. It's a concept. It's not a thing.'

'This evil is a thing,' said Rune. 'A number of things. Thirteen things in fact.'

'Thirteen things?' Will asked.

'Evil in human form,' said Rune. 'The Chiswick Townswomen's Guild.'

12

'Now just hold on there!' Tim McGregor did waving his hands in the air. 'Are you telling me that I am your brother?'

'Half-brother,' said Will. 'Different mums. And I'm just telling you what Rune told to me.'

'But *my* mum and *your* dad? That's disgusting.'

Will shrugged and took a sip from his latest pint of Large. It tasted good. Not as good as Rune's champagne but cooler though and good.

'But if it's true,' Tim made a thoughtful face. 'Then it means that *I* am a descendant of Hugo Rune.'

'We both are. If it's true.'

'But *I* am his magical heir. *Me*.'

Will shrugged once more.

'Cease with all these shruggings,' Tim told him. 'This is incredible. I mean, Rune. Hugo Rune, the greatest magus of the nineteenth and twentieth centuries.'

'I don't know about that. But hang about, Tim. You mean that you have actually heard of Hugo Rune?'

'*Heard* of him?' Tim laughed loudly. And Will recognised that laugh. It was the laugh of Hugo Rune. 'Heard of Rune? The man is a legend in the annuls of the occult. The guru's guru. The Logos of the Aeon. The One and Only. The Lad Himself. The founder of the church of Runeology.'

'There is no such church,' said Will.

'There was.' Tim nodded his hairy head. 'It wasn't too big a church. It only had a congregation of about six. Women mostly. Young women, wealthy young women.'

'Sounds about right,' said Will.

'Hugo Rune wrote *The Book of Ultimate Truths*. *I* have a copy.'

'You have a copy of a book? You never told me this.'

'You said you didn't believe in magic. You'd have sneered if I'd told you.'

Will all but shrugged, but didn't.

'But this is *so* brilliant,' Tim was now all smiles. 'I always knew I was special. But Hugo Rune's magical heir! Fantastic. So, when do we go back into the past? What do I have to do? Will I get to cast spells and stuff?'

'I'm sure you'll get the opportunity to try. But not yet. You have to hear all of the story-so-far first.'

'I've heard enough,' said Tim. 'Finish your pint. Where did you park the time machine?'

'I didn't return here in a time machine.' Will sipped further Large. 'Time machines are old-fashioned. That's not the way I travel through time now.'

'Oh,' said Tim. 'So how do you do it? By magic?'

'No, not magic. It's done by vegetable, actually. But all that's a year on in the story.'

'A year on?' Tim scratched at his hairy head. 'Are you telling me that you were there in Victorian times for a year?'

Will nodded. 'Haven't you noticed that I look a bit older?'

'I'm a bloke,' said Tim. 'Blokes don't notice stuff like that. Although, perhaps, now that I look at you closely. You didn't have those big Victorian sideburns yesterday, did you? And you are dressed in Victorian costume, which you weren't when you went to the toilet on the tram.'

'The sideburns took me nearly a year to grow.'

'I'm loving this,' Tim rubbed his hands together. 'I didn't like the bit where I got killed next Friday night. But I assume I'll be dodging that.'

Will nodded.

'So I love all the rest. Especially the magic. He actually cast a spell on your knees, did he?'

'I suspect the champagne was drugged,' said Will.

Tim laughed once more. 'It was magic,' he said. 'Rune was one of the greatest magicians of his, or any other, age. He spoke every language known to man and could play chess blindfolded, against six grand masters simultaneously, and beat every one of them, whilst engaging in, shall we say, congress, with a woman in an adjoining room.'

'So he told me,' said Will. 'Although I never actually witnessed such a competition.'

'And darts,' said Tim. 'He played darts with the Dalai Lama. Hands-off darts. Using his powers of telekinesis.'

'I never actually saw that either. Although we did visit the Dalai. Nice chap.'

'*You* visited the Dalai Lama?'

'With Rune. We travelled for nearly a year. Rune was always on the move. Outwitting the forces of evil.'

'Witches,' said Tim.

'Creditors,' said Will. 'Rune never carried money, you see. He said it was beneath him to do so. He said that he offered the world his genius and all he expected in return was that the world should cover his expenses. We stayed in a lot of first-class hotels. But we always had to leave them speedily and stealthily, and under the cover of darkness.'

'But all the time he was teaching you his magic?'

'He informed me that I had to grow *physically* before I could grow *spiritually*. I spent all my time dragging his steamer trunk about.'

'Oh,' said Tim once more. 'But you got to see some amazing sights, I'll bet.'

'That's true enough and we did it in style. We journeyed across the Victorian world, always travelling first class and always failing to pay for our tickets. We crossed China, where we were the honoured guests of the Mandarin. We had to leave in a rush though, because Rune engaged in, as you put it, congress, with a number of the Mandarin's concubines.'

'Top man,' said Tim. 'But there must have been some purpose to all this travelling, other than for evading creditors.'

'I'm sure there was, but Rune did not see fit to confide it to me. I learned a lot though, which might well have been the purpose. I learned how to handle myself, how to mix in society, and it all came in very useful. Shall I continue with the story?'

'Please do so,' Tim raised his glass. 'But promise me that when you've done, you'll definitely take me back into the past with you.'

'That's why I'm here. I need your help, Tim. You're the only person I can turn to. There's big trouble going on back there.'

'Right,' said Tim. 'So continue with your story.'

'Right,' said Will. 'But you must understand that although being with Rune was never dull and did involve a high risk factor, which I found personally appealing, I was trapped in an age that wasn't mine and an age that is not how our history records it. There were wonders back then, scientific wonders, in England at least. It was all very confusing to me and I was homesick. Can you believe that? A chance at real adventure and I got homesick. I missed my mum and dad, and you too.'

'Nice,' said Tim. 'I suppose.'

'And I still didn't understand why the truth about Victorian times had been covered up. I wanted to know *a lot*. Rune said that he had engineered it for me to return to the past, although it was you that he really wanted. And that the intention was for me to aid him in his struggle against the forces of evil, which came in the shape of The Chiswick Townswomen's Guild. But he wouldn't confide his plans to me.'

'Does it all become clear in the story?' Tim asked.

'Sort of,' said Will.

'Then perhaps you should continue the story *now*. Then we can both, you know, whip back in time and stuff. Eh?'

'Right,' said Will once more. 'I'll tell you the lot. I have to or you won't understand. It's exciting stuff. You'll enjoy it. And when I'm done you'll understand what you have to do and we'll return to the past together. Are you all right with that?'

'I'm all right with that.' Tim raised his glass a little higher. 'A toast?' said he.

'A toast?' said Will.

'To the future,' said Tim. 'Which might lie in the past. And to our mutual ancestor, Mr Hugo Rune.'

'I'll drink to that,' said Will.

And he did so.

'The champagne to your liking?' asked Hugo Rune.

Will studied his glass. The light that fell upon it came from one of the crystal chandeliers that hung from the ornately gilded ceiling of the Café Royal, Piccadilly. It was November, the year was eighteen ninety-nine.

'Somewhat inferior,' said Will, as he viewed the rising bubbles in the golden liquid. 'I would hate to take issue with the wine waiter over this.' Will now studied the label on the bottle. 'However, I would suggest that this is not a Chateau Rothschild, but rather a Chateau Vamberry.'

Rune nodded approvingly. Tonight the guru's guru, The Logos of the Aeon, The One and Only, The Lad Himself, wore full Highland dress, for reasons of his own that were not explained to Will, but which were probably something to do with it being Friday. With a tweed bonnet with brooch and eagle's feathers, ceremonial dress tunic of crimson damask, a kilt in a tartan of Rune's own design, a dirk in his left sock and silk slippers on his feet, Rune, as ever, cut a dash.

Will was smartly turned out in a black satin evening suit, white tie and patent leather shoes. Neither he, nor Rune, had actually paid for their apparel.

Will glanced all around and about at his surroundings.

The interior of the Café Royal had come as something of a surprise to him, as he had expected the full Victorian over-the-topness: gilded columns, ornate statuary, marble fireplaces and Rococo furnishings. But there was little of the Victorian left to the décor, except the ceiling and the crystal chandeliers.

The Café Royal had gone post-modern.

The chairs and tables looked to be of the IKEA persuasion. The crockery was white, the cutlery had plastic handles. The walls of this famous establishment had been stripped of their decorative plaster mouldings, painted in pastel shades and hung with huge canvasses.

'The work of Richard Dadd,' said Hugo Rune. 'Her Majesty's favourite artist.'

'And one of mine too,' said Will. 'But Dadd never painted pictures like this. These paintings look more like the work of Mark Rothko. They're just big splodges of colour. They're rubbish.'

Rune put a finger to his fleshy lips. 'Mr Dadd is a most fashionable artist,' said he. 'His latest portrait of the Queen hangs in the Tate. Three gallons of red emulsion slung over a ten foot-square canvas. Not my cup of Earl Grey, to be sure, but fashion is fashion. And by the by, Mr Dadd sits yonder.'

Will turned to view Mr Dadd. 'Which one?' Will asked.

'Short fat fellow, sitting with that womaniser, Wilde.'

'Oscar Wilde?' Will asked.

'That's the chap; dabbles a bit in theatre, when he's not bedding some countess or another.'

'But I thought Oscar Wilde was gay.'

'Oh, he's cheerful enough.'

'I mean, as in him being a sweeper of the chocolate chimney.'

Rune laughed loudly. 'Quite the reverse,' said he. 'A big ladies man is our Oscar.' And Rune caught the eye of Wilde and waved. 'Evening, Oscar,' he called.

Oscar Wilde made a face and raised two fingers at Rune.

'Commoner,' said Rune. 'Still bearing a grudge over the twenty guineas I borrowed from him.'

'Do you know anyone else here?' Will asked, as he viewed the fashionably dressed patrons of the Café Royal.

'Indeed,' said Rune. 'Most, if not all. See that tall fellow lounging by the jukebox; that is Little Tich, who has found fame with his ever-popular Big Boot Dance. And there, the gaunt creature with the long black beard. That is Count Otto Black, proprietor of the Circus Fantastique, who has found fame through the exploitation of freaks, foul fellow that he is.'

Rune pointed out Dame Nellie Melba, who would later find fame as a popular dessert, and Aubrey Beardsley, whose erotic novel *Under the Hill* had given Will a stiffy on the tram in the twenty-third century, and who would later find fame by dying young from TB.

'And that is Mr Gladstone,' said Rune. 'Who will be remembered for his bags. And that is Lord Oxford, who will also be remembered for his bags. And that is Lord Duffle, who will similarly be remembered for his—'

'Bags?' said Will.

'Bags,' said Rune. 'And that is Lord Carrier, and that is Lord Johnny.'

'I think that's enough bags for now,' said Will.

'I agree,' said Rune. 'The secret lies in knowing when to stop.'

'Isn't that Lord Colostomy?' Will asked.

'No,' said Rune. 'It isn't.'

'Why are we here?' Will asked of Hugo Rune.

'Now *that* is indeed a question,' the guru's guru replied. 'A question which has puzzled Man since his genesis. Darwin claims that he holds the answer, but so too does the Archbishop of Canterbury. Both these fellows are good friends of mine, and both are mistaken in their beliefs. The real reason why we are here—'

'I mean, why are *you* and *I* sitting here, *now*, drinking inferior champagne?'

'A far easier question to answer. We await the arrival of the gentleman who invited us here. We are a little early. Cigar?' Rune proffered the open silver humidor which stood upon the crisp white linen tablecloth.

Will shook his head. Rune scooped up a fistful of cigars, placed one in his mouth and crammed the others in his top pocket. 'Magic,' said he.

'Speaking of magic,' said Will. 'You have been promising for some time now, for as long as I have known you in fact, which is over a year, to demonstrate some of yours to me. Perhaps you would care to impress me by improving the flavour of the champagne?'

Rune raised a hairless eyebrow. 'One does not trifle with magic,' said he. 'But see this. And he snapped his right forefinger and thumb, drawing flame between them, from which he lighted his cigar.

'That is a music-hall trick,' said Will. 'I have seen Dan Leno do that.'

Rune smiled as he sucked upon his cigar and then blew hurriedly on his flaming finger and thumb.

'So who *is* treating us to this meal tonight?' Will asked.

'A very close friend.' Rune puffed cigar smoke and spoke through it. 'We were fellows at Oxford together. He seeks success in a different field to myself. He is a man obsessed with logic. I have however helped him out in the past with one or two matters which have proved to be beyond the scope of his logic.'

'So, who is he?'

'You'll see soon enough,' Rune raised his left hand. 'Aha, I sense his approach.'

Hugo Rune arose from his IKEA-looking chair and turned to greet the arrival of a tall, slender gentleman in an immaculately tailored evening suit. He carried a fashionable bag of the Gladstone persuasion.

'William,' said Hugo Rune to Will. 'Allow me to introduce you to my very good friend, Mr Sherlock Holmes.'

Will climbed from his chair to shake the hand of the world's most famous fictional detective. Will's jaw had dropped and his eyes were somewhat wide. It couldn't actually be true, could it?

'Mr Starling,' said Mr Sherlock Holmes. 'I perceive that you have recently been to—'

'China,' Will managed to blurt.

'The toilet,' said Holmes. 'Your fly is still unbuttoned.'

Will hastened to rebutton his fly.

'I have heard much of you,' said Sherlock Holmes. 'Hugo informs me that you are a young man of almost infinite capabilities.'

'He does?' Will glanced at Rune, who put his finger to his lips.

'That you are indeed the fellow I seek,' continued Holmes.

'Really?' said Will. 'I don't think I quite—'

'A pleasure to see *you* once again, Shirley.' Rune offered his hand and Holmes shook it. The manner of the handshake was significant. Its significance was lost upon Will.

'It's Sher*lock*, in public, if you don't mind.' Holmes glanced the Logos of the Aeon up and down. 'I observe that you have gained precisely fifteen and a half pounds since last we met. The travelling life evidently agrees with you.'

Rune perused the great detective. 'And you, I see, have lost a little weight,' he said. 'I trust that you have not raised your dosage above a seven per cent solution.'

'Idleness does not agree with me, as well you know. And by the by, your tailor called in upon me at Baker Street, last week. He asked that he be remembered to you and also that I convey his bill directly into your hands.'

'Which you certainly will *not* do,' said Rune.

'We are gentlemen both. And brothers under The Arch. Might I test a glass of that questionable champagne?'

'Sit yourself down and do so.'

Holmes sat down and so did Rune and so too then did Will. Further champagne was poured and tasted, and commented upon unfavourably, and then a conversation ensued between Holmes and Rune, which Will listened to, but for the most part failed to comprehend.

The conversation was of that special variety which only exists between close and intimate friends. Where a mere word or phrase conjures mutual memories, raising either laughter or sadness. Mostly laughter upon this occasion.

Will watched and listened and shook his head.

It *was* Sherlock Holmes. The *real* Sherlock Holmes. He looked exactly as he did in the Sidney Paget illustrations, which had clearly been drawn from life. Will had read all of the Sherlock Holmes stories. He'd downloaded digital files of their original publications in the *Strand* magazine, from the copies held in the British Library. These files were in his palm-top. Will's palm-top was in Will's pocket.

Will wondered what Holmes might think if Will were to show him these downloaded files. Records of cases that Holmes had yet to be called upon to solve.

It was an interesting thought and one full of intriguing possibilities.

'So, Hugo,' said Sherlock Holmes. 'I regret that I will not be able to join you for supper, so let us address ourselves to the business at hand. You have recommended your magical son to me as the fellow I seek. Are you absolutely certain that he is up to the challenge?'

Rune nodded enthusiastically. 'Absolutely,' he said.

'What is all this?' Will asked.

'It is simple enough,' said Holmes. 'I would take on the case myself. In fact, I feel confident that I could solve it without even leaving the fireside of my sitting room at Baker Street. However, I am somewhat pressed by another urgent matter, which necessitates a trip to Dartmoor.'

'Ah,' said Will. 'I know—' But then he held his tongue.

'You know?' asked Holmes.

'Nothing,' said Will. 'So what is this case that you would like Mr Rune and myself to look into?'

'Not Mr Rune and yourself. Simply yourself.'

'But I—'

'Listen to the gentleman,' said Rune. 'You seek to *find things out*, do you not?'

Will nodded.

'Then this is your opportunity. Pray continue, Shirley.'

'Sherlock,' said Holmes. 'You must understand, Mr Starling,' he continued, 'that I am building a reputation for myself as a consulting detective. The world's only consulting detective. To do this it is necessary that I solve all the cases that are presented to me. But I have recently been inundated with requests for my assistance. Mostly these are trifling matters that can be speedily dealt with. But there are many of them. Too many. Hugo here has assisted me before. He is, as you must know, a man of considerable insight and intuition. And generosity.'

Will raised his eyebrows to this intelligence.

'Hugo informs me that you possess certain skills and that I can trust you to deal with this particular matter.'

'Yes, but,' said Will.

Holmes turned to Rune. 'I am having my doubts,' said he.

'All will be well,' said Hugo Rune, making a breezy gesture before sucking once more upon his cigar. 'The lad is shy. He is overwhelmed at meeting you.'

'That's certainly true,' said Will.

'But if anyone can deal with this case, I guarantee that this someone is William Starling. I know these things. Trust me. I'm a magician.'

'Then I *shall* trust you,' said Holmes. 'The reward is—'

'Let us not speak of rewards,' said Rune.

'As you please,' said Holmes.

'Well, not here,' Rune's voice was now a whisper. 'In private, later on.'

'Quite so.'

'What is this?' Will asked.

'Nothing,' said Rune. 'So, you have the file with you?'

'I do.' Holmes took up his Gladstone bag, opened it and produced a buff-coloured envelope, which he handed to Rune. 'My reputation depends upon this,' he said. 'We understand each other, don't we?'

'We do,' said Rune. 'Brother upon The Square,' and he made a certain sign.

'Then, good.' Holmes rose from his chair. Rune rose with him and the two shook hands once more. The significance of the unorthodox handshake was not quite so lost upon Will this time.

'I look forward to hearing from you once you have solved the case,' said Mr Holmes, now shaking Will by the hand. 'Enjoy your supper, charge it to my account. And so farewell.'

And with that he departed into the fashionable crowd and was gone.

'Nice chap,' said Hugo Rune, reseating himself.

'Nice chap?' Will slumped down and stared at Hugo Rune. 'What did you tell him about me? What is all this about?'

'Calm yourself,' said Rune. 'It is simplicity itself. We require funds.'

'We?' said Will.

'*We*,' said Rune. 'In order to do what must be done. You wish to return to your own time, do you not?'

'I do,' said Will.

'And when we have achieved our goal. Which is to rid the world of an evil presence.'

'The Chiswick Townswomen's Guild?' Will's voice had a certain sneering quality to it.

'You will learn in time the scale of the evil,' said Rune. 'And then you will believe. But we do require funds. And how better to earn these, than for you to take on a bit of detective work?'

'I'm *not* a detective,' said Will. 'What do *I* know about detective work?'

'You came from the future,' said Rune. 'You know all manner of things. You know for instance why Sherlock is going to Dartmoor, do you not?'

'Actually, I do,' said Will. 'I read it. He's going to solve the case of the Hound of the Baskervilles. The butler did it, by the way. It's often the butler who does it.'

'There you are,' said Rune. 'You are possessed of knowledge that is denied even to me. This,' Rune tapped the buff-coloured envelope, 'is a *big* case. A big *historical* case. A famous case. Solve this, gain the reward money, aid me and return to your own time, what could be simpler?'

'Ah,' said Will. 'Now I see. You told Holmes that I could solve the case, because you knew that I could. Because you knew that I'd know who the criminal was, because the case would be history to me. Even if much of history has been erased and hidden.'

'Exactly,' said Rune. 'Although I could have put it somewhat more eloquently. And bear also this in mind. We are acting for Sherlock Holmes; his reputation depends on him solving all the cases that he is given. You wouldn't want to let Sherlock Holmes down, would you? You wouldn't want him to lose his place in history?'

Will shook his head. 'Go on then,' he said. 'Let's have a look in the envelope.'

Rune slid it across the tablecloth. 'Everything depends on this,' he told Will. 'Holmes' reputation, you getting back to the future. Everything. It does. Trust me, it really does.'

Will shrugged and sighed. 'If it's a famous case, then I probably do know,' said he and he took the envelope and opened it.

Will pulled out papers and glanced at them, and then Will began to laugh.

'You know,' said Rune. 'You do know, don't you?'

Will laughed some more and then some more. And then Will stopped laughing and said to Hugo Rune. 'If everything depends on this, we're stuffed.'

'Stuffed?' said Rune. 'Whatever do you mean?'

'I mean,' said Will. 'That we have been given a case to solve that cannot be solved. Is *never* solved.'

'There is no such case,' said Rune.

'There is,' said Will. 'And this is it. The case of Jack the Ripper.'

13

'Excellent,' said Hugo Rune. 'Unsurpassed, incomparable, quintessential and prototypical also.'

Will shook his bewildered head. 'And this would be the Australian aardvark in aspic, or possibly the Bavarian brown bear in blueberry sauce, or even the cranberry-covered Carpathian coypu? Or is it the Dalmatian dog in the Danish pastry?'

A meat feast of heroic proportions spanned the table's distance between himself and The One and Only. Rune had ordered all but everything on the Café Royal's menu.

'Each and all.' The Lad Himself took up a napkin and wiped away jellied eel from the corner of his mouth. 'But above and beyond that, your earlier assertion that the case of Jack the Ripper cannot be solved. It will certainly put the mongoose amongst the cobras when you solve it, don't you think?' And he forked up a helping of fried French ferret and plunged it into his mouth.

Will shook his bewildered head a second time, noting ruefully as he had upon so many previous occasions, that Hugo Rune's mode of food consumption mirrored exactly that of Will's own father. Like father, like son, like father, like son and so on down, or up, the ages.

'The case of Jack the Ripper cannot be solved,' Will said once more. 'It's never solved.'

'Have I taught you so very little?' Rune enquired. He dined from several plates simultaneously and fed as he spoke.

'You have taught me *nothing*,' Will replied. 'Well, perhaps a few things. Which hand to hold my eel fork in, for instance.'

'Then let me tell you this. And I will keep it brief for fear that the grilled goat gets a skin upon its gravy. You, my boy, have been returned to this period in time to use what knowledge you possess in putting things to right. Your presence here affords us the opportunity to change the future. To create a new and better future. To thwart the plans of the evil ones who seek to alter it for their own advantage.'

'The Chiswick Townswomen's Guild.' Will's face once more had a sneer painted over it.

'Evil in human form,' said the sage. 'And pass the sage and onion sauce if you will.'

'I will,' said Will, passing it.

'All right.' Rune poured the sauce all over his hummingbird hotpot. 'In order that you might be returned to your own time it is necessary that we change things. By changing things we change the course of history.'

'I really don't understand.' Will helped himself to a slice of impala. 'It's all rather complicated.'

'It's simplicity itself.' Rune pulled a platter of Jamaican jackdaw in his direction. 'We are going to cause a few ripples in the ice cream of time. According to your history, Jack the Ripper was never brought to book for his horrendous crimes. What if you were to rewrite the menu of history? Strike off the first course and add a delicacy of your own.'

'And that would help to make things right?'

'It's a starter,' said Rune. 'And speaking of starters, did I finish all those kiwi kebabs?'

Will nodded. 'You did. And you ordered a second portion which you similarly consumed.'

'So much to eat, so little time. Life in a coconut shell.'

Will pushed lemur in lemongrass sorbet about on his plate. 'But what I also don't understand,' said he, 'is why both you and Mr Holmes want *me* to take on this impossible case. If Mr Holmes isn't going to take it on himself, why don't you do it?'

'*Me?*' Will now found himself sprayed with half-masticated morsels of marmoset meringue. 'I am a mystic,' quoth Rune. 'A magician. An avatar. A perfect master. I am not a mere detective.'

'But I'll bet you'll take the credit if I *do* solve it,' Will said. 'And all the reward money.'

'What was that, boy?'

'Nothing.' Will helped himself to some neck of newt. 'But the case cannot be solved. So it's all neither here nor there, really.'

Hugo Rune shook his great bald head. 'There is nothing that cannot be done,' he said and again he tucked into his tucker.

They ate on in silence but for Rune's occasional belchings and calls to the waiter for further wine. Will, all alone with his thoughts, pondered upon the situation. What, just what, might happen if the most unlikely event was to occur and he was actually able to bring Jack the Ripper to justice? Jack was one of the most notorious criminals in all history, not because of the scale of his crimes, but because of the mystery that was attached to them, his motives and the fact that he was never caught. History would record Will, if Will could stop Rune taking the credit, pile accolades upon him. He would be forever known as the man who caught Jack the Ripper, when the police *and* Sherlock Holmes had failed. That would be big kudos.

And it *would* change history: a bit, anyway.

But a big bit as far as Will was concerned.

But then, and then a big 'but then' crossed Will's mind.

But then, Jack the Ripper was a psychopathic killer. Not a man to be trifled with. Tackling him would be a risky business: a very risky business.

Did the pros outweigh the cons?

A great big smile spread up either side of Will Starling's face. How often was an opportunity like this ever to occur in a lifetime? Never at all, was the answer to that. But as it had . . . well.

'I'll do it,' said Will.

Rune grinned through a face-load of ostrich à l'orange. 'I knew that you would,' said he.

At considerable length, their vast repast concluded, even down to the wallaby in wild woodbine and the zebra in a basket, Rune called for the bill. He then took issue over the cost and quality of each and every item on it. He called for the manager and took him to task about the quality of the champagne. Then he produced a small bone, which he claimed to be a rat's pelvis, that he said had lodged in his throat during his consumption of the terrapin terrine. He issued protests and threats of litigation and eventually settled 'out of court' for twenty guineas compensation up front and at once.

'A job well done,' said Rune as he and Will left the Café Royal, never again to return.

'Was that really necessary?' Will asked. 'Mr Holmes was paying for the meal.'

'I know,' said Rune. 'But Holmes is a friend and the champagne *was* inferior.'

Will and Rune walked together along the Strand. It was after midnight now. There had been rain earlier but it had since cleared up, leaving only puddles which reflected the glow of the neon lights shining from the bow-fronted windows of the exclusive shops. An electric carriage slid soundlessly past. Within the glazed dome, fashionable fellows joked with painted ladies of the night-time calling.

At Piccadilly Rune and Will halted.

'I am going on to my club now,' said Rune. 'The Pussycat in Greek Street. Perhaps you would care to join me?'

'I think I'll return to our lodgings,' Will said. 'Think things over. Come up with some sort of plan. I have the envelope of case notes. I have all sorts of stuff about Jack the Ripper on file in my palm-top. Most of it is probably rubbish, but you never know. I might come up with something.'

'Good boy,' Rune patted Will upon the shoulder. 'Although you do not have faith in me, I have faith in you. Together we will triumph. This is just the beginning, but it will facilitate the end.'

Will nodded thoughtfully.

'As surely as the errant bicycle is viewed through the veil of cucumber,' said Rune, 'then so does the spotty youth of time dwell upon the doorknob of pasta. Muse upon these truths.'

Will shook his head.

'Good night,' said he.

'Good night,' said Rune, 'and see you on the morrow.'

And so they parted company, Rune, chuckling to himself and steering his sizeable slippers in the direction of the Pussycat Club, and Will heading back to their present humble lodgings in Shoreditch.

Will sat long into the night, a lighted candle as his elbow, his palm-top on his knee and many cockroaches hurrying about their business all around him. He trawled the pages of his files on Saucy Jack. He came up with the usual suspects, shook his head at the conspiracy theories, made notes of all that he considered relevant. He leafed through the case notes, deciphering with difficulty the spidery cursive penmanship of the hardly literate constables and the observational findings of the coroner. At length, when his eyelids began to droop, Will closed up his palm-top, shook vermin from his bed and tucked himself into it still fully clothed.

He blew out the candle and lay in the darkness, wondering where all this might lead to. Concluding that he didn't have the faintest idea, he eventually fell into a deep but troubled sleep.

Sunlight awakened Will. He yawned and stretched and plucked away the web that a spider had woven over his face. Will smiled somewhat at this. There was no explaining Hugo Rune. The guru's guru always demanded first-class treatment, even though he was never prepared to actually pay for it. But still he thought nothing of sleeping in the poorest of accommodation. Although similarly he thought nothing at all about actually paying for that either. The man was an enigma. Charlatan or sage? Will really didn't know. But he certainly had charisma. And charisma is ultimately what sorts out the somebodies from the nobodies.

'Are you awake?' Will asked and he turned to view the wretched pallet of the perfect master. The perfect master however was not to be seen. And his wretched pallet showed no signs of having been slept upon.

'Didn't get back,' said Will to himself. 'Well, he said nothing about us doing a moonlight flit last night, so I assume he must have stayed at his club.'

Will rose and washed his face in a bowl of cold and doubtful-looking water and then he took himself downstairs. There was always the possibility that he could charm the landlady into offering him some breakfast. Not that he felt particularly hungry. Last night's gargantuan feast still padded his stomach. Will paid a visit to a communal toilet of terrible aspect and, once hastily done with his ablutions there, removed himself from the boarding house to stretch his limbs in the street.

It was a long walk to Rune's club and Will did not have the fare for a hansom cab, let alone one of the new electric flyers. So he stood in the doorway of the rooming house, taking in the morning air and the sights and sounds and smells of Victorian London.

'Read orl abowt it! Read orl abowt it!' A paperboy flourished papers. Will recognised the paperboy, the lad who had accosted him upon his undignified arrival in the time machine.

'Good morning, young Winston' said Will. 'We meet again.'

'Gawd lop off me love truncheon,' said the lad. 'I remember you, guv'nor. Care for a paper. It's the *Shoreditch Sun*. First with the news, and the best news there is. And a lady in a corset on page three.'

'No thanks,' said Will.

'Please yourself then. Read orl abowt it!' he bawled once again. 'Hideous murder in Whitechapel. Ripper strikes again.'

'What?' went Will.

'Ripper strikes again!' bawled the lad.

'Not so loud,' said Will. 'But that isn't right. A sixth murder. That's not right.'

'Hideous murder,' bawled the lad. 'Blood and guts all over the place. Police as ever baffled.'

'Give me a newspaper,' said Will.

'Halfpenny,' said Winston.

Will dipped into his pocket and brought out a silver threepenny bit.

Winston snatched it from his hand and trousered it with haste.

'Sorry, no change,' he grinned, handing Will a newspaper.

Will unrolled the broadsheet and cast his eye over the headline and the words that were printed beneath it.

TERRIBLE MURDER IN WHITECHAPEL
Ripper claims sixth victim

Will read the dreadful details. A gentleman had taken his leave from a well-known house of ill repute, after a dispute with the madam of that establishment regarding her charges. He had then apparently been pursued through the night-time streets by Jack the Ripper and brutally done to death. The chase had been witnessed by several gatherers of the pure,* who were working the nightshift. The actual murder had not been witnessed. The body had been later found by a patrolling constable.

'Upon the arrival of the corpse at Whitechapel Police Station, the victim had been positively identified by Inspector Lestrade of Scotland Yard, who was there playing whist with the station sergeant.

' "I knew the murder victim," he told our reporter. "He owed me five guineas. His name was Hugo Rune." '

The newspaper fell from Will's fingers and drifted down into the gutter.

His world was suddenly all in little pieces.

Hugo Rune was dead.

* Collectors of dog shit that was used in Victorian times for the process of tanning kid gloves. It's true, you can look it up in *Mayhew's London*. (I did.)

14

Tim looked appalled. He was appalled.

'Dead?' said Tim. 'Murdered?'

'Murdered,' said Will. 'By Jack the Ripper.'

'You never told me this.'

'I've just told you.'

'But you never told me this earlier. I was getting really excited about meeting him. I'm his magical heir.

'Sorry,' said Will. 'And believe me, I was pretty sorry too. For all the chicanery and the bravado and braggadocio, I really liked him. And all the time I was with him, when I thought that he wasn't teaching me anything, he was, like I said, he was teaching me how to survive. I owe him a lot. *A lot.*'

'But dead. I can't believe it.'

'Sorry,' said Will. 'But he was dead. It was him. I saw the body and I went to the funeral. You wouldn't believe how many famous folk of the day turned up to it. It was a real celebrity gathering.'

'You're being very off-hand about this,' said Tim.

'It did happen a very long time ago. I'm over it now.'

'I'm shocked,' said Tim. 'I'm really shocked.'

'So was I.' Will supped upon his pint of Large. 'But like I say, his funeral. That was really something. Queen Victoria came to it.'

'Queen Victoria came?' Tim's eyebrows were up into his hair.

'Close personal friend, apparently.'

'But Rune didn't die in Victorian times. He lived until 1947, when he died penniless in a Hastings boarding house.'

'In our version of history.'

'Oh,' said Tim. 'I see. But weren't you supposed to be changing history, by catching Jack the Ripper and stuff like that?'

Will winked at Tim. 'Certainly was,' he said. 'I was very angry about Rune being murdered. Very angry indeed. I can't tell you how angry. More angry than I've ever been about anything ever before. I was determined upon one thing and that was to bring Jack the Ripper to justice. He'd committed those other murders, which had nothing to do with me, but this time it was *personal.*

'And when I say, *personal*, I mean *personal.*'

The personal effects of Hugo Rune, the guru's guru, Logos of the Aeon, The Lad Himself and now, in death, the stuff of future legend, were contained within a steamer trunk which stood within the rat-infested hovel that was William Starling's not so home from home.

The reading of Rune's will had been an event that Will would long remember and cherish. Will had returned from it with tears in his eyes, but they were not of sorrow. Rather were they of laughter.

The reading had been held in public. So many were there, in fact, who wished to be present at the reading of this will, that the Royal Albert Hall had been loaned for the occasion by Her Majesty Queen Victoria (Gawd bless Her), who sat in state in her royal box to witness the proceedings.

Rune had left elaborate instructions, which were published in *The Times* newspaper, regarding the reading of his will, and the manner of his interment. The latter was to be a time of celebration, he stated, the celebration of a life well lived in the service of others. His body was to be embalmed in the manner favoured by the pharaohs, dressed in his magical robes, his ring of power upon his nose-picking finger, and seated upon a Persian pouffe within a pyramidal coffin of gopher wood, embellished with topaz and lapis lazuli. This was to be set upon a gun carriage, swathed by the flag of his former regiment, then drawn by six white horses to Westminster Abbey, where a selection of his poetry, including 'Hymn to Frying Pan' was to be read by the poet laureate whilst a choir of virgins sang lamentful anthems to his praise.

Will had been rather looking forward to that, once the reading of the will was out of the way.

And Will was much impressed by the interior of the Royal Albert Hall, with its terracotta reliefs depicting the arts and sciences of all ages. He looked with appreciation upon the tiers of boxes and galleries, which allowed the seating of some seven thousand individuals around the central arena. And he gazed up in some awe at the great dome of wrought iron and glass. He had visited it before with Rune to attend a gala ball and hear Dame Celia Asquith sing an operetta by Gilbert and Sullivan, which had also impressed him considerably.

There had been so much of old London that Will had wished to see: the British Museum, the Tate Gallery, the Victoria and Albert

Museum. Rune had taken him to each in turn and spent much time explaining to Will the whys and wherewithals and what-abouts of classical architecture, sculpture, fabric, fashion, and art, art, art. Rune's knowledge of all the arts was indeed profound, and whilst he had stoically refused to offer Will any insights to the magic he claimed to possess, he was always vociferous in expounding upon what he knew of other matters. And Will had taken in the knowledge he had been offered, gratefully. 'Education,' Rune had told him,' is what remains after you have forgotten everything that you have been taught.'

Will considered this an erudite statement.

Will was certainly fond of the Royal Albert Hall, and certainly amazed by the folk who filled it to hear the reading of Rune's will. They were not the cultured folk who attended the opera, the top-hatted dandies and gorgeously attired ladies. These people were strictly of the lower orders. Tradespeople.

Will, who could by now identify a tradesman by the manner of his garb, spied hat-makers, silversmiths, manufacturers of occult paraphernalia, vintners, brewers, book-binders, milliners, cobblers, hoteliers, inn-keepers, boarding-house proprietors, travel agents, shipping clerks, and sundry others. Many sundry others. There was not a free seat in the house.

There was an air of expectancy in that great domed room, an atmosphere that could have been cut with a cheese knife, all of which would have no doubt tickled Mr Rune.

And there was no doubt at all, that for this moment, and this moment alone, all of Rune's creditors were assembled in the selfsame place.

Mr Richard Whittington, the Lord Mayor of London, had been given the unenviable job of reading the will. He wore his robes of office and after ringing his big hand-bell in the fashion of a town crier and calling for order, broke the seal upon the envelope that had been lodged with Coutts' bank, withdrew the parchment contained within and read aloud the words printed there upon.

'This is the last will and testament of I, Hugo Artemis Solon Saturnicus Reginald Arthur Rune, Magus to the Hermetic Order of the Golden Sprout, Twelfth Dan Grand Master of the deadly art of Dimac, Logos of the Aeon, Lord of the Dance, King of the Jungle, snake-charmer, unicyclist, three-way cross-channel swimmer, Mr Lover Lover, Wild Colonial Boy, and one Hell of a Holy Guru, being of the soundest mind ever lodged within the human form and signed in my own hand in the presence of His Royal Highness, Prince Albert

Saxe Coburg Gothe, and our most Regal Majesty Victoria. May the Gods bless Her.' At the mention of the monarch's name, the crowd removed its collective headwear and bowed its collective head.

The Lord Mayor of London read aloud the will of Hugo Rune.

'I have nothing.

'I owe much.

'The rest I leave to the poor.'

Will, who had learned from Rune always to take the seat nearest to the door, 'in case some unforeseen unpleasantness might occur', was the first out of the door and so not only avoided potential injury during the ensuing riot, but also potential immolation during the conflagration which followed, and which indeed consumed the Royal Albert Hall. Will had glimpsed, upon his departure, Her Majesty making her own departure from the Royal Box. To Will's great amusement, he noted that Her Majesty was also, upon this occasion, *amused*.

Rune did not get the funeral he'd been hoping for. He was cremated at the expense of Hastings Borough Council. Although many close personal friends, the Queen included, did attend the funeral. The general public, in particular members of the trading class, were excluded.

And now it was all done and Will was alone, alone in the hovel with Rune's steamer trunk. And Will was wondering what he should do about it and its contents. Whose were they now? Were they his? He was after all, Rune's heir. But here was an anomaly. Rune had apparently died wifeless and heirless. No one had come forward and none had been mentioned in Rune's will. Perhaps the answers to the many questions Will had, might be found within the steamer trunk.

There was no doubt in Will's mind that Rune had possessed wealth. He was born of noble stock, a member of the landed gentry. He was *not* the son of a brewer, as he had originally told Will. His entry in *Who's Who* filled three whole pages. Will had always considered Rune's refusal to pay for anything an amusing, if somewhat dishonest, affectation, curiously typical of the very rich, who have been notorious throughout history for failing to pay their bills.

The chances that the trunk was crammed not only with Rune's clothes but indeed with countless stocks and shares bonds, jewels of high value and large denomination money notes seemed most probable to Will.

And as Will was a stranger in a strange land and presently without funds, hungry and awaiting the knock upon the door that presaged eviction into the street, now would be as good a time as ever to open up the trunk and take a look inside.

And after all, Will had dragged that trunk across five continents and never been granted a peep within. Rune had kept the key upon a chain around his neck. Will had not been able to gain possession of this key.

Will sighed, rose from his verminous pallet, took up the crowbar he had 'acquired' and gazed down at the trunk.

'Mr Rune,' he said, 'I am going to open your trunk. You will pardon me for this, I trust. I swear that I will avenge your death and bring your murderer to justice. But in order to do this, I require funds. If, to this end, I am forced to sell your clothes and whatever magical accoutrements are held within this trunk, so be it. I am hoping, however, that this trunk contains treasure. And that's all I have to say really.' Will might well have crossed himself after this brief speech, but instead he made the sign of the pentagram as he had seen Rune do upon many occasions, mostly before a moonlight flit.

And then Will put his crowbar to the lock of the steamer trunk and forced it open. He put the crowbar aside, applied his hands to the lid, and lifted it.

A curious fragrance breathed out from the open trunk, as of lilacs; the 'odour of sanctity' that issues from the incorruptible bodies of the saints. Will sniffed this fragrance. 'It pongs of his aftershave,' said Will.

And then Will delved into the trunk. He heaved out Rune's clothes: the hand-made shirts, and vests, (no underpants, for Rune had always gone 'commando'), socks, garter-straps and spats. And suits: the Boleskine tweed six-piece suit, the linen tropical number, Rune's pink chiffon evening dress. There were papers, many papers, but most of these were unpaid bills. And then there were books. Will did what you did with books, Will pored over them. Tomes they were, books of magical lore. Here was Joseph Glanvil's *Saducismus Triumphatus* and also the *Daemonolatreia* of Remigius, the 1595 Lyons edition; and *The Book of Rune*, and inevitably *The Necronomicon* of the Mad Arab Abdul Alhazred. Will knew of *The Necronomicon*, because, let's face it, *everyone* knows of *The Necronomicon*. He set it aside for a later bedtime read and proceeded with his search for Rune's hidden wealth.

It did not appear to be forthcoming.

He came across Rune's swordstick, the slim ebony shaft topped by a silver skull. Will twirled it between his fingers. He'd always rather fancied that cane.

There were boxes now, beneath where the books had been stacked. Cufflinks; many, many sets of cufflinks. Will viewed these approvingly. Some were set with diamonds and emeralds. There was wealth here. And watches, gold hunters, several embossed with Masonic symbols set about their faces in substitute for numbers. And there were the golden brooches and the watch chains.

'There is money here,' Will smiled to himself. 'He certainly favoured a bit of jewellery.'

Will opened box after box after box. Many great rings displayed themselves, magical rings, inscribed with enigmatic symbols, inlaid with cabochons and turquoise and lapis lazuli. Will gasped anew as each new treasure revealed itself. There *was* wealth here, great wealth: the legacy of Hugo Rune. Will plucked a ring at random from its box and put it onto his finger. The ring was far too big for his slender digit, but Will blew upon the ring and buffed it on his sleeve. 'Splendid,' he said. He took up another and another until his hands could hold no more. 'Thank you, Mr Rune,' said Will. 'None of this will be wasted, I assure you.'

Will let the rings drop from his fingers onto his bed and sought further treasure. Only one box remained in the trunk. Will fished it out. It was larger than a ring box, and weighty too; of considerable weight in fact.

'This has to be it,' said Will. 'The mother lode.'

And Will sought to open the box, but could not.

Will puzzled at this. There was no sign of a keyhole. It was just a box with a lift-up lid; a curious box though; an interesting box. Will studied the interesting box. It was of tanned hide, tanned pink hide. Will could not guess from what manner of beast this hide had been extracted, but there was something about it which Will found unsettling.

Regarding the dimensions of the interesting box, it was cuboid and about ten centimetres to a side. Upon its lid was an engraved brass disc. Will studied the engraving upon this disc: a name, a single name.

And lo, this name was Barry.

'Barry,' read Will. 'Now I wonder who Barry might be. Some former owner of this box, I suppose. So how do you get it open?' Will fought with the box but it was an unequal struggle. The box would not be opened. Will took out his pocket knife and selected a suitable blade. He struggled and forced, and the blade sheared off and almost took his eye out.

'Right,' said Will. 'Well, I'm not going to be beaten by a little box.

If I can't pry you open, then I'll stamp you open. Even the most vigorous stamping is unlikely to damage a diamond.'

'No chief, don't do that.' The voice was a tiny little voice and came, it seemed, from far away.

'Who said that?' Will span around. His box-free hand became a fist. 'Come out wherever you're hiding.'

'I'm not hiding, chief. I'm nestling.'

'Who said that?'

'It's me, chief. In the box. I'm Barry.'

'Barry?' Will held the box at arm's length, peered at it, lifted it to his ear and gave it a little shake. 'Barry?' he said once again.

'Yes, chief; Barry. Please stop jiggling me about.'

'Wah!' went Will and he flung the box across the room. Across the room was not too far. The box bounced off a damp-stained wall and fell to the uncarpeted floor.

Will lifted his foot and prepared to do stampings, this time not in the cause of finding hidden wealth but rather to destroy whatever lurked within the pink skin box.

A creature? A demon? A witch's familiar? Will didn't know just what.

'Ooh that hurts,' the tiny voice came from the box. It jangled Will's nerves something wicked. 'Don't stamp on me, chief. I'm *your* buddy now. And I'd really appreciate it if you'd let me out of this box.'

Will was getting a real sweat on. 'Who are you?' he asked in a tremulous tone. '*What* are you?'

'I'm Barry, chief. Please don't stamp on me.'

Will stared down at the box. 'Are you a genie?' he asked.

'A *what*, chief?'

'A genie,' said Will. 'I've read about genies, they're magical entities trapped in bottles or lamps or suchlike. When you release them they grant you three wishes.'

'Ah,' said the tiny voice. 'I hear where you're coming from. Genie would be one way of putting it.'

'So you'll grant me three wishes?' Will was warming to the idea.

'I'll certainly give it my best shot.'

Will stooped and gingerly took up the box. He put it once more to his ear. 'You promise?' he said.

'No probs, chief. I'll promise you anything you like.'

'So how do I open the box?'

'Just give the lid a twist, it's a screw-on, you schmuck.'

Will stared at the box. 'What did you call me?' he asked.

'Nothing chief. I said, just give the lid a twist. It's a screw-on. *Too stuck.*'

'I'm sure that's *not* what you said.'

'Well, please yourself, chief. If you have no use for three wishes. Like I don't think!'

'All right. Hold on.' Will pondered, as one would in such a situation; a situation, which it has to be admitted, probably wouldn't come up in the normal course of one's lifetime more than, maybe, the number of times one might find oneself called on to solve the case of Jack the Ripper. There could be danger in this box. Something horrible might lurk within. Opening this box would be risky business.

It would be a big risk.

Will gave the lid of the box a twist, and it fell aside, to reveal—

'A sprout,' said Will, in considerable amazement. 'You're a sprout.'

'Of course I'm a sprout,' said Barry. 'You were expecting, perhaps, a genie!'

15

'A sprout.' Will lifted the sprout from its box and cradled it on the palm of his hand. 'A talking sprout.'

'I think we've established that, chief,' said the talking sprout.

'But, a sprout,' Will had genuine awe in his voice. 'A talking sprout.'

'Yes, yes, chief. Let's not make a big thing out of it.'

'But, I mean, you're a sprout. And you can talk.'

'Oh dear, oh dear,' said Barry the talking sprout. 'Did we suck too many lead soldiers when we were a lad?'

'What?' went Will.

'Or perhaps you were dropped at birth, that would always do it.'

'What are you saying?' Will's fingers tightened on the sprout.

'Oooh!' went Barry. 'Don't do that, please, no.'

Will's grip slackened, slightly.

'I'm trying to remain cool, calm and collected here,' Will told the sprout. 'I'm sure that I'm not hallucinating you.'

'He never mentioned me, did he?'

'Who?' asked Will.

'My master. Hugo Rune.'

'No,' said Will. 'He never did.'

'Typical,' said Barry. 'Please stop with the squeezing, will you?'

Will released his fingers. He peered at the little green spheroid and shook his befuddled head. 'I'm talking to a sprout,' he said. 'I don't know what to say.'

'You could say, "pleased to meet you, Barry" and then, in about ten minutes time, you could say, "thank you very much for saving my life".'

'What?' Will went.

'No, chief, not *what*. "Pleased to meet you".'

'No,' said Will. 'About saving my life.'

'A thank-you will suffice, so get a move on, then.'

'What?' went Will once again.

'Monosyllabic,' said Barry. 'The lad is a numbskull.'

'What did you say?'

'What I'm saying, chief, is that big trouble is heading your way, so if you know what's good for you, you'll scoop up everything that's worth taking from Rune's trunk in your mouldy-looking bed blanket and have it away on your toes through the window.'

'*What?*' went Will, once again.

'Trouble,' said Barry. 'Big trouble. On its way now. I know these things. Trust me, I'm a sprout.'

'Right,' said Will. 'Right.'

'Then get a move on.'

'Right, said Will.

'I really mean it,' said Barry. 'It's on its way up here.'

Will's gaze turned towards the door. From beyond it came sounds of something being smashed and heavy footfalls crunching on the rickety stairs. And Will could smell a horrible smell issuing through the crack beneath the door. A horrible smell that he knew all too well, so to speak.

'Right,' said Will once again and he thrust Barry back into his box and Barry's box into his pocket. Then he dragged the steamer trunk across the floor and rammed it up against the door. Rune's jewellery was already on the bed, so Will snatched up the magic books and tossed them onto the blanket. He considered the clothes, but they were of no use to him. And what of his own belongings?

Something struck the door a heavy blow.

'William Starling,' called a voice, a deeply-timbred voice with a rich, Germanic accent.

'Oh no,' went Will, and he gathered up the blanket, hastily knotted its corners, snatched up Rune's cane and fled to the window.

Further blows rained upon the door. Wood splintered, hinges gave. Will struggled to open the sash but it was jammed shut by years of accumulated grime. Will might have tried the crowbar, but there just wasn't time, so he took as many steps back as he could within the tiny room, rushed forward and dived through the unopened window – which was three storeys up.

Now it only happens in movies, because movies are movies and real life is something else entirely. In movies, if the hero dives out of the window, then there is always something soft below to cushion his fall:

an awning, a pile of cardboard boxes, a passing wagon loaded with hay, an open-topped truck delivering mattresses; or a stunt mat.

But real life *is* something else entirely.

In real life there would be a row of spiked railings, a concrete area strewn with broken glass, a pit full of alligators, or, as happens on most occasions, the usual gang of cannibal bikers, or a flock of blood-crazed rabid chickens.

Will smashed through the window and plunged three floors to his almost inevitable doom. The awning slowed his descent. He ripped through that, however; struck the pile of cardboard boxes,* bounced from these onto the passing hay-filled wagon, slid from that onto the open-topped truck that was delivering mattresses and from there toppled down to the stunt mat that someone had dumped upon the pavement.

'Phew,' went Will, as he rose unscathed to his feet – to be promptly set upon by a flock of blood-crazed rabid chickens.

'Wah!' went Will as he fought himself free and took to his heels up the street.

Eight minutes later Will sat, all sweaty and breathless in a tavern called the Scurvy Stump and Lettuce. It was a Thames dockside tavern, the haunt of bargees and lightermen, pirates and ne'er-do-wells, smugglers and brigands, and gatherers of the pure. The tavern reeked of ship's tar and tallow, shag smoke and brandy, bad breath and armpits, and unwashed bottoms too. It echoed with the coarse discourse of burly sea-faring types, and the talk was all of yardarms and spinnakers, top sheets and anchor chains. And of bilges and brigs, and the new electric warships that the Royal Navy had upon trials, whores and whorings, and how well Brentford might fare in the FA Cup.

A one-eyed, one-legged barlord lorded it behind the bar, and a lady in a straw hat and Salvation Army uniform, moved about amongst the nautical clientele selling copies of the *War Cry*. Will, looking somewhat out of place in his funereal costume, sat in as dark a corner as he could squeeze himself into, but one that was near to the door. The blanket bag was between his feet, Rune's cane at his elbow, a mug of grog before him on a stained and rugged table, and a pink box was held between his trembling hands.

Will twisted open the lid and peered in at the recumbent sprout whose name was Barry.

'Thank you very much for saving my life,' Will whispered.

* It was a very big pile!

'You'll have to speak up a bit, chief,' chirped Barry. 'A bit of a din in this pub, don'cha know.'

'I don't want to speak louder.' Will raised the open box to his face. 'I don't exactly wish to be seen talking to a sprout.'

'Oh, excuse me,' said Barry. 'Not posh enough for you, eh?'

'That's not what I mean and you know it. But thank you again for saving my life.'

'At your service, chief. I suppose you'd like me to send you on your way home now.'

'I'm homeless at present,' said Will, dismally.

'I mean to your own home, in your own time.'

'What?'

'Please, not with the whats again. I can send you home if that's what you wish for.'

'Oh,' said Will. 'Then you really are a genie.'

'I'm a Time Sprout,' said Barry. 'From the planet Phnaargos. Brought here on official business to the twentieth century. Got knocked off course, though. Been helping out Mr Rune.'

'I really don't understand,' said Will, who didn't.

'It would take too long to explain now, chief. But if you want to go home, just give me the word and we're off.'

Will pondered. He placed Barry's box onto the rugged tabletop, took up his mug of grog and sipped at it. It was not at all bad, considering all the bits and bobs that were floating about on its surface. Will wiped a wrist across his mouth and replaced the mug. 'I can't go yet,' he said.

'What's that, chief? I thought you'd be eager to be away from here.'

Will shook his head. 'This is absurd,' he said. 'This is madness. A time-travelling sprout. Madness. I must have gone mad.'

'You're fine, chief, you're fine. I'm sure it's a bit of a shock, but you're fine. Trust me, I'm a sprout.'

'Well, I can't go just yet. I've sworn to avenge the death of Mr Rune. To bring Jack the Ripper to justice.'

Barry whistled. 'You really don't want to get involved in that,' he told Will. 'Let me take you back to your own time, that would be for the best.'

'I'm staying here,' said Will, 'until I've done this.'

'You really don't know what you're getting yourself into, chief.'

'I don't care. I've made up my mind. It's a matter of honour, if you like.'

'Good lad, chief. I respect that. And it's what I hoped you might say. So it means that I've finally found the right fellow. Pop me into your ear and we'll get started.'

'What?' said Will.

'Chief,' said Barry. 'Could you drop the "whats"?'

'Sorry,' said Will. 'But what are you talking about?'

'You've had my box open too long. I can't survive in the air for more than a couple of minutes. You'll have to stuff me into your ear. That's the way I do business.'

'No,' said Will and he shook his head. It was a very definite shake. 'I have no intention of stuffing you into my ear. You wouldn't fit anyway.'

'I'll meld in; it will be fine. Trust me.'

'I don't trust you. We've only just met.'

'I saved your life, didn't I? And I can help you out. You'll find I'm a really helpful chap.'

'No,' said Will. 'It's out of the question.'

'Then I'm sorry, chief. For the both of us. You'll never return to your own time and, as for me—' Barry made little coughing sounds – 'I'm a goner chief, sorry.' And, 'cough cough cough,' went Barry some more. And, 'croak,' and, 'gasp.'

'Stop it.' said Will. 'I don't believe you.'

Barry made a ghastly strangulated sound. And his leafy person began to visibly wilt.

'Stop it,' Will plucked Barry from his box and shook him about. A big bargee caught sight of this and looked on with interest. He nudged a smaller campanion and pointed.

'Wake up!' Will shook Barry about some more.

'Fading fast, chief, goodbye.'

'Stop it! Stop it! Oh dear me!' Will took the sprout and pushed it against his right ear. There was a kind of sucking sound and then a terrible plop.

'Oooooh!' went Will.

'Bugger me backwards,' quoth the big bargee. 'Did you see that, Charlie, or are me peepers playing pranks upon me brain box?'

'See'd it meself,' said Charlie. 'Pushed a gherkin right up his nose.'

'No he didn't.' The big bargee smote his smaller counterpart. 'It was a little cabbage what he had, and he rammed it into his ear'ole.'

'Why would he want to do that?' Charlie asked. 'Gherkin up your nostril makes good sense, done it many a time meself down in the horse latitudes. Staves off the scurvy and clears the sinal passages. Or is that a cantaloupe I'm thinking of, or possibly an aubergine?'

'You, boy,' called the big bargee. 'Undertaker's lad. What did you poke in your ear just then?'

'Ooooh!' went Will once more and he clutched at his head.

The big bargee approached Will's table. 'Come on lad, out with it.'

'Can't get it out,' Will groaned and clawed all about his head.

'Calm down, chief,' came a voice from inside it.

'Aaaagh!' went Will. 'Come out of me.'

'What are you up to?' The big bargee reached out a large and tattooed hand.

'Get it out of me,' wailed Will, leaping to his feet.

'Calm down, chief, I'm nice and comfy in here.'

The small bargee called Charlie said, 'Put your finger up your empty nostril then blow down the other.'

'It ain't up his 'ooter,' said the big bargee, 'it's in his lug'ole.'

'Get it out!' Will began to beat himself about the head with his fists. Which drew the attention of the one-eyed barlord.

'Now now now!' this fellow shouted. 'What's all this commotion?'

'Lad's got a cucumber stuck up his arse,' said the small bargee.

'It was never a cucumber.' His larger companion smote him once more.

'And stop with the smiting.' The small bargee kicked his persecutor in the ankle.

The one-eyed barlord reached under his bar counter for his peacekeeping knobkerry.

Will howled and beat some more at his head.

'Ow!' went Barry. 'Stop doing that.'

The big bargee hit the small bargee and the one-eyed barlord hopped over the bar, most nimbly for a peg-legged man.

Will lurched forward, overturning his table and spilling grog over bargees great and small. The one-eyed barlord swung his knobkerry and brought down the lady in the straw hat.

'Get out of my head!' shouted Will.

The big bargee punched the small bargee and the small bargee took a swing at Will.

'Incoming!' cried Barry. 'Duck, chief.'

Will ducked and the small bargee's fist swung harmlessly by.

'See how helpful I am,' said Barry. A three-legged stool sailed through the air and knocked Will from his feet.

Will collapsed onto his blanket bag.

'I think we'd best make tracks, chief, places to go, people to see, all that kind of stuff.'

'Get out of my head,' wailed Will, wriggling a finger into his right ear.

'No can do, chief. Fatal consquences and all that. But I'll be no bother and I don't take up much room.'

The one-eyed barlord now took to kicking Will with his timber toe. But then he went down amidst the growing number of flailing fists.

'We really should be on our way,' counselled Barry. 'Bring your blanket bag of goodies and Mr Rune's cane.'

Will now hastened to oblige.

As further fists were thrown and mighty oaths given voice, as bargee belaboured bargee and Jack Tar battered Jack Tar, pure-gatherer struck pure-gatherer, and a wandering bishop who was in the wrong pub punched Popeye the sailor man, Will crawled away to take his leave in the manner known as hurried.

16

'Well,' said Barry. 'Thanks be to me for getting you out of that spot of bother unscathed.'

'I'm not talking to you,' said Will. 'And you're not staying in my head.'

'Pardon me, sir,' said the gentleman behind the counter of Asprey, as he viewed the somewhat bedraggled figure that stood before him. The gentleman behind the counter was not truly a gentleman. He was an automaton, although not a scary black-eyed, evil-smelling grim satanic automaton. He was an elegant well-spoken upmarket model: a Babbage 1900 series. 'Pardon me, sir,' he said once again.

'Nothing,' said Will. 'I wasn't talking to you.'

'As you please, sir. So what is it that you require?'

'A pencil,' said Will. 'A really sharp one.'

Asprey was a wonderful shop, *is* a wonderful shop and hopefully will *always* be a wonderful shop. Asprey is set in the heart of Mayfair, a glorious emporium where are to be found porcelain and silverwares, antique books and travelling cases, china and crystal, guns, games and goblets; and a range of stylish automata on the first floor. Everything is beautiful at Asprey, especially the pencils.

'Certainly sir,' said the liveried gentleman's gentleman.

'Now hold on, chief,' said Barry. 'What do you need a pencil for?'

'I'm going to stick it in my ear and winkle you out.'

'Pardon me, sir?'

'Not you,' said Will. 'Just sell me the pencil, please.'

'And sir wishes to poke it into sir's ear?'

'I've a foreign object lodged in there.'

'Then perhaps sir should see a surgeon, rather than risk serious injury.'

'Just sell me the damned pencil.' Will made a very fierce face.

'As you wish, sir. Would you care to have it wrapped?'

Will made an even fiercer face.

'He's right, though, chief,' said Barry. 'You *will* injure yourself. Can't we just talk this over, sprout to man, as it were?'

'No,' said Will. 'You tricked me. You're some kind of evil parasite.'

'Well really sir. There's no need for that.'

'I'm not talking to *you*!'

Well-dressed patrons raised their noses and muttered 'disgraceful' and 'commoner'.

'And you lot can mind your own business.' Will was now most unsteady on his feet. He raised and shook a feeble fist.

'Forget the pencil, chief,' said Barry. 'You don't even have enough cash on you to pay for it. Or perhaps you were thinking to charge it to Mr Rune's account.'

'Actually I was,' said Will.

'But Mr Rune's dead, chief. What you *really* need is a bit of peace and quiet. Why don't we hock a pair of Mr Rune's cufflinks and check into the Dorchester?'

'What?' went Will.

'Here we go with the "whats" again. Time goes slipping by and if you really want to avenge Mr Rune's death you really should be concentrating on the job in hand.'

'I don't feel at all well,' said Will.

'Take a nap then, chief. Leave it to me.'

Will almost said, 'what?' once more.

But he didn't. Instead he just fainted dead away.

He later awoke to find himself lying on a most comfortable Regency rosewood bed in a private suite at the Dorchester.

It was an elegant suite, elegantly furnished, with a carpet of William Morris design, a George III satinwood dresser, a Louis XVI mahogany desk, a French ebonised and Boulle breakfront side cabinet, with brass mouldings, and gadrooned plinth, whatever that may be; and a settee and chairs in the style of Thomas Hope, whoever he may be.

And then Will *did* say 'what' once again.

'What am I doing here?' he said, and, 'How did I get here?'

'Ah, we're back in the land of the living are we?' The voice of Barry was once more in the head of Will.

Will made dismal groaning sounds.

'But no more cheerful I perceive,' Barry chuckled. 'For your information, I sort of animated you while you were out cold. Hocked the cufflinks and the rings, opened a bank account and deposited the money in Coutts', then got you to book yourself in here. What a nice chap I am, eh?'

'*What?*' Will's eyes were now very wide. 'You *animated* me? Like a zombie?'

'Hardly that, chief. Well, a bit like that, I suppose. You will find that your knees are a bit grazed. It took me quite some time to get all your odds and bods coordinating properly. I'm afraid I bumped you into a doorpost or two. But I got the hang of it in the end.'

'This is a nightmare' Will began to weep.

'Oh I don't know, chief. I think it's a pretty nice room. And it's got a bath. And frankly you need a bath. You're definitely a bit niffy. What with all the excitement and underarm roll-on deodorants not being invented yet. And everything.'

'I can't go on.' Will drummed his fists on the scented bed linen.

'Then have another kip and I'll take care of your bathing.'

'No you damned well won't.'

'The ingratitude of some people.'

'Please get out of my head.'

'I'm sorry, chief. I told you, I can't. But I *can* help you. And I will. We're one now. Your problems are my problems, so to speak. And I'll help you avenge Mr Rune's death *and* get you back to your own time. That's a pretty good deal, isn't it?'

'If it's true,' Will blubbered.

'It is true. And I've already got you started. Although you weren't aware of it, you called in at a cartographer's shop, a gentleman's outfitters and a purveyor of pistolry on your way here.'

Will shook his miserable head and asked, 'Why?'

'You'll be wanting a map of the Whitechapel area, new clothes and a gun. I was just doing what you'd naturally have chosen to do for yourself.'

'Oh,' said Will. 'Well, naturally, yes.'

'And you had dinner, because you were hungry. All meat, I hasten to add. I personally find the concept of eating vegetables positively obscene, don't you, chief?'

'Well,' said Will.

'I knew you'd agree. So, after you've had your bath, we can get started. What do you say?'

'Would you mind coming out of my ear while I have my bath?'

'Oh I see. You're a bit embarrassed about me being in your head and looking through your eyes and seeing your private bits.'

'Actually I am.'

'Well forget it, I've already seen them. And so has the young woman you picked up after dinner last night.'

'*What?*'

'Well, I wanted to know what, um, *doing it* as a human being felt like. You and I really enjoyed it, although naturally you won't remember that you did.'

'No!' and Will wailed some more and went, 'No,' and 'No,' again and again and again.

'But look on the bright side, chief. Your bits are no mystery to me, so you can have your bath without worrying about that.'

And eventually Will did have his bath. He lay in the warm and scented water, reading a copy of *The Times* newspaper. And as it was the first that he'd taken in quite some time, and as Barry *had* seen his bits before and everything, Will really enjoyed that bath. He lay and he soaked and he read the newspaper and life didn't seem too bad.

'So, what's the plan?' Barry asked. 'To apprehend Saucy Jack. What do you have in mind?'

'Ah,' said Will laying aside his newspaper, which was growing rather soggy about its bottom regions. 'Well.'

'Not really anything then.'

Will sponged at himself. 'You tell me,' he said. 'You seem to know everything about everything. And you know something about this Jack the Ripper business, don't you?'

'I know some, chief. Which was why I told you that you really wouldn't want to get involved.'

'So, what do you know?'

'He kills people, chief. Carves them up something wicked.'

'And that's all you know?'

'You don't pick up too much about current affairs when you're locked in a box at the bottom of a steamer trunk.'

Will rose from his bath, climbed out and wandered dripping in search of a towel.

'Why were you in the box?' he asked Barry. 'Why weren't you inside Mr Rune's head?'

'Mr Rune and I had a bit of a falling out. He made rather a lot of demands. A very single-minded fellow, Mr Rune.'

Will said no more, found towels and dried himself.

And then he flung the towels down onto the carpet of William Morris design and his naked self into an armchair.

'Look at me,' he said to Barry. 'You're in there, peering out of my eyes. Look at me and tell me what you see.'

'About your bits, chief?'

'No! Not my bits! About *me*!'

'Well, chief, I see what you see. A long skinny boy, healthy enough, but a bit sallow-complexioned. Probably from your late-night exertions. But a nice enough lad, if perhaps a bit—'

'A bit *what*?'

'A bit lost, chief.'

'Yes,' Will sighed. 'A bit lost is right. I don't know what I'm going to do. I'm caught up in something that I don't understand. If this were a book or a movie, the critics would tear it to pieces, saying that the hero was two-dimensional and the entire sorry business unconvincing and totally plot-led.'

'That's a bit harsh, chief. You didn't have much choice in the matter.'

'Exactly, and I should have a choice. I should be doing something. Making something happen. I don't even think I know who I am any more.'

'Tell me about it,' said Barry.

'Well—' said Will.

'No,' said Barry. 'I meant that rhetorically. I know exactly what you mean. It's just the same for me.'

'Yeah, right,' said Will.

'No, chief, listen. Let me tell you all about myself.'

'It will help, will it?'

'Bound to,' said Barry. 'When you've got troubles, there's nothing better than having someone else tell you all about theirs.'

'I don't believe that,' Will hunched his shoulders. 'But go on, say your piece. Tell me what you really are.'

'I'm a sprout,' said Barry.

Will sighed.

'A Holy Guardian sprout.'

'A what?'

'It's like this, chief. When God created the universe, He did it on what he called the "just enough of everything to go around principle". Personally I think it was more of a theory than a principle, but God knows His own business best. His principle was that there'd be just enough of everything. Enough stars to fill the sky, enough air for people to breathe. Enough water to fill up the sea, that sort of thing.'

'I don't believe in God,' said Will.

'And just enough doubt in mankind's mind to always keep them guessing. But God has never really been what you'd call a forward planner. He gets stuff started, then He sort of loses interest and goes off with one foot in the air and one hand behind His back and does something else.'

'Why with one foot in the air and one hand behind His back?'

'He moves in mysterious ways,' said Barry. 'I thought everyone knew that.'

Will sighed once more and shook his head.

'So things sort of carry on without Him and they tend to get a tad messed up. Which is one reason that the world is always in such a mess. It started off okay, back in Old Testament times, when He had His finger on the trigger and was on chatting terms with the prophets. You see, in those days everyone had their own personal Holy Guardian Angel to try and keep them on the straight and narrow and it worked for the most part. But the population of the Earth grew and grew until demand outstripped supply and there just weren't enough Holy Guardian Angels to go around. Which is how come chaps like me got involved.'

Will sighed once more and once more he shook his head.

'God started rooting around for more Holy Guardian Angels, but you can't just keep creating endless lines of them. So He dug into His garden and began dishing out His vegetables instead. So one person might get a Holy Guardian courgette and another a Holy Guardian turnip.'

'When I do get you out of my head,' said Will, 'I'll have to decide whether I am going to boil or roast you.'

'Chief, I'm trying to tell you all of the truth.'

'Well pardon me,' said Will, 'but I don't believe a word of it.'

'Then you'd prefer a scientific explanation?'

'Yes,' said Will. 'I would.'

'Then try this for size. I am a Time Sprout from the planet Phnaargos.'

'You told me that before and I didn't believe it then.'

Barry now sighed, but he didn't shake his head. 'I come from the future,' he said. 'Not the same future as you do. An alternative future. In the future I come from your world pretty much ended in the year two thousand, in what we called the Nuclear Holocaust Event. I was sent back in time to prevent that occurring. You see everything that has ever happened on Earth is watched by folk on another planet, who view it as a reality TV show called *The Earthers*. It's always been the most popular show there is, but after the Nuclear Holocaust Event, which got the greatest viewing figures ever, interest fell off, because there weren't that many Earthers left and what they did in that nuclear bunker was pretty dull. So the folk of Phnaargos, who were all vegetable, let me tell you, bred me in their horticultural laboratories, to go back in time and change the plot. Stop the Nuclear Holocaust Event occurring.'

'Yeah, right,' said Will. 'So how did you do that?'

'I was sent to find the one man who was responsible for all the bad stuff in the second half of the twentieth century and persuade him to act differently.'

'Adolf Hitler,' said Will. 'I do know something about history.'

'Elvis Presley,' said Barry. 'You don't know as much as you'd like to think. My job was to persuade Elvis not to take the draft. If Elvis hadn't joined the army, an entire generation of American kids would have also refused to join. There would have been no war in Vietnam and by 1967 Elvis would have been president of the USA.'

'I don't recall reading about this,' said Will.

'Things didn't go exactly as planned. Although you will agree, there was no Nuclear Holocaust Event.'

'So you're a Time Sprout from the planet Phnaargos?'

'Or a Holy Guardian sprout. Elvis Presley's Holy Guardian sprout. Depends on what you choose to believe, I suppose.'

'I think I'll remain unconvinced, if you don't mind.'

'That's fine with me, chief.'

'So, would you care to come out of my ear now?'

'All in good time, chief. After I've helped you out. Because by helping you out, I'll also be helping me out. And I'll be helping everybody out. You see my work here is not yet done. I might have forestalled the Nuclear Holocaust Event, but there's big trouble in this day and age, which is why I'm here. I was on the job with Mr Rune, but now he's gone, I'm on the job with you.'

'How very comforting,' said Will. 'So with you to help me I can probably expect to end up the same way Rune did.'

'If he'd listened to me, he'd have never come to grief. That man was a law unto himself. He refused to take my advice.'

'Refused to stick you in his ear, you mean.'

'That's part of it, perhaps.'

'Well I've had enough.' Will rose from the armchair and took himself over to the tantalus that stood upon the George III satinwood dresser. He poured scotch whisky into a crystal glass and sipped upon it. 'If I can't get rid of you,' he said, 'then understand this. I have had enough of being a pawn in someone else's game. From now on I'm going to do things my way.'

'Oh dear,' muttered Barry.

'What was that?'

'I said, "Oh *cheer*". Three cheers for you.'

'Right,' said Will. 'I'm going to be running this show from now on. We will be doing things my way. And, when I'm done, you can take me back to my own time, *like you promised*. And then you go your own way. Are we agreed on this?'

'I want what you want,' said Barry. 'More than you know.'

Will finished his scotch and poured himself another. 'I'll take that as a yes,' he said. 'And I'll do it without your help.'

'But chief."

'If I need your help I'll ask for it.'

'Be hearing from you soon then, chief.'

'What was that, Barry?'

'Nothing, chief.'

Will dressed in the smart new clothes that Barry had acquired for him.

'I hope you didn't pay for these,' Will said.

'Certainly not, chief. Opened an account for you with one of Mr Rune's tailors. They were happy to offer credit to Lord Peter Whimsy.'

'Who?' Will asked.

'Makes a change from "what",' said Barry. 'It's an alias. Tradespeople are always willing to offer credit to toffs, you know that. And anyway, I didn't think you'd want to give your real name. You wouldn't want any more of those knocks at the door from the black-eyed smelly clockwork chap with the deeply-timbred Germanic accent, would you?'

'Certainly not.' Will admired his suit and matching cap. 'And Boleskine tweed. I always rather envied Rune's suit.'

'I know you did, chief.'

'Hmm,' went Will. 'And so to work. I have the map of Whitechapel, so all I need is the . . . *damn*!'

'The *damn*? Chief?'

'The case notes. Damn. I left them behind when I threw myself out of the window.'

'No probs, chief. I knew you'd need them. I had you sneak back and pick them up. They're over there on the Louis XVI mahogany desk.'

'You were very busy with my body, weren't you?'

'All in a good cause, chief. Your interests at heart.'

'Well, let's have a look at them.' Will gathered up the notes and the map, sat himself down at the Louis XVI mahogany desk, took the fountain pen from his top pocket ('thought you'd need a pen too, chief') and set about studying.

And so Will studied. He studied the map and the case notes. He also studied what files he had contained within his palm-top. And he studied his fingers, and then the ceiling and then the floor.

'How's all the studying coming on?' Barry asked him, at length.

'Fine, thanks,' said Will. And he studied the bottom of his glass.

'Might I make a suggestion, chief?'

'No, Barry, you may not.'

'No probs, chief, you study on, then. Study the curtains, if you feel it might help.'

'Please don't interrupt me; I'm thinking.'

'So sorry, chief. Don't wish to interfere with your thinking. They're nice curtains though, aren't they?'

'Splendid,' said Will. 'But it's not helping. Just be quiet and let me ponder over this. There have to be clues here. There has to be something.'

'They *are* nice curtains,' said Barry. 'Nice pattern.'

'Something obvious,' said Will.

'Very nice *pattern*,' said Barry.

'Something staring me right in the face.'

'Extremely nice *pattern*.'

'Like a—'

'Pattern, chief?'

'Hold on,' said Will, and he studied the map once more. He marked the sites of the five original murders and then he searched for —

'There's a twelve-inch rule in the drawer, chief.'

Will opened the drawer and took out the rule. And then he worked away at the map. And then—

'Aha!' went Will.

'Aha, chief? What is aha?'

'I've found it,' said Will.

'You have, chief. What have you found?'

'A pattern,' said Will. 'I've found a pattern.'

And it *was* a pattern. And so it is to this very day. Simply join the dots, as it were, and see what you will see.

'A star,' said Will. 'A five-pointed star.'

'A pentagram,' said Barry. 'An inverted pentagram.'

'Significant, eh, Barry?'

'Highly, chief. Well done for coming up with it all on your own.'

'And the site of Rune's murder.' Will marked the spot. 'It's outside the pentagram. I wonder—' He drew further lines.

'What are you doing now, chief?' Barry asked.

'Just a hunch. According to the police report, which I managed to acquire a copy of, Rune was pursued for some distance before his murderer caught up with him and did the evil deed. I'm tracing his route; he travelled along here and then there, and then here. What do you make of that?'

'That he had more puff in him than I'd have given him credit for.'

'No,' said Will. 'Not that. He wasn't running in the direction of our lodgings. Although he could have done. So what was he running towards?'

'A police station, chief?'

'No, he passed one, here.' Will drew a line upon the map, from the centre of the pentagram to the site of Rune's murder. 'He was always running northeast. Why would he do that, was he trying to tell us something? What I really need is—'

'A map of Greater London, chief? There's one in the drawer.'

'Thank you.' Will took out the map of Greater London and spread it across the desk. He redrew the line and extended it. 'Well, well, well,' said Will. 'What do you make of that Barry?'

'What exactly should I make of it, chief?'

'See where the line goes to?'

'Well, I do chief, but I don't quite see—'

'Buckingham Palace,' said Will.

'Well, yes, chief, it does, but if you carry the line on, I think you'll find—'

'Buckingham Palace,' said Will once again. 'And there's enough stuff written to suggest that there was some kind of scandal involving a member of the Royal household. A child born out of wedlock to a prostitute, that sort of business, and—'

'If you extend the line, chief, I think you'll find it leads to—'

'Perhaps that's what Rune was trying to tell us, Barry. That's why he ran in that direction.'

'No, chief. I'm sure that—'

'Stop it, Barry.'

'But chief.'

'Barry, just stop it. You're simply miffed because I found this out without your help.'

'As if you did, you—'

'We'll take a cab straight over there, ask a few questions.'

'An omnibus would be cheaper.'

'An omnibus it is then.'

'The number 39 goes that way, chief. And then it continues in a northeasterly direction, the same direction as the line on the map, until it terminates at *Chiswick*.'

'A number 39 it is then.'

'Terminates at *Chiswick*, chief. *Chiswick*.'

'A number 39 it is then.

'To *Chiswick*, chief?'

'To Buckingham Palace.'

'Oh dear, oh dear, oh dear.'

17

Will settled himself into a front seat on the open upper deck of the Chiswick omnibus. The bus was a three-storey vehicle, electrically powered.

Ground floor, first class, with cocktail lounge, served by a cocktail waiter.

Second floor, middle class, with lounge bar, served by a suited barman.

Third floor, working class, with a pile of beer crates in one corner, booze by the bottle, served by a toothless hag.

'Care for a pint of old Willydribbler, dearie?' enquired this hag, leaning over Will's shoulder and showering him with flecks of jellied eel.

'No thanks, missus,' said Will. 'Have to keep a clear head, off to see the Queen, you know.'

'We'll forget all about those two large scotches you had back at the Dorchester shall we, chief?'

'Silence, Barry.'

'What's that, dearie?'

'I said nothing, thank you.'

The hag shuffled off to serve a party of Japanese sightseers.

And Will took in the sights and sounds of London. The bus was travelling slowly down the Strand and Will looked out upon the swank storefronts.

There was Mr Dickens' famous Old Curiosity Shop. And there was Woolworths, the Kwik Fit Fitter, and there was the Little Shop of Horrors. And there was a Babbage superstore, with a range of automata displayed in its front window; many different varieties, none of which were black-eyed and monstrous. And there was the Electric Alhambra, where Little Tich was topping the bill and performing his ever popular Big B . . .

'Fine view,' said the man on the seat next to Will.

'It certainly is,' said Will.

'And how would you know that?' asked the man. 'I haven't given it to you yet.'

'Pardon me,' said Will. 'I don't think I quite understand you.'

'Ignore him, chief: "nutter on the bus". There's always one. It's a tradition, or an old charter, or something.'

'Silence, Barry.'

'And my name isn't Barry,' said the man.

Will glanced at the man. He was an average-looking man: average height (even when sitting down), average weight, average face, averagely dressed. He raised his average hat to Will.

'I'm The Man,' said he.

'Really?' said Will, and he addressed his attention once more to the scenery.

'The Man,' said The Man once more. '*The* Man.'

'I'm sorry,' said Will, 'but I really don't understand. And I'd prefer to be alone with my thoughts at the moment, if you don't mind.'

'You can't let an opportunity like this slip by,' said The Man. 'Not when you meet The Man.'

'The Man?' asked Will.

'The Man on the Clapham Omnibus,' said The Man. 'Don't say that you've never heard of me.'

'Fair enough,' said Will. 'I won't.'

'The Man on the Clapham Omnibus,' said The Man. 'It's me, it's really me.'

'But this is the Chiswick omnibus.'

'It started off at Clapham,' said The Man. 'And to Clapham it will return. With me on board. As I have been now for more than thirty years.'

Will raised an eyebrow beneath his tweedy cap. 'Why?' he enquired.

'Vox pop,' said The Man. 'I am the voice of the people. I *am* public opinion. When I'm not on the bus, do you know what I am?'

Will shook his head.

'I'm The Man in the Street,' said The Man. 'Same fella, it's me.'

'Very pleased to meet you.' Will now found his hand being shaken.

'So go on. Ask my opinion. Ask for my fine view.'

'About what?' Will wrenched back his hand and crammed it into his pocket.

'Anything you like, and I'll give you my uninformed opinion.'

'But why would I want to have it?'

'Was that your first question?'

'No, it wasn't.'

'So why did you ask it?'

'Would you please be quiet?' asked Will.

'Was *that* your first question?'

Will sighed. Deeply. 'Sir,' said he. 'I must inform you that I am a master of Dimac, the deadliest form of martial art in the world. I was personally trained by Mr Hugo Rune.'

'Gawd rest his Dover sole,' said The Man, 'scoundrel that he was. Or loveable rogue, if you prefer. Although he was a toff and toffs ain't worth the time it takes to wipe your arse with a copy of *The Times*. In my opinion.'

'I didn't actually ask for your opinion,' said Will.

'I don't always have to be asked. I give my opinions freely. There's no charge, although a small gratuity is never refused.'

'As I was saying,' said Will, 'about the Dimac. My hands and feet are deadly weapons. With little more than a fingertip's touch I could disable and disfigure you. So please, as the popular parlance goes, put a sock in it!'

'How about a tour then?'

'I'm on my way to Buckingham Palace.'

'Me too. Well, passing by there. But I could give you a talking tour on the way. Point out places of interest, tell you all about this wonderful city. You ain't no Londoner, is you?'

'Actually, I'm from Brentford,' said Will.

'Ah,' said The Man. 'Wonderful place. Believed to be the actual site of the biblical Garden of Eden.'

Will shook his head. A swooping pigeon laid a dropping on his cap.

'Damn!' said Will.

'That's good luck,' said The Man.

'Good luck?'

'Good luck it hit you and not me.'

Will took off his cap and wiped its top beneath his seat.

'To your right,' said The Man, 'Trafalgar Square.'

'I've been to Trafalgar Square before,' said Will.

'Know all the statues, then?'

'Well, no. No, I don't.'

'Then let me introduce you.' The Man pointed. 'We are now passing the statue of Lord Palmerston, who will be remembered for his cheese.'

'That's Parmesan,' said Will.

'And there you see the statue of Lord Babbage, great genius of our age. Without him the British Empire wouldn't be what it is.'

'And what is it?' Will asked.

'Spreading all the time, across the world and upwards. The British Empire will continue to expand until it encompasses the entire globe, before moving on to the stars.' The Man pointed upwards. 'Tomorrow the moon; the next fortnight, the stars.'

'Tomorrow the moon?' said Will.

'Well, not actually tomorrow; the launching is in a few days' time, but you know what I mean,' said The Man.

'To the *moon*?'

'Where have you been, mate? Don't you ever read the news or listen to the wireless?'

'Well,' said Will. 'I haven't much, actually, though I really should do, I suppose.'

'Well, we have Lord Babbage to thank for it all. With the help of Mr Tesla. That's his statue there, by the way. Though he's a Johnny foreigner, so we don't care much for him.'

'A lunar flight,' Will mulled this over. Jules Verne had written about that. So had H.G. Wells. Fact, not fiction.

'I was there when they launched Her Majesty's Electric Airship *Dreadnaught*,' said The Man. 'Took a day off being The Man on the Clapham Omnibus or The Man in the Street and became A Face in the Crowd. Made a change. And spectacular it was. And I saw the assassination attempt and how Captain Ernest Starling of The Queen's Own Electric Fusiliers bravely gave up his life to save Her Majesty the Queen, Gawd bless her. We just passed his statue in Trafalgar Square too. Posthumously knighted, he was, which makes him *Sir* Captain Ernest Starling, I suppose.'

'What?' went Will. '*What?*'

And memories once more returned to him, of his noble ancestor, *and* of his noble ancestor's meeting, in the waiting room of Brentford station with a certain Hugo Rune, now also dead and gone.

'I remember that.' Will buried his face in his hands.

'Easy now, chief,' said Barry.

'Shut up!' cried Will.

'Sorry,' said The Man. 'What did I say?'

'Nothing,' said Will. 'Nothing. Captain Ernest Starling. He was my—' Will paused.

'Not your daddy?' said The Man. 'Gordon Bennett's old brown trousers! I should have spotted the resemblance. You're the dead spit.

Blimey, it's a pleasure to meet you and shake your hand.' The Man dragged Will's right hand from his face and shook it warmly.

The driver's voice came over the omnibus speaker system.

'Buck House,' said the driver's voice. 'Toffs off, if you please.'

'I have to go,' said Will, rising. 'But thank you very much. It's been a pleasure talking to you.'

'Any chance of a gratuity?' The Man stuck his hand out.

'Certainly,' said Will and he dug into his pocket and brought out a silver threepenny bit.

'Your generosity is only exceeded by your personal charm and good looks,' said The Man, accepting the coin and trousering it.

'Thank you,' and Will took his leave.

'Ugly sod,' The Man called after him.

And so Will found himself standing outside the gates of Buckingham Palace. Buckingham Palace looked pretty much as Buckingham Palace has always looked and probably always will look, but for the occasional difference in the colour of the railings. This season's colour was presently black, because black was always the new black as far as Queen Victoria was concerned.

'So now we're here, chief, what do you propose to do?'

'Go inside,' said Will. 'Search for clues.'

'You're on a total wrong'n, chief.'

'I'm doing this my way, Barry.'

'They'll never let you in, chief. You're a commoner.'

'You don't think I can pass myself off as Lord Peter Whimsy?'

'No,' said Barry. 'I don't.'

They were changing the guard at Buckingham Palace. A young lad was peering through the railings. His name was Christopher Robin. He'd come down with his nurse called Alice to watch them go through their changes.

Will marched past the young lad and approached the newly changed guard.

'I'd like to see the Queen please,' said Will.

'Hold on a mo.' The guard fiddled with his suspender belt. 'I'm not quite changed yet,' he said.

Will looked on in amazement.

'Dyslectic clerk,' said Barry. 'At the Ministry of Defence. The regiment was supposed to be called The Queen's Own Home Foot Regiment, but he put it down as The Queen's Own Cross-dressing

Nancy-Boy Shirt-lifting Fusiliers. Easy mistake to make if you're a dyslexic, I suppose.'

'That's not funny and it's not clever, Barry.'

'You're right there,' said the guard. 'And how did you know my name was Barry?'

'Lucky guess?' said Will.

'Amazing,' said the guard, now done with his adjustments and smoothing down his corset. 'So bugger off, will ya?'

'I'm here to see Her Majesty, Gawd bless Her,' said Will. 'It's very important.'

'It always is.' The guard took various items from his handbag and began to powder his nose.

'I have to see Her Majesty *now*.'

'Ooooooo,' went the guard. 'Get her. Mince off, will ya? Ya can't come in.'

'Please tell Her Majesty I'm here,' said Will.

'You're wasting your time, chief.'

'Keep out of this, Barry.'

'It's not my job to keep out of it,' said the guard. 'It's my job to keep riff-raff like you out. Although if you'd care to hang about, we might go for a drink later. I know a little club in Soho, the Brown Hatters. I might treat you to a cocktail.'

'Give it up, chief, you're beaten.'

'I'm not,' Will whispered. And then he said. 'Very well done, guard. I will commend your vigilance to Her Majesty. And now you can let me through the gates. I am William Starling, son of Sir Ernest Starling of The Queen's Own Electric Fusiliers who valiantly gave up his own life to save Her Majesty from the assassin at the launching of the *Dreadnaught*.'

The guard stared at Will. And then he blinked and stared again. And then he put away his make-up and said, 'Bugger off.'

'What?' said Will.

'Only joking,' said the guard. 'Recognised you immediately.'

'No you didn't,' said Will.

'Do you want to go inside, or what?'

'I do,' said Will.

'Then do.'

'So what now?' asked Barry, as Will marched across the parade ground and up to the big front door. 'This is such a waste of time.'

'I'm doing it my way, Barry. And I'll thank you to keep out of it. The Queen has her own special surgeon, does she not?'

'Of course she does, chief. Sir Frederick Treves.'

'Do you think he owns a pair of very long tweezers?'

'Sure to, chief.'

'Think about it, Barry.'

'Ah yes, chief, I get you. I'll just keep quiet then.'

Will knocked upon the big front door. After no great length of time, a liveried automaton of the stylish and non-threatening persuasion opened it. Will stared at the liveried automaton.

'You're all covered in liver,' said Will.

'And?' the automaton enquired.

'Oh I see,' said Will. 'Dyslectic clerk at the Ministry of Defence?'

'No,' said the automaton. 'Fancy-dress ball.'

'Right,' said Will. 'Well, I am William Starling, son of the late Sir Captain Ernest Starling, who nobly laid down his life for Queen and country. I'm sure you know the one.'

'I do,' said the liveried automaton. 'But why are you not in fancy dress?'

'But I am.' Will did a kind of a twirl. 'Can't you guess what I've come as?'

The liveried automaton cocked his head upon one side and viewed the uninvited guest. 'Ah yes,' said he. 'Most subtle, most amusing. Do come inside.'

'Ludicrous,' said Barry.

'Tweezers,' whispered Will.

'I think I'll take a nap now,' said the sprout.

The interior of Buckingham Palace was something to behold. Will beheld it and whistled.

It had been designed by Sir Joshua Sloane, who would later be remembered for his Rangers. He'd done Buck House in the 'Palace Style', very heavy on the gold leaf and the chandeliers and the statuary and the plush fitted carpets, not to mention the ormolu-mounted kingwood and marquetry commodes, with the blind fret-carved friezes, flanking broken scroll pediments ornamented with gold japanned paterae and fluted balusters, rendered in the style of Thomas Chippendale (who, with the aid of his brothers, would later find fame for dancing about in front of drunken young women and whipping out his todger [nice work if you can get it!]).

The entrance hall was about the size of Victoria Station, its walls dressed with many huge canvasses, the work of Mr Dadd in his 'you chuck it on and I'll spread it' period, which was to say, his present period.

Will whistled once again.

'Very good,' said the liveried automaton. 'The whistling goes with your costume, are you a professional actor?'

'No,' said Will. 'I'm a time traveller, on a mission to catch Jack the Ripper.'

'Most amusing, sir. I must introduce you to Mr Oscar Wilde. I'm sure the two of you will have much to talk about.'

'I doubt that,' said Will. 'I'm easily bored. Might I just peruse the guest list. I feel that one or two of my old friends may be here.'

'Certainly. Sir.' The liveried automaton took up a clipboard from one of the ormolu-mounted kingwood and marquetry commodes (the one on the right-hand side of the front door as you're coming in) and offered it to Will.

Will perused and returned it. 'Thank you,' said he. 'Now if you will just steer me in the direction of Her Majesty.'

'As you wish, sir.'

The liveried automaton led Will through rooms filled with many wonders.

These had the looks of engineeriums. Mighty machines of shining steel and buffed-up brass, all cogs and flywheels, pistons and ball-governors, rose in the midst of these rooms. The air was heavy with the rich smell of engine oil and of ozone, which has something to do with electrical jiggery-pokery.

'Her Majesty appears to show a great deal of interest in electronics,' Will observed.

'The future lies in technology,' the liveried automaton replied. 'And as long as the Crown holds every patent, the British Empire will continue to expand until it encompasses the entire globe, before moving on to the stars.'

'Do you have a brother?' Will asked.

'No, sir. I'm an automaton.'

'Then I perceive that you reside in Clapham and travel here every day upon the omnibus.'

'Gawd bless my soul,' said the liveried automaton. 'You're a regular Miss Shirley Holmes, ain't you, sir?'

'The man's an amateur,' said Will.

'We're all gonna die,' said Barry.

'Tweezers,' whispered Will.

'Talking in my sleep,' said Barry. 'Zzzzzzz.'

'The Great Hall,' said the liveried automaton. 'You'll find Her Majesty somewhere in here. I'll have to leave you now, sir. I'm on door duties.'

'Fine,' said Will. 'Thank you very much. See you on the way out, or perhaps I'll catch you on the Clapham omnibus some time.'

'I'll look forward to it, sir. Farewell.'

Will gazed into the Great Hall. It was a very wonderful Great Hall.

The ceiling was a magnificent dome, painted in the style of Michelangelo, but with more cherubs and a great deal more naked folk indulging in what toffs euphemistically refer to as the pleasures of the flesh, but what the commoners call shagging. The ceiling had been designed by Mr Aubrey Beardsley, but he hadn't actually done any of the painting himself, because he had a bit of a cough. His brother Peter (who would later find fame playing football for Liverpool and earning fifty-nine caps for England) had done all the colouring in.

The walls of the Great Hall were hidden beneath swathes of red toile de Jouy fabric, which presented a most lustrous effect. The furnishings were splendid, and resembling, as they did, those in the famous apartments of Louis de Champalian, there is no need for description of them here.

So, all in all, it was a pretty natty Great Hall.

It was also a very crowded Great Hall, and it swelled with swells and glittered with the glitterati. Wilde was holding court before a bevy of breathless beauties. Wilde had come dressed as the Pope, who in turn had come dressed as Wilde. Count Otto Black was to be seen, clad in the star-spattered robes and conical hat of Merlin the magician. He was chatting with Queen Victoria herself, whom Will was surprised to see wore nothing but a diaphanous gown and a pair of high-heeled clogs.

Little Tich was there, of course, wearing his now legendary ever-popular big boots. Will was slightly disappointed to observe that they were not quite so big as he'd hoped they'd be. But then, you can't have everything, and Will consoled himself with the fact that he had at least caught a glimpse of Queen Victoria's muff.

Dadd was there, dressed as a packet of pork scratchings. And there were countless others, far too many for Will to count, although he was looking for one in particular.

A minion in a gorilla suit approached Will. The minion bore a silver tray with glasses of champagne. Will helped himself to one of these, took it up and sipped at it.

It was quite exquisite.

Will took another sip and said, 'Oh yes.'

This was really something. *Really* something. Will had seen a lot of somethings during his travels with Hugo Rune. He had dined with potentates and emperors, and even with the Pope in Rome. (Will recalled how he had warned the Pope about the growing threat of vampires, who had been misidentified as saints, and wondered whether the Pope had paid any heed to his warnings.) And Will had visited many palaces. In fact, Will had done a whole lot of wonderful things with Mr Rune, the importance and relevance of which were only now becoming apparent to Will.

Rune had taught him how to fit in, and a whole lot more than that.

But for all that whole lot more, Will had never seen anything quite so splendid and eccentric as this, and as his eyes took it in, his brain did somersaults, which awoke the snoozing sprout, who was similarly impressed when he peered out through Will's eyes.

'This is good,' said Barry, 'if perhaps a little silly. Isn't that the Duke of Wellington, who, if I'm not mistaken, will later go on to find fame as a lightweight summer sandal with a Velcro strap? Why is he dressed as a grandfather clock?'

Will shrugged. 'Just go back to sleep, Barry. I am going to mingle and learn what there is to be learned.'

'And after that we can leave here and get back on the trail of Jack the Ripper.'

'Tweezers, Barry.'

'Good night, chief.'

Will grinned. He felt confident that the word 'tweezers' would now be figuring prominently in his future conversations with Barry.

'Don't forget the law of diminishing returns,' said Barry.

'What?' went Will. 'Can you read my thoughts too?'

'No,' said Barry. 'But that one was pretty damn obvious.'

'Good night, Barry.'

'Good night, chief.'

And so Will mingled.

Will mingled with members of the French aristocracy. They had come dressed as the cast of *Joseph and the Technicolor Dreamcoat*, which was having its very first run in London's West End. Will conversed with them in the fluent French that Hugo Rune had taught him. The members of the French aristocracy were much taken with Will. They talked a lot to him. Their talk seemed mostly concerned with the spread of the British Empire.

Will asked whether they'd come here by bus.

Will learned that they had not.

Will enjoyed a conversation with a Chinese trade delegation. They were pleased to meet an Englishman who could speak Mandarin. The spread of the British Empire bothered them, they told Will.

The Greek ambassador shared a joke with Will. Did the spread of the British Empire give him cause for concern, Will asked. The Greek ambassador said that it did and praised Will for his grasp of the language.

Will sat apart from the crowd of partying folk and took stock of the situation, *his* situation.

He really *did* teach me, thought Will. Rune. He may not have chosen to share his magic, if he did have any magic, but I really have learned so much. He prepared me. That's what he did, prepared me. And I'll just bet that he would have shared his magic, if I'd been his magical heir. But of course I'm not; Tim is.

And Will thought about Tim and how he missed Tim and how he'd really like to tell Tim all about this, and if it were possible, bring Tim back here and show it all to him.

But then Will thought about the job he had to do. The job he had sworn to do; bring Jack the Ripper to justice, and then, *with* the help of Barry, go home.

So what was he doing here?

Will knew exactly what he was doing here. And it had nothing to do with meeting the Queen, or searching for clues in the palace.

'Might I sit beside you?' A soft voice spoke at Will's ear, a soft and lisping voice, a voice with a certain pain in it. Will looked up and found himself staring at a black mask; a sack more like, with a single eyehole cut into it. This sack hung about a head which seemed grossly overlarge. Some eccentric costumery, Will supposed. The figure who wore the sack upon his head was stunted, bowed; there was something altogether uncomfortable about his posture.

'Please do,' Will smiled. 'Sit yourself down.'

'My thanks.' The figure seated himself, awkwardly.

Uncomfortably, Will noted the feet of the figure. They seemed huge in comparison to his height.

'I am pleased to make your acquaintance,' the lisping voice said slowly. 'My name is Joseph Merrick.'

'Please to meet you, Mr Merrick,' said Will. 'I am William Starling, son of the late Sir Captain Ernest Starling. I am puzzled by your costume; what exactly have you come as?'

'I have come as myself. This is a carnival of curiosities and I am surely the greatest curiosity of this age.'

'I don't know what you mean,' said Will.

'You do not recognise my true name. Then perhaps you might recognise my professional name. I am known as the Elephant Man.'

'The Elephant Man!' Will stared at the Elephant Man. 'I have heard of you. I've read about you. This really is a very great pleasure.' Will extended his right hand for a shake. Joseph Merrick extended his and Will shook it.

'Are you enjoying the ball?' Will asked.

'Oh yes, it is wonderful, wonderful. Everyone had been very kind.'

Will nodded, and smiled in that excruciating sympathetic/condescending manner that folk just can't help doing when confronted with a freak.

'I hate that smile,' said Joseph Merrick.

'Sorry,' said Will. 'But you are having a good time?'

'Splendid,' the Elephant Man nodded his oversized head. 'And I'm hoping to score later. I've been chatting up the Belgian ambassador's wife and I'm taking her back to my room at the London Hospital later.'

'What?' went Will.

'They can't resist me. And they can't help themselves wondering, what's his tackle like? Is he hung like an elephant?'

Will opened his mouth, but could find nothing to say with it.

'Got any tottie sized up for yourself?' asked Mr Merrick.

'Well, no,' said Will. 'I hadn't really thought about it.'

'You're not in The Queen's Own Cross-dressing Nancy-Boy Shirt-lifting Fusiliers, are you?'

'Certainly not.'

'Well, there's plenty of pussy going begging. And these posh bints bang like an outhouse door, if you know what I mean.'

'I think I have to be going,' said Will and he rose to his feet.

'Well, don't be a stranger now. My light's always on. Bedstead Square, back of the London Hospital. You can shin over the railings. And I'm always up for a threesome.'

'Good luck to you,' said Will. 'And goodbye.'

'I'm not *him*, you know,' said Mr Merrick. 'I know some folk think I am, but I'm not.'

Will turned back. 'Him?' he asked. 'What do you mean?'

'You know who I mean: Jack the Ripper. I know there's been talk. Rumour. Every murder has been committed within a ten-minute walk from the London Hospital. Some folk even say it's Sir Frederick Treves, the Queen's physician. He arranged for me to take refuge at the London Hospital, you know. So very kind. But it's not him and it's not me either.'

'I don't think anyone has ever had *you* down as Jack the Ripper,' said Will.

'Well I think that's most unflattering. But then it's obvious who the murderer really is, isn't it?'

Will sat back down again. 'Is it?' he asked.

'Of course it is.'

'So who is Jack the Ripper?'

'*Was*,' said Joseph Merrick. '*Was*, because he did himself in. Committed suicide, he did. Sickened by his own crimes he took his own life.'

'Really?' said Will. 'So you know who it was?'

The Elephant Man nodded his bulbous bonce. 'Plain as the great big nose on my face,' said he. 'His name was Hugo Rune.'

18

'It *wasn't* Hugo Rune,' said Will. 'I was with him during the time that the murders were committed. We were in Tierra del Fuego.'

'Oh,' said the Elephant Man. 'Then I must have been misinformed. That's the last time I travel on the Clapham omnibus.'

Will sighed deeply. 'I should have expected this,' he said, 'as soon as I decided to strike out on my own.'

'It's my turn not to understand.' Mr Merrick lifted his champagne glass, passed it under his head sack and slurped upon it noisily.

'Running gags,' said Will. 'I've read about them, but never encountered them before, in the flesh, as it were.'

'Speaking of flesh,' said Mr Merrick, 'there's a couple of right crackers over there; why don't we move in as a team and have a pop at them?'

'I'm here on important business,' said Will.

'And you can't fit in time for a shag?'

'Well,' said Will. 'I have to confess that it's been a very long time since I've had a shag.'

'How long?'

'More than three hundred years.' Will couldn't count the woman Barry had picked up the previous night, because he couldn't remember her.

'Are you an associate of the Comte de St Germain? I see him over there, chatting up Her Majesty.'

'I've never heard of *him*,' said Will.

'Claims to have discovered the philosopher's stone and the elixir of life. Claims to be two thousand years old and to have met Christ.'

'You're kidding me,' said Will.

'I am not possessed of a sense of humour. And when you clock my boat race, you'll see why.'

'I've seen photographs,' said Will. 'Although I'm sure they don't do you justice.'

'They do. I look like shit.'

'But you're still a big hit with the ladies.'

'Every cloud has a silver lining. Or, as I like to put it, every skirt has a pink one. So shall we have a pop at a couple? There's two over there. Although I don't like the look of your one.'

'All right,' said Will. 'I can spare a little time.'

'Suffer from premature ejaculation, do you?'

'Your conversation is somewhat coarse,' said Will.

'If you think *that's* coarse, you should see my—'

'What?' Will asked.

'Let's go and pull.'

'All right,' said Will. 'Let's go.'

And they *did* pull. Will was amazed. His one wasn't a catwalk model but later, in Mr Merrick's room at Bedstead Square, she proved herself to be a willing and imaginative lover. And what Mr Merrick got up to, Will didn't know. It sounded like a lot of fun by all the noise of it, but Will really didn't want to look.

Will slept very soundly after everything was done, and was somewhat surprised to suddenly awaken in the dark.

Will didn't say, 'Where am I?' for he knew just where he was, but he wondered what had woken him and why.

Curious sounds came to Will in the darkness. Hissing sounds and clickings and the sounds of whispered words. Will raised his head and eased himself away from the sleeping female at his side.

The hissings and clickings continued and so did the whispered words. Will rose from the hospital bed.

A door was ajar; a wan light shone through the ajarness. Will stealthily crept towards it.

'Ground control,' he heard words whispered. 'Ground control to Major Thomas.'*

Will peered through the gap between doorframe and door.

Mr Merrick sat at a table. Before him was a complicated-looking piece of apparatus. Some kind of radio transmitter, Will correctly assumed, but not of a type he'd ever seen before.

'Ground control to Major Thomas,' said Mr Merrick once more.

'Major Thomas speaking,' a voice replied. 'What do you have to report?'

* You can't say Major Tom. It's an infringement on copyright and you have to pay royalties, so stuff that!

'The date for the moonship launch is confirmed.'

'Well, you'll just have to stop it happening, won't you?'

'I can't do that,' said Mr Merrick. 'How can I do that?'

'Blow it up. I don't care.'

'I'm hardly equipped to blow it up, am I? I'm not a trained assassin. I'm just a spy.'

'And a pretty rubbish one,' said the voice of Major Thomas.

'Well, that's hardly my fault. You said that the alien-human hybridisation programme would make me indistinguishable from a normal human being. That wasn't exactly true, was it?'

'A bit of a glitch in the system, but you have achieved a certain celebrity. You're a darling of royalty. You have connections in high places. That's worked out much better than we could ever have hoped for.'

'That's all right for you to say. I have to cart this big huge head around.'

'Just stop the launch,' said the voice of Major Thomas. 'We don't want the British Empire builders blundering onto our moon base.'

'I have certain connections in the London underworld,' said Mr Merrick. 'Anarchists. I will arrange to have a bomb placed in the moonship, to explode when the countdown reaches zero!'

'Splendid. That will do nicely. Is that all that you have to report?'

'Well, actually, no, it isn't. The British Empire's space programme may be a threat to our home planet Mars, but there is an even greater threat. It is not the British government we have to fear. It is the power that lies behind the British government.'

'Her Majesty Queen Victoria?'

'Not her,' said Mr Merrick. 'A cabal of witches. They are up to all manner of wickedness. Their evil extends throughout this society and their power grows ever stronger. I hear rumours from my informants that these witches seek to take control of the government. They disguise their evil by passing as the seemingly benign middle class ladies of a philanthropic chit-chat and charity organisation called the Chiswick Townswomen's . . . just hold on, will you?'

'What's going on?' asked Major Thomas.

'I thought I heard something.'

Will edged away from the open door, returned to his bed and feigned sleep. He heard the approach of the Elephant Man, the shuffling feet, the movement of fabrics. He felt the warm breath against his cheek, and smelled it also. It smelled of woman.

Will made snoring sounds.

The breath left his cheek. Mr Merrick moved away and Will heard a door shut behind him.

'And what do you make of *that*?' Will asked.

'Zzzzzzzzzzzz,' went Barry.

'So let me just get this straight,' said Tim McGregor, downing Large and running a knuckle over his mouth. 'Sorry to interrupt you in mid-chapter as it were. But your tale seems to have entered other dimensions. We now have Barry the Holy Guardian sprout or Phnaargian genetically-engineered Time Sprout, depending upon your particular take on reality, or otherwise. And Mr Merrick, the Elephant Man, who is a human-alien hybrid spy.'

'Yes?' said Will. 'So?'

'Oh nothing.' Tim shrugged and tucked back the hair that now engulfed him. 'So what happened next? Did you go to the launching of the Victorian moonship?'

'Not yet,' Will's glass was once more empty. 'That hasn't happened yet in the time I've returned here from. I think I might go on to halves now,' he said. 'Or I will shortly be too drunk to continue with the telling of my tale.'

'Right,' Tim drained his glass to its naked bottom. 'But this Barry, whatever he might be. Is he still inside your head?'

Will nodded and tapped at his earhole. 'Still in there,' said he. 'Which is how I came to be here with you.'

Tim cocked his head upon one side and peered thoughtfully at Will. 'Would you like me to winkle him out?' he asked. 'I'd be happy to let him nestle in my bonce, if you want. I'm ever so keen to get going on whatever it is we're supposed to be be getting going on.'

'Oh no,' said Will and he shook his head vigorously.

'Easy, chief,' said Barry. 'I was having a nap.'

'Sorry, Barry,' said Will.

'Did he speak to you?' Tim made a most excited face.

'He rarely shuts up. But I'll hang on to him for now. I've grown somewhat attached to Barry. We've been through a lot together.'

Tim shrugged once more and took himself off to the bar.

'Are you sure we really need *him*?' Barry asked. 'I can find you far better, I really can.'

'We do,' said Will. 'I'm still running things, remember?'

'As if you are, chief.'

'What was that?'

'I said, "Of course you are, chief".'

'Well I *am* and that's that. I'll tell Tim the story and then we'll all go back and sort out the last part. And then you and I can go our separate ways.'

'I might take Tim up on his offer, chief.'

'I thought you'd been having a nap.'

Tim returned with the drinks. 'I just love this pub,' he said, placing two pints upon the table.

'I asked for a half,' said Will.

'The part-time barman wouldn't hear of it. Heroes drink pints, he said. *And* he sells pork scratchings. Imagine that. Pork scratchings!' Tim waved a packet at Will.

'This wombat is thrilled by pork scratchings.' Barry wriggled about in Will's brain.

'We don't have pork scratchings any more,' said Will. 'There aren't any pigs any more.'

'You're not all vegetarians, I hope,' Barry now shivered.

'Most foods are synthetic,' said Will.

'You're talking to him again, aren't you?' Tim sat himself down. 'Could I see him if I peeped in your ear?'

'I'd rather you didn't.'

'Okay, fine by me. So, go on with your tale.'

'Well,' said Will. 'I have to tell you, I wasn't feeling too well.'

'Nerves, I suppose.' Tim took up his latest pint and supped upon it. 'What with you knowing that another Victorian Terminator robot might well be on your tail.'

'That constantly worried me.' Will glanced towards the saloon bar door. 'I was always looking over my shoulder. But it wasn't that.'

'So, go on.'

And Will went on.

Will awoke in Mr Merrick's spare bed in Bedstead Square, at the London Hospital, Whitechapel. A now unappealing woman snored on top of him. Across the room, on a somewhat grander bed Mr Merrick slept in a seated position, his knees drawn up and his monstrous head resting upon them. It was the first light of day now and in that first light, Will viewed the full grotesquery of Mr Joseph Carey Merrick: the horrible pendulous flaps and folds of skin, the spongiform eruptions, the grubby underwear. And *this* man was a big hit with the ladies!

Will yawned silently and then took to gripping his forehead. It was possibly the worst hangover he'd ever had. Whatever had he been drinking last night? Will took to shivering. Medical alcohol, that was it. Laced with absinthe and mescal. *A Merrickan Express*, Mr Merrick had called it. Because it gets you into the 'Love Tunnel' and makes you 'Elephant's trunk'. And it had.

Will now dimly remembered his former awakening. And the business of Mr Merrick and the transmitter. That *had* been true, hadn't it? Or had he dreamed it? Had it been the drink? Will didn't know for sure.

To be absolutely certain, he'd have to get another look into the adjoining room where the equipment had been. Will tried to rise, but the recumbent female weighed heavily upon his chest. Will eased her off and she made curious whimpering sounds. Will swung his legs down from the bed, rose with difficulty and staggered as quietly as he could across the room to the door in question.

Will reached out to the doorknob.

And then Will groaned.

There was no doorknob, as there was no door.

'No door,' whispered Will. 'Barry, are you awake?'

'Keep the noise down, chief. I've got a right hangover here.'

'*You've* got a hangover?'

'I sustain myself on your vital juices, chief. Which means I'm pretty pickled. Can we get out of here and have some coffee? And some breakfast too?'

'Not yet. Something very weird happened last night.'

'You are the master of understatement, chief. You had a foursome with the Elephant Man and a couple of foreign princesses. I'd head on out before the paparazzi arrive, if I were you.'

'There was a door here and—'

'Did it open into another world, chief? Was there a big lion and a witch?'

'There was some very strange equipment.'

'I'll just bet there was. Thankfully, I slept through that bit.'

'Oh, forget it.'

'Consider it forgotten, chief. So breakfast, is it? Sausages, eggs, bacon. No tomatoes, no mushrooms, no potatoes.'

Will shuffled back to his bed, found his trousers, shirt, cravat and shoes, and tweedy cap, dressed and quietly took his leave.

19

Whitechapel was beautiful at this time of the morning. But then so many places are. Unlikely places, even scrapheaps and abattoirs, have a romantic quality about them at sun up. It's probably down to the fresh air and the silence and the light.

Will wandered through the deserted streets.

It was all rather magical, but Will's head hurt him very much.

A potato lay in the gutter and, much to Barry's horror, Will kicked it along before him.

'So what are your plans for today, then, chief?' asked the sprout. 'Scarf down a big boy's breakfast, then back on the omnibus and off to—'

'Wimpole Street,' said Will. 'That's where we're going.'

'But why are we going there, chief? It's so obvious that Mr Rune was pointing you towards—'

'Chiswick?' Will dribbled the potato along the pavement.

'Finally sunk in has it, chief? And kindly leave that poor spud alone.'

Will paused in mid dribble and took in big-breath-lungfuls. They never really help when you have a hangover, but you feel compelled to take them nonetheless.

'I will get to Chiswick in my own good time,' said Will. 'And if those witches really exist and are the terrible threat to society which Rune considered them to be, perhaps I'll look into the matter.'

Barry made oh dear, oh dearings.

'But I don't believe that witches were responsible for the brutal murdering of five women. Witches, as far as I understand them, have strongly-held feminist convictions.'

'But you joined up the sites of the murders, chief. You saw the inverted pentagram. That spells witchcraft, whichever way you care to spell it.'

'I could have joined the sites together to form almost anything,' Will said. 'A pentagon, for instance.'

'Well, yes, chief, I suppose you could.'

'And I could have chosen any point to draw a line to the site of Rune's murder. The permutations are endless.'

'So hang about, chief. Why then did we go to Buckingham Palace?'

'Because there was someone I hoped to meet there.'

'Her Majesty the Queen, Gawd bless Her?'

'No, Barry, one of her guests. According to the copy of *The Times* that I read while having my bath at the Dorchester, he was to be at the ball. You might or might not recall that I checked the guest list when we entered the palace. He was on the list. He was not, however, at the ball.'

'Okay, chief, I'm intrigued now. Who is it?'

'Aha.' Will tapped the potato with a polished toecap and continued his wandering along. 'When you saw the line on the map, all that you could see was that it led to Chiswick. I saw something else. Rune wasn't giving us a clue. Rune was trying to reach the house of his friend, to take shelter there. He nearly made it too; the house is only two streets away from where the murderer caught up with him.'

'So, who is it, chief?'

'I haven't quite finished yet. I know that this friend of Rune's lives in Wimpole Street, because I've read his biography. He lives next door to a family called Barrett. I have a very good memory for this kind of detail. And I've been really wanting to meet him ever since I found myself in this day and age.'

'Yes, all right, chief; you're very clever, I'm sure.'

'Thank you, Barry.'

'But if you knew the address, why didn't we go there first?'

'Because he was supposed to be at the ball! Are you losing the plot, Barry?'

'Not just me, I'm sure,' said the sprout.

'What was that?'

'Nothing, chief.'

Will booted the spud across the deserted street. 'And Starling scores the winning goal for Brentford,' he cried, and then he wished he hadn't, and clutched at his head once again.

'What?' went Barry.

'Did I just hear you say, "*What*"?'

Barry took to a sulking silence and Will wandered on.

At length Barry tired of his silence. 'All right, I give up,' he said. 'Who *is* it we are going to see?'

Will whispered the name to Barry.

'Complete waste of time, chief. No point at all in going to see him.'

'Really, Barry, and why do you say that?'

'Because he was just a friend of Rune's. He won't know anything. It's Chiswick we should be going to. The witches, that's what this is all about.'

'I'd like a word with this chap first.'

'But he's a nutter, chief. A loony, trust me.'

'A quick chat, that's all.'

'It's a waste of time. We should be pressing on.'

'You seem very definite about this, Barry.'

'I just think we should be pressing on.'

'And I think we should do things *my way*.'

'Oh dear, oh dear, oh dear.'

Will found the house without difficulty. An elegant ivy-hung Georgian dwelling, it looked much the same as it had when pictured in the biography Will had downloaded into his palm-top, but for the neon up-lighters and the rather swish electric carriage with the blacked-out windows which stood outside. Will slicked down his hair with spittle, straightened his cravat, squared his shoulders and pressed the button, which activated the electric doorbell. In a distant part of the house the opening notes of Beethoven's Fifth Symphony chimed out.

Will waited a while and then rang the doorbell again.

'He's out, chief. Let's be on our way.'

'It's early, Barry; he's probably still in bed.'

'So let's have breakfast and come back later. Or better still not at all.'

'You really don't want me to meet this man, do you, Barry?'

Barry returned to his sulking silence.

'There's a window open up there,' said Will, peering up.

Barry returned from his sulking silence. 'Don't even think about it, chief. Not with our hangover.'

But Will was already on the ivy. He struggled and climbed and struggled and climbed some more.

'Someone will see you, chief.'

'Please be quiet, Barry.' Will reached the window ledge, eased himself into it, stooped, slid up the sash window and with difficulty and care, to equal degree, succeeded in entering the house.

'This is so bad, chief. This is trespass.'

'Sssh!' Will shushed him.

'Well, don't say I didn't warn you.'

The room Will now found himself in was an elegant study, cum laboratory, cum workroom. Leather-bound books bricked its walls and the early morning light fell upon a workbench loaded with much strange apparatus. The room was filled with many interesting items and Will found interest in each and every one of them.

Will peered at this and that. And then Will touched this and that.

'Don't touch that,' said Barry.

So Will touched this instead.

'*Chief!*' Barry piped, with a very shrill, 'chief'. 'Chief, get out of here at once. Big trouble's coming. I can feel it.'

'Don't try to trick me, Barry,' Will whispered.

'No, I'm serious, chief. Something's not right. In fact something's very wrong. And that very wrong something is heading our way.'

'I'm not listening to this. I'm not—' And then Will heard it, and saw it also – the polished doorknob turning on the door.

'Don't worry, Barry. I expect it's just the master of the house. I'll apologise for breaking in, I'm sure he'll understand.'

Will smiled towards the door, and the door swung open, but no one stood in the opening.

'Hello,' called Will. 'Hello Mr—'

And then something struck Will hard in the face and knocked him from his feet. Will went down in a confusion of gangly limbs and hit the wooden floor.

'Who did that?' And 'Ouch, oh damn, oh ouch,' went Will.

A cold wind seemed to engulf him and Will was hauled aloft. He could feel the fearsome force, but could not see his attacker.

'Who are you?' howled Will as he found himself being flung across the room. '*What* are you?' Will tumbled through the open doorway and out into the corridor beyond. It was a charming corridor. Its walls were decorated with William Morris wallpaper and hung with family portraits. Brass wall sconces held scented candles, which favoured the air with delicate fragrances of musk, vanilla and White Rose of Cairo.

The charm of the corridor was however lost upon Will, who collided with a wall and sank once more to the floor.

'Don't hit me any more.' Will's arms flailed away at his unseen attacker. And suddenly a voice spoke at his ear.

'A common criminal,' said this voice, 'who dares to enter here. What is your name, boy?'

'Will,' went Will. 'Will Starling.'

'I am the guardian of these premises, Will Starling. You have chosen the wrong house to rob.'

'I'm no robber,' Will protested. 'I've come to speak to Mr—'

But once more Will was hauled aloft and this time flung down the stairs, which was very painful, especially when you have a hangover.

Will lay flat upon his back at the bottom of the stairs, panting and gasping and groaning by turns. This was not at all good. In fact, this was very bad indeed. Will tried to rise but a terrible pressure forced down upon his chest.

'I must punish you,' said the voice, 'so that you desist from your evil ways, so that you never steal from honest folk again.'

'I'm not a thief,' Will put up his hands to fight off his unseeable assailant and found himself gripping *something*. Will gripped at this something with all his might and fought to remove it from his chest.

A Dimac move, known as *The whip of the wild weasel's wanger* and taught to him by Hugo Rune, entered Will's mind and Will twisted and snapped something invisible.

'Oooooow!' howled the voice. 'My ankle, you've broken my bally ankle.'

Something crashed down beside Will and Will fell upon this something and punched it and punched it and punched it until it made no further sounds.

Sunlight fell in through high casement windows into a pleasant front sitting room. It lit upon an elegant Georgian fireplace, with an ormolu clock of the French persuasion ticking away on its mantelshelf; numerous over-stuffed comfy-looking chairs, an escritoire, a folio stand and a whatnot loaded with whatsits.

The sunlight also lit upon something altogether strange, something that was now bound to a chair in the middle of the room.

The upper parts of this were white and man-shaped.

The lower parts were invisible. The man-shaped something struggled. The man-shaped something had a handkerchief stuffed into its mouth.

Will Starling sat in another chair facing this man-shaped something. Will Starling said, 'I'm very sorry it had to turn out this way, sir. And I'm very sorry that I broke your ankle.

'Mmmph,' went the man-shaped something.

'I'll take the gag out of your mouth,' said Will, 'if you promise not to shout. You will promise that, won't you, Mr Wells? You are Mr H.G. Wells, aren't you?'

What could be seen of Mr H.G. Wells nodded its head.

Will removed the gag. 'I had to sprinkle you with talcum powder,' he said. 'I got it from your bathroom. Floris of Jermyn Street talcum. Personal blend; you have very good taste. Mr Rune had his cologne and lavender water blended there.'

'Get me to a hospital,' wailed Mr H.G. Wells. 'I am seriously injured.'

'It doesn't look too bad,' said Will. 'But then, I can't see it. It's invisible.'

'You sadistic fiend.'

'You started the fight,' said Will. 'I was only defending myself. You threw me down the stairs, I'm bruised all over; I could have been killed.'

'So much the better for it,' hissed Mr Wells.

'You're not a very nice man,' said Will. 'And I was so looking forward to meeting you.'

'Untie me,' wailed Wells. 'I'm in agony.'

'No you're not,' said Will. 'I administered some morphine that I found in your bathroom cabinet. I'm sure you're not hurting at all. And I will see that you get medical attention if you really want to go to hospital, in your present physical condition, you being invisible and everything.'

'I'll deal with my ankle myself,' said Wells. 'Just release me.'

'I don't think that would be for the best; you might shake off the talcum and attack me again.'

'You have my word as a gentleman that I will not.'

'And I value your word,' said Will. 'But you will remain bound until I take my leave. It's nothing personal. Well, actually, it is.'

Wells struggled some more, but Will had done a good job with the tying up.

'I am sorry,' said Will. 'I hoped we'd meet under more civilised circumstances. I did knock at the door.'

'I don't answer my door. You can see why.'

'I'm amazed,' said Will. 'And very impressed. I mean, I've read all your books, including *The Invisible Man*, but I didn't think it was true. I thought it was fiction.'

'Fiction?' said Wells. 'What are you talking about?'

'You are one of my favourite novelists.'

'Novelist? I am not a novelist. I am a scientist.'

'Yes, well, certainly. Rune told me all about the time machine.'

'You are acquainted with Rune?'

'I am his magical heir,' said Will. 'I have spent the last year travelling with him. He taught me many things, including Dimac.'

'Set me free,' said Wells.

'All in good time,' Will sipped upon something.

'What are you drinking there?' Wells asked.

'I believe you'd call it "hair of the dog",' said Will. 'I've a terrible hangover, which hasn't been helped by the beating you gave me. I helped myself to the bottle of port on the escritoire there.'

'My vintage port. My Corney and Barrow 1807. That cost me thirty guineas.'

'Oh dear,' said Will. 'I didn't look at the label. But I should have recognised it. Rune and I shared a bottle at Claridges, although we didn't actually pay for it.'

'For the love of God,' wailed Wells. 'If you've opened it, then at least have the common decency to let me sample a glass.'

'It might not to go too well with the morphine.'

'I care not,' said Wells. 'I am beyond all caring.'

Will went over to the escritoire, poured some port for Mr Wells, held the glass to his mouth and let him sip it.

'It's not as good as I'd hoped for,' said Wells.

'The 1809 is much better.'

'You certainly know your vintages, young man.'

'I had a good teacher. But alas he is now dead. And I am sworn to avenge his death and bring his assassin to justice.'

'Jack the Ripper,' said Wells. 'The very thought of that monster abroad on the streets sends a chill into my heart. Give me a little more port.'

Will did so.

'It's why I'm here,' said Will, sipping further port. 'I believe that Rune was trying to reach your home when his attacker caught up with him.'

'I believe that too. More port, if you please.'

Will administered more port.

'It is deeply regrettable that Rune never reached here,' said Mr Wells. 'Particularly so because he had promised to pay me back a sum of money he had borrowed and also to aid me in my present predicament.'

'Your being invisible, do you mean?'

'Of course I do.'

'But why do you call that a predicament? It's an incredible scientific achievement.'

'Science is bunk!' cried Mr Wells. And he spat as he cried it. 'I put my faith in science. I believed that the world could be explained according to scientific principles. I was wrong.'

'How so?' Will asked.

'Because this world does not function according to scientific principles. It functions according to magic.'

'Oh,' said Will. 'Really? Do you think so?'

'Look at me,' said Wells. 'Look at what little you can see of me. I never intended to become invisible. I wanted to become taller. The little you can see of me is short, is it not?'

'Not *that* short,' said Will. 'I've seen shorter.'

'Only at the circus. I worked on a growth serum. To alter my metabolism and increase my height. It failed dismally. The result you see, or don't see, before you.'

'And being invisible is a *bad* thing?'

'Have you ever tried to shave yourself when you can't see your reflection in the mirror? You cannot imagine how awful it is to be invisible.'

'I can imagine what fun it might be,' said Will.

'Oh yes. Such as creeping into ladies' rooms and watching them undress.'

'Things like that,' said Will.

'I am a scientist, not a voyeur.'

'Quite so,' said Will.

'Do you think I would gain pleasure by sneaking unseen into Buckingham Palace and positioning myself upon her Majesty's toilet, so that she sat down unknowingly upon me and did her business?'

'Absolutely not!' Will made a disgusted face. 'Such a thought never entered my head. Are you all right, Mr Wells?'

Mr Wells had a curious expression upon what could be seen of his talcumed head. An expression of ecstasy.

'I'm fine,' said Wells, doing snappings-out-of-it. 'Fine.'

'And Rune was going to return you to visibility, through some means or another?'

'Through magic,' said Wells. 'Which seems to triumph over science at any given opportunity.'

'But you invented the time machine. That's a triumph of science if ever there was one.'

'If only that were true.'

'But it worked. I know it worked. I came here in it from the future.'

'Not through any efforts of mine,' said Mr Wells.

'But you invented it.'

'But it didn't work.'

Barry stirred in Will's head. 'I've been out for the count, chief. What happened, are we all right?'

'I'm just having a little chat with Mr Wells. Please be quiet, Barry.'

'Aaagh!' went Barry.

'Aaagh!' went Mr Wells.

Will scratched at his aching head and then he peered at Mr Wells. 'Why did you just go, "aaagh!"?' he asked.

'You spoke the name Barry.'

'I did,' said Will.

'Barry,' said Mr Wells. 'He's in *your* head, isn't he?'

'He might be,' said Will. 'What is it to you?'

'The time machine,' said Mr Wells. 'He was the power behind it. He made it work.'

'Barry did?'

'He's a loony, chief,' said Barry. 'And why is he all talcumed up? And why has he got bits missing? And oh dear, oh dear, oh dear.'

'What do you mean, Mr Wells?' Will asked.

'Forget whatever he means,' said Barry. 'Let's get out of here, chief. Things to do, places to go. Chiswick, for instance.'

'Be quiet, Barry.'

'Inside your head,' said Mr Wells. 'Your poor fool.'

'Hold on there,' said Will.

'Let's be off,' said Barry.

'No, I want to hear what Mr Wells has to say.'

'I don't.'

'Then go back to sleep.'

'That thing,' said Mr Wells, 'that thing in your head was the power behind my time machine. I was working on the project but getting nowhere. Rune came round for dinner. He needed money, but I was disinclined to lend him any, as I had done so before on several previous occasions and failed to receive repayment. Rune told me that he could make my time machine work if I advanced him one hundred pounds. He was a very persuasive speaker. I gave him the money.'

'And Barry made the time machine work?'

'It was nothing, chief, I can't take all the credit.'

'*Credit?* Mr Wells' time machine brought that terminator robot thing into the future to kill me. And that's why I'm here, now.' Will had a very fierce face on; thankfully for Barry he couldn't see it.

'You're getting it wrong, chief,' the sprout protested. 'It's not how you think, it wasn't my fault.'

'So whose fault was it?'

'Search me, chief.'

'I'm going to release you now, Mr Wells,' said Will. 'Don't get me wrong; I don't trust you. You seem like a very bitter individual to me.'

'You'd be bitter too if you were in my position.'

'Well, be that as it may, I am going to release you. It's time Barry and I had a long talk.'

'You won't get much truth out of him.'

'I think I might. Do you possess a pair of tweezers? A *long* pair?'

'I do,' said Mr Wells.

'All right, chief, I'll tell you whatever you want to know.'

Will thought about this. 'I'm not even certain that I know what it is I want to know.'

'Fair enough then, chief, so let's get on our way.'

'Ask him about his twin brother,' said Mr Wells.

'Damn,' said Barry.

'Cough it up,' said Will.

'Family business,' said Barry. 'You wouldn't be interested.'

Will reached down and untied Mr Wells. 'I'll help you up,' said he. 'Let's find your longest tweezers.'

'All right, chief, I'll tell you everything.'

'Everything?' Will asked.

'Everything,' said Barry.

20

Mr Wells now sat in a comfy fireside chair, cushions all about him, his invisible broken ankle swathed in bandages and resting on a Persian pouffe. Will stoked up the fire and settled into a chair of similar comfort opposite the partially visible man.

'So, Barry,' said Will. 'Would you like to tell me all about it?'

'Not really, chief.'

'Well, that is neither here nor there, nor anywhere else for that matter. Just tell me the truth and all of the truth.'

'And we'll keep it between the two of us, yes, chief?'

'I don't think so. Mr Wells seems to know something about this. I'd like him to hear it too.'

Mr Wells toasted Will with a glass of vintage port.

'All right then, chief. Tell you what, close your eyes and let your jaw go slack and I'll work your vocal cords.'

Will shook his head and sighed. 'If it will save time, then I will.' And so Will closed his eyes and slackened his jaw.

And Barry manipulated Will's vocal cords.

'We must be off,' said the voice of Will. 'Goodbye now, Mr Wells.'

'No!' Will's eyes became widely open. 'Just tell the truth and let's be done with it.' And he closed his eyes and slackened his jaw once again.

And in that cosy room, with the comfy chairs and the dancing firelight and the light of the morning entering the windows, Barry told his tale through the mouth of Will Starling.

'Firstly,' he said. 'You have to understand that none of this is my fault. Well, possibly some of it is, but most of it isn't. You can look upon me as not just a Holy Guardian sprout assigned to bring comfort to a single individual, but as more of a Holy Guardian of the World sprout, a sprouty soldier of fortune on constant assignment to the forces of goodness and purity.'

Mr Wells made groaning sounds.

'Your ankle paining you?' Barry asked.

'Your banal conversation,' said Mr Wells.

'But it's true,' said Barry. 'It really is. As a scholar you must surely know that since the time of Christ, and possibly even before, mankind has been under the constant belief that it is living in the End Times; that the Apocalypse and Armageddon, and things of that nature generally, are about to occur.'

'This is indeed so,' said Mr Wells. 'End Time cults have existed throughout history. There have been countless false messiahs, preaching that, "the end is at hand". All have been wrong, however.'

'On the contrary,' said Barry. 'Most have been correct. Mankind stands teetering on the edge of destruction. It always stands teetering on the edge of destruction. Always has, probably always will.'

'Stuff and nonsense,' said Mr Wells. 'Amply proven by history. We are still here, are we not?'

'Only because of the likes of me.' Barry now moved Will's hand towards his mouth and poured port into it.

'Oi!' said Will, regaining control of himself. 'Cut that out. Just do the talking.'

'There is always some terrible conspiracy,' Barry continued. 'Always some fiendish plot on the part of the forces of evil to destroy mankind and unleash chaos upon the world. Always. The likes of me are forever engaging in titanic struggle against the likes of them. We thwart their sinister plots and save mankind from extinction. Why only last month—'

'Only last month you were in Rune's steamer trunk,' said Will, before relaxing once again.

'Chief, I can travel through time. I could pop off this moment, do things for years and years in another time and then be right back here a split second later, before you even realised that I was gone. *There*; I did it, then.'

'Tell us about your brother,' said Mr Wells. 'I am sure Mr Starling would like to hear all about him.'

'I would,' Will agreed.

'Then just slacken that jaw and listen, chief.'

Barry continued with the telling of his tale. 'I can't do anything without human help,' he said. 'I need a "host" to work with, as it were. Someone enlightened, who can actually hear the voice of their Holy Guardian. Most folk cannot. Choosing the right host isn't easy, which is why some of my kind come to grief. They fall in with the wrong crowd, like my brother has a habit of doing, and then the trouble starts.'

'I spy a flaw in your line of debate,' said Mr Wells. 'Surely *everyone*, according to reasoning, has a Holy Guardian Angel, be it angel or vegetable, assigned to them at birth.'

'That's the way God does business,' said Barry. 'Well, not God exactly, because He doesn't get around to doing much of anything nowadays, but one of His operatives, in a department, in heaven, somewhere.'

'But *everyone* has one.'

'Yes,' said Barry. 'I told you that.'

'So where is Mr Starling's? When you moved in, did you evict the previous tenant?'

'Ah,' said Barry.

'Ah,' said Mr Wells.'

'Allow me to explain,' said Barry. 'Evicting the previous tenant, as you put it, is not something to be entered into lightly. It can have a dire effect on the "host". Conflicting voices in the head, that kind of thing. It will be called schizophrenia in a few decades from now. It's a tricky business. I am here at this present time because of the *big trouble* that is here. Mr Rune, for all his unconventional behaviour, was one of the good guys. He was dedicated to the fight against evil. I sought him out to help. But his Holy Guardian, Gavin the gooseberry—'

'*What?*' went Will.

'Slacken up, chief.'

Will slackened up.

'Gavin the gooseberry wasn't having any of it. He thought he knew best. So I manifested in physical form to Mr Rune during one of his many abortive conjurations. But he didn't trust me, and he kept me in a box. I was trying and trying to win him over and let me come inside. I could have made short work of that Gavin, sprout against a gooseberry, no contest! But however it didn't come to pass, because Mr Rune had a plan of his own and it so happened that my plan and his plan joined together perfectly. Rune sought knowledge of future events, very possibly to lay bets upon race horses, but I'm sure also to aid the forces of good. I suggested to him that although it was a radical thing to do, I might be persuaded to bring someone back from the future; someone who would have knowledge of past events which were still future events to Mr Rune. If you understand me.'

Mr Wells nodded and sipped port.

'And this was the clever bit,' said Barry. 'Rune wanted to bring back his magical heir, a descendant of his. The last of his line, in fact.'

'Tim.' Will worked his own mouth.

'Tim,' said Barry. 'But, as you know, there was a bit of a balls-up and you were brought back instead.'

'A moment please,' said Mr Wells. 'If you hatched up this plan with Rune, why was I brought into this?'

'You were working on a time machine,' said Barry. 'And Mr Rune wanted to borrow a hundred quid. There's nothing more to it than that.'

'Scoundrel,' said Wells. 'Outrageous!'

'And a terrible mistake all round,' Barry continued. 'I allowed myself to be placed in that machine. Allowed my time-travelling powers to be harnessed but not under my control. The machine was stolen, and used by the forces of evil against Mr Starling, because he had found evidence that the history he had been taught was incorrect, and his returning here would have an effect on changing things back to the way they should be. It's all rather complicated. But the point I'm trying to make, and in answer to your question about previous tenants, is this. Mr Starling turned out to be the ideal candidate, because he doesn't have a Holy Guardian of his own. In his age there are no more Holy Guardians, because in his age there is no more God.'

'What?' went Will.

And 'What?' also went Mr Wells.

'In the age you come from, chief, there is no record of the incredible technological achievements of this age, am I right?'

'You are,' said Will.

'Because history will be changed in the year 1900. Everything will change as if none of the amazing things, the electrical automobiles, the *Dreadnaught*, the moonship that is soon to be launched, ever happened. The human race will take an evolutionary step backwards. This will lead to terrible things happening. Amongst those terrible things, and in fact the most terrible of them all, will be the death of God.'

'God cannot die,' said Mr Wells.

'I agree,' said Will.

'You do?' said Barry.

'I do,' said Will. 'He can't die, because He doesn't exist.'

Barry had a right royal struggle to slacken Will's jaw once again. 'Exactly, because if no one believes in Him, He effectively ceases to exist. But whether you do or do not believe in God, chief, you know that history was changed. You're here now, you can see how things really are. You can't deny that, can you?'

Will just shook his head, slowly and thoughtfully.

'Something happens to change it all, to wipe out all records of what really happened here. All but a tiny detail here and there, like the digital watch the chief here discovered on a Victorian painting. One or two little things slipped through the magical net somehow. And the evil ones who stole the time machine tried to put that right, destroy the evidence and wipe out all knowledge. So far they've failed to do that, which means that we still have a chance at this minute to save the future from being interfered with. And to save good old God too. He's not a bad old stick; He doesn't deserve to get the chop.'

Will would have spoken, but he was speechless. Mr Wells, however, was not.

'I recall,' said he, 'that you prefaced this tale with the words, "You have to understand that none of this is my fault". And you have enforced this by telling us that although you were the power behind the time machine, you had no control over where it was sent.'

'Mr Rune set the controls,' said Barry. 'He worked out the equations.'

'Rune told me that,' said Will, 'when I first met him. I crash-landed in a street. Rune told me the calculations were slightly out. I don't recall *you* being amongst the wreckage, though, Barry.'

'Had to make a *timely* departure, chief. A drayman's horse nearly stepped upon me.'

'No, no, no,' said Will. 'None of this makes any sense. If you wanted to be inside *me*, as *my* Holy Guardian, why didn't you do it then?'

'You weren't ready, chief. You were pretty confused, finding yourself in the Victorian era and everything. And you needed time with Mr Rune, so he could teach you stuff. Prepare you for the fight.'

'He taught me a lot,' said Will. 'No magic, though.'

'He taught you Dimac,' said Mr Wells, ruefully rubbing at his bandaged ankle.

Barry cleared Wills's throat. 'Can I just ask one question?' he asked. 'Mr Wells, how did you know about my brother?'

'Rune told me, over a very expensive dinner at one of his clubs, which *I* paid for. Rune liked to pontificate, to boast of his knowledge. "Science is bunk," he said to me. "Do not be fooled by scientific achievement; it has magic at its core." I didn't believe him then, of course. We were celebrating the fact that the time machine was completed. I did not know then that the only reason it was completed was because Barry here had been installed within it by Rune. And I *had* parted with the one hundred pounds. And he couldn't resist telling me. He told me all about you, *and* your brother. Barry's brother, Mr Starling, was another of God's little helpers, but he came to a sorry end.'

'A very sorry end,' said Barry. 'Got cooked in the Great Fire of London. He persuaded his host there, a baker named Wilkinson, to get the fire started to purge London of the plague. The plague would have wiped out the entire country if it hadn't been for my brother.'

'And,' Mr Wells continued, 'Rune told me that he had arranged with Her Majesty that we would demonstrate the time machine before her at Buckingham Palace the following day. When we returned here after the meal, the time machine was gone.'

'Hold on,' Will's voice was now once more under his own control. 'This all makes some kind of sense, if Rune had already set the controls, and these "forces of evil" had found out about his plan. All they had to do was put their terminator robot in the driving seat and send it off on its way while you were out at dinner celebrating. Is that what happened, Barry?'

'Near as damned, chief. I've been trying to figure it out myself. I know I travelled into the future and back, but who was at the controls, I don't know. If I'm not inside a human, then I can't see through their eyes. But I do know that Rune was being constantly followed. Time and time again I warned him, but he always boasted that he was invulnerable to attack. Sadly he was proved wrong on that account.'

And Barry relinquished his hold upon Will's vocal cords.

Fire crackled in the grate. Will rose, fetched the port, refreshed Mr Wells' glass and also his own. He returned to his seat and sat down upon it.

'Well,' said Will.

'Well,' said Mr Wells.

'I really don't know what to say and what to do next.'

Mr Wells dusted talcum from his hands. His port glass hovered in the air. 'I do not know what to believe any more,' he said. 'I am a man of science, or perhaps I should say, *was*. If only I could claim that I achieved this dismal state of invisibility through science, then I would argue science over superstition. But sadly I cannot. My present state of being was not achieved through the administration of a medical decoction. I fear that I hold a certain degree of responsibility for your present predicament, Mr Starling.'

'I don't understand,' said Will.

'I brought the evil to you.'

'I *really* don't understand.'

'I travelled in the time machine myself,' said Mr Wells. 'Before my dinner with Rune. Before the machine was stolen.'

'You did?' said Will. '*When* did you go to?'

'I went forward into the latter part of the twentieth century. I only altered the date Rune had set. Not the location. I travelled forward to Brentford, and I became involved in a number of most extraordinary adventures, before I returned here. Ten minutes before Rune arrived to take me to dinner, I met two remarkable fellows in Brentford; a Mr Pooley and a Mr Omally. But I have reason to believe now that I did not return from that time alone. Someone, or something, returned with me. And that someone or something absconded with my time machine.'

'How can you be sure of that?' Will asked.

'Because that someone or something dropped something when they stole the time machine. And I found it and I used it, which is why I am now invisible.'

'And what was this something?' Will asked.

'A computer,' said Mr Wells. 'A miniature computer. It took me considerable time to fathom its workings, but when I did, I discovered that it contained a veritable storehouse of arcane knowledge: certain mathematical formula, mathematical and magical formula.'

Will shook his head. 'Will you show this to me?' he asked.

'No,' said Mr Wells. 'I destroyed it. Cast it into the fire.'

'Why?' Will asked.

'Fear, I suppose.'

'What did it look like?' Will asked.

'It was about this size.' Mr Wells motioned with invisible fingers. 'You pressed it in at its lower edge and the top slid aside. On the inside of the inner lid were a number of markings. A serial number.'

Will dug into his pocket and brought out his palm-top. 'Did it look anything like this?' he asked.

Mr Wells stared at Will's palm-top. 'It looked exactly like that,' he said.

Will pressed the lower edge of his palm-top and the top slid aside. 'Do you remember the serial number on the inside of the inner lid?' he asked.

'I do,' said Mr Wells. 'It was 833903.'

Will studied the number embossed upon his palm-top. He really didn't need to study it, he knew it well enough by heart.

'Oh dear, oh dear, oh dear,' said Will.

21

Will had breakfast with Mr Wells. He cooked up a big boy's breakfast, which included mushrooms, tomatoes and potatoes. He and Mr Wells enjoyed it thoroughly.

'So what *will* you do now?' asked Mr Wells, upon the completion of their considerable repast.

Will wiped a napkin over his mouth. 'Continue,' he said. 'Search for Rune's murderer. I have sworn to do this and so I shall.'

'And for all the rest?'

'If it is connected, and I agree that perhaps it might well be, then I shall do what I can. You had my palm-top computer, which somehow came from the twentieth century, which means that I must have been there, or will be there, or something. I'm sure it will all become clear eventually. But can I ask you this? Might I rely upon your assistance if the need should arise?'

'You feel now that you can trust me?'

'I have no reason not to. I will ache for some time from the violence you visited upon me, but your port has at least cleared my hangover.'

'I thought you a potential assassin,' said Wells. 'You can understand that.'

'I can.' Will rose from his chair. 'I will take my leave now. Will you be all right, with your ankle and everything?'

'I will telephone for the services of my good friend Dr Watson.'

'Not *the* Dr Watson.'

'*The*,' said Wells.

'You'll have to call someone else,' said Will. 'He's away with Mr Holmes, solving the case of the Hound of the Baskervilles. The butler did it, by the way.'

'My turn to be speechless, I think,' said Mr Wells.

'A pleasure to meet you,' said Will. 'Farewell.'

'So, where are we off to now, chief?' asked Barry, when Will was once more in the street. 'Chiswick, is it?'

'No,' said Will. 'I don't think so.'

'But, chief, I've told you everything. We're on the same side, we share the same goals. Sort of.'

'Barry,' Will spoke behind his hand to avoid the attention of passers-by, 'we will do things my way or not at all. You are free to depart whenever you wish.'

'You won't get back to the future without me, chief.'

'Perhaps I'm not bothered,' said Will. 'Perhaps I like it here. I'm used to it now, and frankly, it's better than the time I come from. Much more exciting.'

'Come off it, chief. You don't mean that really.'

'Maybe I do, maybe I don't, but I won't be bullied by you. Since I've put myself in charge, I've found out all manner of things. I think I'll just carry on doing things my way.'

'Then we're all doomed,' said Barry.

'What was that?' Will asked.

'I said, "then we're all doomed", as it happens.'

'We'll see,' said Will. 'We'll see.'

Will hailed a hansom and returned to his room at the Dorchester. Here he bathed and then dressed himself in one of the morning suits from the extensive range of clothing that Barry had acquired for him. Will took up Rune's cane, twirled it between his fingers and examined his reflection in the cheval glass.

'Very dashing, chief. A regular dandy, you are. So what do you have in mind to do next?'

'A visit to Whitechapel police station,' said Will. 'We will see if any new clues have turned up regarding the Ripper murders.'

'A waste of time, chief. You *know* that they haven't.'

'I can no longer trust history, Barry. I will follow the case. There has to be a reason why those women were murdered. And if, and I mean *if*, the same murderer killed Hugo Rune, then we'll see what we shall see.'

'But chief, come on, the witches, the forces of darkness. The End Times at hand, the death of God, the—'

'My way, Barry. My way or not at all. If the case can be solved. I will solve it.'

'How, chief? How will *you* solve it?'

'By deduction, Barry. The science of deduction. I've read all the Sherlock Holmes books. I know his methods.'

'So you are now a consulting detective?'

Will took up the envelope of case notes. 'I'm Will Starling,' he said. 'Associate of Mr Sherlock Holmes of Baker Street, and out to make a name for myself in history as the man who brought Jack the Ripper to justice.'

'Oh d—'

'Don't say it,' said Will.

'I'm sorry, chief.'

'That's better.'

Whitechapel police station was a dreary-looking building, constructed of grimy London Stocks and painted all around its wooden bits with dull grey paint. It did have the big blue lamp outside, but there was just no cheering it up. It was dull, and it was dreary, it was grim.

Will entered the grim police station. It's interior was stark and joyless: faded oak-panelled walls, what were now old-fashioned gas lights, a miserable desk that barred the way to depressing offices beyond. A sleeping policeman lay slumped upon a sorry chair behind this miserable desk.

A sad brass desk bell stood mournfully upon this miserable desk.

Will struck the button of this sad brass desk bell.

The sleeping policeman awoke.

'Let's be having you!' he cried as he awoke. 'You're nicked chummy. Put your hands up, it's a fair cop.'

'Good day to you,' said Will.

'Ah.' The policeman focused his eyes. 'Good day to you too, sir.'

The policeman raised himself from his chair of gloom and Will stared at the policeman. 'I know you,' he said. 'I know you from somewhere.'

'Constable Tenpole Tudor,' said the constable. 'I never forget a face, and I don't know you.'

'Starling,' said Will. '*Lord* William Starling, son of the late Sir Captain Ernest Starling, hero of the British Empire. I am an associate of Mr Sherlock Holmes of Baker Street.'

'Never heard of him,' said Constable Tenpole Tudor.

'Your superiors have; they placed this case file in his hands, and I am dealing with it now.' Will placed the envelope upon the miserable desk, the constable turned it towards himself and gave it a peering at.

'The Ripper,' said he, and then he began to laugh.

'Why do you laugh?' Will asked. 'This is no laughing matter.'

'I laugh,' said the constable, 'because we've already caught the blighter. Less than an hour ago. We have him banged up in the cells even now. That's why I laugh.'

'You have *caught* Jack the Ripper?'

'Didn't give up without a struggle. Took four officers to bring him down.'

'And you have him in custody? Here? Now?'

'Down below in the cells. Presently being interrogated by Chief Inspector Samuel Maggott.'

'Samuel Maggott?' said Will. 'Of DOCS?'

'Docs?' asked the constable. 'I wouldn't know about any docs. The fiend might need a doctor by the time we've finished with him though. Doesn't seem too keen to confess to his evil crimes.'

'But you're sure you have the right man? How can you be sure?'

'Covered in blood, he was. And raving too. Well he was at the time, when we caught him. "I did it", he shouted. "I had to. God made me do it." Can you imagine that? God made him do it? That's a new one, ain't it?'

'It will stand the test of time,' said Will. 'Can I see him?'

'See him? Why would you want to see him?'

'Because I was assigned to this case. Look, there's a letter in this envelope. Passing the case on to Mr Holmes. He passed it on to me.'

'A lot of passing about,' said the constable. 'That's not how things are done through official channels.'

'Yes it is,' said Will. 'That's always how it's done.'

'Is it?' asked the constable. 'Well, nobody's ever told me. All I ever get is orders from above.'

Will paused.

'Oh I see,' said the constable. 'I suppose you're right.'

'Then I can see the suspect?'

'The murderer, you mean.'

'The murderer, then.'

'Well,' said Constable Tenpole Tudor, and he rubbed his thumb and forefinger together in a significant fashion. 'I don't know. Just letting anyone in. That might be more than my job's worth. I just don't know.'

Will reached into his pocket and brought out a golden guinea. 'See this,' he said.

'I do,' said the constable.

'Then take me to the murderer's cell and perhaps I'll show it to you again.'

'This way, sir,' said the constable and he raised a depressing flap upon his miserable desk and led Will down to the cells.

The down-to-the-cells way was all that Will might have expected, had he been expecting it: dark, dank, damp and dripping stone walls; sounds of steel doors clanging in the distance, horrid smells, slimy steps.

'Like the décor?' asked the constable. 'We've just had it redecorated. Chap off the wireless. Laurence Llewellyn-Morris.'

'Very, er, atmospheric,' said Will, stepping over something vile that lay upon a step.

'A bit too modern for my taste,' said the constable. 'I prefer things traditional. Can't be having with this trendy stuff. It was all aluminium tiles and pine decking down here before.'

'Please lead on,' said Will. 'I'm becoming confused.'

'We've had them all down here,' said the constable, as he led on. 'Sweeney Todd, the demon barber of Fleet Street, Sawney Bean, the Galloway cannibal; the Count of Monte Cristo, the Prisoner of Cell Block H. And *the* Prisoner, of course, played by Patrick McGoohan.'

'What?' said Will.

'I'm a member of the fan club,' said the constable. 'Six of One; you get a badge and everything. I'd send away for the t-shirt, but they're a bit expensive.'

'Chief,' said Barry. 'There's something very wrong here, we should be going, I think.'

'I know what you mean,' Will whispered.

'Oh and Hannibal Lecter,' said the constable. 'He's a real terror. We have to keep him in a straitjacket with a leather mask, or he'll bite your face off. Happened to Constable Colby last week. He was token policewoman; took the mask off to give Mr Lecter's teeth a clean. Bad mistake that.'

'Away, chief,' said Barry. 'Now.'

'I think I'd like to see the prisoner,' said Will.

'Mr McGoohan, your lordship?'

'No, Jack the Ripper.'

'That's what you're,' the constable tapped at his nose, 'you know, bribing me for.'

'It's official business,' said Will. 'But you will be recompensed for your trouble.'

'That's it, your lordship "Recompensed". Good word, that.'

'Please just lead the way,' said Will. And the constable continued with his way-leading.

'Now down here,' he said, 'there used to be all big cells, very spacious, en-suite bathrooms and that kind of thing, but Mr Llewellyn-Morris split them up, made them more down-market. Newgate chic, he called it. Retro-look. Ah, here we are. Would you like to go in?'

They had stopped before an iron door, an iron door with one of those little grilles upon it with the sliding panel that you can move aside to have a peep into the cell and a good old gloat if you're that way inclined.

'Could I just have a peep through the little grille?' Will asked.

'Certainly, your lordship. And have a good old gloat too if you wish. I always do. The captured villain on the inside, the good fellow on the outside, that's always worthy of a good old gloat in my opinion.'

'A peep,' said Will. 'I'm not ready for a gloat just yet.'

'Please yourself,' said the constable. 'And I suppose that really *you* don't have anything to gloat about. After all, *you* didn't catch Jack the Ripper. I did.'

'You said it took four of you.'

'But I caught him. Wandering in the street, burbling like a mad man. Covered in blood from head to toe. I'll take the credit. My name will go down in history for this.'

'Well done,' said Will, but not with enthusiasm.

'So have a little peep, your lordship, and then we'll settle up.' And the constable rubbed his thumb and forefinger together once more.

'Indeed we will.'

The constable pushed the little sliding panel aside and Will peered through the grille and into the cell.

Within the tiny wretched-looking cell sat two men, either side of a table, one the suspect, the other Chief Inspector Samuel Maggot.

Will viewed the suspect. He was strapped into a straitjacket. There was much blood upon the straitjacket. There was much blood upon the suspect also. It was clotted into his hair. It was all around the edges of his face also. The suspect's face was contorted, madly contorted.

'It wasn't me,' he was yelling. 'You don't understand,' he was yelling. 'You have to do something,' he was yelling also.

The suspect's yelling hurt Will's ears. And Will's face made a very pained expression. But it wasn't the yelling that did it. It was the suspect.

Will stared at the suspect and Will's mouth opened.

'Chief,' said Barry. 'I see that. Do you see that?'

'I see that,' Will whispered.

'But chief, it's . . . it's . . .'

'It's me, Barry,' said Will. 'That man in the cell is me!'

22

'Well that's handy, chief,' chirped Barry. 'You've got an evil twin and he's Jack the Ripper. Case solved, then. Let's head for Chiswick.'

'Stop it!' Will made a fist and struck his temple with it. 'That man in the cell is *me*.'

'Could be a great-granddaddy, chief.'

'It's *me*. I know it's *me*.'

Constable Tenpole Tudor stared Will up and down and then gently eased him aside and had a good peer through the little metal grille.

'I'll be a red-nosed burglar!' said he. 'There's a definite resemblance and no doubt about it. Do you want to put your hands up to being an accessory and come quietly with me? Or would you prefer to enjoy the privilege accorded to the titled classes of this time, tip me a guinea and stroll away unmolested to your London club?'

'The latter indeed.' Will peeped once more into the cell and Will had a good old tremble going. 'It's *me*,' he whispered to Barry. 'It *is* me. What are we going to do?'

'*We*, chief? I thought you were calling all the shots now.'

'I must interview the suspect, constable,' said Will.

'You'll have plenty to choose from then, your lordship.'

'What?' said Will.

'If you want to interview a suspect constable, half of the constables here are decidedly suspect.'

Will looked at the constable.

And the constable looked back at Will.

'Sorry,' said the constable. 'Couldn't resist it.'

'But it wasn't funny.'

'Maybe not to you,' said Constable Tenpole Tudor. 'But to me, it was hysterical. I'm all torn up inside over it, me. Can hardly keep a straight face. You can never beat a little humour to lighten a stressful situation.'

'Let me speak to the prisoner,' said Will.

'Mr Patrick McGoohan, your lordship?'

'Hit him, chief,' said Barry. 'Employ your Dimac. Put this dullard out for the count. The Count of Monte Cristo, if you like.'

'The other day,' the constable continued, 'I was in this hardware shop, needed some nails, see. And I said to the chap behind the counter, "I'd like some nails please". And he said, "How long would you like them?" And I said—'

' "Forever",' said Barry. ' "I want to keep them." That's quite a good 'n.'

'It's rubbish!' said Will.

'No,' said the constable. 'That's not what I said. I said, "About six inches will do. Or at least that's what my wife always says!" ' And the constable began to laugh.

'Different punch-line,' said Barry. 'I preferred mine. The element of *time* being involved and everything.'

'And the other day,' said the constable, 'I was playing cards in the jungle with some natives and—'

Will employed a Dimac move known as *The Donk of the Dark Dragon's Doodle*, struck the constable hard in the chin and knocked him to the newly flag-stoned floor.

'Try that for a punch-line,' said Will.

'Nice one, chief. So what now?'

Will rapped the tip of Rune's cane on the steel cell door.

The yelling which hadn't ceased, but which hadn't been mentioned because it would have interfered with the achingly funny dialogue, stilled away to nothing at all. And a voice called, 'What is it, constable?' It was the voice of Chief Inspector Samuel Maggott.

'Special visitor, sir.' Will did his best to imitate the constable's voice. 'Sent from Scotland Yard to interview the prisoner. Member of the aristocracy.'

'Let him in, constable.'

'Very good, chief.'

Will knelt, relieved the constable of his keys and, after several attempts, selected the correct one and managed to open the door. He eased himself inside, calling ' "wait for me in the corridor, constable",' over his shoulder.

Samuel Maggott turned in his chair and stared up at Will.

'By the—'

But he said no more as Will made free with his Dimac. This time the move was *The Terrible Twist of the Tiger's Todger*. It involved the same fist and the outcome was identical. Samuel Maggott toppled from his chair and lay very still on the floor of the cell.

'You're a regular twelfth-dan master, chief,' said Barry.

'Just leave this to me.'

Will sat himself in the now vacant chair and stared at the jacketed prisoner. The jacketed prisoner stared back at Will and there was fear in his eyes.

'Just be calm.' Will raised his hand. The prisoner flinched and Will lowered it again. 'Who are you?' he asked.

'Who are *you*?' Will's living double replied.

'My name is William Starling.'

'No.' The prisoner struggled and struggled. 'This is some trick. You're trying to drive me insane. You're not me. You can't be me.'

'Me?' Will shook his head slowly. He trembled now from blondy head to patent leather toe. 'Are you *me*?'

'You're one of them. Pure evil. Just kill me. I won't tell you anything.'

'Nobody's going to kill anyone. And I'm certainly not going to kill you.'

The two men looked at each other. Both were scared. But one was on the point of terror.

'What do you want from me?' The prisoner's teeth chattered together. 'How did I get here? Where am I? *When* am I?'

'Ah,' said Will. '*When?*'

'Chief, we really should be going. The lads from Scotland Yard are probably on their way here now. Things won't look good for you, trust me on this.'

'I'm not leaving him here.'

'Then bring him with you. But let's get out of here now.'

'Right,' Will jumped to his feet. 'I'm getting you out of here. Come on now.' And he reached out his hand towards the prisoner.

'No!' Barry's voice echoed in Will's head, causing him to drop his cane and clasp his hands over his ears. 'No, chief. Don't touch him.'

'Not so loud.' Will clawed at his head.

The prisoner looked on with a horrified expression.

'You mustn't touch him, chief. I've just had a terrible thought.'

'Tell me something new.'

'Oh ha ha ha, chief. A little humour to lighten a stressful situation. But I'm not kidding you. Don't touch him. Under no circumstance touch him.'

'Why not?' Will asked.

'Because if it *is* you, there's no telling what might happen. Well, actually, there is and it's not good, I can tell you.'

'I don't have time for this.'

'You do, chief. And *time* is what it's all about. This could be *you*, due to some time-travelling anomaly. And if it is, the two yous must not come into physical contact. It's all that time paradox business. Two yous cannot occupy the same space. It would be like matter and antimatter meeting. Big explosion and then no yous at all. Did you ever see *Time Cop*? David Warner was in that and he got pushed into his other self and the two went whoosh. Horrible, it was, but a damn good movie. Actually, David Warner was in several movies with a "time" theme. *Time after Time*, *Time Bandits*—'

Will thought for a moment. It was not a particularly long moment. It was possibly longer than a 'trice', but not as long as 'a mo'. Or perhaps it was the other way around.

'Up!' he shouted at his blood-splattered doppelgänger. 'Come with me, if you want to live.'

'Good line, chief. Wrong movie, but still one of my favourites.'

The prisoner sat shaking. He turned his face away.

'They'll kill you if you stay here,' Will told him. 'It's capital punishment in this era. They'll hang you for being Jack the Ripper.'

'I'm not—' the prisoner groaned.

'Hurry,' Will told him.

The prisoner struggled to rise. Will almost helped him. Almost.

'Keep thinking David Warner,' Barry told him.

'Out.' Will threw open the cell door.

'What happened?' asked Constable Tenpole Tudor, peering dizzily in.

Will felled him with a second blow and snatched up Rune's cane from the floor. 'Out.' He waved the cane at the prisoner. 'Out, and hurry.'

The prisoner stumbled across the cell, he stepped over the unconscious Chief Inspector and then the unconscious constable. Will prodded him into the corridor with the cane. 'Along to the end and up the stairs,' he told him. 'And hurry. I really do mean hurry.'

And along the corridor and up the stairs the prisoner stumbled. He seemed in a state of near collapse and he was buffeted from one wall to another. Will kept prodding and urging and in more than a 'mo', but less than a 'bit', they reached the miserable front desk.

And then Will saw them, through the melancholic front windows of the police station. Two hansom cabs were drawn up outside and folk were climbing down from them: official-looking fellows in high top hats and long dark-jacketed morning suits, and a number of women. Well-dressed women, lavishly-dressed women, but with preposterously slender bodies and tiny pinched faces, these women, four in number they were, looked curiously alike, as if sisters. But—

'Evil,' whispered Will.

'Chief, I can feel them,' Barry said. 'Evil is right. Let's get out the back way and let's make it snappy.'

'Back.' Will prodded the prisoner once more. 'Back through that door there.'

'Leave me alone,' the prisoner howled.

'I'm sorry,' said Will, and he poked him even harder. 'But we are in big trouble here. Just go, if you know what's good for us.'

Into a rear office they went and Will slammed the door shut upon them. The key was in the lock and he turned it.

The office room was gas-lit. Filing cabinets of a doleful disposition lined the cheerless walls and at a disconsolate table sat a young policewoman.

Will stared at the young policewoman.

She was *not* a young policewoman.

She was a young man dressed as a young policewoman.

This young man looked up at Will.

'I know,' he said. 'Don't tell me. What gave it away? The wig, wasn't it? If I've told them once, I've told them a thousand times. If you want someone to play the role of token woman, give them the tools for the job. But do they listen? No. These high heels are crippling my feet, and as to the corset—'

'What is your name?' Will asked. He asked the question in a slow and deliberate voice. He had a feeling that he already knew the answer.

'Policewoman John Higgins,' Policewoman John Higgins replied. 'Who are you and—' He/she glanced from the face of Will to the face of the prisoner and back again.

'No time at all to explain,' said Will, 'even if I could. Undo the prisoner's straitjacket, if you will.'

'I certainly will *not*.' The cross-dressing officer of the law rose from his/her seat and reached for his/her truncheon.

'I don't have time for this,' said Will.

'Stick your hand in your pocket, chief.'

'What?'

'What?' said Policewoman Higgins.

'Just do it, chief, tell he/she that you have a gun in your pocket. Make him or her, or whatever it is, unstrap the other you and open the back door.'

'Good idea.' Will did as he was bid.

'I've a gun in my pocket,' said Will. 'Do what I say, or I'll shoot you.'

And now there came sounds of a handle being turned and then fists being banged on the door that Will had locked, just two 'trices' and three 'half-a-mo's'* before.

The token policewoman raised his/her truncheon and peered at the bulge in Will's pocket. And, as it was impossible at such a moment to resist uttering the now legendary line, uttered it.

'Is that a gun in your pocket, or are you just—'

And Will's finger squeezed upon a trigger and shot the end off the token policewoman's truncheon.

'Gun, then.' Higgins dropped the truncheon and set about releasing the straps which held the other Will's straitjacket.

Fists now rained upon the locked office door and there was a great deal of angry shouting.

'The back door,' Will said, when his other self was unbuckled. 'Unlock it quickly, now.'

'It's not locked,' said token Policewoman Higgins.

'Then come over here.'

'What is it?' The token policewoman teetered in Will's direction.

'Only this, and I'm sorry.' And Will brought him/her down with a Dimac moved called *The Lunge of the Lion's Lingum*, which this time involved Will's elbow, as his fist was growing sore.

Will's other self stood unsteadily rubbing at his wrists and shaking fearfully.

'Out of the door,' Will told him. 'Don't make me hit you too.'

The other Will staggered forward and opened the door. Will pushed him forward with the cane, forward and into an alleyway.

It was an alleyway of heart-breaking dejection.

'Along the alley. To the front of the building,' Will said.

'The *front* of the building, chief?'

'I'm running this, Barry.'

'And most violently too. Lots of pent up aggression coming out. I hope you're not having a psychotic episode.'

'Go on,' Will told his other self. 'Along the alleyway. Quickly.'

* Equivalent to one and a half mo's. Or three quarters of a tick.

★

The street truly bustled with people now.

Many tradesmen hustled as they bustled and called out the Cries of Old London.

'Bluebottles, bluebottles. Get yer luverly bluebottles.'

And so on.

The two hansom cabs still stood before the police station. Will opened the door of the first one and ushered his other self into it. The cabbie looked down through his hatchway at the back.

'Sorry gents,' he said. 'These cabs is taken. Hired by Very Important Folk. Hail another, if you please.'

Will closed the hansom cab's door. His other self sat within, hunched up and cowering. Will stepped around to the rear of the cab. 'Cabbie,' he called up. 'Could you step down here for a moment.'

'How long a moment would that be, sir? More than a "tick", would it be, or less than a "twinkling" or a "flash"?'

'Do I spy a duff running gag?' Will asked. 'Just step down here for a "jiffy", if you will.'

'Oh, I can certainly spare a "jiffy".'

The cabbie climbed down and a Dimac move called *The Wave of the Wombat's Winkie* laid the cabbie low.

'Chief,' said Barry. 'You're not going to—'

'Yes I am.' Will leapt up onto the cabbie's mount and took up the horse's reins.

And then folk issued from the police station: important-looking men in high top hats, and curious pinch-faced women. These wore the most ferocious expressions.

And Will, with a surprising degree of dexterity, which involved holding the horse's reins in one hand, taking up the cabbie's whip in the other, and somehow still managing to keep a hold upon Rune's silver-topped cane, slapped the reins and cracked the whip and shouted, 'Giddy up.'

And the cabbie's horse just stood there, refusing to be moved.

And now the important-looking men and the ferocious-faced females were at the hansom cab and climbing onto it.

'Giddy up!' shouted Will, cracking the whip once more and employing Rune's cane to strike the top hat from the head of an important-looker. 'Get a move on. Hutt! Hutt!'

'Hutt, chief?'

'It's what you say to camels,' Will kicked away the important-looker who was clawing at his leg.

'Try "Hi Ho Silver", chief.'

'And why?' *The Poke of the Porcupine's Pecker*, a shin-move deeply applied, sent another important-looker toppling.

'No harm in trying, chief.'

'Hi Ho Silver!' shouted Will and he cracked the whip once more.

And the cabbie's horse took off in a manner that was not unlike the wind.

'You can't beat a farting horse,' said Barry.

'So *not* funny.' Will clung to the reins and Hi-Ho-Silvered some more.

And important-lookers and ferocious-faced-females fell away as the horse leapt forward, scattering bluebottle-sellers and costermongers and rag men and rabbit-skin hawkers.

The horse traffic was, of course, heavy. There were many carts and carriers and trucks and cabs too.

A prediction was made in the year eighteen ninety, which seemed a most logical prediction at the time, and this prediction was, that with the ever-growing volume of horse drawn traffic in London, by the year nineteen twenty, every street, road and lane in England would be nose to tail in horse-drawn vehicles, and London would be thirty-five feet deep in horse manure. And it *was* a prediction based upon logic.

Will steered the cabbie horse (Silver?) with remarkable skill, about this obstruction and the next, and the next, and the next as well.

'Very impressive, chief,' said Barry.

'Rune taught me to ride in Russia,' said Will. 'We rode with the Cossacks. Visited the Tsar. Had to make an early departure though. Rune behaved in a somewhat inappropriate manner with the Tsarina.'

'There was never a dull moment with that fellow, was there?'

Will now yelled at a pure-gatherer who blocked his passage. 'Out of the way!' he yelled. The pure-gatherer dropped his bucket, but dodged the wheels of the speeding hansom.

'Have we lost them?' Will asked, as the hansom thundered over Westminster Bridge.

'Look over your shoulder and check, chief.'

'No, Barry. I'm asking *you*. Can you feel *big* trouble still following us?'

'I can feel big trouble all around, chief. But specifically following us? No, chief, you've escaped.'

'Good.' Will slowed the cabbie's horse and once across the river, brought it to a halt and allowed it to refresh itself at a public trough.

'Interesting,' said Will, as the horse gulped down its water.

'Not particularly,' said Barry. 'All God's creatures like a drink. Man, especially.'

'Not that,' said Will. 'You know what I mean.'

'Actually, I don't, chief.'

'They were right behind us,' said Will. 'In the second cab. Very close. I thought they were going to catch up with us.'

'You didn't mention it, chief, although I could certainly feel them.'

'But then they stopped, when we reached the bridge. Why did they do that?'

'Because witches cannot pass over running water, chief. It's a tradition, or an old charter, or certain death if you've sold your soul to Satan.'

Will said nothing more and when the horse had drunk its fill he Hi-Ho-Silvered it gently and it trotted on.

'Chiswick, then is it, chief?' asked Barry, at a length that was neither a 'jiffy' nor a 'tick', nor a 'twinkling', nor even a 'mo' and a third.

'Get real, Barry,' said Will.

'They don't come any realer than me, chief.'

'Chap down below.' Will pointed to his passenger. 'Me down below. Another me. Rather a lot of questions to be asked and answered, I would have thought.'

'So not Chiswick, just yet, chief?'

'No,' said Will. 'But somewhere quite close to Chiswick. I'm going home, Barry. Home to Brentford.'

23

Where Kew Bridge meets the Brentford High Road, Will brought the hansom to a halt once more and climbed down from it.

He opened the passenger door and beckoned to his other self.

'Would you please come out?' he asked him.

Will's other self seemed in a state of shock. His face was deathly white and his eyes had the thousand-yard stare.

'Please,' said Will. 'There's another horse trough here. You must clean yourself up, wash away that blood, make yourself look halfway respectable.'

His other self said, 'What?'

'It's definitely you, chief. Same stupid "what".'

'Shut it, Barry.'

Will's other self flinched.

'Please,' said Will. 'I mean you no harm. I'm trying to help you.'

His other self stepped down like a sleepwalker, took himself over to the horse trough and proceeded to splash himself with water.

'He's well out of it, chief,' said Barry. 'Perhaps you should just leave him here.'

'To fend for himself? I think not.'

'Only trying to think about what's best for you.'

'Yeah, right,' said Will. 'But he *is* me. Look at him. Look at his clothes. Those aren't the clothes of this day and age. He's from the future.'

'I'm trying to figure out how this happened,' said Barry. 'And I hate like damn to admit it, but I'm baffled.'

At a length, which will remain forever unquantified, Will's other self completed his ablutions and returned to the cab. Will ushered him gently inside at stick's length and then drove on.

There was no denying the beauty of the Borough of Brentford. But then, until the twenty-second century, there never had been.

Brentford, the jewel in London's crown, slumbered in the early winter sunlight.

The hansom passed the gasworks and Will turned right into the Ealing road. Will let the horse wander where it wished. And soon it wished to stop. So Will let it.

The hansom drew up outside a hostelry, a public drinking house built of London Stock, with hanging baskets of Babylon, which flowered unseasonably and perfumed the air all around.

The public house was named The Flying Swan.

'Ideal,' said Will. 'A drink would not be out of the question.'

And thus, having said this, he leapt down from the cab and secured the horse's reins to an iron bollard.

'Come,' he told his other self. 'If anyone needs a drink, that anyone is you.'

The other Will looked upon The Flying Swan. 'Here,' he said. 'It would have to be here.'

'What?' asked Will.

The other Will hung his head and said nothing more.

The saloon bar of The Flying Swan looked exactly as it had when Will had taken Tim into it many chapters before and some three hundred years into the future. But, of course, as this was the first time that Will had entered the bar, he was not aware that it *was* exactly the same. But it *was*.

Well, not *exactly*, perhaps. The décor was the same, the fixtures and fitting were the same, but they were newer, because this was three hundred years before. The carpet, for instance, that was brand spanking new, although no spanking had actually been performed upon it as yet. And the dartboard was new and the etched glass of the windows was still relatively unstained by tobacco smoke. The Britannia pub tables looked exactly the same though, as did the eight beer-pulls upon the bar counter, and the jukebox in the corner, and the part-time barman, called Neville.

'Gentlemen,' the part-time barman smiled across his polished bar counter. 'Mercy me, two identical gentlemen. Well, gentlemen both, how might I serve you?'

Will glanced along the row of beer-pump handles. Their buffed enamel shone, their silver tips twinkled.

'We have eight hand-drawn ales on tap,' said the part-time barman, proudly. 'More than any other alehouse in the district. Our selection, which exceeds the Wart and Canker by two, the Bleeding Stump by three, the Weeping Gusset by five, the Suppurating—'

'That one,' said Will, pointing. 'Two pints of that one, please.'

'Large,' said the part-time barman. 'A fine choice. None finer in fact.'

And then, with a keen and practised hand, the barlord drew off two pints of the very very best.

'Four pence,' said he and was paid four pence.

Will urged his other self towards the seat in a cosy corner, motioned to him to sit, placed the two pints upon the table and sat himself down.

'Drink,' he told his other self.

And his other self took up his pint glass and supped upon its contents.

'You are safe now,' Will told him. And Will sipped the pint that was his own. 'This is extremely good ale,' he said.

Will's other self said nothing, but he did drink further ale.

'Listen,' said Will. 'I know you're confused. Very confused. But I'm not going to hurt you. You're me, I know that. And I'm you. I came here from the future. You did that too, didn't you? This place, Brentford. This is your home in the future, isn't it?'

'You're not *me*.' The other Will fairly spat the words out. 'You're one of them. Possessed by demons.'

'Nothing possesses me,' said Will. 'I can assure you of that.'

'Damn right, chief,' said Barry. 'You tell him.'

'And yet you dress as they do. And you speak to the demon that you alone can hear.'

'Ah,' said Will. 'That's not what you think. That's Barry.'

'Balbereth, more like.'

'Barry for short,' said Barry.

'Balbereth!' said the other Will. 'You think to taunt me by assuming my form.'

'He's a nutter, chief. You'll get nothing here. It's a waste of time.'

'Déjà vu?' said Will. 'I recall you saying the same about Mr Wells.'

'There,' said the other Will. 'Converse with your demon. I am weak now, but if I had my strength I'd—' And the other Will raised a fist, rose feebly, then sank back into his chair.

'Feisty, ain't he, chief?'

Will did not reply.

'I'll kill you too,' said the other Will. 'You'll die. You'll all die. I'll kill you all.'

'You really don't want to kill me.' Will drank further Large.

'I really do.' His other self did likewise.

'Ask me anything,' said Will. 'Anything that only *you* know. That I couldn't possibly know if I wasn't you.'

'I won't play your evil games.'

Will shook his head. 'I don't know what to say to convince you. But you and I are the same person. We're both here from the future. How did *you* get here; will you tell me that?'

'I need to go to the toilet.'

'All right,' said Will. And, 'Barlord,' he called to the part-time barman, 'where is your gentlemen's toilet?'

'Door to the left there,' the part-time barman pointed.

'Go on, then,' said Will.

'Chief, he'll be out of a window in a shot. It's what you'd do, isn't it?'

'I thought you wanted to be rid of him.'

'Again.' The other Will pointed a feeble hand. 'Again you converse with your familiar.'

'It isn't what you think. I'll accompany you to the toilet.'

'I'll stay here then. I was only hoping to escape through a window.'

'You're me,' said Will. 'And I'm you, somehow, and I don't understand how. Please tell me. I'll let you go if you do. I promise.'

'And why should I believe your promises?'

'What have you got to lose? If I'd wanted to kill you, I could have done it by now. And if I'd wanted to torture some information out of you, I would have hardly brought you into a public bar.'

'Your evil trickery knows no bounds.'

'Oh, I give up,' said Will. 'Things are complicated enough for me already. I really don't need this. Drink your beer and go your way. I have pressing matters to attend to. My mentor was murdered and I mean to bring his assassin to justice. If you're me then you'll survive. I have no idea what you've been through, but it seems pretty bad. But I'd survive it somehow. Drink up and go. I won't try to stop you.'

The other Will considered his pint, then took it up in a trembly hand and drained it to its very dregs, not that there *were* any dregs, this being the finest ale that there was.

'I can leave?' he said.

'Go on,' said Will. 'But please take care. I have no idea how this works. But it might be that if you were to die, I might also. So please be *very* careful.'

'And I can just leave?'

'I've told you that you can. Go on.'

The other Will put his hands on the tabletop and eased himself up. 'Really leave?' he said.

'Just go,' said Will. 'Here, take some money.' And he fished into his pocket.

The other Will sat back down again. 'Silver,' said he, 'give me silver.'

'As you please.' Will fished out a handful of silver coins and dumped them on the table.

'Yes,' said the other Will. 'All right. Yes.'

'You like silver?' said Will.

'You crossed the river,' said the other Will. 'And now you handle silver. You're not one of them.'

'The lad knows his stuff,' said Barry.

Will didn't answer him.

'I'm not a witch,' said Will. 'If that's what you're thinking. I'm you. I'm really you.'

'Thank God.' The other Will put his hands to his face and began to weep.

He sobbed and he sobbed, and Will looked on and didn't know what to say. He'd have liked to have hugged his other self, for after all it *was* him, but he knew that he didn't dare.

'Don't forget about what happened to David Warner in *Time Cop*,' Barry kept saying.

When the other Will had finally sobbed himself dry, he wiped the last tears from his eyes, looked across at Will and said, 'Fetch me another drink.'

'Are you all right now?' Will asked.

'I'll be fine,' said his other self. 'And I'll be a lot finer with another glass or two of this Large inside me. Take the silver and purchase further pints. Go to it, then.'

'Right,' said Will and he took himself off to the bar.

'Your brother seems somewhat distressed,' said the part-time barman, as he pulled two more perfect pints.

'A family matter,' said Will. 'Do you have any pork scratchings?'

'Certainly do,' said the part-time barman. 'Two packets?'

'Yes please.'

Will returned to his table with two pints and two packets. He placed all down and took his seat once more.

'You really don't know, do you?' said his other self as he tucked greedily into the pork scratchings. 'About what happened to *me*?'

'No,' said Will.

'So you've never met the witches? Somehow you got into this time too, but you've never met the witches?'

'No,' Will shook his head. 'But the women who came to the police station, they were witches, weren't they?'

'They were.'

'So, will you tell me your story?'

'I will,' said the other Will. 'And when I'm done, you'll *really* know what kind of trouble the both of us are in.'

'Oh good,' said Will. 'I'll *really* look forward to *that*.'

24

'It's no fun being the Messiah,' said the other Will, tucking into his pork scratchings. 'In fact, it's a really crap job.'

'I'm sure it is,' said Will. 'But what has that got to do with anything?'

'Because *I am* the Messiah. And *it is* a crap job.'

'He's as mad as a bucket of spanners, chief,' said Barry. 'Let's get him committed to a nice lunatic asylum and head on to Chiswick.'

Will ignored Barry's advice and said to his other self, 'What *are* you talking about?'

'The Promised One,' said the other Will. 'That's what they call me. The saviour of Mankind. The lad who travelled back into the past and thwarted the evil witches' schemes to change history. Ensured the wondrous future to come. That's me, for what it's worth.'

'I really don't understand,' said Will, who didn't.

'When I was born, upon the first of January in the year two thousand, two hundred and two' said the other Will, 'there was rejoicing throughout the world. My family had always lived under the protection of the state, but when I was born I was taken into the London fortress, that had been specially constructed for my protection, where I would be taught all about myself. Who I really was and the fate that I was born to. Then, when I was older, and upon the date that was foretold, the third of March, two thousand, two hundred and twenty, I would enter the time machine and be dispatched back here to do my thwarting of the witches and save the world.'

Will shook his head and made a puzzled face. 'I don't get this,' he said. 'You were born here in Brentford, on the same date as me, and you travelled back in time upon the same date as I did. But I've never heard about any of this Promised One business. Which sky tower were you brought up in?'

'I was born just around the corner. Number seven Mafeking Avenue.'

'No.' Will shook his head. 'All the streets around here were demolished in the twenty-first century. There are twenty-three sky towers, a tramway connecting the borough with London Central, some supermarkets, of course, and—'

'No,' said the other Will. 'You fail to understand me. *That* is the future *you* come from. It's not the same future *I* come from.'

'Oh,' said Will. 'Can you just stop there for a moment. I have to use the toilet.' Will got up from his seat and looked down at his other self. 'You won't run away or anything, will you?'

The other Will shook his wretched head and sank further ale.

Will went off to the toilet.

'Can this be right?' he asked Barry.

'I don't know about right, chief, but it can certainly be possible. In fact, if you think about it, it's more than possible, it's probable.'

'So, let me get this straight. *I* travel back here from *my* future, a future that has no knowledge of all the technical wonders that really went on in the Victorian era, because these so-called witches had somehow managed to suppress and erase all the records. And I stop them from doing their dirty work, thereby changing the future, so that the future I come from, the crappy future with the acid rains and everything falling to pieces, never occurs. The future *I* come from ceases to exist. Never exists. And because I have saved the world, as it were, and as this is recorded history, the world is awaiting the birth of William Starling on the first of January, two thousand, two hundred and two. The birth of the hero who saves history. The Promised One. Is that it?'

'Pretty much so, chief.'

'Except that this Promised One isn't actually the real hero. The real hero who does the actual saving of the world is *me*, this *me* in this toilet, not the me sitting out there.'

'I think that's got it, chief. It's *you* who did the saving, not that poor schmuck. He's just a victim of circumstance, really.'

Will shook his head. 'So how did *he* get back here? Whose time machine did he come in? Did you have anything to do with this, Barry?'

'No, chief, not me. Imagine this wet, imagine this dry, cut my imaginary throat if I tell a lie.'

'What?'

'I'm innocent, chief. I don't know how he got back here. Why don't you ask him?'

Will returned himself to the table and sat himself down.

'You don't believe me, do you?' his other self asked. 'You think I'm some kind of raving lunatic. You think I'm as mad as a bucket of spanners.'

'No,' said Will. 'What you're telling me makes some kind of sense. Tell me what you were told, when you were being brought up, about yourself and the things you did, or would do, when you travelled back to the past.'

'Scripture,' said the other Will. 'Holy Scripture. I was brought up on it, as is everyone else.'

'Holy Scripture?' said Will.

'*The Book Of Rune*,' said the other Will. 'The Holy Scripture of the One World Religion, written by the Master himself, Hugo Rune. Are you not a practising Runee?'

'Not as such,' said Will.

'Then, do you never watch the worldcasts on the reality screens? Have you never seen footage of terrorwitch attacks? Seen a spell bomb go off in a shopping plaza? Seen men turn into turnips?'

'This is getting *really* tricky,' said Will. 'In the future I come from things like that don't happen. I can assure you of this. And there is no *Book Of Rune*.'

'In the future *you* come from.' The other Will spoke these words slowly and unsteadily.

'He's clueing up, chief. Perhaps you'd better change the subject; he might become violent.'

'Just tell me,' said Will. 'I need to understand. Tell me about *The Book Of Rune*. I've got a copy of that back at my hotel, but I've never actually read it.'

'All right. *The Book Of Rune* is a book of prophecy. It was published, privately, and at some considerable expense, by an unknown patron. Some believe it was Queen Victoria herself, but no one knows for sure. It was published in eighteen seventy-five and ridiculed by the public. It predicted that a cabal of witches would attempt to take over the world, but they would be—'

'Thwarted?' Will asked.

'Thwarted, yes, by Rune's magical heir, the Promised One, who would travel from the future, do the thwarting and save mankind. And Rune went on to predict the outcome. Incredible technological advances in the twentieth century, based upon the work of Babbage and Tesla. How the Earth survived the Martian invasion, how the British Empire took control of the entire world, as indeed it did and how Runeology would be established as the world religion by the year

2000, which it was, based of course upon the accuracy of his prophecies.'

'The old scoundrel,' said Will, and there was a grin on his face.

'And of course,' the other Will continued, 'my birth, the date of my birth, and the date that I would return to the past and achieve my great heroic feats.'

'It all makes sense, chief,' said Barry. 'And it's pretty damn clever when you come right down to it.'

'All right,' said Will. 'I follow everything you're saying. But tell me about the time machine. Who built that? What powers it? Is time travel common in your future?'

'Common? No.' And now the other Will laughed. But it was a sick laugh and lacked for humour. 'As the predictions proved, one after another to be correct, and Runeology became *the* religion, scientists realised that if the Promised One was to travel back in time to do his heroic deeds, he would need to have a time machine to travel in. Details of the machine's construction were not included in *The Book of Rune*, you see. So scientists set to work. Because it was of major importance, wasn't it? The hero couldn't go back and save the world without a time machine to travel in. It took one hundred and seventy years of work, but at last it was completed and ready. Just one machine. Billions and billions of pounds spent on work and research, just for me.'

'And they sent you back in it?'

'No,' said the other Will. 'I decided not to go.'

'What?'

'*Of course they sent me back in it! I'm here now, aren't I?*'

'Yes, of course,' said Will. 'Sorry.' He finished his pint of Large. 'Same again?' he asked.

'Yes, please,' said his other self. 'And another packet of pork scratchings. Both these packets are finished.'

Will returned to the bar.

'Incredible,' he whispered behind his hand. 'But logical, I suppose.'

'And I bet I don't even get a mention,' said Barry. 'Typical, that is. Rune takes all the credit, gets himself a place in history, fathers a world religion and not a mention of Barry the Holy Guardian sprout, the real power behind the throne.'

'I thought you were a divine entity, dedicated to serving mankind? Forestalling the End Times and so on. Surely you are above praise.'

'Well, naturally, chief. Naturally.' Barry made grumbling sounds.

'Two of similar, would it be?' asked the part-time barman.

'Indeed,' said Will. 'And two more packets of pork scratchings.'

The part-time barman set to doing the business.

'I'm having a real problem with this,' whispered Will. 'I don't like this at all.'

'Then dump him, chief, let's move on and get the job jobbed.'

'It's getting the job jobbed that's the problem.'

'You'll do fine, chief. It's all in *The Book Of Rune*, probably.'

'That's not what I mean. Logically, I *must* achieve these goals, otherwise my other self wouldn't be sitting over there now. But what will happen to *me* once I've achieved these goals? If history is changed and the future is changed, then the future I come from will never occur. I will cease to exist. What happens to my mum and dad and Tim? If I cease to exist, so do they. My other self will return to the future and get all the praise, but what about me? Will I just vanish along with the future I came from?'

Barry gave this some thought. And he gave it some thought in silence.

'And you too,' whispered Will. 'You don't come from his future. You'll cease to exist too.'

'God's garden!' went Barry. 'Which is why I won't get a mention in *The Book Of Rune*, I'll bet.'

'Difficult times for us both,' whispered Will.

'There you go,' said the part-time barman. 'Two pints of Large and two more packets of pork scratchings. One and two pence please.'

Will paid up, took his purchases and returned to his table.

His other self was staring at Will, rather hard.

'Are you okay?' Will asked.

'I'm—' His other self made stutterings. 'I'm beginning to figure this out. 'It's you . . . isn't it . . . it's you.'

'I'm me,' said Will. 'And so are you.'

'You're the Promised One. You returned to stop the past from being changed. Returned from your future.'

'This would seem to be the case,' said Will.

'Then all the horrors I've suffered. They're all *your* fault!' The feeble fists were waving once again.

'Calm down,' Will told the waver of the feeble fists. 'It's not my fault. How was I to know that some alternative future would be brought into being and that you would exist?'

'You destroyed my life. You destroyed it before I was even born.'

'Your life isn't destroyed. In fact, it seems that you have enjoyed a life of rare privilege. A great deal better than my life.'

'What? Born to fulfil a destiny that was not of my own choosing? Schooled to a fate that was laid out for me? Never allowed friends in case they were witches dedicated to my destruction? Watched over twenty-four hours a day? Never knowing a moment of privacy?'

'I've known hardship,' said Will. 'Attacks have been made on my life.'

'You deserve whatever you get. It's all *your* fault.'

'You ungrateful sod,' said Will. 'You'd be nothing if it wasn't for me.'

'Chief, don't go down this route. It's a hiding to nowhere.'

'And you keep out of it,' said Will.

'Aha!' said his other self. 'Again he speaks to his familiar. I know what you are. You are the Evil One. I am Will Starling and you are the Anti-Will!'

'Turn it in,' said Will, 'or I will have to give you a smack.'

'No, chief, don't touch him. Remember David Warner. Keep thinking David Warner. Never touch your other self.'

'I'm trying to help you,' said Will. 'I'm not the Anti-Will. I am you and you are me. Different futures. Same fellow. We must help each other. We must try and work this thing out.'

'I hate you,' said the other Will.

'That's ridiculous. And it's unfair.'

'Do you have any idea of what I've been through?'

'No,' said Will. 'I haven't. What *have* you been through?'

'Hell,' said the other Will. 'I've been through Hell.'

'I'm sure whatever it was, it wasn't *that* bad.'

'Look at me.' The other Will fluttered his wobbly hands about. 'Look at the state of me. I've been through horrors you wouldn't believe.'

'Would you like to tell me about them?'

'No,' said the other Will. 'I wouldn't. I'd like a bath. I'd like a good meal and then I'd like to hide somewhere safe. Somewhere safe and comfortable. And I'd like to stay there, all on my own, forever.'

'You wouldn't rather just help me get the job jobbed and then return to the future in glory.'

'Return to the future in glory? Are you mad?'

'It's what I'd do,' said Will. 'I'm sure they're getting a reception committee ready for you even now. Parades through the streets, gala dinners, lots of willing groupies. In fact—'

'Won't work, chief.'

'What won't?' Will whispered behind his hand.

'What you're thinking. That *you* return to *his* future and take all the praise if he's not keen. Wouldn't work. *You* can't travel into *his* future.'

'It was just a thought,' whispered Will.

'Mad,' said the other Will. 'Quite mad.'

'Why is it mad?' Will asked.

'Because it's not what happens. It's not what is written in *The Book Of Rune*. The Promised One returns to the past and thwarts the schemes of the evil witches. But he does not return to glory in the future. He dies in the past. Dies in an act of supreme heroism. Gives up his life for the cause of mankind. There's no going back to the future for either of us. We die here.'

'We *what*?'

'Die,' said the other Will. 'Not much of a future, is it?'

25

'But,' said Tim McGregor. 'I mean— Well, die in the past? I mean, you're here now. You didn't die in the past, did you? I mean—'

Tim was sitting in the very place that the other Will had been sitting, three centuries before. It was even the same chair. Will had sat him down there on purpose, of course. Same chair. Same table. Same pub. Same part-time barman actually, but we'll have to get to *that* at some other time.

'Pretty complicated stuff, eh?' said Will. 'Which is why I wanted to go on to drinking halves. I was involved in all this, and *I* have a problem following the plot.'

'Tell me about the chaps at the police station,' said Tim. 'Constable Tenpole Tudor, and Policewoman Higgins and Chief Inspector Sam Maggott. They were from here, right? From now. What were they doing back there?'

'I'll get to that at some other time.' Will chewed upon Tim's pork scratchings. 'These taste exactly the same,' he said. 'But listen, you can imagine my dilemma, can't you? What was I to do? I was sworn to hunt down Rune's murderer—'

'I assume that *wasn't* your other self. He wasn't Jack the Ripper.'

'No,' said Will. 'He wasn't. But, you see, I'd now got myself in pretty deep. Obviously I would do things that would change the future. Obviously, because there was my other self sitting right where you're sitting now. But I wanted to do things of my own free will. Be in charge of my own destiny. Be in control.'

'But hold on,' said Tim. 'Surely the future didn't get changed. I've never seen a copy of *The Book Of Rune*. There's been no war with Mars, or the British Empire ruling the world. Nothing has changed. But, fair dos, you're trying your best to explain it all. So what happened next, and what *had* happened to your other self in the past?'

'Well, what happened next wasn't too much fun and what had

happened to him was no laughing matter at all. You see he'd travelled to the past and—'

'They were waiting for me,' said the other Will. 'The witches. They'd read *The Book Of Rune* too, hadn't they? They knew exactly when I'd arrive. And where. In a rented room in Miller's Court. The room rented by Hugo Rune. He was supposed to be waiting for me there, with a bottle of champagne to toast my safe arrival. But he wasn't there.'

'No,' said Will, 'he was out buying the champagne, or at least *acquiring* champagne. I doubt that he actually paid for it. I met him outside in the street. That's where I appeared.'

'Yes,' said the other Will. 'That would be it. *You* would be the one who met him and was taught by him.'

'Please go on with your story,' said Will. 'There may be a way out of this for both of us.'

'There's no way out. We're doomed.'

'Not necessarily so.'

'That's what I thought. I had a plan you see. When they escorted me to the time machine to send me off to save the world and die in the process, I didn't struggle, I didn't try to escape. I behaved with dignity, because I had a plan.'

'Go on,' said Will.

'Escape,' said the other Will. 'Escape from them. My watchers and my protectors and the witch assassins who were constantly trying to kill me. I planned to escape from them all. I couldn't do it there in the future, but I reasoned that I could in the past. I'd let them send me. I couldn't stop them. But once I was here, I figured that I'd do things my way. I wouldn't play their games. I'd play *my* games. I'd just vanish. No heroics and no death for me. I'd get myself a quiet little job, settle down and marry a nice Victorian girl. Have some kids; maybe they would be my own great- great- great- and-whatever-grandparents. But I wouldn't get involved in any world-savings.'

Will shrugged and smiled a little too. 'That's probably what I would have done,' said he.

'That's exactly what you would have done, chief,' said Barry.

'So what happened?' Will asked.

'I've told you what happened, they were waiting for me. The moment I appeared in the time machine they grabbed me and the time machine.'

'Hang about,' said Will. 'The witches captured you and they

captured the time machine. When I first met Rune and he took me to his lodgings, his room was a mess, he said the witches had been there. They captured you there, did they?'

'That's what happened,' said the other Will.

'So the witches then had their own time machine?'

'Obviously.'

'Obviously,' said Will with some degree of thoughtfulness. 'Except that I have been told another story entirely. All about a time machine that was built here in the Victorian era and then was stolen. All sorts of things in fact.'

'I don't know what you're talking about,' said the other Will. 'There's only *one* time machine.'

'Then I have been lied to,' Will wiggled his finger into his right ear. 'In fact I've been told a right pack of lies.'

'No, come on, chief, it's not what you think.'

Will turned his face away from his other self. 'It's exactly what I think,' he said. 'You lied to me, Barry. All that talk about you being fitted into Mr Wells' time machine.'

'I was,' said Barry. 'Well, for a bit anyway, so Mr Wells could have a little test of it himself. Rune knew he wouldn't be able to resist it and Rune wanted to borrow some more money from him.'

'So *you* never travelled into *my* future?' It wasn't *you* who brought me here?'

'No, chief. The witches sent their terminators in your other self's time machine.'

'Then why didn't you tell me this?'

'Because, chief, I was hoping that you'd never bump into your other self. He's just complicating the issue.'

'So you knew he was here all the time?'

'I might have, chief.'

'*You might have?*'

'You're at it again,' said Will's other self. 'Conversing with your demon.'

'I'm *not* conversing with a demon!' Will turned back to his other self. 'It's not like that. Although,' and he said these words to himself, '*I'm beginning to wonder.*'

'I heard that, chief. And it's not true. I'm one of the good guys. I'm just trying to protect you.'

'Perhaps,' said Will and he turned back to face his other self. 'Please tell me,' said Will, 'what happened to you, after you arrived in this time? These witches, they captured you?'

'Yes, that's what they did. They were waiting for me in Rune's lodgings. They grabbed *me* and they took the time machine. I was captured. I was helpless.'

'So why didn't they just kill you and have done with it?' Will asked.

'Good question, chief.'

'Good question,' said the other Will.

'So what's the answer?'

'I'm the answer,' said the other Will. 'I told them the truth. That I didn't want to be any Messiah. That I just wanted to be left alone. I was terrified by them. They're horrible. Fearful. They couldn't understand that. They were expecting some kind of fearless superhero. And they kept asking me about a painting, called *The Fairy Feller's Masterstroke*. It's mentioned in *The Book of Rune*. But I told them I'd never heard of, nor seen, such a picture, because I haven't. So they sent a robot into the future in the time machine. But the time machine returned without it, so they sent another one and the time machine never returned. But it did return, didn't it, and you were in it.'

Will nodded, thoughtfully. This *did* seem to tie up a lot of loose ends. 'So then they just kept you imprisoned,' he said.

The other Will nodded, glumly. 'They tormented me, forced me to stitch Chiswick Townswomen's Guild needlepoint cushions for them, and stuff lavender bags. They even made me judge the most-blackest black cat competition.'

'Doesn't sound all that bad,' said Will.

'And they kept me in a cage and fed me on rats.'

'Rats?'

'And worms,' said the other Will.

'Nasty,' said Will.

'Very nasty,' said the other Will. 'For months and months and months in a filthy cellar. In a cage. I planned my escape. Rats' jaws I used. To saw through the bars. Hundreds of rats' jaws. It took me over a year, but I finally escaped.'

'That's dreadful,' said Will. 'Really dreadful.'

'And it's all *your* fault.'

'It's not *my* fault. But how did you come to be covered in blood and arrested as being Jack the Ripper?'

'I didn't know what to do. The only thing I could think of was to find Hugo Rune. Try and reason with him. I was pretty messed up. I *am* pretty messed up.'

'I see,' said Will. 'And after the witches discovered that you'd escaped, they went looking for you and I suppose that eventually they came to the conclusion that you'd go looking for Hugo Rune, which is why they sent one of their robots to Rune's room, which was where *I* was. Which is when I met Barry.'

'Barry, your demon?'

'He's *not* my demon. But you were arrested, covered in blood. What happened to you?'

'I saw it,' said the other Will. 'I was hiding in an alleyway. I saw it all. I was out of my mind. I'd been imprisoned, tortured, fed on rats and worms, but I'd escaped and then I saw *that*.'

'What did you see?' Will asked.

'I saw *it*. The thing that killed those women. I saw it kill Hugo Rune. I saw it. I saw it kill and I was showered with the blood of its killing.'

'It?' said Will. 'A robot, was it?'

'Not a robot. Not a person. Something far worse. Something utterly monstrous. I saw it. And then I blacked out. I don't know what happened after that. Days must have passed, and the next thing I knew I was being hauled into the Whitechapel police station, accused of being Jack the Ripper. I even thought I was, when they arrested me.'

'And then I rescued you from the cell.'

The other Will hung his head. 'That's it,' he said. 'That's what happened.'

'But what was this thing? This thing that killed those women and killed Hugo Rune. If it wasn't a robot and wasn't a man?'

'What was it?' the other Will stared at Will with wide mad eyes. 'What do you think it was? What is it that witches worship? What is it that seeks to control this world? Reorder history so that *it* is in control? Not any man and not any robot. That thing I saw was the devil himself, Will.

'That thing was Satan.'

26

'Satan,' said Will, and he sighed. It was a long sigh, a deep sigh, a heartfelt sigh. It was the sigh of one who had had quite enough. 'I've had quite enough,' said Will.

His other self looked on. Somewhat bitterly, Will felt. Somewhat accusingly.

'Listen,' said Will. 'It's not my fault. Do you understand this? *It's not my fault.*'

'It *is* your fault,' said the other Will. 'You got me into this mess and you have to get me out.'

'Why *me*?' Will threw up his hands, spilling his drink all over himself. 'Damn,' he continued, 'look at what you've made me do, all over my expensive suit.'

'Expensive suit? My clothes are in tatters, covered in blood and you have the nerve to—'

'Stop,' said Will. 'Just stop. It's clear that you've been through terrible times. The rats and the worms and everything.'

'And the needlepoint,' said the other Will. 'And having to stuff those lavender bags.'

'All right, you suffered dreadful privations. But *I* wouldn't be here if it wasn't for *you*. It was *your* time machine that brought *me* here. If anything, it's all *your* fault.'

'I don't really think that follows, chief. If it's anyone's fault then the blame must lie with—'

'Shut up!' shouted Will. 'It's not *my* fault and it's not *your* fault. If it's anyone's fault, it's Hugo Rune's fault.'

'The Master was faultless,' said the other Will. 'It says so in Scripture.'

'But he wrote the Scripture!'

'Then it must be true, mustn't it? Scripture doesn't lie.'

Will dusted beer froth from his shirt front. 'Scripture doesn't lie, eh?' he said thoughtfully. 'And your entire future society is based upon this Scripture, is it?'

'It brought peace to the world.'

'It brought you here to die.'

'That's all *your* fault.'

'Turn it in,' said Will. 'This is getting us nowhere.'

'Perhaps you should just put him out of his misery, chief. Get someone to employ the Dimac Death Touch for you. It's being cruel to be kind.'

Will thought the words 'SHUT UP!' as loudly as he could.

'Wah!' went Barry. 'Don't do that, chief. It gives me a headache and as I'm all head, that's a lot of ache.'

'I don't mean you any harm,' said Will to his other self. 'In fact, quite the reverse. I don't want you to die here. I don't want anyone to die.'

'I want plenty of people to die,' said the other Will. 'All those witches that tormented me. I want them to die. I'll kill the lot of them if I get the chance.'

'Really?' said Will. 'You'd do that, would you?'

'Slow down, chief. I know what you're thinking.'

'I'd kill them all,' said the other Will.

'Then maybe I can help you out of this. I have something in my head.'

'An idea?' said the other Will.

'Not as such.'

'Forget it, chief. I'm not going into his bonce, it's already occupied and anyway, he's stone bonker.'

'Do you have a long, sharp pencil about your person?' Will asked.

'No, chief, let's be reasonable about this.'

'But you both share the same goal,' Will whispered into his hand. 'You could train him up, Barry. He is *me*, isn't he?'

'No, chief. We're a team, you and me. You can't break up a team. It's like Marks and Spencer, or Burke and Hare, or even Jekyll and Hyde, who live just around the corner; we—'

'SILENCE!' Will thought. 'All right,' he said to his other self. 'We will speak more of these things. For now I can say only this, trust me. I am you and you are me and there is no point in us arguing. I suggest we return to my hotel room.'

'Why?' asked the other Will.

'So you can take a bath, have a shave, eat a splendid lunch and so that *I* can have a flick through *The Book Of Rune*. It does tell exactly how *you* thwart the witches, doesn't it?'

'It tells exactly how *you* thwart them,' said the other Will.

To add an extra something to the drive back, Will steered Silver the horse around the Borough of Brentford first, to take in more of its beauty. And as both Wills still felt somewhat dry of throat, they also took in some of Brentford's other drinking houses. Although not any of those that the part-time barman of the Flying Swan had mentioned. They visited the Four Horsemen, the Shrunken Head and the Princess Royal.

They ran their way through the fine and hand-drawn ales of Brentford, savouring each and every drop that they didn't spill down themselves. And as the hours passed and the glasses emptied, talk became merrier and the many troubles the two of them shared were pushed somewhat to the side, although Will remained ever at arm's length of his other self, for fear of the terrible *Time Cop*/David Warner consequences that might occur should they actually touch each other.

'Chiesh,' went Barry. 'I'm somewhat schoozled here, shouldn't we be getting back?'

'So, I was doing *The Times* crossword, the other day,' said Will. He and his other self now sat in the Hands of Orloc, which is in Greendragon Lane, on Brentford's east side. 'And I managed to answer every single clue, except one.'

'And what was that?' The other Will quaffed further ale. He had a healthier pallor now, which is one more reason for drinking beer, as if one more should be needed.

'Overloaded postman,' said Will.

'Overloaded postman?' The other Will stroked at his chin and missed. 'Overloaded postman? How many letters?'

'Thousands!' Will spluttered laughter into his beer. 'That was why he was so overloaded.'

'Thousands,' said the other Will. 'It must have been a very large crossword.'

'No,' said Will. 'It was a joke. Overloaded postman. Thousand of letters. Get it?'

'What *is* a postman?' asked the other Will. 'A man who sells posts, would it be?'

'It's a joke.' Will wiped beer froth from his mouth. 'A joke. Surely you know what a joke is.'

'I don't feel quite right,' said the other Will. 'Is there something wrong with this cordial we've been drinking?'

'It's beer,' said Will. 'You're getting drunk, that's all.'

'Drunk?' said the other Will. 'What is drunk?'

'What is drunk? Don't they have booze in your world?'

'Booze? There is *no* booze in my world. Booze is evil. There has been no booze since the mid two-thousands. Is that what we've been drinking? *Booze*?'

'No booze?' Will said back in his chair. 'You come from a world without booze?'

'Booze is forbidden. It says so in Scripture. The Master foreswore all hard liquor. He lived upon dry bread and water all his life, and only the occasional sprout to give him iron.'

'What wash that?' slurred Barry.

'Foreswore hard liquor?' Will laughed heartily. 'That's a joke if ever I heard one. And what about the bottle of champagne he was going to greet you with?'

'I don't understand. Although I feel, I don't know, I feel—'

'Happy?' Will asked.

'Yes, that's it. That must be it. I've heard of happy, but I've never experienced it before.'

'*Never?*' Will's face fell. 'You've never been *happy*?'

'I've seen people laughing. Lots of times. But I never knew why they laughed. They never laughed when they were with me. They always had grave expressions.'

'Now *that* is evil.'

'But I do feel it. I feel – happy. Can I have some more of this booze?'

'But it's against Scripture.'

'Stuff Scripture!' said the other Will. 'Stuff everything. I won't play by the rules of Scripture. I'll be free of Scripture. I'll be free of everything.'

'Once you've thwarted the witches,' said Will.

'Once *you've* thwarted the witches. Tell me another joke. I don't want to think about witches. We weren't thinking about witches, were we? We were thinking about being happy.'

'We were,' said Will. 'I'll get us in another drink.'

And he rose unsteadily and went off to do so.

The other Will sat staring dreamily into space.

'I think things are going rather well, squire,' said a voice in his head. 'I think we can pull this thing off and come up trumps all round.'

'Who said that?' The other Will's eyes widened and he stared all around and about.

'It's me, squire. Larry, your Holy Guardian sprout. I've been trying to get through to you for ages. The beer has eased the passage, as it were.'

'Who's saying this?' The other Will's head turned this way and that.

'Me, Larry, Barry's brother. They thought I was done for in the Great Fire of London, but I wasn't and now I'm in your head. I'm your protector. We can beat this other schmuck, we have him eating right out of our hands. Well *your* hands; I don't have any.'

The other Will clutched at his head. 'I am possessed!' he howled, which drew the attention of several other patrons of the Hands of Orloc, amongst them a big bargee and his smaller counterpart, who had stopped off for the night in Brentford (which is upon Thames), and a lady in a straw hat, who was hawking copies of the *War Cry*.

'Great scabs of scurvy!' said the big bargee. 'Tell me, Charlie; ain't that the bloke we had a punch-up with the other day?'

'The undertaker's lad, with the parsnip up his bum?' said his smaller companion. 'I do believe it is.'

'Get out of my head!' cried the other Will, beating at his temples with his fists.

'Don't go all stone bonker, squire,' said Larry. 'I'm one of the good guys, I'm here to help.'

'I am cursed.' The other Will beat some more at his temples.

'Definitely the same geezer,' said the small bargee. 'Must tread the boards. Seems to have only the one act.'

Will eased himself between big bargee and small. 'Excuse me gents,' he said. 'Beer coming through.'

'Gawd damn my eyes,' said the big bargee. 'It's another of them and just the same.'

Will glanced up at the big bargee.

'Oh,' said he. 'It's you.'

'Can I interest you in a copy of the *War Cry*?' asked the lady in the straw hat to Will. 'It's to help our missionaries save the savages of darkest Africa. I'm hoping they'll save a couple for me.'

'What?' said Will.

'Get out of my head!' shouted the other Will.

'Here,' said a gatherer of the pure who had wandered far from home upon this day in search of the white stuff,* 'I recognise that voice.'

* It was the white dog poo they collected in those days for the tanning. You just don't see white dog poo about any more, do you?

'I saw him first,' said the big bargee.

'And me second,' said his smaller counterpart.

'I know *you*,' said the lady in the straw hat to Will.

'Chiesh,' said Barry. 'I think I'll take my nap now.'

'Squire,' said Larry. 'Stop beating at your temples. It's rocking me all about.'

'Aaaaagh!' went the other Will.

'Oh dear, oh dear, oh dear,' said Will.

And then as surely as night follows day, or seagulls follow a mackerel boat, or the dustcart follows the Lord Mayor's show, or drunken girls wearing halos and angels wings and enjoying a hen night in Brighton sing 'follow the leader, leader, leader,' before getting ruthlessly shagged by young men who have been following *them* from bar to bar all evening, a bit of a fight got started.

And things got somewhat out of hand.

And.

'Lord Peter Whimsy,' said the presiding magistrate, Mr Justice Doveston, at the Brentford Magistrate's court, as this was the name Will had given to the police who had arrested him. 'You are charged with the following crimes. That you and your twin brother entered the local hostelry known as the Hands of Orloc in Greendragon lane, in or about the time of eight thirty yesterday evening, in a state of advanced inebriation and did there cause a common affray. That you did employ Dimac, the deadliest of all the martial arts, whereby a fingertip's pressure can maim and disfigure, upon Mr Michael Mugwump, otherwise known as the big bargee; Mr Charles Windsor, otherwise known as his smaller counterpart, constables Norman Meek and Reginald Mild. Mrs—'

A cough from the gallery was silenced by an usher of the court.

'—otherwise known as the lady in the straw hat, Mr Nigel Dempster, society columnist for *The Brentford Mercury* newspaper—'

'Eh?' said Will. He sat as far as he could from his other self upon a bench in the dock, flanked by burly police constables; burly police constables who sported bandaged heads and bruised chins; burly police constables named Meek and Mild.

'– the cast of the musical *Joseph and the Technicolor Dreamcoat*, which is presently enjoying its first run in the West End, and sundry others—'

'I never hit anyone called Sundry Others,' said Will.

The magistrate consulted his notes. 'Ah no,' he said. 'It's not "sundry others", it's Mr Montague Summers, historian and occultist.'

'He had it coming,' said Will. 'He hit me with his rhythm stick.'

'Three fat persons, click, click, click,' sang Barry.*

'And "a wandering-minstrel-I-a-thing-of-heirs-and-braces",' said the magistrate. 'Who is a dyslexic.'

'He hit me first,' said Will. 'With his janbo.'

'And so, how do you plead?'

'Innocent,' said Will. 'My brother and I were set upon by ruffians; we were only defending ourselves.'

'And the two policemen, constables Meek and Mild, whom you laid unconscious when they arrived upon the scene of the disturbance?'

'I did no such thing,' said Will.

'A bystander says that a friend of his saw you.'

'That's hearsay,' said Will.

'No,' said the magistrate, 'Hearsay was a short-lived, manufactured vocal harmony group. You are, however also accused of assaulting Little Tich, the popular music hall entertainer.'

'He stood upon one of my big boots,' said Little Tich, poking his nose over the gallery rail.

'Never laid a foot on him,' said Will. 'This is all a case of mistaken identity.'

'Might I approach the bench, your honour?' said a gentleman in a gown and a wig and a pair of high-heeled boots.

'And who might you be?' asked Mr Justice Doveston.

'I am the counsel for the defence, Freddie "the loser" Lonsdale.'

'Eh?' said Will.

'Do I know you?' asked Mr Justice Doveston.

'Of course you do, your honour,' said Freddie. 'I only live around the corner. I'm the duty counsel for the defence. When I'm not gathering the pure.'

'Are you a Freemason?' asked the magistrate.

'Not as such,' said Freddie.

'Then things look very bad for your client.'

'On the face of it, yes,' said Freddie. 'But you never know, I might strike it lucky this time. Sooner or later I'm bound to get it right.'

'I admire your spirit,' said the magistrate. 'Although you smell a bit iffy. But I don't think you'll win this one, and the penalty for common affray is death.'

'It never is,' said Freddie.

* Which is allowable and not a breach of copyright.

'It is, today,' said Mr Justice Doveston, 'because today is Tuesday.'

'Ah,' said Freddie. 'I see. That makes sense. Still, I'll try my best, and if I foul up again, well, tomorrow is another day. Wednesday, I suppose.'

'If I might approach the bench,' said another fellow.

'And who might you be?' asked the honourable one.

'Gwynplaine Dhark,' said the fellow. 'Freemason and counsel for the prosecution.'

'He's one of *them.*' The other Will shrank down upon the bench that he shared with Will. The other Will was holding his head; he had the first hangover of his life. It was a blinder, but at least, now sober, he could no longer hear the voice of a certain Larry.

'*Them?*' whispered Will.

'Them,' said the other Will. 'The witches. That man is in league with the devil. He made me judge the most-blackest black cat competition.'

'What?' went Will.

'What was that?' asked Mr Justice Doveston.

'I object,' said Will, rising to his feet.

'Shut it,' said Constable Meek, applying his truncheon to Will's head.

'Ow!' went Will, sitting down again.

'I *do* object,' went Will, standing up again.

Constable Meek raised his truncheon once more.

'Less of that please, constable,' said the honourable magistrate. 'You can do that at your leisure down in the cells, but not here.'

'Your honour,' said Mr Gwynplaine Dhark. 'I was summonsed here late last night from Scotland Yard, when the mugshots of these twin malcontents were faxed over there from Brentford police station. One of these men is an escaped criminal, who broke out of his cells at Whitechapel police station. He is indeed none other than Jack the Ripper.'

'Ooooooh!' went the folk who packed the gallery.

'Knew it,' said the lady in the straw hat, who sat among them. 'The one in the smart suit, it'll be. There's something about his eyes. He's got murderer's eyes. You can always tell. My late husband had burglar's eyes. And he was a cutlery salesman. Which is the exception that proves the rule, in my opinion.'

'Madam,' said Mr Justice Doveston, 'I must ask you to remain silent, or I will be forced to have you thrown from the court and into a muddy puddle.'

'You have lovely eyes, your honour,' said the lady in the straw hat. 'Blue as a bruised behind and clear as an author's conscience.'

'Thank you,' said the magistrate. 'You can stay. And I'll see you in my chambers at lunchtime.'

'Your honour,' said Mr Gwynplaine Dhark, 'I don't think it will be necessary to keep you until lunchtime. I have here a crudely forged document signed by Her Majesty herself, God bless Her, to the effect that both the accused are to be transported at once to Tyburn for immediate public execution.' Mr Gwynplaine Dhark handed this document to the magistrate.

'Seems sound enough to me.' Mr Justice Doveston exchanged a Masonic wink with the counsel for the prosecution.

'No!' cried Will.

And 'No!' too cried the other Will.

And down came two truncheons in perfect harmony.

'Well, I'm done here,' said Freddie 'the loser' Lonsdale. 'You can't win them all. Or in my case, none at all. Such is life.'

'Taken like the man you are,' said Mr Gwynplaine Dhark. 'I can get you a front row seat at the execution, if you'd like one. Bring the wife, it's always a good day out.'

'Thank you very much indeed.'

'I object!' Will covered his head with his hands to shelter his skull.

'Object?' said Mr Doveston. 'It's a bit late for objections, surely? You should be showing remorse, it might lighten your sentence.'

'Really?'

'No,' said the magistrate, 'only joking.'

And he laughed.

And Mr Gwynplaine Dhark laughed. And Freddie 'the loser' Lonsdale laughed. And the constables laughed. And the lady in the straw hat laughed. And the big bargee and the small bargee and all the folk in the public gallery laughed too.

'I don't think I'll ever get the hang of humour,' said the other Will.

'I *do* object,' said Will. 'Please hear me out.'

'Go on then,' said the magistrate. 'I'm a fair man. Say your piece and then I'll pass sentence and we'll send you off to your execution.'

'I need a moment,' said Will. 'Just a moment. I have to think.'

'Would you like me to adjourn the court?' Mr Justice Doveston asked.

'Yes please,' said Will.

'Then I will.'

'Thank you,' said Will.

'Only joking.' And all and sundry, including Mr Montague Summers, laughed again.

'Lost on me,' said the other Will.

'Just a moment,' said Will. 'Please, just a moment.'

'Clerk of the court,' said Mr Justice Doveston. 'I am going to give the accused "just a moment". How long will that be, exactly?'

The clerk of the court flicked through legal tomes. 'Well,' said he, 'in Bacon versus the British Empire, the defendant, accused of subversion and intent to knob one of Her Majesty's (God bless Her) ladies-in-waiting, was granted a "moment" to reconsider his statement, that "she was gagging for it." The "moment" in question was precisely two "ticks" and three quarters of a "jiffy".'

'And is that a precedent?'

'Well, I can refer you also to Shields versus Carroll, two pugilists who both sued the other for "hitting in the face in the ring". On that occasion—'

'I'm bored,' said Mr Justice Doveston. 'I will grant the accused three "ticks", one "jiffy" and "half-a-sec"', because I'm such a very nice man.'

'He is,' said the lady in the straw hat. 'Lovely eyes. Just like my Malcolm, although he was a bit weird. Had this thing about tubas, thought they were golden toilet bowls. He went to see the London Symphony Orchestra play one night and—'

'Madam,' said Mr Justice Doveston.'

'Sorry, your worship,' said the lady in the straw hat.

'Right then,' said Mr Justice Doveston. 'Three "ticks", one "jiffy" and "half-a-sec" ' starting—' And he took out his gold Babbage Hunter digital watch and scrutinised his face. 'Now.'

There was silence in the court and all eyes turned towards Will.

Will raised a hand to cover his mouth. The wrist of this hand wore a handcuff. As did Will's other wrist.

'You have to do something for me, Barry,' whispered Will.

'Zzzzzzz,' went Barry.

'Barry, wake up. This is important.'

'Only joking, chief. I'm on the case.'

'Then you have to do something for me *now*. You're supposed to be my Holy Guardian sprout and a time travelling sprout, to boot. Get me out of here.'

'No sweat, chief. We're out of here.'

'*And* my other self.'

'What, chief?'

'Well, I can't just go without him, can I? They'll execute him.'

'Nothing I can do about that, chief, sorry.'

'Work your magic, Barry. Get us both out of here.'

'No can do, chief. If he didn't have a sitting tenant in his head, then I could do it. I could move two people through time simultaneously. But he does have, so I can't.'

'Well, stir the tenant into action, time's running out.'

'Time's running out,' said Mr Justice Doveston.

'Tell you what, chief. I'll just take you and—'

'That won't do, Barry. I can't just leave my other self to die. I can't. That's all there is to it. But, hold on, you've given me an idea, a brilliant idea. We'll *whisper, whisper, whisper.*'

'Why all the *whisper whisper whisper*, chief?'

'Because I don't want to ruin the surprise.' Will whispered some more.

'That's a bad idea,' said Barry. 'In fact, that's a *really bad* idea.'

'Time's up,' said Mr Justice Doveston. 'I trust you made good use of your three "ticks", one "jiffy" and 'half-a-sec"'.'

'I did,' said Will, who now it appeared, wore a complete change of clothing. 'I have decided to discontinue the services of my counsel, Mr Freddie 'the loser' Lonsdale and engage a new counsel for the defence.'

'Is that allowable?' Mr Justice Doveston asked the clerk of the court.

The clerk of the court consulted further legal tomes.

'Well,' said he, 'in the Crown versus Hill, the defendant Mr Graham Hill, manager of the Big Cock Inn, Tillet, Herts, who had been accused of an anarchist bomb outrage upon the German Embassy, there was—'

'I'm yawning again,' said Mr Justice Doveston.

'It's all above board,' said the clerk of the court. 'And on the square and on the level and Masonic things of that nature generally.'

'Then I have no objection. Wheel in your new counsel for the defence, Lord Whimsy. If he's suddenly on hand. *Is he?*'

'He is, your honour.' Will rose to his feet, and smiled towards the door of the court. 'I would like to introduce my counsel for the defence. Mr Timothy McGregor.'

27

The door of the courtroom opened and Tim McGregor appeared in the opening. Tim smiled upon the assembled multitude, at the magistrate and the gathered everybodies and up at Will. It was a somewhat sheepish smile. It somewhat lacked for confidence.

'This is such a bad idea, chief,' said Barry. 'I could have got you anyone: the now legendary Mike Mansfield, solicitor to the stars; Robert Shapiro and "The Dream Team" – they got O.J. Simpson off; or Vincent Lugosi, or Rumpole of the Bailey, or even Quincey – he never loses a case. Or Boyd QC, or Kavanagh QC. But you choose your mate Tim.'

'He's my half-brother and my best friend,' said Will. 'And I've told him everything now. And I had to go forward and save him anyway. I couldn't let him get killed.'

'But he knows nothing about being a counsel for the defence.'

'He'll do okay. And remember I'm doing things *my* way.'

'And brilliantly too, I don't think.'

'What was that, Barry?'

'I said, "brilliantly too, you won't sink".'

'As if you did! You sarcastic little sod.'

'What was that, chief?'

'Nothing, Barry.'

'Your honour,' said Tim McGregor, mooching into the courtroom. He wore his long black leather coat and had fastened his abundant hair behind his head in an abundant ponytail. He carried a bulging briefcase and continued with his smiling. 'My client has acquainted me with the details of this case and I feel that I can offer a defence that will prove to exonerate him and his brother of all charges.'

Mr Gwynplaine Dhark glared at Tim.

Tim felt his bladder pressing for an adjournment to the gents.

'I object,' said Mr Gwynplaine Dhark.

'Upon what grounds?' asked Mr Justice Doveston.

'Upon the grounds that this may prove prejudicial to myself.'

'These are somewhat unusual grounds,' said Mr Justice D. 'Do we have a precedent for them?'

The clerk of the court consulted his tomes once again.

'No, don't bother,' said Mr Justice Doveston. 'Frankly, I can't be arsed to listen. Let's hear Mr McGregor out. Hear what he has to say.'

'Thank you, your honour,' said Tim. 'I will seek to prove that my client is an innocent man. And so is his twin brother. That they have been wrongly accused and that a conspiracy exists to overthrow the British Government, destroy the technology of the British Empire and plunge the world into a new Dark Age. And that the root cause of this conspiracy is a cabal of witches who represent themselves as The Chiswick Townswomen's Guild.'

'Grrrr!' went Mr Gwynplaine Dhark.

'This sounds most interesting,' said Mr Justice Doveston. 'Will it take long, do you think?'

'A couple of months, perhaps,' said Tim. 'I'll be calling a lot of witnesses, including Her Majesty the Queen (God bless Her), Lord Charles Babbage, Mr Nikola Tesla, Mr Sherlock Holmes, and countless others.

'Sounds like a lot of fun,' said the magistrate. 'We don't usually get a group of celebrities like that in this courtroom.'

'I object,' said Mr Gwynplaine Dhark. 'This counsel is only seeking to muddy the waters. This is an open and shut case. Tyburn's tree awaits these madmen. It is time for them to dance a jig for Jack Ketch.'

'Well, naturally I appreciate that. But imagine having Her Majesty—'

'God bless Her,' said all those present.

'Quite so,' said the magistrate. 'Imagine having Her Majesty right here in this courtroom.'

'I can imagine that,' said Mr Gwynplaine Dhark. 'Legs in the air and backwards over the bench.'

'Pardon me?'

'It is outrageous, your honour. Her Majesty would never consent to give evidence.'

'She already has,' said Tim. 'I've just come from Buckingham Palace. And I've spoken, by telephone, to all the others; twenty-three in all. I am well prepared.'

'See,' said Will to Barry. 'Tim's on the case.'

'This is never going to work, chief.'

'It will, Barry. And with no violence and killing and with me and my other self walking free from the court and not dying. And the witches getting arrested and—'

'Dhark the warlock too?' said Barry. 'He'll just put his hands up and be led quietly to the cells, will he?'

'One thing at a time, Barry.'

'You're on such a wrong 'n here, chief.'

'Well, it can't hurt to give it a go.'

'And I shall go on to prove—' – Tim McGregor had continued speaking throughout Will's brief conversation with Barry '– that Mr Gwynplaine Dhark is none other than a warlock working for Satan himself, and so must be put to torture and burned alive at the stake.'

'That sounds like a lot of fun, too,' said Mr Justice Doveston.

Mr Gwynplaine Dhark glared even harder at Tim, and Tim felt boils breaking out around his willy.

'This is never going to work, chief,' said Barry. 'This is such a bad idea.'

Will whispered once more behind his hand. 'I have no intention of being executed,' he whispered, 'nor letting my other self get executed. And if this cabal of witches really exists, and some psychopathic killer, who my other self thinks is Satan, is connected with them, well, let's get it all out in the open. Let's bring them all into this court. Let's see what happens.'

'It's a really duff plan, chief.'

'And you had a better one?'

'It's all in *The Book Of Rune*, chief.'

'Which you'd neglected to mention.'

'It would have been cheating. But I'd have got you through it without *The Book Of Rune*. Got you to do the right thing.'

'And I'd have ended up dead.'

'Not necessarily so, chief. Your other self would, but that's his fate. We can't mess around with that.'

'I can do what I want, Barry. And I want to do things my way.'

'It will end in disaster, chief. Let me get you out of here, now.'

'Get *us* out of here, now. My other self and me.'

'Can't do it, chief, sorry.'

'Then we'll just have to do things my way.'

Barry made groaning sounds.

'And save the world,' Tim was still continuing.

'Do *what*?' asked Mr Justice Doveston.

'My client,' said Tim McGregor. 'He will save the world. This is his destiny. His fate, we can't mess about with that.'

'We'll see,' said Mr Gwynplaine Dhark.

'I think,' said Mr Justice Doveston, that I will adjourn the court now. It's getting near to lunchtime and because of the nature of this case, I feel it best that members of the paparazzi and the British Broadcasting Company wireless service be alerted. This will give the Borough of Brentford the kind of publicity it has always needed. People don't appreciate Brentford, they don't understand it. A case like this will put Brentford on the map.'

Mr Gwynplaine Dhark made snarling noises. Sulphurous fumes issued from his mouth. The whites of his eyes became black.

'So,' said Mr Justice Doveston. 'Court adjourned for two hours. Lady in the straw hat up to my chambers for a bit of how's-your-father. And Mr Dhark—'

'Yes your honour?'

'Clean your teeth,' said the magistrate. 'Your breath smells something wicked.'

The cell had been recently decorated in pastel shades with a nautical theme. A lifebelt framed the window, through which could be seen that tent of blue the prisoner calls the sky. Several driftwood boats hung upon the wall beside the door and the customary straw pallet had been replaced by a hammock. Upon this hammock sat the other Will. Upon a throw rug with seagull motifs sat Will and lounging by the door stood Tim, attempting to smoke a Victorian cigarette and grinning all over his face.

'Isn't this just entirely brilliant?' said Tim, coughing somewhat.

Will managed less than half a smile.

The other Will managed nothing but a frown.

'But it is,' Tim gave the cell a twice-over, for he had already given it the once. 'I'd imagined rats and water dripping down the walls.'

The other Will made groaning sounds.

Will said, 'You are up for this, aren't you, Tim?'

'I am,' Tim grinned if anything more broadly. 'And this *is* brilliant. Thanks for bringing me back here with you from the future. I'm loving this, I really am.'

'I haven't introduced you,' said Will to the other Will. 'This is my—'

'Brother,' said the other Will. 'It has to be; he looks just like *my* brother. Apart from the silly hair and the ridiculous coat.'

'Your brother has those, does he?' Tim asked.

'No,' said the other Will. 'You do.'

Tim's grin hardly faded. 'He's as much fun as you said he was,' he said to Will. 'So what's going to happen next?'

'Shall we have a look at *The Book Of Rune* and find out?'

'That's cheating, chief.'

'I'm doing things my way, Barry.'

Tim delved into his briefcase and pulled out *The Book Of Rune*. 'Picked it up from your room at the Dorchester, as you requested. There's a bit of bother there, by the way. Apparently you paid a week up front when you arrived at the hotel, but your cheque bounced. I don't think you'd better go back.'

'Perfect,' Will sighed.

'You didn't *really* want to pay for the room, did you, chief?' Barry asked. 'You are Rune's magical heir, well, sort of. You're following in his footsteps. Your money's in a different account.'

'Let's have a look at the book,' said Will and Tim handed it over.

'You're wasting your time,' said the other Will. 'There's nothing about this in Scripture.'

'There isn't?' said Will.

'Of course there isn't. I know Scripture by heart. I've had it drummed into me all my life. Do you think that if it said I'd get drunk in a Brentford pub, get arrested and then put on trial for my life, I would have let it happen?'

'Well, I'd like to see exactly how I'm supposed to do the thwarting of the witches.'

'Thwarting,' said Tim. 'I like that.'

'We're frankly sick of the word,' said Will.

'Then you could use "confounding" or even "trouncing" or even "vanquishing". Or "creaming". That's a good word, one of my favourites.'

'I've never heard you use it.'

'One of my *new* favourites.'

Will flicked through *The Book Of Rune*. 'My goodness,' he said. 'This is all terribly exciting. It reads like a Lazlo Woodbine thriller.'

'Never heard of those.' The other Will jiggled about on the hammock. 'I'm really hungry,' he said. 'Do you think they'll serve us lunch, or will they just starve us?'

'I've already ordered lunch,' said Tim. 'A delivery from The Flying Swan. It's called a sowman's lunch. It includes a lot of pork scratchings. But go on, Will. What's a Lazlo Woodbine thriller?'

'Stumbled on them by accident,' said Will, 'when I was downloading books from the British Library. I was looking for stuff by Sir

Arthur Conan Doyle, and the Woodbine books had been filed there by mistake. Woodbine was a nineteen fifties American genre detective, the greatest of them all. He worked only four locations: his office, where clients came over to offer him business; an alleyway, where he got into sticky situations; a bar, where he talked toot with the barman; and a rooftop, where he had the final confrontation with the villain. Who always took the big plunge to oblivion at the end. *The Book Of Rune* reads just like one of these thrillers.'

'So,' said Tim, 'are you going for Woodbine or are you going to stick with the Sherlock Holmes technique?'

'I'm going to stick with the Will Starling technique. I'm doing things my way.' Will pushed *The Book Of Rune* into his pocket. 'Let's see what we can pull off in the courtroom, eh, Tim?'

'No sweat,' said Tim and he made an 'O' with his thumb and forefinger. 'After all, we've spent ages planning this, haven't we?'

'*Have you?*' asked the other Will. 'How did this come about?'

'I, er, did a little time-travelling,' said Will. 'From the court a few minutes ago. Surely you noticed that one moment I was wearing my somewhat besmutted morning suit and the next I was, as I am now, rather nattily dressed in this Boleskine three-piece.'

The other Will shrugged. 'I thought I was just hallucinating. This hangover is wrecking my brain. But how did you travel through time, did you reacquire my time machine?'

'No,' said Will. 'But I don't want to bore you with the details.'

'But I *want* to be bored by the details. You travelled through time and you didn't take me?'

'I couldn't,' said Will. 'It was only possible for one of us to go.'

'Then it should have been me. Remember, I'm the innocent party. Let me travel through time *now*.'

'It can't be done,' said Will.

'This is outrageous,' said the other Will and he made a very grumpy face.

There came a knock at the cell door, followed by the sound of a key turning in the lock, followed by the opening of the door and the entrance of a portly gentleman wearing, amongst other things, a chef's hat and a leather apron. He carried a food hamper. 'Good day gents,' said he. 'I'm Croughton the pot-bellied potman from The Flying Swan. And I bring you your lunch.'

'Splendid,' said Will.

'Give it to me, please,' said the other Will. 'I will eat my fill and you can share whatever remains.'

'We'll all have fair shares,' said Will.

'That is fair shares. I am the Promised One. I eat before lesser folk.'

'He's losing it again, chief,' said Barry. 'Get Tim to give him a little smack.'

Will took the hamper, opened it and shared out its contents. Croughton the pot-bellied potman bowed and departed, closing the cell door behind him. The other Will sat on the hammock, folded his arms and sulked. At length however, he unfolded his arms and ate.

'That Gwynplaine Dhark is pretty scary,' said Tim, between munchings. 'If he really is in league with the Devil and the witches, he could well be ordering up another demonic clockwork terminator, even as we speak.'

'He's in league with the Devil, all right,' said the other Will, who had finished munching and now was supping from a bottle of ale. 'We're all going to die and it's all your fault. He'll have us all killed!'

'Not if I can help it.' Will now took to supping ale. 'We'll beat him and we *won't* die. Trust me, I've no intention of dying just yet.'

'Trust him,' said Tim. 'He means what he says. We have a plan. Two plans in fact. A plan "A" and a plan "B". Plan "A" is an absolute blinder.'

'What about plan "B"?' asked the other Will.

'Plan "A" is an absolute stonker,' said Tim. 'We'll get you out of here.'

'What about plan "B"?' asked the other Will, once again.

'You'll really love plan "A",' said Tim.

The other Will finished his ale and uncorked another bottle. 'My hangover is leaving me,' he said. 'Order some more ales; we can drink them during the afternoon.'

'I doubt whether the magistrate will allow that.' Will sought his second bottle of ale, but found that his other self had acquired it. 'And give that back to me.'

The other Will said, 'No,' and shook his head.

'Give him a smack, please, Tim,' said Will.

And Tim would certainly have done so, had not the cell door opened once again to reveal two large constables, wielding truncheons and carrying an assortment of handcuffs and leg irons. 'Time to go, lads,' one of the constables said. 'The hangman awaits.'

'We'll see about *that*,' said Will.

28

Numbers in the courtroom had increased significantly since the lunchtime adjournment. Gentlemen of the press, clad in their distinctive white trousers, striped blazers and straw boaters, now crowded into the public gallery and milled about in the doorway. Other gentlemen from the British Broadcasting Company, dressed in sombre black morning suits, had erected microphones all about the courtroom and were bivouacked wherever they could, adjusting sound levels on complicated-looking equipment which bulged with valves and doodads. The poet laureate was making a guest appearance as a roving correspondent. And then there were locals. Many locals, drawn by the promise of scandal and controversy as the moth of fable (or otherwise) is drawn unto the flame.

There were also certain others in the courtroom, certain others who occupied the very front row of the public gallery: six women all in black, well-dressed women, lavishly dressed women, but with preposterously slender bodies and tiny, pinched faces. The clerk of the court called, 'All rise', and those who were able to do so, did so.

Mr Justice Doveston elbowed his way through the crush. 'Get out of my chair, damn you,' he told a blonde Swedish weather girl, whose agent had advised her to make an appearance, 'just in case'. The blonde Swedish weather girl vacated the magistrate's chair and sank from view beneath his bench/table/desk or whatever the word is for the piece of furniture magistrates sit behind.

'And get out from behind my wardrobe,' said Mr Justice Doveston, who didn't know either. The blonde Swedish weather girl departed, flashing her smile at the press photographers.

Mr Justice Doveston settled into his chair. He had a somewhat dishevelled look to him and there were traces of lipstick on his wig. 'All sit down,' he told the court. And all that could, sat down.

Mr Justice Doveston smiled all round the courtroom. 'This is a bit more like it,' he said. 'I'm very pleased to see so many members of the press favouring these proceedings with their presence. And the gentlemen of the British Broadcasting Company.' And he tapped his microphone with his gavel, raising a scream from a sound engineer, who tore off his headphones and took to hopping about.

'Now then, now then,' said Mr Justice Doveston, in the manner that would one day be favoured by the now (then) legendary Sir Jimmy Saville. 'How's about that, then, eh?'

'Don't you worry about anything,' said Tim to the heavily manacled Will. 'I'll have you both out of here and walking the streets as free men in no time at all.'

'It will probably take *some* time,' said Will.

'Oh, yeah, some time. But not much. A couple of months at most.'

Tim McGregor struggled through the crush to approach the magistrate's bench. 'If I might just speak to you for a moment, your honour,' he said.

'Ah,' said the magistrate. 'Mr McGregor, I was hoping I'd bump into you again.'

'Well, I *am* the counsel for the defence.'

'And you'll have to be an exceedingly good one.'

'I'm sure I will be, your honour.'

'Because, frankly, I'm rather miffed about Freddie "the loser" Lonsdale being dismissed from the case.'

'The defendant's decision, your honour.'

'But I've just been informed by Freddie that he is my cousin.'

'Oh,' said Tim.

Mr Gwynplaine Dhark was suddenly at Tim's side. 'I'd like to call my first witness, if I may, your honour,' said he.

'Ah, Mr Dhark. Well, of course. Someone famous, I trust.'

Tim looked Mr Gwynplaine Dhark up and down. He literally exuded evil. It seemed to ooze from the very pores of his skin. A terrible darkness surrounded him and a terrible coldness too.

'Brrr,' went Mr Justice Doveston. 'Won't someone turn up the heating. And the lights also, it's growing rather dark in here.'

'Your honour,' said Mr Dhark, his lips drawn up into a smile that exposed his pointed yellow teeth. 'I would like to call Master Makepiece Scribbens.'

'Makepiece Scribbens?' said the magistrate. 'I don't think I've ever heard of him.'

'But surely you have, your honour. He's a local celebrity.'

Mr Justice D shook his bewigged bonce.

'It was in all the papers. Your honour must surely have heard of cases in the colonies when young children, separated from their parents in forests and jungles, have been adopted and raised by wolves.'

'I do believe I have,' said the magistrate, in his best speaking voice and into his microphone. 'And also gazelles, and also apes. Wasn't there that Lord Greystoke chap?'

'Indeed there was, your honour. Master Makepiece Scribbens' family was involved in a freak electric dibber accident on Brentford allotment. His parents succumbed; Master Makepiece, a tiny helpless babe, was left alone and friendless. He would certainly have died had he not been taken in, nurtured and raised by snails.'

Mr Justice Doveston wiped a tear from his eye. 'That is a most moving account,' said he. 'And this poor mite can offer some pertinent testimony in this case?'

'Indeed, your honour. He witnessed the incident in its entirety. And being raised by snails he is a perfect witness, because he cannot tell a lie.'

Mr Justice Doveston nodded thoughtfully. 'Snails are renowned for their honesty,' he said. 'As the old adage goes, "What a snail knows not of honesty, a fly knows not of deceit".'

'Your honour couldn't speak more truth. Does your honour not perhaps have a little snail in himself somewhere?'

'Flatterer,' said Mr Justice D.

'What?' went Will.

And 'What?' went the other Will also.

And 'I object,' said Tim McGregor.

'And why?' asked the magistrate.

'I'm not entirely certain,' said Tim. 'But I don't like the sound of this snail boy.'

'Ooooooooooooooooooooooh!' went the crowd.

And 'Ooooooooooooooooooooooh!' went the gentlemen of the press also, and the chaps from the BBC and even the blonde Swedish weather girl, although she made more of an 'Ooh', and threw her head back when she did it.

'*What?*' said Tim.

'Impugning the reputation of snails for truth-telling,' said the magistrate. 'You're stepping on slippery ground.'

'Whatever,' said Tim. 'Then I don't object. In fact I welcome this witness. Wheel the blighter in.'

'Ooooooooooooooooooooooh,' went all concerned again.

'Ow!' went the blonde Swedish weather girl, and she slapped a reporter who was touching her bum.

'What?' went Tim once again. 'What is everyone ooooooooo-oooooooooohing for, this time?'

'Wheelchair-bound,' said Mr Gwynplaine Dhark. 'A rather tasteless remark on your part.'

'But,' said Tim. 'But.'

'Call Master Makepiece Scribbens,' called the magistrate.

'Call Mr Monkfish Scrivvens,' called the clerk of the court, who had a boil in his left ear.

'Call Mrs Mavis Wiverns,' called a court bailiff at the door, who had a wart on his bottom that was being treated by acupuncture.

'Calling occupants from interplanetary craft,' called a constable in the corridor, whose great grandson would one day find fame writing lyrics for The Carpenters.

The courtroom door was open
The crowd was silently stilled
The atmosphere was electric
All hearts were thricely thrilled
And from beyond the corridor
Came the sound of squeakity-squeak
And closer and closer and closer came someone
A man? Or a monster? A freak?

'It doesn't have to be done in verse,' said a BBC sound technician.

'But I am the poet laureate,' said the poet laureate. 'And I'm going out live on air.'

'Sorry,' said the sound technician. 'Please carry on.'

'I can't now; I've lost my muse.'

'Perhaps you left it in your other kilt,' said the sound technician.

'I'll go and have a wee look,' said the poet laureate, the Great McGonagall.

And into the courtroom came Master Makepiece Scribbens, the Brentford Snail Boy.

All eyes were turned towards the door, but upon his entrance and upon the sight of him many eyes turned away in horror. But most of these soon turned back, because, well, you'd just have to have a good old look, wouldn't you? After all, he *was* raised by snails.

'I do hope this is going to be worthwhile,' said Mr Justice Doveston. 'There's been an awful lot of build-up.'

'Trust me,' said Mr Gwynplaine Dhark. 'I'm a Queen's Counsel.'

A nanny pushed the wheelchair. She was a very pretty young nanny, bright of eye and rosy of cheek. Her name was Miss Poppins.

Her wheelchair-bound charge was neither bright of eye, nor rosy of cheek. A blanket covered the most of him and the most of him it covered seemed lumpen and shapeless. The little of him that was visible, to whit the head region, was puffy and bloated. His eyes were scarcely visible beneath folds of pale flesh. The cranium was bald and a curious musty odour breathed out from him. The wheels of the chair left twin slimy trails upon the courtroom floor.

'Mr Monkfish Scrivvens,' said the clerk of the court, 'will you please take the witness stand.'

The Brentford Snail Boy's mouth, two flabby flaps of skin, moved and sought to push out words, but failed.

'This looks like being a bundle of laughs,' Will whispered to Tim.

'We're in big trouble here, chief,' said Barry.

'You have to be kidding, right?'

'Damn right, chief.'

'So why did you say it?'

'Because I haven't said anything in ages and I'm not too keen on Mollusc Man getting all the attention.'

'Can you actually take the witness stand?' Mr Justice Doveston asked the Brentford Snail Boy.

'Pish.' The word emerged from the blubbery lips. 'Pish, pash, posh.'

'He's eager,' said Mr Gwynplaine Dhark. 'I'll help him to the stand. Miss Poppins, if you will assist.'

'Super-cali-fragically,' said Miss Poppins and the two of them eased the invalid from his wheelchair and carried him to the witness stand.

'Pesh,' said the Brentford Snail Boy.

'My pleasure,' said Mr Gwynplaine Dhark.

'Let the witness take the oath,' said Mr Justice Doveston, fanning at his face with his gavel. 'He smells rather iffy, let's get this done.'

'Ah, no,' said Mr Gwynplaine Dhark, taking several steps back from the Holy Book and crushing the feet of spectators. 'He cannot swear upon the Bible. He has no concept of Christianity, although the nuns at Saint Sally of the Little Buttocks are presently engaged in converting him. He can only swear upon a box of salt.'

'Salt?' asked Mr Justice D.

'Snails fear salt,' said Mr Gwynplaine Dhark. 'And slugs also, you know what happens if your pour salt on slugs.'

'Squesh,' went the Brentford Snail Boy.

'Ah yes,' said the magistrate. 'Horrible business. He can swear upon the salt then, not that he needs to, but it's protocol. And personally, and no offence meant, Mr Scribbens, I like salt. I'm very partial to salt. Particularly on a portion of cod and chips.'

'Me too,' said Mr Gwynplaine Dhark, running a forked tongue about his lips. 'And I also like plenty of vinegar.'

'Oh yes, vinegar, too.'

'They put it on a sponge,' said Mr Gwynplaine Dhark. 'And offered it to Jesus when he cried out on the Cross that he thirsted.'

'I don't think that has any relevance,' said the magistrate.

'None whatever,' said Mr Gwynplaine Dhark. 'I just like thinking about it.'

'HP sauce,' said the clerk of the court.

'What?' said the magistrate.

'HP sauce, your honour. On the cod and chips. There's nothing like HP sauce.'

'You're right there. It's a pity we've just had lunch. Let's go and have fish and chips later.'

'And pickled onions.' The clerk of the court brought out the official box of salt that was kept for such occasions as this and offered it to the witness, who shied away at its approach.

'He is greatly afeared of the salt,' said Mr Gwynplaine Dhark.

'But he loves a bit of lettuce,' said Miss Poppins positioning herself behind the Brentford Snail Boy.

'Please do the reciting of the oath and things of that nature with the witness,' the magistrate told the clerk of the court.

'Certainly, your honour. Will the witness, please raise his right hand?'

Miss Poppins lifted the Snail Boy's right hand.

'Repeat after me,' said the clerk of the court. 'I swear to tell the truth, the whole truth, and nothing but the truth, so help me, or I may be doused in salt, soused with garlic and lightly pan-fried and served with a hollandaise sauce upon a bed of tossed green salad.'

'Poosh,' said the Brentford Snail Boy.

'He certainly does,' said Mr Gwynplaine Dhark.

'I object again,' said Tim McGregor.

'And why this time?' asked the magistrate.

'Because anyone can see where this is going. The witness makes incomprehensible pssshing sounds and the counsel for the prosecution interprets them as suits himself.'

'You wouldn't do that, would you?' the magistrate asked the counsel for the prosecution.

'On my word, your honour.'

'That was an ambiguous answer,' said Tim.

'Poosh,' said the Brentford Snail Boy.

'You're so right,' said the magistrate. 'I wish I'd said that.'

'*What?*' said Tim.

'I wish I'd said *that,*' said Will.

Mr Gwynplaine Dhark approached the witness stand.

'Ow!' 'Ouch!' 'Oh!' went those who stood in his way as he did so.

'You are Master Makepiece Scribbens of number nine Mafeking Avenue, Brentford?' he asked.

'What?' said the other Will.

'Pssssh,' went the Brentford Snail Boy.

'And did you witness the altercation that occurred last night in the Hands of Orloc public house, Brentford?'

'Pssssh,' went the Brentford Snail Boy, dribbling somewhat as he said it.

Miss Poppins took out a white linen handkerchief, wiped the witness's lips and then popped a spoonful of sugar into his mouth.

'It helps the medicine go down,' she explained.

'Would you be so good as to describe, in your own words, what took place in The Hands of Orloc?' Mr Gwynplaine Dhark asked the witness.

'This should be thrilling,' said Tim.

'Pusssssssh,' said the Brentford Snail Boy.

'I can scarcely believe my ears,' said the magistrate. 'And where were you when you witnessed these alarming events that you have given us such a precise and detailed account of? And which prove absolutely the guilt of the twin accused.'

'Psss,' said the Brentford Snail Boy.

'Really?' said the magistrate. 'Half way across the ceiling ignoring the unwelcome attentions of a sparrow-hawk. Your bravery is an example to us all.'

'I object again,' said Tim McGregor.

'Upon what grounds, this time?' asked the magistrate.

'Because this is absurd. He's making silly noises and you're pretending to understand him. There's no justice in this.'

'I believe,' said Mr Gwynplaine Dhark, 'that the counsel for the defence does not speak mollusc.'

'I certainly don't,' said Tim. 'And nor do you, this is all nonsense.'

'I hardly feel that such damning evidence as this can be called nonsense,' said Mr Justice D. 'In fact, I believe that you are in contempt of court. I will have to ask you to withdraw from the case.'

'No way,' said Tim. 'I have heaps of famous witnesses to call, the Queen and everything. You wanted a trial that would bring some publicity to the borough and you are going to get it. This man,' Tim pointed at Mr Gwynplaine Dhark, 'is going down. Big time.'

'He doesn't even speak the Queen's English,' said Mr Gwynplaine Dhark. 'He is totally incompetent. And according to Master Scribbens' eloquent testimony, he was also an accomplice. He should be taken at once to the cells and from there to Tyburn to join the evil twins upon the scaffold.'

'I agree,' said the magistrate. 'Much as I would have enjoyed meeting the Queen. Or indeed watching you burn at the stake if you'd lost the case. The witness's evidence is damning. I think we'll have all three executed this very afternoon.'

'Then fish and chips afterwards,' said the clerk of the court.

'No!' Will cried. He rose from his bench and flinched in expectancy of his imminent truncheoning-down. 'This isn't right. The Snail Boy is lying. The ceiling in the Hands of Orloc is far too low. If he'd been on it we would have been bumping into him.'

'What have you to say about *this*?' the magistrate asked Snail Boy.

'Posssh,' said the Snail Boy.

'As high as *that*?' asked the magistrate. 'Eight miles high? That's a very high ceiling.'

'See what I mean?' cried Will. 'And we do have really famous witnesses to call.'

'We'll call them to attend your execution then,' said the magistrate. 'It will be a star-studded extravaganza. The blonde Swedish weather girl can pull the lever. Would you like that, my dear?'

'I'd like that very much,' said the blonde Swedish weather girl. 'Nothing I like more than pulling on a big stiff lever.'

Mr Justice Doveston put on his black cap. 'It is the verdict of this court,' said he, 'that you and your evil twin are guilty of all the charges and—'

'Tim!' shouted Will. 'I think we'd better go to plan "B"!'

'Plan "B",' said Tim. 'Are you absolutely sure?'

'Never been surer.'

'Okay,' said Tim. And he reached into his briefcase.

And drew out a gun.

And he pointed the gun at Mr Justice Doveston.

'Free the Brentford Two,' said Tim. 'Or I will be forced to shoot you dead.'

29

'Hands up!' Tim levelled the pistol at Mr Justice Doveston. It was a blinder of a pistol, a phase-plasma pistol (in the forty-watt range) with laser sighting and everything. Will and Tim had stopped off in the twenty-first century to acquire it. The little red laser dot jiggled about on the magistrate's forehead.

'This is unacceptable behaviour,' complained Mr Justice D. 'Put down that pistol at once and hand yourself over to the constables.'

'I'll shoot you dead.' Tim cocked the trigger. It was one of those hair triggers.* The pistol went off. Tim fell back and so too did Mr Justice Doveston. Mr Justice Doveston's wig was on fire.

'Arrest this man!' cried Mr Justice Doveston.

'Oh no, you don't.' Tim had fallen back into the crowd, but was on his feet with remarkable speed. 'Put your hands up now and have the constables release the prisoners.'

Mr Justice Doveston battered away at his smouldering wig. 'My best wig. You maniac.'

'Next time, it's your head,' said Tim, putting a very brave face on things, considering just how terrified he was. 'It would have been your head that time, but the tracking's slightly off.' Tim whispered the words, 'thank the Goddess,' in completion of this statement.

'All right.' The magistrate raised his hands. 'Constables release the prisoners.'

The crowd had remained strangely silent throughout all this, or perhaps not so strangely. After all, when confronted by a lunatic with a pistol, don't most of us go somewhat quiet? Whilst silently wetting ourselves.

'Everybody else *out*!' cried Tim. 'Out of the courtroom, all of you.'

'I'll lead the way,' said Mr Gwynplaine Dhark.

* Not to be confused with a hairy trigger, which is a variety of Siberian mountain horse. Or a willy.

'No,' said Tim. '*You* stay. Your honour, tell everybody else to leave.'

'Everybody else leave,' said Mr Justice Doveston.

But nobody moved. Tim glanced all around and about. 'Are you free yet?' he called out to Will.

'No,' Will called back.

'Tell the constables to hurry up,' Tim told the magistrate.

'Hurry up, constables,' said this man.

But the constables seemed disinclined to obey.

'What is wrong with you please?' Tim asked. 'I'll shoot the magistrate dead.'

Silence reigned.

Tim glanced about some more.

'Don't you care?' he asked.

Heads shook slowly. Shoulders shrugged. Someone mumbled, 'not much, really.'

'All right then.' Tim turned his pistol upon Mr Gwynplaine Dhark.

Heads continued to slowly shake and shoulders to shrug. Someone else mumbled, 'Go on then shoot him.' And several people chuckled.

'Incredible.' Tim did further glancings, and then he sprang forward, clawed himself over the witness stand, snatched up the box of salt and held it over the head of the Brentford Snail Boy.

'Booooo!' went the crowd, 'Poor show,' and 'Rotter.'

'Ah,' said Tim. 'Got your attention now. Clear the court. All of you. Apart from the constables, you free the prisoners. Hurry now, or the Snail Boy gets it.'

And so did they hurry. They really hurried. They pushed and barged and elbowed and fought to escape from the court. Mr Gwynplaine Dhark was trodden down by the onrushing masses and Will and his other self found themselves free at last. (Sweet Jesus, free at last).

'Shall I go too?' asked the magistrate.

'You might as well,' said Tim.

'Shall I send you the bill for the refurbishment of my wig? Or would you care to settle up now? Actually, it's probably better that you settle up now, because it's unlikely that you'll escape from this courtroom alive.'

Tim raised an eyebrow.

'I'll just go then,' said the magistrate.

'I'll help him,' said Mr Gwynplaine Dhark, rising from the floor and patting dust and dirt away from his dire person.

'You stay,' said Tim. 'We want words with you.'

'What about *me*?' asked Miss Poppins. 'Would you like me to stay?'

Tim smiled Miss Poppins up and down, in a lingering kind of way. 'I'd love you to stay,' said Tim.

The door of the courtroom closed behind the last of the leavers, a gentleman of the press, who had managed to shoot off a couple of pictures before his departure.

Another silence settled upon the courtroom. It was broken in less than a 'jiffy' and a 'trice', by the voice of the other Will.

'And *that* was plan "B"!' The other Will rolled his eyes. 'Most inspired, I don't think.'

'Tim did very well,' said Will. 'He handled it very well indeed.'

'Thanks,' said Tim, and he twirled the pistol on his trigger-pulling finger and winked at Miss Poppins.

'You're all dead men,' said Mr Gwynplaine Dhark. 'The magistrate was correct in his statement. You'll never leave this courtroom alive.'

The other Will pointed a shaky finger at the counsel for the prosecution. 'Please shoot this monster,' he said to Tim.

'Now, now.' Mr Gwynplaine Dhark waggled an unshaky finger. 'You'd better behave yourself, or there'll be no rat for your dinner tonight.'

'*Shall* I shoot him?' Tim asked Will.

Will shook his blondy head. 'Not unless you *have* to,' he replied. 'You don't really want to shoot someone, do you?'

'Not really,' said Tim.

'Psssssh,' said the Brentford Snail Boy.

'Oh sorry,' said Tim and he put down the box of salt. 'I wouldn't really have poured it on you.'

'Passh.'

'No problem.'

'Eh?' said Will. 'You don't really understand what he's saying, do you?'

'Stop all this nonsense,' said the other Will. 'Shoot that evil warlock. Or give me the gun and I'll shoot him.'

'Calm down,' said Will. 'Nobody's shooting anyone.'

'Then I'll just leave,' said Mr Gwynplaine Dhark.

'Shoot him if he tries to leave,' said Will.

'You will certainly die,' said Mr Gwynplaine Dhark.

'Lock him in a cell,' Will said to Tim.

'Good idea,' said Tim. 'Come on, you; move.'

★

'Er, chief,' said Barry, when Tim and Mr Dhark had left the courtroom. 'As things seem to have gone arse-upwards here, what exactly are you planning to do next?'

Will whispered behind his hand. 'Shut up, Barry,' he whispered.

'But chief, the local constabulary will be tooling up outside. There may well be another demonic terminator robot thingy on the way. The street will be filled with crowds and press. Things don't look altogether hopeful.'

'I know what I'm doing, Barry.'

'But chief, I could just whip you back in time a couple of days and you'd never have to bother with any of this. You could do things differently.'

'I'm not stupid,' whispered Will. 'I know that. And don't think it hasn't crossed my mind to whip back in time a bit further and save Hugo Rune from getting murdered.'

'Ah,' said Barry.

'Yes, ah,' whispered Will. 'But you won't let me do that, will you?'

'My remit embraces certain parameters, but beyond them I cannot go.'

'So we'll do things my way for now, and if I really foul up, which I won't, then I'll ask for your help.'

'*Again*,' said Barry.

'We picked up Tim, because *I* wanted to. I'm in charge here.'

'Yeah right,' said Barry.

'What was that?'

'I said "*you're right*".

'As if you did.'

'Have you quite finished?' asked the other Will.

'Excuse me?' said Will.

'Talking to the demon in your head. I heard you.'

'He's *not* a demon,' said Will.

'He's *not*, squire,' said Larry. 'He's just my twatty brother.'

'Leave me alone!'

'I'm sorry,' said Will.

'Not you.'

'What?'

'I'm struggling,' said the other Will and he made struggling motions with his hands. He sort of mimed struggling, although not particularly well. 'There's one of them in me. It's driving me insane.'

'His Holy Guardian is speaking to him, chief.'

'You've a voice in your head?' Will asked.

'I can hear it, it speaks to me.'

'Don't be alarmed,' said Will. 'It's all right. It's your Holy Guardian. You have nothing to fear.'

'I have *everything* to fear, and so do you.'

'All done,' said Tim, returning to the courtroom. 'So what are we going to do now? You don't have a plan "C" do you?'

'Don't need one,' said Will. 'What we want is publicity, right? To expose the witch cult, if it really exists.'

'It exists,' said the other Will. 'How can you doubt it?'

'Okay. I'm *not* stupid. I'm well aware that the witch cult conspiracy business *is* what all this is about, whether they are *real* witches or not. But the best way to deal with them is to expose them to the public. I'd hoped to do it through the court case, but this is even better. A courtroom siege, a hostage situation; this will stir up the media. We'll get our say on prime-time radio.'

'They'll kill us,' said the other Will. 'They'll send in the army and shoot us all dead.'

'Not until we've had our say on the BBC.'

'You're wasting your time,' said a little voice.

'Who said that?' asked Will.

'I did,' said the Brentford Snail Boy. 'You're wasting your time. It won't work.'

'You can speak,' said Will.

'Of course he can speak,' said Tim. 'He makes those pssh noises, then he whispers. That's how the magistrate heard him. I heard him when I was up there with him.'

'That is so crap,' said Will.

'Your plan won't work,' said Master Makepiece Scribbens.

'And why?' asked Will. 'I think it's a great plan. No violence and lots of press coverage.'

'Firstly,' said Master Makepiece Scribbens, 'you know *nothing* about the witches. A few theories, is all you seem to have. Everyone has theories. And secondly, *they* will never let you broadcast your theories to the nation. *They* control the media. You're wasting your time.'

'Hm,' said Will. 'So what do *you* know about all this? You lied in the court.'

'I had no choice. They threatened to kill me.'

'Fair enough,' said Will. 'But what do you know about these witches?'

'As much as *he* does,' said the Brentford Snail Boy, raising a wobbly hand and pointing one of its shapeless fingers towards the other Will. 'I was caged up in the cell next to him. I used to listen to him screaming. I played dumb. They thought I was an imbecile.'

'Why did they capture *you*?' Will asked.

'They didn't capture me. They borrowed me from the circus, Count Otto Black's Circus Fantastique.'

'Count Otto Black,' said Will. 'I know that name. I saw him at the Café Royal on the night that Hugo Rune was murdered, and then at Buckingham Palace. Does he have something to do with all this?'

'He has everything to do with everything,' said Master Scribbens. 'Count Otto Black is the King of all the witches. You could never have won this case, even with all the witnesses you hoped to call. Count Otto holds the ear of Her Majesty the Queen (Gawd bless Her). He is above the law, which is why you will never be heard. You have to get out of here, or you will surely die.'

'Your thoughts on this, Barry,' said Will.

'My thoughts are that I thought you were doing things *your* way, chief.'

'I am,' said Will. 'All right. Then we have to get out of here.'

'Will,' said Tim. 'You could just make the broadcast yourself. The BBC men have left all their equipment behind.'

'And say you did,' said Master Scribbens. 'What can you really say? What can you really prove? What do you really know?'

'We have to get out of here,' said Will.

And then a voice entered the courtroom. Entered *was* the word. This voice entered loudly, dramatically. It was a very noisy voice.

It came through one of those police bullhorns, electric bullhorns, state-of-the-Victorian-art-technology. It said: 'Give yourselves up, you are surrounded,' very loudly indeed.

Tim began to panic, as did the other Will.

They panicked in different ways. Tim flung his hands in the air, one holding the gun and the other not, and began to spin around in small circles. The other Will clapped *his* hands over his head and assumed the foetal position.

'Release the hostages,' called the voice through the state-of-the-Victorian-art police bullhorn. It was the voice of Chief Inspector Samuel Maggott. 'Release the hostages or we storm the building and shoot everyone, hostages included, just to be on the safe side.'

'Your thoughts on *this*, chief,' said Barry.

'We're going to plan "C",' said Will.

★

There was now a big presence all about the Brentford court house: a big crowd presence, a big media presence, and a big police presence. The big police presence had a lot of state-of-the-Victorian-art weaponry to its account. It is recognised and understood by experts in the field of antique weaponry that the Gatling gun was the nineteenth-century progenitor to the General Electric Minigun, that now legendary weapon, favoured by Blaine in *Predator* and Arnie in *Terminator 2*.

But, as it must now be understood by all, history cannot be trusted. And so several M162 Babbage Miniguns were being moved into strategic positions around the courthouse, much to the delight of the crowd, which was really looking forward to watching those bad boys being put into service.

Tim took a peep through a window.

'Cops,' said he.

'How many?' asked Will.

'All, I think.'

'Plan "C" it is then,' said Will.

'And what exactly is plan "C"?' Tim asked.

'Release the hostages,' said Will.

'If I might make a suggestion,' said Master Makepiece Scribbens.

There were an awful lot of guns trained upon the court house door when it opened; an *awful* lot of guns, an awful lot of *awful* guns, terrible guns; hideous, heinous, horrible guns. They all took aim and they all cocked but happily none of them had a hair trigger.

Three figures issued slowly from the courtroom, heads bowed down, cowering somewhat. Miss Poppins pushed the wheelchair containing the Brentford Snail Boy, smothered by blankets. Mr Gwynplaine Dhark, head bowed, arms raised, followed on behind.

The police cordon parted to let them through.

The crowd beyond parted also.

And then the Babbage Miniguns opened up upon the building.

And they did it style. They fairly stuffed that courthouse.

The crowd cheered wildly, and waved Union Jacks. Why? Who knows; crowds often do! The policemen launched mortars, employed flamethrowers, flung grenades, lobbed in canisters of nerve gas and other weapons of mass destruction. And when it was finally assumed that nothing above ground level could possibly have lived through the holocaust, they moved in to search for what might be left of the bodies.

★

Beyond the crowd, and someways far down the Brentford High Road towards Kew Bridge, Miss Poppins said, 'That was a good plan.'

'As long as they're safe,' said the Brentford Snail Boy.

'They'll be safe enough,' said Miss Poppins. 'They're locked in the cell downstairs. The police will release them.'

'Then I think that we can say that plan "C" was a definite success.'

A hansom cab was passing and Miss Poppins hailed it. 'Piccadilly, cabbie,' said she.

'You've a very manly voice for a nanny,' said the cabbie.

'Sore throat,' said Will, for it was he. 'Now all aboard. We're out of here.'

30

When your credit no longer holds good at the Dorchester, move on to the Savoy. And when the Savoy refuses to cater to your needs without further payment, then call upon Simpsons to accommodate you. And when Simpsons will no longer do this, and threatens to retain your luggage and personal effects subsequent to the settling of your bill, then it is time to take humble lodgings in Whitechapel, or board a steamer across the Channel to begin once more at the top.

So much, Hugo Rune had taught to Will.

But, as Rune had worn out his welcome at all of London's top hotels several years before Will met him, and as Will could no longer return to the Dorchester, it was at the Savoy that Will chose to spend the night with his companions.

'Lord Peter Whimsy,' said the other Will as Will had instructed him to do, 'travelling with my charge, Master Makepiece Scribbens, the famous Brentford Snail Boy, and his nurse and nanny, Miss Poppins. A three-bedroomed suite, if you will.'

The benign automaton desk clerk at the Savoy smiled obsequiously and turned the visitors book in the other Will's direction for him to sign. 'Your luggage, your Lordship?' he asked.

'I am Lord Peter Whimsy!' said the other Will. 'I do not have *luggage*. Whatever I require is tailored to my needs, as and when I require it. And I require it now. Have a tailor, a shoemaker, and a representative from Asprey sent up to my suite at the soonest.'

'Yes, your Lordship.'

The suite was splendid enough in its way: three bedrooms and a bathroom leading from a central sitter, with a well-stocked mini-bar and a great deal of comfortable furniture.

Tim sprawled upon a box ottoman.

'I hope the tailor doesn't take too long,' said he. 'Being dressed as the Brentford Snail Boy really doesn't suit my image.'

'Oh, too bad,' said Will. 'I just love being dressed as Miss Poppins.'

'I think it looks rather good on you.'

'I'm fine with Mr Gwynplaine Dhark's outfit,' said the other Will. 'And I will rejoice forever in the memory of him handcuffed in that cell wearing nothing but his underpants. Thank you, at least, for that.'

'I'm glad it made you happy,' said Will.

'Momentarily. But I'm gloomy enough now because by now our escape will have been discovered. And we will be at the top of the most wanted list. We're in bigger trouble than ever.'

'Don't go putting a downer on things,' said Tim, fishing into the mini-bar. 'We're free, we escaped, and it was all down to Will.'

'It was all down to Master Makepiece Scribbens,' said Will. 'It was his idea.'

'Our pictures will be in all the papers tomorrow,' said the other Will. 'We should flee to France, or America, or Australia.'

'Do you have a plan "D", Will?' Tim asked.

'In a few minutes from now,' said Will, 'in fact, in possibly less than a "trice" and a "twinkling", a tailor and a shoemaker and a representative from Asprey will arrive. This is Victorian London. Our new clothes and shoes, accoutrements, cufflinks and whatnots will be ready for us by the morning. When we have them, we will leave. I have to sort out all this witch business, I know I do. I know that it's me who has to do the thwarting. And I know that I *will* do the thwarting, because if I didn't, then my other self here wouldn't exist. I have to do it, no matter what it means for me.'

'And me,' said Tim. 'What about me? If you do this, then the me that is me may cease to exist.'

'Which is why I have to do it *my* way. Not as it is written in *The Book Of Rune*.' Will pulled *The Book Of Rune* from his bodice and flung it onto the bed. 'I have to save both our futures somehow.'

'How?' Tim asked.

'I don't know, but if I do it differently, things will be different. Perhaps both futures will exist. Perhaps both futures always existed. I don't know. This is very complicated, Tim, and I don't understand it. I'm just making it up as I go along.'

'Like the author,' said Tim.

'What author?' asked Will.

'Any author,' said Tim. 'They just make it all up as they go along.'

'No they don't,' said Will. 'Authors research everything. They plan every chapter, paragraph and sentence. They never waste a word. That's what makes them such very special people.'

'Turn it in, chief,' said Barry. 'Everyone knows that authors are a lot of drunken bums.'

'All I know,' said Will, 'is that I'm really messed up. Rune has been murdered. The witches are on to me. There's trouble after trouble. But I *will* sort it, somehow.'

'You won't,' said the other Will. 'We'll both die. You cannot cheat your fate and neither can I. And believe me, I tried.'

'And you'll keep on trying,' said Will. 'Because you are me and that's what we do.'

A knock came at the door.

Tim drew out his pistol.

Will made him put it away. 'It'll be the tailor and the shoemaker and the representative from Asprey,' he told Tim, and to his other self Will said, 'let them measure you up and order two suits of clothes. I'll go and hide in the bathroom until they're gone, I don't want to be seen dressed like this.'

Tailors and shoemakers and a representative from Asprey entered. Measuring ups were done, accoutrements, cufflinks and whatnots were chosen. Tailors and shoemakers and the representative from Asprey departed.

'What now?' asked Tim.

'Dinner,' said Will returning from the bathroom. 'I believe that the Savoy serves a particularly fine cod and chips. We'll have some sent up.'

They wined and dined and then they wined some more, and brandied also. And when the brandy was gone they emptied the mini-bar.

And the other Will cheered up once more and even laughed at a joke Tim told him that concerned a pop star and a plastic surgeon, although he didn't really understand it. And when they all had finally drunk themselves to oblivion, they slept where they sat, or lay, for it had been, all in all, a stressful day for them.

Although possibly less stressful than the days that were to follow, like the following one, for instance.

31

A loud and lusty bout of door-banging tore Will from the amorous arms of Morpheus.

'What?' went Will, in some confusion. 'What is going on?'

'Porter,' called a voice. 'Porter, your lordship.'

'No,' went Will. 'I don't want any porter, nor any ale at all for that matter. I've drunk quite enough.'

'*I'm* the porter, your lordship. Your apparel and accoutrements, cufflinks and whatnots have just been delivered.'

'Ah.' Will blinked his eyes and sought to focus them. 'Please leave them outside. I'll fetch them in a minute.'

'As your lordship pleases.'

'What is going on?' Tim awoke in slightly less confusion, but then, Tim was a hardier drinker than Will. 'Why is the world upside down?' he asked.

Will sought to focus his eyes upon Tim. 'It's you,' he explained.

'Oh yes, you're right.' Tim righted himself. 'That was a good old piss-up,' he said.

'Our new clothes have arrived.' Will arose from the carpet and clicked various joints. 'It will be a pleasure to put on a pair of trousers.' Will rubbed at his forehead. 'We didn't do anything stupid last night, did we?'

'Not that I recall.' Tim, now in the upright position, parted his hair and beard. 'No, I'm sure that we didn't.'

'Good,' said Will. 'Where is my other self?'

Tim fumbled up a glass and set to filling it from the dregs of various others that littered the suite. The suite was no longer quite so swish as it had been when Will's party entered it. The suite now had the look of a Holiday Inn hotel room that had played host to a heavy metal band on tour, although it lacked for sleeping naked females.

Sadly.

'Where is he?' Will asked.

'Perhaps in the bathroom.' Tim shambled to the bathroom and pushed open the door. 'Not here,' he said.

Will peered under the ottoman. 'And not here either. In one of the bedrooms?'

Will and Tim checked the bedrooms, and returned once more to the sitter.

'Any luck?' said Tim.

'None,' said Will.

'He'll be around. Perhaps he's in the mini-bar.'

'That's not very likely, is it, Tim?'

'Why not? You got in there last night, didn't you?'

'Ah,' said Will. And he checked the mini-bar.

His other self was *not* in the mini-bar.

Nor was he anywhere else in the suite.

'Perhaps he's gone down for breakfast,' said Tim, tossing back a cocktail of gin dregs and ginger beer. 'That hits the spot,' he continued.

'Oh dear,' said Will. 'What's this?'

Upon the mantelpiece of the previously unmentioned Louis XV Carrara fireplace, with the serpentine mouldings and the scrolling foliate friezes, an envelope leaned against the similarly unmentioned Louis XIV scarlet Boulle mantel clock, with the Berainesque panels, inlaid with pewter and brass, and the gilded central finial figure in the shape of a dancing bear.

Will took down the envelope and read what was written upon it.

'To Will,' he read.

'It's for you,' said Tim.

'Thanks, Tim.' Will opened the envelope and took out a sheet of paper. Savoy stationery. Will now read aloud the words that were written upon this.

' "Dear Will",' he read.

'It's for you too,' said Tim.

'Turn it in, please.'

'Sorry,' said Tim.

' "Dear Will,

"By the time you read this letter I will be gone."

'It's a "dear John" letter,' said Tim. 'Why's it addressed to you?'

'Tim,' said Will, 'I have learned Dimac. Be silent now or you will in future walk sideways in the manner of a crab.'

'That's a bit harsh,' said Tim, jiggling bottles and coming up trumps with a measure of crème de menthe.

' "I no u hv mi intres at ?",' Will continued. ' "But I hv 2 go." This seems to be written in code.'

'I think that you'll find it's written in "drunk",' said Tim. 'Give it to me.'

Will handed Tim the letter. 'Let's have a sip of the crème de menthe,' he said and Tim let him have a small sip.

' "I know you have my interests at heart," ' Tim translated. ' "But I have to go. I will be far away from here by the time you read this. Don't waste your time trying to find me. Perhaps we will meet again once *YOU* have thwarted the witches. Best wishes, Will." '

'No,' said Will, and he tore the letter from Tim's hands. 'He can't do that. He'll come to grief. He can't survive by himself. We have to find him.'

'It's all for the best, chief,' said Barry.

'Shut up, you,' said Will.

'I didn't say anything,' said Tim, 'although if I had, I'd have probably said that it was all for the best.'

'We have to find him,' said Will once more. 'I'll call room service.'

'How will that help?'

'I need another drink.'

'Oh good,' said Tim. 'I'll join you.'

Will phoned down for breakfast. He ordered a bottle of champagne and a jug of iced orange juice. Well, a Buck's Fizz *is* breakfast, isn't it?

The lad who brought the tray up also carried in the new clothes from the corridor. He had been trained in the arts of multiple carrying at a special academy in Greenwich.

'Impressive carrying,' said Will.

The boy looked Will up and down. 'Thank you, madam,' he said.

'Give the lad a tip please, Tim,' said Will.

'Fair enough,' said Tim. 'Stay away from Brentford,' he tipped the lad.

'Most amusing,' said Will on the lad's rather grumpy departure, 'but this is really bad.'

'Looks good to me.' Tim popped the cork from the champagne and decanted the bubbly into the nearest glasses.

'I mean, my other self. We'll have to find him.'

'And where would we look?' Tim handed Will a glass of champagne. Will would have topped it up with orange juice, but there wasn't any room.

'Our pictures will be in all the papers,' said Will. 'The police will catch him in no time.'

'Then, fine,' Tim swigged champagne. 'We'll wait until they do, then liberate him. We're pretty hot stuff on liberation.'

'And what if Count Otto and his witches get to him first?'

'Chief,' said Barry. 'You could easily forestall that by getting to *them* first.'

'I have to think.' Will took up a new suit of clothes and took himself off to the bathroom for a shower, a shit and a shave.

He presently returned, well shaved and dashing, to find Tim grinning foolishly at him.

'You've drunk all the champagne,' said Will.

'Damn right,' said Tim.

'Then sleep it off again. I'm going for a walk.'

'Is that safe?'

'I need some fresh air. I'll be careful.'

Will took the lift down to the reception area. The lift boy grinned up at him. Will avoided his gaze, but the lad just kept grinning.

'What are you grinning at?' Will asked.

'It's *you*, isn't it, sir?'

'What?' said Will.

'You, sir. It *is* you. Could I have your autograph?'

'My autograph? Why would you want that?'

'To prove that I met you, sir. I will treasure it, pass it on to my first-born son, when I have one.'

'What?' said Will once again.

'Well sir—' But the lift had reached the ground floor and the lift boy pressed back the retractable brass gate.

Will left the lift and entered the Savoy's lobby.

The lobby was crowded with people; smartly dressed people, expensively dressed people, and people of all nationalities. Will even recognised one or two of them: the Greek ambassador and a member of the Chinese trade delegation that he'd met at Queen Victoria's fancy dress ball. And as he left the lift, the heads of these people turned. And the voice of the lad who had delivered Will's champagne and accoutrements was heard to cry out, 'There he is. I told you it was him.'

'Oh dear,' said Will. 'Oh dear, oh dear, oh dear.'

And he hastened his footsteps and prepared to make a run for it.

And 'Hoorah!' went the expensively dressed people, and they clapped their hands together and cheered.

Will went 'What?' for the umpteenth time that morning and pushed through the crowd, which patted his back and shook his hand and wished him the very bestest of luck also.

And when Will reached the Savoy's front doors, these were opened for him by twin doormen, who raised their thumbs and wished him good luck.

Will stumbled out into the street beyond.

That street was the Strand.

He shook his head and scratched it also and glanced back over his shoulder.

Folk were crowded against the now closed doors, waving and cheering. Will shook his head once more and stumbled on.

On the corner of Oxford Street stood a newsboy. 'Read orl abowt it!' he cried. Will straightened his sagging shoulders and approached the newsboy. The newsboy viewed his approach.

'Gawd lather my love muscle,' said the newsboy.

'It's *you*, again,' said Will. 'Winston.'

'And it's *you* guv'nor. And I never knowed. Gawd bless you guv'nor and Gawd save the Queen.'

Will patted his pockets for change, but his new suit contained none at all.

'On the 'ouse guv'nor,' said the newsboy, handing him a paper. 'And might I shake yer Alice also?' He stuck out his grubby mitt and Will shook it.

'And to think,' said the newsboy, 'that I 'ad you down as a Berk.* Looks can be deceiving, eh?'

'I have no idea what you are talking about.'

'Come on, guv'nor; you're looking for your arse† in the paper, ain't ya? And it's there, right on the front page.'

Will groaned.

'And a regular 'ero you are, and I never knowed.'

'Eh?' went Will and he unfolded the broadsheet.

'MOONSHIP LAUNCH TODAY,' ran the banner headline.

'Oh yes,' said Will. 'The launch. In all the excitement I'd forgotten about that. But—' And then he glanced down the front page. And then he saw the photograph – his photograph – and he read the copy beneath it.

It had nothing to do with his trial in Brentford, nor his hostage taking, nor his escape.

* Berkshire Hunt: Fool (loosely speaking).

† Arsenic and Old Lace: Face.

Nor in fact, did it have anything to do with him whatsoever.

Will read the copy:

HERO OF THE EMPIRE

Colonel William Starling, of The Queen's Own Aerial Cavalry, and son of Captain Ernest Starling of The Queen's Own Electric Fusiliers, posthumously awarded the Victoria Cross for his valiant act of heroism, in saving the life of Our Regal Majesty from an assassin, during the launching of the *Dreadnaught*, will today pilot Her Majesty's moonship, *Victoria*, on her maiden flight to the moon. Colonel William Starling has been in training for many months and hopes are high for the success of the flight to the moon, where Colonel Starling will plant the Union flag and claim the moon as the first off-world colony of the British Empire.

Will stared at the picture once more and then he stared at it again. The resemblance to himself was uncanny, but for the colonel's somewhat more splendid sideburns. 'Colonel William Starling,' mumbled Will. 'Son of Captain Ernest Starling, my great-great-great—'

'Great 'ero of the Empire,' said the newsboy. 'D'ya fink there's blokes up there, Colonel?'

Will mouthed a silent 'What?'

'On the moon? The theory that extraterrestrial life might exist is 'ardly new, is it, Colonel, guv? And this world of ours is literally littered with ancient monuments of gargantuan proportion that defy rational explanation and seem to point to an extraterrestrial 'ypothesis. For instance, the great pyramid of Cheops, the monuments at Karnac. Even our own Ston'enge. Do you not think it possible that members of an advanced cosmic civilisation landed upon this planet in the distant past?'

Will clipped the newsboy about the earhole.

'Shut it,' said he.

'Thank you very much, guv'nor,' said the newsboy, rubbing at his ear. 'To say that I 'ave suffered child abuse from an 'ero of the British Empire will look very good on my CV when I apply for that assistant curator's job at the Tate Gallery that I'm up for next week.'

Will stalked away, and as he stalked away, he leafed through the broadsheet. There were no pictures of the real him. Not even a mention of the events the day before in Brentford.

Master Scribbens had been right. Nothing to do with the trial had reached the media. Although. Will found a small article on the back page:

POET LAUREATE GOES STONE BONKER.

This told how the Great McGonagall had supposedly forced his way into a BBC studio the previous day and broadcast a bogus report about a fictitious trial in Brentford before dying in a freak electric lawnmower/microphone accident. Will raised his eyebrows to this.

A gent in a top hat, fly-fronted beaver-skin ulster coat and spats saluted Will. 'My very best wishes upon your historic voyage,' said he. Will sidestepped this gent and returned to the Savoy.

The expensively dressed folk of all nations were no longer to be seen. The desk clerk waved at Will and wished him all the best.

Will signed an autograph for the lift boy and returned to his suite.

Tim wasn't sleeping. He was up and about. He hadn't bathed and he never shaved, but he was all togged up in his brand new suit.

'You look rather perky,' said Will, 'for a man who's just downed a bottle of champagne.'

'I drank the orange juice,' said Tim. 'Full of vitamin C, sobers you up in an instant.'

'Does it?' said Will.

'Not really. I'm still as pissed as a pudding.'

'Well, read this. It will sober you up.'

Tim read the front page. 'My goodness,' he said. 'Electric garters that cure arthritis. What will they think of next?'

'Not the adverts. The copy.'

Tim read the copy. 'By the Goddess,' he said. 'Colonel William Starling, that would be—'

'One of my ancestors.'

'This is a surprise.'

'Isn't it.'

'Yes,' said Tim. 'But it shouldn't be, should it. I mean, you took the Retro drug, didn't you? You should be able to remember about this. Does he get to the moon okay?'

'I don't know,' said Will.

'But you must know.'

'It doesn't work like that. When I got back here into the past, all I could remember was what had happened to my ancestors up until the *now* I was *now* in. The future beyond has yet to happen, so those memories have yet to exist. Do you follow what I'm saying?'

'No,' said Tim. 'Well, sort of. But then you must have been able to remember that this Colonel William was training for the space programme.'

'Strangely,' said Will, 'I've had other things on my mind. But we have to get to the launch. I told you about the Elephant Man. He means to sabotage it, blow up the moonship when the countdown reaches zero. And you know what that could mean, don't you?'

Tim nodded thoughtfully. 'No,' he said. 'Not really.'

'My ancestor,' said Will. 'Colonel William Starling. My many times great-grandfather. If he was to die then—' Will drew a finger over his throat 'No more Starlings. No more *me*.'

'Oh,' said Tim. 'I get you. This isn't too good, is it?'

'It's about as bad as it can get, if things weren't already bad enough.'

'It's no problem,' said Tim. 'Phone the police. Tell them what you know. Have them arrest the Elephant Man.'

'Yeah, right,' said Will.

'But why not?'

'Because he's a celebrity. A friend of Her Majesty the Queen.'

'The Goddess bless Her,' said Tim. 'Phone *Her* then.'

'Her Majesty, who is apparently a good friend of Count Otto Black, also. I can't trust anyone, Tim.'

'You can trust me.'

'Yes,' said Will. 'I can.'

'Brilliant,' said Tim. 'I'm loving this. Sorry about the trouble you're in and everything. But I'm *loving* all this. Time travel. Alternative histories and futures. Robots and aliens and witches. Being here in the past with my bestest friend. I'm sorry, Will, but to me this is absolutely brilliant.'

'Glad you're enjoying it,' said Will.

'I'm sorry, but I am.'

'Just one thing,' said Will. 'Bestest friends and all that. But you seem to have forgotten something. You're also my half-brother. If *our* many times grandfather dies, then neither of us will exist.'

'Call for a cab,' said Tim. 'We can't just sit around here chatting. We have pressing business to attend to.'

'Brilliant,' said Will.

'Now *this* is brilliant,' said Tim, and he peered through the passenger window and out at the clouds.

'We are now flying,' called the cabbie through his little glass hatchway, 'at an altitude of three hundred feet at a cruising speed of eighty-five miles per hour. Our estimated time of arrival will be about half past ten.'

'Brilliant,' said Tim once more. The aerial hansom was a splendid affair, powered by Tesla turbines which drew their transmitted energy from the great sky towers. The seating was sumptuous; all overstuffed leather and polished brass fittings. The driver sat up front and he whistled as he flew.

'Present state-of-the-Victorian-art,' said Will. 'I've never travelled in one of these before; they're brand new.'

'Only picked up mine last week, Colonel,' said the cabbie. 'I know tourists still favour the old horse-drawn hansom, and many of the toffs don't feel safe travelling above ground level except in airships, but the future of public transport lies in aerial cabs; that's my conviction.'

'Goes to show how wrong you can be,' whispered Tim. 'We don't have these in our age.'

'Don't have the technology,' said Will.

'But we must have.'

'No, we don't. Look down there.' Will pointed. 'See those?'

'I do,' said Tim. 'What are they?'

'They are the Tesla towers, I told you about them. The country is dotted with them; they are linked to power stations. They broadcast electricity on a radio frequency. This cab picks up the transmission of energy; it powers the engine. No batteries to weigh the craft down you see; that's how it can fly.'

'Incredible,' said Tim. 'And we don't have this technology in our age because it was somehow erased from history.'

'In the year nineteen hundred, as far as I can figure out. Remember how I got into all this, in the first place? The digital watch in *The Fairy Feller's Masterstroke*?'

Tim nodded thoughtfully.

'Mind you,' the cabbie called back, 'I don't actually have any idea how to land this thing. It's the first time I've actually flown it.'

'I'm sure you will do fine,' said Will.

'What?' said Tim.

'I would have waited a bit,' said the cabbie. 'Had a bit of a test drive from my back garden. But when I heard the call go out on the old CB that Colonel Will Starling wanted a lift to the launch site, what with there being no other cabs available as *everyone* was heading for the launch site. Well, I upped for Queen and country, and Gawd bless me, if we all die in getting you there, then I've still done my duty, haven't I?'

'*What?*' said Tim once again, but with greater emphasis.

'Where exactly *is* the launch site?' Will asked.

'You're a caution, Colonel,' said the cabbie. 'As if you don't know.'

'Pretend I don't,' said Will. 'Where is it?'

'Penge,' called the cabbie. 'I hear it's a very nice place, although I've never been there myself. The grounds of the Crystal Palace. Might I ask you something, Colonel?'

'You might,' said Will.

'Do you think there's blokes up there, on the moon, Colonel? The theory that extraterrestrial life might exist is hardly new, is it? And this world of ours is literally littered with ancient monuments of gargantuan proportion that defy explanation. For instance, the great pyramid of Cheops, the monuments at Karnac. Even—'

'Fly on,' said Will.

The Crystal Palace.

Ah!

How wonderful was that?

Extremely wonderful, beautifully wonderful, *wonderfully* wonderful. The Millennium Dome? Spht!*

Five thousand nine hundred feet in length, over thirteen million separate panes of glass, entirely lit within by neon.

The air cab dropped down towards the Crystal Palace in a somewhat faltering manner. It did cruisings-in, followed by severe pullings-up. It did comings-round-again, followed by further and even more severe pullings-up. It did droppings-down-slowly, followed by frantic pullings-away. It did.

'Aaaaagh!' went the cabbie as Will shimmied into the driving compartment and flung him out through the driver's door.

'That was a bit harsh,' said Tim.

'He'd have killed us.'

'I think you just killed him.'

'He fell into a pond. He's okay.'

'And so you know how to drive this thing?'

'I'm willing to give it a go.'

Tim hid his face, put his hands together and recommended himself to his deity.

Will brought the air cab down into the lake amongst the concrete dinosaurs.

'Oh very good,' said Tim, peeping up. 'We've survived.'

* Spitting sound.

'Have a little faith.' Will climbed out of the cab and into the water. 'It's cold,' he said. 'But not deep.' And he waded ashore.

They were certainly there in their thousands. The glitterati of Victorian society. The expansive lawns were bespattered with them, seated in groups about their picnic hampers and gingham tablecloths.

Will and Tim did meltings into the crowd.

'No doubt you have some kind of plan,' said Tim. 'Would you care to favour me with it?'

'Get up front,' said Will. 'Keep an eye out for the Elephant Man. We have to get the launch postponed until the spacecraft can be checked for any bombs.'

'Fair enough,' Tim said. They were threading their way through the picnicking celebrities. Will had his head well down. Tim had his up; he was enjoying everything.

A voice on the public address system announced that the gallant pilot was now approaching the rostrum. The crowd cheered wildly.

Tim and Will threaded their ways onward.

It was a beautiful day. Considering the lateness of the season and everything. Very warm, very sunny, very clement. Ahead the moonship rose, glittering in the sunlight.

It was a proper Victorian moonship, with proper big fins, proper pointy top and proper portholes, lots of proper portholes.

'That is an amazing bit of kit,' said Tim. 'Do you think it will actually fly?'

'It will, if I have anything to do with it.'

'That's not what I meant. Look at it, Will. It's a Victorian spaceship. The Victorians didn't have spaceships. I'm becoming unsure about any of this. Perhaps ours is the *right* future. Perhaps none of this should really have happened.'

'What are you saying?' Will asked.

'I don't know. I'm not sure, but this can't be really real, can it? All this is more like a dream. None of it ties up, somehow.'

'Please don't confuse the issue even further, Tim. We're here to see this moonship take off safely and our many times great-grandfather in it. Whether it's really real or not, whatever that means, I can't go into now.'

'Nice day for it,' said Tim. 'Shall we get up as close as we can?'

'That's the idea.'

And so they moved forward, furtherly threading their way. They passed by a group of Pre-Raphaelite painters living it large with hampers of champagne.

'Sorry,' said Tim, as he stood upon the foot of Dante Gabriel Rossetti.

And then finally, when they could thread their way no further, they stopped – beside the twenty-foot-high electrically charged fence.

'This would be an obstacle to our further threadings forward,' said Tim. 'How are we going to get around this?'

Will stared up at the fence. Little blue crackles of electricity moved all around and about of it, saying in their own special way, 'just you try it, buddy'.

'They've somewhat stepped up security,' said Will, 'since the assassination attempt at the launching of the *Dreadnaught*. They're not taking any more risks on the life of Her Majesty.'

'Gawd bless Her.'

'Shut up.'

'Sorry.'

'We'll just have to go around it.'

'We don't have much time,' said Tim.

'Don't we?' said Will.

'Counting down,' came a voice over the public address system. 'Ten . . . nine . . . eight . . .'

Will looked at Tim.

And Tim looked at Will.

'Do something,' said Tim.

'Seven . . .'

'I don't know what to do.'

'Six . . .'

'Ask Barry to help.'

'Five . . .'

'I'm not asking Barry.'

'Four . . .'

'But he could . . .'

'Three . . .'

'I'm not going to ask him. There has to be a way . . .'

'Two . . .'

'Do something!' Tim now assumed the foetal position.

'One . . .'

'Perhaps if I . . .' said Will.

And, 'ZERO.'

And, 'KABOOOOM!'

32

The explosion erupted.

The moonship was torn into fragments. Shards of metal blasted in every direction. Ten million panes of glass fragmented in the Crystal Palace. Courtiers flung themselves in front of Her Majesty.* Beyond the electrified perimeter fence Will and Tim were bowled back by the force of the blast, and rich and and famous folk who sprawled upon the clipped lawns were swept away as if painted dollies before the hand of a petulant child. The bandstand collapsed, spilling musicians. A mushroom cloud rose into the sky.

All was chaos and destruction and devastation.

Will raised his head. His hair was scorched, his face somewhat reddened, but he seemed otherwise uninjured.

'Tim,' he called. 'Tim.'

Folk were fleeing now. Some of them were on fire. Will caught sight of Oscar Wilde, his trousers ablaze, and Lord Babbage and Mr Tesla and, it seemed, every notable body of the age, running and screaming and patting at their burning bits and bobs. It was mayhem.

'Bugger me,' said Tim, raising himself from beneath a fallen section of bandstand and freeing himself from beneath his hair. 'Will?'

'I'm here,' Will dusted debris from his person. 'We're both here. Both *still* here.'

'But the moonship? Our many times great-granddad?'

'I don't know,' said Will.

'But he couldn't have survived.'

'I just don't know.'

'Let's get out of here,' said Tim.

'We can't. People are injured. Many people. We'll have to help.'

'You're right.'

A wild-eyed and trembly Queen Victoria was being escorted away

* Gawd Bless Her. Take it as read.

from the scene of devastation. Military fellows were stumbling about, helping up the fallen. The Crystal Palace itself was now ablaze.

Tim pointed towards it. 'I remember being taught in history about that burning down,' he said, 'although it seems that they got the date wrong *and* the circumstances.'

'We really *should* get out of here, chief,' said Barry. 'Leave this to the professionals. You don't know anything about first aid.'

Will pressed his fists to his temples. '*You* could have prevented this,' he shouted.

'*Me*, chief? But you didn't ask. You're doing things your way, remember?'

'Take me back then, ten minutes into the past and I'll stop it from happening.'

'No can do, chief. That's not the way it works. I can't do anything to change what's *already* happened. Only what *might* happen.'

'Are you okay?' Tim asked.

'Of course I'm not. Are you?'

'Anything but. So should we help?'

'No,' Will shook his head. 'We couldn't stop *this*. But we'll stop what is to come.'

'I don't think I quite follow you.'

'I'm angry now,' said Will. 'I'm very angry. Come on. Follow me.'

Joseph Carey Merrick was putting the finishing touches to the paste and paper model he had been constructing of the Tesla dynamo factory, the rooftops of which he could see from his lodgings in Bedstead Square. The miniature radio mast he held between tweezers dropped from them as Tim and Will burst into his rooms.

'You bastard,' said Will. 'You murderous bastard.'

'William' said the Elephant Man, 'you startled me.'

'Blimey,' said Tim. 'You're one ugly mother-f—'

'Leave this to me,' said Will and he approached Mr Merrick. 'You didn't attend the launching of the moonship,' he said.

'I make few public appearances,' said Mr Merrick. 'I remain shy. You can understand that, considering my appearance. Most folk find it troubling.'

'You feared for your miserable life.' Will was upon him now; he dragged the cripple to his feet.

'Unhand me,' cried Mr Merrick.

'You had the moonship rigged with a bomb. People died. Many people.'

'Please let me go. My body is frail.'

'I will wring the life from it.'

'I saved your life. Yours and millions more.'

'You killed my great- great- great- grandfather.'

'That doesn't make sense,' said the Elephant Man.

'No it doesn't. But you killed all those people.'

'I had to do it. How did you know?'

'I heard you,' said Will. 'Three nights ago, when I was here with you, I heard you communicating with your alien controller.'

'Please let me go. You're hurting me.'

'I could kill you,' said Will. 'With nothing more than a fingertip's pressure. I am a master of Dimac.'

'Taught to you, no doubt, by my old friend Hugo Rune.'

Will let the Elephant Man drop. He sank back into his chair.

'Speak to me.' Will swept aside Mr Merrick's model building, reducing it to destruction.

'I have worked for months upon that.'

'You're next,' said Will. 'Tell me everything, or I will surely kill you.'

'And so you should. I welcome death. Can you imagine what it is like to be me?'

'You seem to do all right with the ladies.'

'Yes, but apart from that.'

'Just speak to me,' said Will. 'And quickly.'

'Iyomcwmctykttami.'

'Not *that* quickly.'

'If you overheard me communicating with my controller,' said Mr Merrick, 'then you know the truth about my identity. I am half man and half what you call alien. Martian to be precise.'

'Real Martian,' said Tim. 'Not in *our* future.'

'What is this man saying?' Mr Merrick asked.

'Never mind,' said Will. 'Continue.'

'The folk of Mars do not wish for war,' said Mr Merrick.

'No one's declaring war on Mars,' said Will.

'The British Empire will,' said Mr Merrick. 'They declare war upon everybody. They extend their Empire mercilessly. On and on, within five years it will encompass the globe. But it must not extend beyond Earth into space. Not to Mars. The British Empire's space programme must be halted.'

'You can't halt progress,' said Will. 'Well, I mean, well, you *shouldn't*.'

'I must,' said Mr Merrick. 'That is my mission. If I fail and the British Empire extends to Mars, then the Martian army will invade Earth and destroy every human upon it.'

'You'll lose,' said Will. 'I've read Mr H.G. Wells' book. I know how it ends.'

'I fail to understand you.'

'If Mars invades Earth,' said Will, 'Mars will fail. All the Martians will die.'

'And many men too.'

'And many men too,' said Will.

'And I do not wish for that to happen. Do you?'

'No,' said Will. 'I do not.'

There was a bit of a silence.

And then Tim broke it.

'Are you going to kill him, then?' Tim asked.

'Are we going to kill him then?' a pinch-faced woman enquired of another pinch-faced woman. The two of them were staring down at Colonel William Starling, who lay prone upon the cold stone floor of the cell at Brentford nick.

'Turn him over,' said a pinch-faced woman.

Another pinch-faced woman turned over the Colonel with her boot.

'It isn't him,' she said.

'Isn't him?' another pinch-faced woman asked.

There were four of them, all women, and all pinch-faced.

'Isn't him?'

'Look at the magnificent sideburns. He could hardly have grown them overnight, could he? It's not him.'

'Then it's one of his ancestors.'

'Which means that if we—'

'Exactly.'

'Then shall we?'

'Shall we *what*, ladies?' asked Constable Meek, entering the cell.

'Nothing, constable, but this is *not* the man you want.'

'Eh?' said a cabbie, entering hot on the heels of the constable. 'But it looks just like him. His photo is here on the front page of the *Brentford Mercury*.' The cabbie held up the newspaper. 'You're not trying to swindle me out of my one thousand quid, are you?'

'Sideburns,' said a pinch-faced woman pointing to the front-page photograph. 'This man had much larger sideburns. He could hardly have grown them overnight, could he?'

'Are you sure they're real?' asked the cabbie. And he knelt down and gave them a tug. 'Damn,' he continued. 'They are. And there was me thinking that I'd be able to give up cabbying and indulge myself in a brief but exotic life of drunkenness and debauchery.'

'Such is life,' said a pinch-faced woman, 'but not yours, it would seem.'

'Ned Kelly said that,' said Constable Meek. ' "Such is life," he said, when the hangman topped him. So, should we set this fellow free?'

'Release him into our custody. We'll take care of him.'

'I'm very upset about this,' said the cabbie.

'You can drive us to Chiswick,' said a different, but curiously similar pinch-faced woman. 'We will give you a very large tip.'

'Then I'll just have to make do with *that*, I suppose.'

'Splendid,' said another pinch-faced woman. 'Carry him out then.'

The cabbie, aided by a constable, set to the carrying-out.

'Put him back,' said another constable, barring the way of all in the corridor beyond the cell.

'What is this?' asked the constable who was helping with the carrying-out.

'We have to hold this man for questioning. He answers to the description of a fellow who was observed in the company of several others, urinating upon a burning gatherer of the pure, stoning a tramp who was looking at him in a funny way and throwing an old lady from Kew Bridge for a reason that probably seemed appropriate at the time.'

'A regular villain,' said the constable, letting his end of Colonel William drop to the cold stone floor. 'Back to the cell with this scoundrel.'

'Damn,' said a pinch-faced woman, but which one it was remained unclear.

'Damn,' said Will.

'Damn?' said Tim.

'He's right,' said Will. 'Whether we like it or not, Mr Merrick probably did the right thing.'

'But all those people dead. All those people injured.'

'It could be *very* much worse. If *Mars Attacks*.'

'It could,' Mr Merrick agreed. 'And it would be very much worse.'

'So are we just going to walk away from this?' Tim asked. 'Walk away from *him*? Even though he's responsible for all those deaths?'

'What would *you* do?'

Tim thought and then he shrugged his shoulders.

'Let's go,' said Tim.

33

Three and a half hours earlier, Colonel William Starling of the Queen's Own Aerial Cavalry Regiment had awoken to the sounds of an instrumental rendition of Little Tich's ever popular Big Boot Dance, issuing from his Babbage digital alarm clock. This clock, a present from his now late and lamented daddy, had been given to young William upon the occasion of his sixth birthday. William reached out a hand and silenced the clock.

He blinked his eyes and focused them and took in his present surroundings. These were *not* his barracks at Queen's Gate. William scratched at his blondy head and his prodigious sideburns and then memories returned to him: memories of the night before, the riotous night before.

He had been taken 'out on the razzle' by the chaps of the officer's mess, to celebrate the moon launch of the morrow. Much champagne had been imbibed, many guineas had been squandered at a Notting Hill gaming hell, named Barnaby Rudge's Electric Fun Palace, and much clubbing had been done at the Burlington, Stringfellow's and at the Pussycat Club. And there had been much whoring too, at Madame Lorraine Loveridge's establishment in Bayswater. But beyond this, things were blurry for William.

He dimly recalled a urinating competition which involved an attempt to extinguish a gatherer of the pure whom Binky Hartington had set on fire for a bit of jolly. And then there was the stoning of a tramp who had looked at them in what they considered to be a funny way. And an old lady had been thrown into the Thames from Kew Bridge for some reason that now escaped William, but had seemed appropriate at the time.

All in all, it had been a memorable evening, although no less memorable than any other Tuesday night, when the regiment was down from the sky and billeted in Queen's Gate.

William arose from the bed and stretched his lanky limbs. His regimental cronies had brought him back here, to his childhood home at number seven Mafeking Avenue, Brentford and laid him to rest upon his childhood bed. William glanced down and noticed that he wasn't wearing any trousers, and that his genitals had been painted with boot black.

'Damn poor show,' said Colonel William Starling, examining his blackened bits. 'Tarring a fellow's chappie when he's in the land of Nod. Although,' and here he paused and clenched his buttocks, 'it could have been a lot worse. "Chunky" Wilberforce could have rogered me rigid and I'd not have known a damn thing about it.'

'Willy dear,' a voice called up to him. 'Are you out of your bed yet? It's a big day for you, remember?'

'The mater,' said Colonel William. 'I shall be down in an instant, mother of mine, just as soon as I've had a wash and brush-up.'

'It's kippers and jam,' called his loving mother. 'Your favourite.'

'My favourite is pâté de fois gras smeared upon a maiden's nipple, you common old cow,' muttered Colonel William. 'My very favourite,' he called down.

Getting dressed proved to be something of a problem, for Colonel William's trousers were nowhere to be found. His boots were there, patent and polished, complete with their golden spurs with airship motif, but of trousers, Colonel William's bedroom was a regular Mother Hubbard's cupboard.

'Damn poor show,' said the Colonel once again, and with no propriety-brand cleaning products to hand, he strode down the stairs to breakfast, sans trousers and dark as a nigger's* nadger about the nadger regions.

William scarcely glanced at the pictures that hung upon the gaily-papered staircase wall. These were all of his father, the late Captain Ernest Starling, who had been posthumously awarded the Victoria Cross for saving the life of his monarch during the launching of the *Dreadnaught*.

The son of a national hero was Colonel William and he had every intention of eclipsing his father's fame and winning for himself a very large place in the history of The Empire.

Colonel Will entered the front parlour. It was decorated in the suburban chic of a time two decades before, quilted Farnsbarns ruff-tuckers with extended dolly-frames and overlarge splay-footed finials

* It must be remembered that in Victorian times such terms as nigger, darkie, savage and coon were considered politically correct. And the word spastic was still a term of endearment, although mostly favoured by gyppos.

in the style of Marchant; a Dutch crimping cabinet, with the original geometrically glazed sodium foils, a matched pair of Cheggers, a filigreed muff tunnel, and a dining table and six chairs that were recognisable as 'Olde Chameleons'.

Upon the table was the morning edition of the *Brentford Mercury*. Colonel Will's mother, who had been decanting kippers from the Babbage low-fat fryer to the Babbage electric hostess trolley, caught sight of her son's naked loin area and all but fouled the fish.

'Hell's handbags!' shrieked she. 'Oo, pardon my French.'

'No, pardon me, mater,' said Colonel Will. 'The chaps played a prank upon me.'

'Boys will be boys,' said the lady of the house. 'I recall the regimental dances that your dear dead daddy and I used to attend. Not a pair of trousers left on a man after the clock struck ten.'

'I shall need to borrow a pair of the pater's kecks, if I'm to look respectable for the launching,' said Colonel Will, seating himself at the head of the table.

'His dress uniform is mothballed in a trunk in the loft. I know he'd be proud for you to wear it.'

'Damn good show.' Colonel Will took up a knife and fork and his mother served him kippers from the hostess trolley.

And then she hovered over him, wringing her veiny hands and cocking her head from side to side in that way which mothers always do when they gaze proudly upon their only sons.

'Sit down and join me, mater,' said Colonel William.

'Ah, no dear,' said his mother. 'I'd rather not sit down, if you don't mind.'

'And why is that?'

'Well, let us just say that your chum Chunky stayed rather long last night. After he'd put you to bed, he plied me with cherry brandy and one thing led to another, and I don't think I'll be riding my bicycle for at least a week.'

'Quite so,' said Colonel William. 'I'd prefer not to hear the details.'

'So I'll just stand,' said his mother. 'And hobble when I need to get from A to P.'

'Surely that's A to B.'

'More kippers?' asked his mother.

'I haven't started upon these yet.'

Colonel William's mother smiled warmly upon her son, then hobbled off to P.

She returned to find that the Colonel had finished his kippers and jam, and most of the cornflakes too. And was now engrossed in the *Brentford Mercury*. 'Do you know anything about *this*, mater?' he asked her.

'Yes dear, it's a newspaper.'

'Its contents,' said Colonel William.

'News, dear.'

'Today's news!'

'No dear. There's no telling what that might be.'

'Well, I damn well know what it *should* be, but it is not.' Colonel William made a very fierce face.

'You seem upset,' his mother observed.

'Damnedly right! I was informed by the Ministry that every newspaper in the land would be carrying my photographic portrait upon its front page this morning. This newspaper, however does not.'

'It's the *Brentford Mercury*,' said the mother of Colonel William. 'And this *is* Brentford. Things are done differently here. Brentford does not have much truck with the outside world. Not much lorry either, nor wagon, nor handcart, nor even—'

'Cease your babbling, woman.'

'That's no way to speak to your mother.'

'No, damn me, it is not. My apologies, mother of mine, but this leading story, it is an outrage. A libellous outrage. I shall sue this newspaper for every penny it has.' Colonel William flung the offensive tabloid to the gaily-patterned carpet (an original Trumpton with the classic 'Dancing Dan goes doolally' design). His mother stooped with difficulty and retrieved it.

JACK THE RIPPER ESCAPES FROM BRENTFORD COURTHOUSE

read the headline, and then there was a considerable amount of text, written in that style which is known as 'purple prose.'

And then there was a single photograph of—

'But it's *you*,' said the mother of Colonel William. 'Your photographic portrait *is* upon the front page.'

'That is *not* me!' cried her son, rising hastily from his chair and striking his painted genitalia upon the underside of the dining table in the process. 'It's not me, it's urrgsh!' And he took to clutching at his damaged parts.

'Well, this Mr Urrgsh looks very much like you! Except that he doesn't have such magnificent side-whiskers.'

Colonel William's eyes were crossed. 'Damned slur!' he cried. 'The work of subversives. Enemies of the Empire. A witch plot, I'll wager.'

'A *what*, dear?'

'Nothing, mater.' Colonel William bent double and took to the taking of deep breaths.

'You said a witch plot,' said his mother. 'It will be that Chiswick Townswomen's Guild up to their unspeakable wickedness again, I wouldn't wonder.'

Colonel William raised his red-rimmed eyes. 'What did you say?' he asked.

'The Chiswick Townswomen's Guild,' said his mother. 'Would you like me to put some turpentine on your bits?'

'What?'

'To remove the boot black. If I had a silver sovereign for each time I had to de-black your daddy's bits with turps, I'd have enough to buy myself a diamond-encrusted handbag in the style of Wainscott and a pair of Le Blanc and Sons ivory clogs.'

'No, no.' Colonel William flapped his hands about. 'I have to know what you're talking about. And I do *not* mean regarding the turpentine.'

'Actually it's called turpentine substitute,' said his mother. 'Although I've never been certain exactly what it's a substitute for. I know they have substitutes in football but—'

'Enough.' Colonel William straightened himself up. 'Speak to me only of witches,' said he. 'And in a coherent manner, or surely I will dash out your brains with the Babbage electric waffle iron that hangs beside the brass companion set in the Mulbury Turner fireplace, with the scroll fandangos and moulded jiz-fillets.'

'You mentioned witches,' said the Colonel's mother. 'Why did you mention witches?'

'Because, mater,' Colonel William sighed. 'Not that I should be telling you this because it's top secret, but—'

'A cabal of witches exists, intent upon destroying technological society and so by altering the future.'

'*What?*' went Colonel William once more.

'Your father told me all about it. He was assigned to a special unit.'

'I knew nothing of this.'

'You were only a child when he died so valiantly saving the Queen, Gawd bless Her. Are you in a special unit too?'

'No.' Colonel William was fully erect and his shoulders were back. 'But such matters are discussed in the officers' mess. It is well-known that such plots exist. But as to who is doing the plotting; that is another matter.'

'You should have asked me then, dear. I went to school with most of them, evil harpies that they are. And you believe that they are responsible for this?' And Colonel William's mother tapped at the *Brentford Mercury*.

'What other explanation could there be? To besmirch the reputation of the moonship's pilot by accusing him of being Jack the Ripper.'

'Well, I suppose that's *one* explanation.'

'And you know, *for certain*, that the Chiswick Townswomen's Guild is to blame?'

'Absolutely certain. I'd have told your father, had he ever asked me. But he never did. "A woman's place is in the home," he used to say, "with her face in the pillow and her bottom in the air".'

'I must relay this intelligence at once to the appropriate authorities.'

'I'm sure they already know, dear. I expect they have wives of their own, at home with their bottoms in the air.'

'*About the witches.*'

'They never marry, dear.'

'Fetch father's trunk at once,' said Colonel William. 'I must make haste to the Crystal Palace.'

A half of a morning hour later, Colonel William stood before the wardrobe mirror in his mother's bedroom and examined his reflection.

He looked truly magnificent. His father's uniform fitted him precisely. The dry cleaners had got most of the blood out of it and the invisible menders had mended the terrible rendings of cloth invisibly. But for the strong smell of turpentine substitute that now surrounded him, Colonel William was every bit a military gentleman, even though it was only a Captain's uniform, rather than the far more flamboyant Colonel's kittings.

Colonel William placed his father's bearskin helmet upon his head, straightened the sabre, tucked a silver-mounted swagger stick beneath his left armpit and clicked his military heels together. 'Your Majesty,' he said. 'I have the pleasure to inform you that the threat posed by witches to yourself and your Empire no longer exists. A special unit, led by myself upon my successful return from the moon, has cleansed your realm of evil. A knighthood did you say? I would be honoured to receive it. And your daughter's hand in marriage? Ma'am, you flatter me too much, but I am more deeply honoured and happy to accept.'

'Your cab's here,' the Colonel's mum called up the stairs. 'He says to get your arse in gear because he has a busy morning.'

'Damned impudence,' said the Colonel, and offering his reflection a smart salute, he took himself down to the cab.

It was a *Babbage Electric Wheeler.* The nineteen hundred series. The cabbie leaned against the bonnet smoking a Wild Woodbine. 'Morning guv'nor,' he said in the manner of cabbies everywhere.*

'Into your driving seat, my man,' ordered the Colonel. 'And convey me at speed to the Crystal Palace.'

'Off to the launching, is it?' The cabbie tapped ash from his cigarette.

'And get a move on.' Colonel William stood before the passenger door, waiting for the cabbie to open it. 'I was given to believe that *you* were in a hurry.'

'Nah, not really. That was just to wind you up.'

'Kindly open the passenger door.'

'Lost the use of your 'ands 'ave you?'

'You surly lout!'

'Life's a laugh, innit?' The cabbie swung open the passenger door and Colonel William climbed into the cab. His mum came out to give him a nice wave off.

'Are you not coming too?' Colonel William asked her.

'No thank you, dear. You know what it's like. If you've seen one moon launching, you've seen them all.'

'But this is the first one.'

'So I don't want to spoil myself for the rest.'

'Damned idiot woman.' Colonel William tapped briskly upon the glass partition that separated the cabbie from himself. 'Crystal Palace, as fast as you can.'

'Send me a postcard from the moon,' called his mother.

'Good grief!'

The cabbie engaged the *Babbage's* electric drive system. Electrical power, broadcast from a nearby Tesla tower, set wheels in motion and they were off.

'You didn't answer me,' called the cabbie over his shoulder.

'You didn't ask me anything,' replied Colonel William, settling back upon padded leather cushions and taking in the view of the streets that he'd played in as a child.

'I asked you whether you were off to view the launching,' called the cabbie.

'Hardly to view,' Colonel William called back. 'I am the pilot of the moonship.'

* Except outside the Greater London area.

'You never are!' The cabbie glanced into his driving mirror.

'Indeed I am!'

'Well I never. They should have put your picture in the paper.'

'Grrrr!' went Colonel William.

'Although.' The cabbie glanced down. Upon the polished Bakelite dashboard of his cab was his copy of today's *Brentford Mercury*. Upon it's front page was *that* photograph.

The cabbie glanced once more into his driving mirror. Although it wasn't so much of a glance this time, more of a stare.

'Keep your eyes on the road!' called the Colonel, as the cab struck a cyclist a glancing blow and sent him into a hedge.

'Right, sir,' said the cabbie, but his eyes darted once more towards the paper's front page, and towards the text which Colonel William had not read in full; to the bottom of the text in fact, the bit that mentioned the reward, the one thousand pounds reward, generously donated by the Chiswick Townswomen's Guild for the recapture of Jack the Ripper.

'Bless my soul,' said the cabbie. 'This is my lucky day.'

'What was that?' called Colonel William.

'Nothing guv'nor. You just sit back there, have a bit of a snooze if you like. It will be a long journey, but I'll get you there as quickly as I can.'

'I shall,' called Colonel William. 'I'm still somewhat groggy as it happens. Bit of a late night with the chaps. A quick forty winks will sharpen me up for my flight,' and the Colonel snuggled himself down and closed his eyes.

'We'll see all about that, *Jack*,' muttered the cabbie and he pressed the button that engaged the cab's central locking system. The clicking of the passenger door locks went unheard by Colonel William who was settling into slumber.

'And out you come, my laddie!' Colonel William was suddenly rudely awakened. Rough hands were being laid upon him. Pullings were occurring, hither, to and thus. 'Don't make a fight of it, or we'll have to truncheon you down.'

Colonel William looked up. A constable, with bandages showing from beneath his regulation helmet, had him by the throat.

'Unhand me, you oaf!' cried the Colonel.

'That's it. Constable Meek, club this villain senseless.'

'With the greatest of pleasure,' and the clubbing-senseless began.

And it didn't end within the cab itself. It continued in the street, and into the Brentford police station, and then down to the cell, and then in the cell, where savage bootings were added to the clubbings senseless.

'Why are you doing this?' moaned Colonel William, who still had some degree of senseness to his account.

'You won't escape from us a second time,' said Constable Meek joyfully putting the boot in once more.

'I'll definitely get my thousand pound reward, won't I?' asked the cabbie, putting in a boot of his own.

'Why?' called Colonel William. 'Why?'

But then a truncheon *really* went down, and the Colonel's lights went out, without any ten-nine-eight-seven-six, but only with one big *ZERO*.

34

The afternoon papers will filled with the tragedy.

MOONSHIP HORROR
Dozens dead and hundreds injured

And speculation was being given its evil head.

It was another assassination attempt upon the Queen, said some. The work of anarchists, said others, or Johnny foreigner, said still others. But one thing was clear in the minds of all the writers. This was *not* an accident. British technology did not fail in such a spectacular and terrifying manner. The moonship had been sabotaged, and the chief suspect had already been named, by most of the papers: Colonel William Starling of the Queen's Own Aerial Cavalry Regiment.

He had failed to appear at the launching. A regimental colleague, a noble officer by the name of Algernon 'Chunky' Wilberforce, had stepped in to save the day and pilot the ship. 'Chunky' Wilberforce was to be awarded a posthumous VC.

The villain of the piece was clearly Colonel William Starling. His photograph *dis*-graced the front pages of every afternoon newspaper, but for the *Brentford Mercury*, which featured the first chapter of the Brentford Snail Boy's autobiography.

Plain Will Starling sat with Tim in the public bar of the Golden Rivet, Whitechapel. Plain Will Starling munched upon pork scratchings, his munchings punctuated by great drafts of porter. Plain Will Starling was a very worried young man and one having difficulty munching his scratchings.

'Take your muffler off,' Tim told him.

Will readjusted the muffler that covered his face. 'I can't,' said he. 'Look at the afternoon newspaper. I now have the face of public enemy number one.'

'Seems very unfair on our great-however-many-times-granddad.' Tim was presently unmuffled, but then it wasn't *his* face on the newspaper. 'You don't think he did it, do you, Will?'

Will sighed. 'We *know* he didn't,' he replied between muffled munchings. 'Joseph Merrick, the Elephant Man, did it.'

'We should turn him in to the police.'

'We've been through all that. Stop it.'

Tim made a thoughtful face and pushed back handfuls of hair. So what do you propose to do next?' he asked.

'What would *you* do next?'

Tim made another thoughtful face, but it was indistinguishable from the first. And just because you make a thoughtful face, it doesn't necessarily mean that the thoughts going on in your head amount to very much.

'Well,' said Tim, thoughtfully.

'If you want my opinion, chief,' said Barry.

'I don't,' said Will.

'Don't what?' Tim asked.

'Barry was asking whether I wanted his opinion.'

'I'd like to hear it,' said Tim.

'Well I wouldn't. The way *I* see it, is this.'

Tim prepared himself to listen. He made a thoughtful, *listening* face.

'I haven't a clue,' said Will. 'I'm sorry to say it, but I'm totally lost. My other self is missing, our many times great-grandfather is missing. You and I are both wanted by the police, *me* somewhat more than you, it appears. We have Martians squaring up to attack Earth if the British Empire launches another moonship. We have witches up to goodness knows what evil. And let's not forget those terminator robots. I'm sure I'm due for another visitation from one of them quite soon. And there's Rune dead, and for all of my other self's talk, I really have no definite idea who Rune's murderer is, nor why he murdered those women. And that's probably not even the worst of it.'

Tim swigged away at his porter. 'This stuff's very poor,' said he. 'The beer really *is* best in Brentford.'

'I think it might be a while before we go back there for another tasting.'

'We could get the Savoy to order us some.'

'We can't go back to the Savoy, I'd be recognised at once.'

'Chief, if I might just make a suggestion.'

'Please be quiet, Barry.'

'But, chief.'

'No Barry,' said Will. 'Let's be positive here, Tim. Let's think this through. What is the easiest option to take?'

'Well,' said Tim and he made his face again.

'Do nothing,' said Will. 'Nothing.'

'But I wasn't going to—'

'I mean, *I* do nothing. What if I was to return to the future, but a day before I discovered the Babbage watch in *The Fairy Feller's Masterstroke*. And then, what say if I *don't* discover it. I ignore it, pretend I've never seen it. Then none of *this* would happen. We wouldn't be in this mess.'

Tim thought about this. 'Can't be done,' said he. 'And I'll tell you why. If you return to the future to a time *before* you left it and came here, the original you would be already there. You met your original you on the tram, didn't you? There can't be two yous in the future, can there?'

'That wouldn't be so bad,' said Will. 'I'm sure we'd get on okay.'

'It's a smelly idea,' said Tim. 'You've met your other self, here in the past. You know that he comes from a different future. And a much better one than ours. Our future is rubbish: poverty, overcrowding, everyone bloated on synthetic food, chemical rains scalding the pavements, constant surveillance. Our future sucks. It's a dystopia. Your other self's future is a utopia. It's a much better option.'

'But if I save the other future, you and I will cease to exist.'

'So we'll never know the difference, will we? And I'll be born in the other future. That won't be so bad.'

'It will for *me*,' said Will. 'I'll be the Promised One. I don't fancy that for a future.'

'One out of two's not so bad. Think of the rest of us. Don't be so selfish.'

Will threw up his hands. 'It's hopeless,' he mumbled. 'Whatever I do, I'm going to end up in the poo.'

'Then do the right thing. Thwart them witches.'

'Stuff the witches,' said Will. 'And stuff the so-called utopia. Our future isn't *that* bad.'

'It's worse than you know,' said Tim. 'I've been thinking a lot about this. About what Barry told you about the death of God. You know that I'm interested in all this kind of business. Always have been, probably because *I'm* Rune's magical heir. But religion has always fascinated me. Remember when you switched those paintings in the Tate's archive and you saw those two women and I told you that *they* were witches and they had a lot of power? And I told you how I'd gained promotion because I'd put on my application form that I was a Pagan.'

'Yes, but—' said Will.

'Just hear me out, please. Think about the future we come from. No one actually worships God or Jesus any more. The churches are all franchised by IKEA or NIKE or ADIDAS or VIRGIN, and that's *not* the Virgin Mary. The services have all been changed. The hymns are advertising jingles. The folk in churches aren't worshipping God any more, or *any* God. They're not worshipping anything. They're just endorsing companies. Major corporations. And who are running the executive boards of these corporations? Witches, that's who. I know this for a fact.'

'So what does it really matter?' Will asked.

'To an atheist it wouldn't matter. But if you believed in God, it would. There is a theory, and it's a very ancient theory, that Man and God are co-dependent upon one another. One cannot exist without the other. Without Man, God has no one to worship Him; therefore He is God to no one, and as such does not exist. God created Man to worship Him, to acknowledge His existence, to be a testament to His existence. The Egyptians worshipped Ra and Horus and Isis. Those gods were real to the Egyptians, those gods existed to them. But the temples of Ra and Horus and Isis were eventually overthrown; those gods were no longer worshipped, so what of those gods now?'

'They never existed,' said Will.

'You can't prove that,' said Tim.

'You can't prove that they did.'

'Please just listen to me. If gods *did* exist, would you find the theory of co-dependence feasible?'

Will shrugged. 'Why not?' he said. 'It makes some kind of sense.'

'So if it made sense with Ra and Horus and Isis, then why not the God of the Israelites and his son Jesus Christ? If no one believes in them any more or worships or acknowledges them any more, then they would cease to exist also, wouldn't they? They'd die.'

'I suppose they would,' said Will.

'So, if *you* believed in them, you wouldn't want that to happen, would you?'

'Of course I wouldn't,' said Will.

'So, if you personally could do something to stop that happening you'd certainly do it.'

'I certainly would,' said Will.

'Such as, doing what you have to do to stop the witches messing with the future and wiping out all memories of Victorian super technology.'

'I suppose I'd have no choice,' said Will, 'if I believed in God and God's continued existence depended upon it.'

'But you don't believe in God,' said Tim.

'I don't,' said Will.

'*Even though you have one of His Holy Guardians in your head!*'

Tim fairly shouted these words at Will and these shouted words drew the attention of other patrons of the Golden Rivet. Amongst these were a big bargee, his smaller counterpart, a gatherer of the pure and a lady in a straw hat who was selling copies of the *War Cry*.

'Well,' said Will, and beneath his muffler, he made a thoughtful face.

'Well?' said Tim.

Will gave Tim a good staring at. 'Are you telling me,' he asked, 'that you think this is what it's all about?'

'It's what Barry told you it's all about.'

'He didn't explain it the way you have.'

'I would have, chief, if you'd given me a chance.'

'It's absurd,' said Will. 'Ridiculous. And more than that, it's unfair. I, an atheist, am expected to single-handedly save the life of God.'

'It does have a certain irony,' said Tim. 'But not single-handedly, Barry and I are here to help you get the job jobbed.'

'Why do I not find this comforting?'

'Listen,' said Tim. 'I didn't believe in God. My mum's a Sister of Sainsbury's, like your mum. I was brought up in that faith. I signed up as a Pagan to advance my career. Now I realise what I really did. Satan's powers on Earth have always been kept at bay by God, because Satan had far fewer believers, worshippers. But with God out of the picture and the witches worshipping Satan, then Satan has all the power. He's in control. Our society is falling apart; things are worse every day. The new day's always worse than the day before. It really *is* a dystopia, Will, and it's turning into Hell on Earth.'

'All right,' said Will. 'Stop. Stop. I get the picture.'

'And do you believe what I'm saying?'

'I don't know,' said Will. 'I'm not sure.'

'You must believe in Barry. He talks to you.'

'That doesn't mean that he's a Holy Guardian. He might be a demon.'

'Oh, so you believe in Satan? If you believe in Satan, then you must believe in God.'

'Aha!' said Will. 'Then that's the flaw in your theory. The witches must believe in God also. And so if there's still folk who believe in him, he won't die.'

'I think you'll find it's all to do with the worshipping, the acknowledging of him as all-powerful.'

'Maybe Barry's not an angel or a demon,' said Will, who wasn't giving up without a struggle. 'Maybe he's something else entirely.'

'And what might that be?' Tim sank more porter and wrung out the drippings from his beard.

Will made a *very* thoughtful face beneath his muffler. 'Maybe he's an alien,' said Will. 'Like Mr Merrick.'

'Well,' said Tim. 'Mr Merrick certainly did have a few sprouty bits about himself, but I don't think it's very likely, do you?'

'It's as likely as your theory. Barry originally told me that he was a genetically engineered time sprout from a planet called Phnaargos.'

'I was winding you up, chief,' said Barry. 'You're beaten and you know it. I'm the real McCoy. I'm one of God's little helpers. And I have the Big Figure's interests at heart. I know He's been a bit lax with managing this planet. His well-known hands-off approach to Godship. He leaves it to fellows like me to be the voice-of-the-conscience and try to keep folk on the straight and narrow. But I don't want Him to pop his almighty clogs. I'd be out of a job, for one thing. I'd have to defect to the other side, or they'd see to it that I got mulched into the Great Compost Heap in the Sky.'

'I need to think about this,' said Will.

'You need to act,' said Tim, 'not think. Do your stuff. Get the job jobbed. Save the future. Save God. I reckon you'd earn yourself some big kudos with God if you pull this off. If you were to die in the process of pulling this off, I reckon there'd be a lot of jolly awaiting you in heaven.'

'And *that's* supposed to make me feel better?'

'There's no pleasing some people,' said Barry.

'There's no pleasing some people,' said Tim.

'All right!' said Will. 'Stop. Stop, the both of you.'

'The both of you?' The big bargee peered down at Will. 'It's you again, ain't it?'

Will looked up at the big bargee. And then Will groaned. 'You don't know me,' he said.

'I do, mister. I recognised your voice. And I recognise this bloke with you, your defence counsel, the one who took the hostages. Take off that muffler, let's 'ave a look at your mug.'

'I've got a skin disease,' said Will. 'You wouldn't want to see my face.'

Tim looked up at the big bargee, the big bruised-looking bargee, the big bruised-looking bargee that had been in the Brentford courtroom.

'Show me your face.' The big bargee dug into his sailcloth trousers and brought out a copy of the morning's *Brentford Mercury*. It's *you*, mister. And there's a thousand quid reward on your 'ead.'

'Please go away,' said Will. 'I don't have time for this. Consider yourself to be a running gag that's run its course and have it away upon your toes.'

'Is it him?' asked the lady in the straw hat.

'I'm taking care of this,' said the big bargee.

'There's a ten thousand pound reward for his capture,' said the lady in the straw hat.

'It's *one* thousand quid,' said the big bargee. 'It's in the paper.'

And he flashed his paper.

'It's *ten* thousand,' said the lady in the straw hat. And she drew from her handbag *her* newspaper and flourished it at the big bargee. Her newspaper was a copy of *The Times*, a late-afternoon edition. It had upon its front page a picture of Colonel William Starling, Britain's Most Wanted Man. He had a ten thousand pound reward upon *his* head.

'Muffler,' said the big bargee.

'No,' said Will.

'I'm warning you, mister.' The big bargee placed his paper on Will's table and raised his fists in a threatening manner.

Will rose carefully to his feet.

'Easy,' whispered Tim. 'We don't want to cause a scene, now do we?'

Will slowly removed his muffler.

'Oh dear,' said Tim.

'Gotcha,' said the big bargee.

But Will shook his head. 'Do you recall what happened to you the last time we met?' he asked. 'Do you not recall the battering I gave you?'

The big bargee sniffed through his broken nose.

'Do you really want some more?' Will asked.

The big bargee stroked his grazed chin with a bruised knuckle. 'There's a one thousand quid reward on you,' he said.

'*Ten* thousand,' said the lady in the straw hat.

'My friend and I are leaving now,' said Will. 'If you attempt to stop us—'

'I'll shoot you,' said Tim and he drew out his pistol.

'Fair enough,' said Will. 'That will save me the effort.'

'But—' went the big bargee. 'But—'

'I'm sorry,' said Will. 'But I have to go. I'm off to save God and the future.'

35

'Bravo, chief,' said Barry, when he, Will and Tim were several streets away from the Golden Rivet and walking unfollowed. 'I think you handled that very well. And I'm glad that at last you've come around to doing the right thing.'

'Tim,' said Will, 'down here'. And Will steered Tim into an alleyway. 'I am just going to have a few words with Barry. Keep a look out for trouble, will you?'

'Will do,' said Tim.

Will walked a few paces further. 'All right,' he said to Barry. 'I will get the job jobbed, but I'll do it my way. Take me to the future so that I can get myself an arsenal of formidable hardware, then convey me to the exact time and place when these witches will be casting their spells or whatever they do to change the future. Then I'll blast the lot of them and we can all go home to bed. Or whatever.'

'Ah, chief,' said Barry.

'Ah, Barry?' said Will.

'No can do,' said Barry. 'Not the last bit anyway. That would be cheating. That would be like Divine Intervention. That's not in my remit. I can't do that. I can advise you, if you'll take my advice, which you haven't done so far. But I can't actually put you in the right time and the right place. Until *you* know what the right time and the right place is. You have to find that out by yourself. Sorry.'

'That is *exactly* what I thought you'd say.'

'Sorry, chief.'

'Then do something else for me.'

Tim turned. 'The coast is clear,' said he. And, 'Oh my – *God*, who are you?'

'It's me, Tim.'

'You? Who you?'

'It's Will,' said Will.

'No it's not.'

'It is.' Will grinned at Tim. And Tim recognised the grin. But he didn't recognise much else. Will had changed – dramatically. He was—

'Older,' said Tim. 'You're older. You're *old*.'

'I'm *not* old,' said Will. 'I'm six months older. I've been in the future for six months, growing this beard and getting myself all prepared.'

Tim, peered hard at this slightly older Will. 'What exactly have you been up to?' he asked.

'I've been to the future,' said Will. 'The other future. Not our future. I had to persuade Barry to take me, he didn't want to do it. But I did persuade him and it *is* a good future. In fact, it's an incredible future, apart from the worshipping of Hugo Rune that goes on there. We'll have to put a stop to *that*. But I stayed there for six months. Grew the beard.' Will stroked at his long blondy beard. 'And the hair.' Will stroked at this also.

'It's a better beard than mine,' said Tim. 'And your hair's longer.'

'They have very advanced cosmetics in the other future. Their shampoos enhance hair growth. There's no more baldness. You see, I couldn't do anything here if I'm on the Most Wanted list. I had to change my appearance. And I had to learn too, all about those witches, and do research and train my body.' Will raised his right arm. 'Feel the muscles,' he said. 'They have very effective steroids in that future. You can just buy them over the counter.'

Tim felt the muscles. 'Big muscles,' he said. 'I don't know whether I think they suit you.'

'I like them. I had to prepare myself for the getting of the job jobbed. I'm all prepared now.'

'I like the get-up,' said Tim.

Will was dressed in a ground-length coat of black leather, white lacy silk shirt, black leather waistcoat, black leather trousers, black leather boots. Well, if you *are* going to be a hero and save the world, you really have to do it dressed in black leather.

Everybody knows *that*!

'It's the only way, isn't it?' said Will. 'I styled the coat on yours. Took the bespoke tailor two months to get it right.'

'But you weren't even gone for a moment.'

'Six months,' said Will. 'Six long months. I missed you, I really did.'

'Sorry that I didn't get the chance to miss you.' Tim shook his head and pushed away his hair. 'This is intense,' he said.

'A witch-finder is always intense,' said Will.'

'A what?'

'Witch-finder,' said Will. 'Will the Witch-finder. That's me. Seek 'em out and destroy 'em, that's my mission.'

'Right,' said Tim. 'Well, I don't know quite what to say.'

'Don't say anything then. Just follow me. We're off to hunt witches.'

Will led Tim from the alleyway and off at the briskest of paces.

'Can I say something now?' Tim asked, as he did his best to keep up.

'Go on,' said Will.

'Where exactly are we going now?'

'To my manse,' said Will.

'Your what?'

'My manse. A magician always has a manse and so too should a witch-finder. Who is in turn a magician of sorts, a white magician. You must know the kind of thing, Tim. You've watched the movies: a Gothic pile with an extensive library of occult books and a veritable museum of curious artefacts.'

'And you have one?'

'I've done my research. I know where there is one. It's not a Gothic pile though. It's an elegant Regency dwelling, it's presently unoccupied, and it's ours for the taking. We're entitled to it.'

'Will,' said Tim. 'I have to say that I have no idea what on earth you're talking about, or exactly what you're up to. But I have to tell you this. I'm loving it.'

'Splendid,' said Will and he marched on ahead.

Tim followed on behind. 'Loving it,' he said once more.

Will hailed a horse-drawn hansom. 'Brentford, please,' he told the cabbie. 'The Butts Estate, Brentford.'

And an hour and a 'smidgen' later, the cab drew up outside an elegant Regency house in Brentford's Butts Estate, and Will and Tim climbed down from it. Will paid off the cabbie and Tim stared up at the imposing house.

'One classy dwelling,' said he. 'And nobody lives here?'

'Not for years.'

'And you're going to break in?'

'No, I have a key.'

'Lead on,' said Tim. 'I'm loving it.'

Will swung open the wrought-iron gate and marched up the gravel path.

'Are you sure nobody lives here?' Tim asked, 'because the lawn is newly cut and the garden well tended.'

'No one lives here,' said Will. 'But behold who did,' and he drew Tim's attention to a small engraved-brass plate upon the panelled front door.

Tim stared and said, 'Rune. The plate says "Hugo Rune".'

'His home,' said Will, 'and possibly his best kept secret. I knew there was more money somewhere. It took a lot of research to uncover the location of this house, this manse. He kept it a very closely-guarded secret. Didn't want its contents to fall into wrong hands in the event of his untimely death. I traced his strongbox to a left-luggage locker in Euston station. The front door key was in it. Shall we go inside?'

'If you think it's okay,' said Tim. 'I mean, there won't be traps and things in there, will there?'

'I wouldn't be at all surprised.'

'Then perhaps I'll just wait out here until you've disabled them.'

'We'll go together,' said Will. 'Remember this is your home as much as mine. Probably more so, as *you're* his magical heir.'

Tim made sighing sounds. 'I am confused about that,' said he. 'Surely our great-great-and-so-on- granddad is Colonel William Starling. Where exactly does Rune fit into his family equation?'

'That doesn't take too much imagination, does it?' said Will. 'You didn't know who your *real* father was, did you? I think Rune was Colonel Starling's grandfather.'

'Then he sent his own son, Captain Starling, to his death to save Her Majesty at the launching of the *Dreadnaught*. You told me that you remembered that when you took the Retro drug.'

'This really isn't the time for that conversation. Let's go inside.' Will placed the key in the front door lock and gave it a forceful twist. Tumblers engaged, levers moved and the lock gave forth to a satisfying click. Will pushed upon the front door. 'We're in,' said he.

And they were.

They stood now in a broad hallway. The mounted heads of numerous exotic animals peered sightlessly from the walls. Tim examined that of a mammoth. 'Bagged by Rune in Siberia, 1852, it says on this little plaque. And this dodo – Mauritius, 1821. And surely this is the head of a unicorn. Narnia, 1818, it says here. He favoured a bit of big-game hunting, did Rune.'

Will nodded and peered at the horns of a dilemma.

'It's all very clean.' Tim stroked the beak of a mounted griffin's skull. 'I would have expected cobwebs at the very least.'

'It *is* clean,' said Will and he drew a finger along the polished cranium of a hippogriff. 'No dust at all.'

'Magic, do you think?' Tim asked. 'Some spell that repels dust and maintains the garden?'

Will shook his head. 'I think not,' said he. 'Come on.'

Tim followed Will along the hall and into a large and splendid study.

'Whoa,' went Tim. 'Now you're talking.'

The room was about as broad as it was long, and as high as it was broad. And its broadness and its longness were packed with wonderful treasures. On every wall were cases loaded with marvellous books, the spines of which twinkled with gemstones and gilded ornamentations. And there were furnishings of abounding richness, golden thrones and couches, sofas piled with cushions of silk and satin and cloth-of-gold. And there were countless beautiful artefacts displayed in glass-fronted cabinets, and antique weapons and suits of armour and statues of the religious persuasion.

'Rather special, isn't it?' said Will. 'I don't think I expected quite so much.'

'This collection must be worth a fortune.' Tim picked up a gem-encrusted Fabergé roc's egg and stared at it in wonder. 'He could probably have paid off all of his debts just by selling this one piece alone.'

'I think he considered that never paying for anything added to his charisma.'

'He must have paid a lot for *this*.'

'You think so?'

Tim shrugged. 'And look at that.' Tim drew Will's attention to an elaborately decorated golden casket with a cut crystal lid.

'Very special,' said Will. 'That's a reliquary, containing, if I'm not mistaken, the beard of the prophet Mohammed's wife.'

Tim raised his eyebrows into his hair. 'And now all this is *ours*?'

'To use in the right way.'

'Can I keep this Fabergé egg, as a souvenir?'

'Put it down,' said Will. 'Remember what we're here for, saving God and the future and everything.'

'But I could keep this. It wouldn't matter really, would it?'

'It would.'

Tim stared at Will. 'You said that without moving your lips,' he said.

'That's because *I* didn't say it,' said Will.

'Then who—'

Tim turned and Will turned also.

In the doorway of the study stood the ancient gentleman. He was liveried as a footman, but in an antique costume of the pre-Regency persuasion: green velvet frocked coat, with slashed sleeves and emerald buttons; red silk stockings and black buckled shoes. His hair was long and white. His face was old and wrinkled.

'Who are you?' Will asked.

'My name is Gammon, sir. I am Mr Rune's retainer.'

'Ah,' said Will. 'Then I'm very pleased to meet you, my name is—'

'I know what your name is, Mr Starling. And I know why you're here. All has been kept in readiness for your arrival.'

Will looked at Tim.

And Tim looked at Will.

'Loving it,' said Tim.

36

'If you gentlemen would be so gracious as to beseat yourselves, I will hasten to bring you beverages,' said Gammon, and he indicated an ebonised sofa, bowed deeply and departed the study.

Will and Tim exchanged glances, then the both of them sat down.

'He's a weirdo,' said Tim.

'Not so loud,' said Will.

Presently Gammon returned, bearing a silver galleried tray which supported a dusty bottle, a brace of Georgian rummers and an ornate corkscrew, fashioned in the shape of a dragon. Gammon set down the tray upon a gopher-wood side table, took up the ornate corkscrew and then struggled to withdraw the cork.

'Let me,' said Will, rising.

'My thanks to you, sir. I am not as young as I once was, but nor am I as old as I might yet become.'

'Absolutely,' said Tim.

Will took the corkscrew, drew the cork. Sniffed it and held up the bottle. 'No label,' said he.

'The Master set it aside for you. He thought that you would appreciate it.'

'Indeed.' Will trickled wine into a rummer, held it towards the light, gauged its colour, took another sniff and then a sip. And then a bigger sip.

'Well,' said Will. 'A 1787 Chateau Lafitte claret. A most superior vintage.'

Gammon nodded his ancient head. 'The Master taught you well,' said he.

Will filled both rummers. 'Will you join us?' he asked Gammon.

'Oh no, sir. My palate is not what it was, although it *is* probably better than it eventually will be. Such fine wine would be wasted upon me.'

'As it will upon Tim,' said Will. 'But do have some if you fancy it.'

'No, sir.'

Will handed a rummer to Tim and they both enjoyed the wine.

'So,' said Will, licking his lips. 'You have clearly been expecting me, Mr Gammon.'

'The Master had the gift of prophecy, sir. All is predicted. Surely you have read *The Book Of Rune*.'

'Several times,' said Will. 'This encounter however is not chronicled there. It is my intention to use these premises as a base for our operations. Do you have any objection to this?'

'On the contrary, sir. I have everything prepared for you. The icons, the hacking weapons, the—'

'Magical accoutrements?' Tim asked.

'Of course, sir.'

'Brilliant,' said Tim. 'I've been really looking forward to getting my hands on some magical accoutrements.'

'Sir,' said Gammon to Will, 'I assume this gentleman to be your manservant, yet you feed him upon the finest wine and allow him to make such outrageous statements.'

'He's not my manservant,' laughed Will. 'He's my half-brother. He's Mr Rune's magical heir.'

'Oh, I am so sorry, sir. My apologies for such an oversight. So *you* are *his* manservant.'

'Let's not go any further with this.' Will sipped wine. 'And I have sufficient weaponry of my own, as it happens. But, as a matter of interest, who employs you now that Mr Rune is dead?'

Gammon put a wrinkly finger to his wrinkly lips. 'Please do not use the word *dead* when speaking of the Master.'

'He definitely *is dead*,' said Will. 'I attended his funeral.'

'I too, sir, but I still find it impossible to believe. The Master assured me that he was immortal.'

'He had a penchant for exaggeration,' said Will.

'But he had discovered the philosopher's stone. Distilled the elixir of life.'

'I don't think he was telling the truth,' said Will.

'But I also drank of the elixir.'

'Then keep your fingers crossed,' said Tim. 'And always sniff the milk before putting it in your tea.'

Gammon made a bewildered face.

'Tell me something,' said Will. 'You might know the answer to this. For all the research I did, I could never trace either Mr Rune's birthplace, nor the date of his birth. Do you know?'

Gammon shook his snowbound head. 'He did not confide such personal details to me, sir. But then I was only in the Master's employ for some two hundred years.'

'What?' went Will.

And Tim coughed wine up his nose.*

'*I* exaggerate, of course,' said Gammon.

'Of course,' said Will.

'It would be one hundred and ninety years at most.'

Tim shook his head and pushed away his hair and then he said with a grin. 'Did he ever pay you at all during this time?'

Gammon made a thoughtful face, but it was hardly a patch on those that Tim was so good at making. 'I did once broach the subject of my salary,' said he. 'About one hundred and fifty years ago. The Master assured me that a cheque *would* be in the post.'

'Perhaps it got lost,' said Tim, grinning further. 'But you never know, it might turn up.'

'It didn't today,' said Gammon. 'I looked on the mat.'

'So,' said Will. 'This is all hugely enjoyable, but—'

'It is for *me*,' said Tim. 'I'm loving it.'

'— but,' Will continued, 'Tim and I have pressing business. We have witches to thwart.'

'You are then already skilled in the necessary arts?'

'To a degree,' said Will. 'I have done a *lot* of research. I know what I'm dealing with. And I'm well tooled up.'

Gammon shook his head once more and this time tut-tut-tutted.

'Why do you do this tut-tut-tutting?' Will asked. 'I'll get by.'

'Not without a period of intensive training.'

'And *you* can provide this training?'

'That is why I awaited your arrival, sir.'

'No need,' said Will. 'I know all the basic stuff about thwarting witches, driving horseshoe nails into their footprints, manufacturing witch-bottles from urine and fingernails and so on.'

'That is *very* basic stuff, sir. I would not wish to open a book upon your chances of success, let alone your survival.'

'You think so?' said Will. 'Well, check this lot out,' and he flung open his long leather coat to expose a veritable armoury of weapons. Tim looked on approvingly.

Upon his hips, Will wore a brace of pistols. He drew one from a holster and twirled it upon his finger. 'This pistol,' said he, 'contains—'

* Tim's nose.

'Bullets forged from silver chalices, inscribed with the sign of the cross and blessed by the Pope?' asked Gammon.

Will nodded.

Gammon shook his head.

'Then this.' Will reholstered his pistol and whipped a stiletto from his belt. 'Fashioned—'

'From nails and timber reputed to come from the True Cross?'

Will nodded once more.

'Then this.' Will reached for something else.

But Gammon said, 'I'm so sorry, sir. Clearly you have done a considerable amount of research, but I suspect that your researches have been into witches of the medieval persuasion.'

Will nodded. 'Yes,' he said.

'You will be dealing with modern witches, sir. Thoroughly modern witches. It is no longer bell, book and candle, nor phials of the Virgin Mary's tears.'

'Aw,' said Will.

'You haven't?' said Tim.

'Paid a fortune for them,' said Will.

'Nor,' said Gammon, 'threads from the Holy Shroud of Turin, woven into the undergarments.'

'Damn,' said Will.

'In your underpants?' said Tim. 'Isn't that blasphemous?'

Will waggled the claret bottle at Gammon. 'Are you telling me,' he said, 'that none of these things will be any good against witches?'

'The pistols would no doubt prove effective in regards to shooting them dead, sir. But it's doubtful whether you would ever get the opportunity to test this proposition. Personally I would advise the icons, the hacking weapons—'

'The magical accoutrements,' said Tim.

'I suspect that your definition of these differs from my own,' said Gammon. 'And if you will pardon my forwardness, I will take the liberty of suggesting that we have spoken enough of these things and that it might be better if I were to show you rather than try to explain.'

'Please do,' said Tim, putting down his glass and rubbing his hands together.

'Sir?' said Gammon.

'Go ahead,' said Will.

'Then follow me, please.' Gammon turned upon an antique heel and shuffled from the study. Will topped up his glass and Tim took his up for a topping also.

'Follow the leader,' said Tim. 'And I'll follow you.'

In the hallway, Gammon produced a ring of keys and introduced one to the lock of a low iron-bound door. The door swung open to the sound of suitably dramatic creaking noises. Gammon reached into the darkness, threw a switch. Neon lighting illuminated a stone stairway that led down and down and down and down some more.

And Gammon hobbled down this stairway, followed by Will and Tim.

'I had the lighting installed myself,' said Gammon, when they had descended a considerable distance. 'I know that candles tend to make for a more forbidding atmosphere, but if you'd fallen down these steps as many times as I have—'

'Is it much further?' Will asked.

'Much,' said Gammon.

'I don't fancy walking all the way back up again,' Tim said.

'Nor me, sir,' said Gammon. 'That's why I always take the lift.'

As all good things must come to an end, so too did the stone stairway.

Tim looked up at the big door that lay (or rather stood, or perhaps, more precisely *hung*) before them.

'That's a big door hanging there,' said Tim.

'Don't be fooled by it,' said Gammon. 'It's not so big as it thinks it is.'

'Is it just me?' Tim asked, 'or do things always get whacky the moment we go underground? Remember the police station and all that interior-decorating nonsense?'

'*You* weren't at the police station,' said Will.

'See what I mean?' said Tim. 'Continuity and logic all go to pot underground.'

'A consequence of time travel,' said Gammon, selecting a key about four feet in length from his key ring. 'Something to do with the transperabulation of pseudo cosmic antimatter.'

He turned the key in the miniscule keyhole and gave the door a little nudge with the toe of his buckled shoe.

'Gentlemen,' said he as he threw another switch and brought neon tubes stuttering to light. 'The adytum. The naos. The cella. The Master's Sanctum Sanctorum.'

Tim looked in.

And Will looked in.

And then Will looked at Tim.

And Tim looked at Will.

'It's—' said Will.
And, 'It's—' said Tim.
'A computer room,' said Gammon.

37

'A computer room,' said Will, now inside the computer room.

'A computer room,' said Tim, now also inside the computer room.

'A computer room,' said Gammon, now entering the computer room. 'Haven't either of you ever seen a computer room before?'

'Well, yes,' said Will, seating himself in a steel swivel chair upholstered in royal blue leather, 'but not in this day and age.'

'But surely anyone who is anyone has a Babbage nowadays? There's one in every well-to-do household. And these are the top of the range. The 1900 series.'

Will did big shruggings. 'I've never seen anything like these,' he said, and he ran his fingers lightly over the keyboard of the nearest computer. It was of the manual typewriter persuasion, wired to a magnificent brass-bound processor bustling with valves. The monitor screen was set into a mahogany cabinet. The mouse was a silver pentacle.

Tim sat down upon another chair and faced another keyboard. 'I'm definitely loving *this*,' he said.

'Five computers,' said Gammon. 'Macro processor, Babbage 1900s, linked to the Information Super Side Street: the Empire-net. My knowledge of such matters is great, although not so great as it yet might become.'

'Just one thing,' said Tim. 'And don't get me wrong, I *am* loving this, but I definitely recall something about icons and hacking weapons and magical accoutrements.'

'Computer terms, sir,' Gammon stepped forward, tapped at the keyboard. The screen before Tim lit up. 'Those are icons,' he said, and he pointed.

'Okay,' said Tim. 'I know what a computer icon is.'

'Splendid, sir, and—'

'Ah,' said Tim. 'Hacking weapons, as in computer hackers?'

'Sir *does* know about computers.'

'And the magical accoutrements?'

'Has sir never heard the phrase, "the magic of technology"?'

'He has you by the short and curlies there,' said Will.

'Hardly an expression you'd normally use.' Tim raised an eyebrow beneath his hair. Will raised one beneath *his*.

Tim tapped at a key or two.

'If you'd allow *me*, sir,' said Gammon, leaning over his shoulder and breathing upon him that particular variety of halitosis which is the exclusive preserve of the elderly, 'I'll put us online.'

'Online,' said Tim fanning at his nose. 'How cool is this?'

'I've been working on my own household page,' said Gammon.

'*Home* page,' said Tim.

'Household page,' said Gammon. 'Ten thousand things you've always wanted to know about Gammon, but were always too polite to ask. I'm up to five now.'

'Five *thousand*?'

'No, *five*, sir. Do you think your question merits number six?'

Tim shook his head.

'Is there a Hugo Rune home page?' Will asked.

'Indeed, sir. The Master was always adding to his pages. Many pages, many, many pages; many, many, many—'

'I get the picture,' said Will. 'Might we see it?'

'Restricted access only, sir. Perhaps, when you have completed your intensive training.'

'This really isn't helping.' Will swivelled about on his chair. 'It's all very impressive, if somewhat unlikely, but what is the point? How is this going to help with me getting the job jobbed?'

'As I said to you, sir, you are dealing with modern witches. Thoroughly modern witches. These witches do not prepare their magic spells with toad's blood and bubbling cauldrons. They do it through computers.'

'They never do?' said Tim. 'Not in this day and age, surely.'

'Hold on,' said Will. 'Are you implying that they do in *ours*?'

Tim shrugged. 'I've heard rumours. Magic is a very precise science. If spells really work, they can only be made to do so by casting them correctly: pronouncing every syllable with absolute exactness, the precise intonation, accent, everything. A syllable wrong and the whole thing goes bum upwards. Spells are a formula to bend and mould space. You can't just read them from the paper; that will never work.'

'I have found no evidence to support the theory that spells *do* work,' said Will. 'I've read a lot of books on the subject. *A lot*. But I have no tangible proof.'

'They work,' said Gammon. 'Magic works, I can assure you of that. In nearly two hundred years of service with the Master, I have witnessed many inexplicable things and I have observed the power of magic. Mr Tim is correct; the secret lies in the technique, in the precision. This precision can be achieved by programming a computer to so achieve it.'

'And that is what you intend to train me to do?'

'No, sir. The Master's intention was to hack into the witches' computer network. Allow me to show you.' And he leaned once more over Tim's shoulder, breathing further halitosis.

'Impressive,' said Tim, fanning once more at his nose.

'You'll have to pardon my slowness, sir. My fingers are not as young as they were.'

'Nor as old as they yet will be.'

'Please don't take the piss, sir.'

'Sorry,' said Tim.

Tim's screen lit up with a sepia display. It had much of the look of an embroidered cushion cover to it. A central inverted pentagram, with goat's head motif, was encircled by lettering and surrounded by four skeletons holding handbags.

Will peered at it and read the letters. 'The Chiswick Townswomen's Guild,' said he. 'If it's really a coven of witches, surely the inverted pentagram and the goat's head are a bit of a giveaway.'

'This is a *restricted* site, sir. The Master hacked into it.'

'I see.' Will saw. 'So what is on this restricted site?'

'Absolutely no idea, sir. This is as far as the Master got. He was never very comfortable with computers. His fingers were rather large for the keyboard.'

Will laughed. 'He'd have been at home in our age,' said he. 'Big fat keypads.'

'Hang about here,' said Tim. 'This all makes sense, doesn't it?'

'Does it?' asked Will.

'Of course it does,' said Tim. 'Rune wanted his magical heir to continue with his work. And that's me, right?'

Will nodded.

'And why did he need his magical heir? Don't say anything, I'll tell you. Because in the time we come from computers are far more advanced than this. And what am *I*, Rune's magical heir, skilled at? Computers, that's what.'

'So am I,' said Will.

'You're rubbish,' said Tim. 'All those books you downloaded into your palm-top from the British Library. You'd never have got away with that if I hadn't hacked into their system and covered up for you.'

'You never told me,' said Will.

'I'm your friend,' said Tim. 'I did it because I didn't want you getting into trouble. We were like brothers. That was before I knew we *were* brothers. But the point is, Rune couldn't hack into the witches' system. Perhaps no one in this age could. But *I* could. It would be as easy as can be.'

'So why did he cart me around the world for a year?'

Gammon affected a knowing smile. 'Everything the Master did, he did for a reason. Everything he taught you, he taught you for a reason. Everything you have learned, you have learned for a reason. Everything—'

'All right,' said Will. 'Stop now.'

'The two of you are here together now,' said Gammon. 'Reason enough, I believe.'

'Right then,' said Tim and he interlocked his fingers and made cracking sounds with them. 'Let's have a hack at these witches.'

Will shrugged towards Gammon. 'This will probably take *some* time,' he said. 'Would you care to show me your household page?'

'*Home* page,' said Gammon. 'I like the sound of Mr Tim's suggestion. I'll put it to my chums next time I'm in the cyber restaurant.'

'Café,' said Will. 'You can have that one on me.'

'Café restaurant?' said Gammon. 'I don't think that scans, as our colonial cousins might say.'

'Show me your home page,' said Will.

And Gammon showed Will his home page.

And it was really, really dull.

'Why is your favourite colour *puce*?' Will asked.

'It's not *really*,' said Gammon. 'I only put that to make myself sound more exciting.'

'It's *black*, really, isn't it?'

Gammon nodded gloomily. 'You've seen the future,' said he. 'Tell me that one day black will *not* be the new black.'

'In the nineteen eighties it's *grey*,' said Will.

'That's not much of a consolation.'

'Things are likely to change.'

'Eureka!' cried Tim.

'Already?' cried Will.

'No,' said Tim. 'Just thought I'd get you going.'

'Fact number three,' said Gammon. 'Favourite song.'

'Let me guess,' said Will. 'Little Tich's ever-popular Big Boot Dance.'

'How ever did you know?'

'It's a gift,' said Will. 'No doubt inherited from Hugo Rune.'

'Would you care for a go at fact four? Favourite present British monarch?'

Will stroked at his magnificent beard. 'Would you care to give me a clue?' he asked.

Fact five, that Gammon's favourite employer was one Hugo Rune, had as much surprise about it as a *Blue Peter* presenter's cocaine habit.

'Eureka!' cried Tim once again.

This time Will ignored him.

'No, *really*. Eureka,' said Tim. 'I've cracked it. We're in.'

'Oh,' said Will and he wheeled his chair upon its castered feet in Tim's direction.

'Ingenious encryption,' said Tim. 'Based upon the Kabbalah.'

'I've read the Kabbalah,' said Will. 'Couldn't make any sense of it though.'

'Not many can,' said Tim. 'It's purposely obscure and designed to confuse. But it's not actually an occult work at all; it's a cookery book. The entry code to the witches' restricted computer files is a recipe for plum jam.'

'I'd have got it eventually,' said Will.

'You wouldn't,' said Tim. 'But here it all is. Care for a look?'

'Indeed.' Gammon now leaned over Will's shoulder, favouring him with his dire breath. Gammon viewed the screen.

It was covered in little icons, in the shape of bats and pumpkins, cauldrons and black cats, and broomsticks. Below each of these were little titles: *My incantations. My book of shadows. My favourite curses. My wart charms.* And so on and so forth, and not very funny at all.

'Cool,' said Tim. 'What shall we go for?'

'If I might make a suggestion,' said Gammon. 'Select *My World Domination Proposal.*'

'Good choice that,' said Tim and he moved the silver star-shaped mouse.

Tim read, and then he paused before reading further. 'I can't read this,' he said.

Will peered at the screen. 'It's Latin. I can read it.'

'Then please do.'

Will read it.

'Out loud,' said Tim.

Will read it out loud.

'Translated into English,' said Tim.

Will translated it into English.

'That's incredible,' said Tim.

'It is,' said Will.

'Could you explain it to me?' said Gammon. 'My English isn't all that good.'

Will sighed. 'What it says is this—' he said.

'It says here,' said a pinch-faced woman, who sat at a computer screen not at all dissimilar to the one that Tim and Will now sat at, 'that someone is hacking into our restricted files.'

Another pinch-faced woman leaned over her shoulder. The breath of this pinch-faced woman made Gammon's smell like fresh-baked bread by comparison.

'Locate the intruder,' said the smelly-breathed one.

The seated pinch-face tapped away at her keyboard. 'The Butt's Estate, Brentford,' said she. 'See the street plan. That house right there.'

'Call up the land registry,' said she of the smelly breath. 'Let us see who owns this house.'

'Won't take a moment.' The sitter tapped further keys. 'Aha,' cackled she. 'According to this, the owner-occupier is one Hugo Rune.'

'Rune.' The smelly-breather spat out the name, as one might spit out a maggot from a Granny Smith. 'Our would-be nemesis from the future must be at Rune's manse. We will deal with this directly.'

And with that said, she picked up a telephone receiver, cunningly fashioned into a facsimile of a stallion's plonker, and dialled out a three-digit number.

Somewhere another telephone rang and another receiver was lifted. And then a dark voice, a sinister voice; a darkly sinister voice said, 'Count Otto Black.'

'Your Highness,' said she whose breath smelled none too sweet. 'Our enemy has hacked into our restricted files.'

'And there you have it,' said Will to Gammon.

'I almost do,' said Gammon. 'Explain the last part again.'

'The witches have formulated a spell,' said Tim. 'Using their computer system. They intend to employ it on the last day of this year, when the clock strikes midnight.'

'The witching hour,' said Gammon.

'Exactly. What would be more appropriate?'

'This spell will infect every piece of Victorian electro technology, anything linked to the Tesla broadcast power system. Everything. It will destroy *everything*. Wipe it out as if it had never existed. Every Tesla transmission tower. Every wonder created by Lord Babbage. Everything. Effectively erase it all from history. It's a very serious spell. The most serious and potent spell ever formulated, in my opinion.'

'The stroke of midnight,' said Gammon. 'On the last night of the year.'

'The last night of *this* year,' said Will. 'This year 1899. It's what we might call a Millennium Bug.'

38

'Surely, sir,' said Gammon. 'It would be a Centennial Bug, not a Millennium Bug. The Millennium is not due for another hundred years.'

'Millennium Bug sounds much more dramatic,' said Will.

'Yes, sir, but it is technically incorrect.'

'Just leave it,' said Will.

'As you wish, sir. And so, can Mr Tim disable this Millennium Bug?'

'Of course.' Tim plucked at his beard. 'Given time, but I doubt very much whether it's even programmed into their system yet. If it were me, I'd leave it until the very last minute before programming it in, in case there was someone like me thinking to sabotage it.'

'Surely you'd want to test it,' said Will. 'To make sure that it worked.'

Tim shook his head. 'This is a bit different from your everyday computer virus,' he said. 'If it involves magic, and this is Big Magic, then I'll bet it involves all manner of big things; alignments of the planets, a series of rituals, probably even a human sacrifice.'

'You are joking, surely.'

'Mr Tim is *not* joking,' said Gammon. 'And there have already been five such sacrifices.'

'What?' went Will.

'The Ripper murders, sir. Surely you are aware of them.'

Will made a thoughtful face.

'Why are you scowling?' Tim asked.

'I wasn't scowling, I was making a thoughtful face.'

'That's not how you do it,' said Tim. 'You do it like this.'

'Very good, sir,' said Gammon.

'Thank you, Gammon,' said Tim.

'Stop this,' said Will. 'It's not funny and it's not clever. You think that the Ripper murders were definitely human sacrifices?'

'No doubt of it, sir. If you join up the sites of the murders on a map you will see that an inverted pentagram is formed.'

'Yes,' said Will. 'I know.'

'But of course you would, sir. The Master informed me that you had agreed to take on the case. Any suspects?'

Will sighed.

'Quite so, sir,' said Gammon.

'Tell you what,' said Tim. 'I'll crack on here, see what I can come up with. Why don't you carry on with Gammon's website? I'm looking forward to reading the answer to question six, "What is Gammon's favourite proprietary brand of pork scratchings?" '

'Good idea, sir,' said Gammon.

'Not so good idea,' said Will.

'I could get supper on,' said Gammon.

'Good idea,' said Will. 'I'll help you.'

'I'd rather that you didn't, sir. I can manage quite well on my own. I've been years getting that kitchen exactly the way I want it.'

'I'll help *you* then, Tim.'

'I can manage.' Tim rattled away at the keyboard. 'Go and play in Rune's study, or something.'

'Oh all right. Lead the way to the lift, please, Gammon.'

Gammon led the way.

And while Tim busied himself at the keyboard and Gammon busied himself in the kitchen, Will, without anything in particular to busy himself with, loafed about in Rune's study.

He ran a finger, beringed with a circlet of varnished gristle (which a talisman salesman in Cairo had assured him was nothing less than the Holy foreskin of St Thomas, the very sight of which would strike fear into the most fearsome of witches), along the leathern spines of a row of antique tomes and plucked one out at random: *The Autobiography of Casanova*.

Will sat himself down next to the fire and idly leafed through it. The book, a first edition, was actually autographed. Will whistled. This book alone would be worth a fortune in the twenty-third century. Rune had amassed a most remarkable collection.

Will gazed at Casanova's signature, a flamboyant piece of calligraphy, and at the date 1792. Will read the dedication above the signature.

To Hugo Rune, who introduced me
to the pleasures of the flesh.
From your disciple,
Giovanni Jacopo Casanova

'What?' went Will. And he looked once more at the date. That couldn't be true, could it? The inscription had to be a forgery. Will put the book aside, rose from his seat and selected another at random.

I'm the Pope and You're not! The life and merry times of Rodrigo Borgia, Pope Alexander the Sixth. 1492.

Will read what was written on the flyleaf.

For Hugo, who –

'No!' went Will. And he struggled to pull an enormous tome from the bottom shelf. He laid it out upon the floor and opened it.

The Domesday Book, signed in the hand of King William himself.

To my dear friend Hugo,
for all his help in putting this together.

'No!' and Will pulled another one and then another.

It *couldn't* be true.

It just couldn't.

Rune had to have forged these signatures.

A bound manuscript of Shakespeare's *The Tempest* bore the inscription: *Thanks for the inspiration, Hugo.*

Will slammed it shut.

'Ah,' said Gammon entering the study with a tray. 'I see you are admiring the Master's library sir. Five thousand volumes, and each with a personal dedication to the Master.'

'It can't be true,' Will shook his head and replaced *The Tempest* onto its shelf. 'He couldn't really have lived for hundreds and hundreds of years.'

'And why would that be, then, sir?' Gammon placed the tray upon a padouk wood and ivory-mounted chess table, that had been a gift to Hugo Rune from Genghis Khan. 'Muffins?' he asked.

'Impossible,' said Will.

'You haven't tasted them yet, sir.'

'Not the muffins. You know what I'm talking about.'

'Sir,' said Gammon, 'you stand before one of the most valuable book collections in the world. I believe that you must be aware that the Master was, how shall I put this, *careful* with money. Do you really believe that he would have amassed such a collection of priceless tomes and then defaced and devalued them by forging signatures and dedications into them?'

Will made a very thoughtful face.

'Good face, sir,' said Gammon. 'And, as our American cousins might say, right back at ya!'

'But I just can't believe it.'

'Sir.' Gammon buttered muffins. 'I informed you and Mr Tim that I had been in the Master's employ for nearly two hundred years. During this time I have kept diaries. Daily diaries. They are all in my room. Perhaps you might care to examine them. They might blunt the edge of your scepticism.'

Will shook his head. And he sniffed the muffins, took one up and munched upon it. 'How old *was* he?' Will asked between munchings.

'I really couldn't say, sir. He once informed me that he was Christ's thirteenth disciple – his spiritual adviser, in fact – but that he'd asked for his name to be left out of the New Testament for personal reasons.'

'That's rather unlikely, isn't it?' Will finished his muffin and licked at his fingers.

'How so, sir? His name does not appear in the New Testament, which rather proves the truth of his statement, I would have thought.'

Will shook his head. 'No,' he said.

'Although,' Gammon glanced about the library shelves, 'I'm sure there's a first draft of the New Testament somewhere here. Written in Christ's own hand and dedicated to—'

'Stop it,' said Will. 'I fear that my brain is about to explode.'

'Above the fireplace there,' said Gammon, 'hangs the very sword that cleaved the head from John the Baptist. The Master was not present on the night of that tragedy, or he would no doubt have prevented it. He did however later have, I believe it is called, a *fling* with Salome. She gave him the sword as a souvenir.'

'Enough,' said Will.

'Another muffin?' asked Gammon.

'No! Yes!' Will took another muffin and returned to his fireside chair.

'Sir,' said Gammon. 'Sir, I know everything about you. Everything. I was in constant communication with the Master during all of your time here. I know, for instance, that you imbibed a drug called Retro.'

'Yes,' said Will. 'I did. What about it?'

'This chemical released the memories of your ancestors that were previously locked away in your brain, am I correct?'

'You are,' said Will.

'Then surely the Master's memories were unlocked to you. The countless years of his remarkable existence.'

'No,' said Will. 'I recall the memories as far back as Captain Starling, father of Colonel Starling who should have piloted the moonship today and whose present whereabouts are unknown to me.'

'Captain Starling was the Master's son, although he never knew it. And the Master allowed his own son to die, saving Her Majesty the Queen (God bless Her).'

'All right,' said Will. 'I understand what you are saying. But this is fantastic stuff. Unbelievable stuff.'

'Sir, but for the Master, have you ever met and spoken to any of your ancestors?'

'No,' said Will, and he rose and helped himself to another muffin. 'I wanted to, of course, but Rune advised me against it. He said it might be dangerous for them.'

'And so indeed it might be, it certainly proved disastrous for the Master.'

'You're not suggesting that it is *my* fault that he was murdered?'

'Well, sir, I—' But Gammon's words were brought short by the ringing of the front doorbell.

'I wonder who that might be?' wondered Gammon.

'If Tim were here,' said Will, 'he'd probably make the suggestion that it was the postman with a cheque for your back wages.'

'Do you think it might be, sir?'

'Stranger things have happened,' said Will. 'To me, in the last half an hour, for instance.'

'Then if you'll pardon me, I shall answer the door.'

'And I'll have just one more muffin.'

Gammon shuffled from the study and Will wolfed down the final muffin and gave his fingers a final thorough licking.

Will heard the sound of the front door being opened and then soon after being closed again.

And then Gammon returned to the study.

'Most strange, sir,' said he. 'I opened the door, but there was no one there. Children playing Knock Down Ginger, perhaps.'

'Perhaps,' said Will. 'Are there any more muffins?'

Gammon cast a rheumy eye over the empty platter. 'I see that you have eaten Mr Tim's muffins also,' said he.

'Have to keep my strength up,' said Will. 'Witch-finding is a hungry business.'

'Quite so, sir.'

And then the doorbell rang once more.

'Shall I ignore it this time?' Gammon asked.

'Never mind,' said Will. 'I'll go.'

'Oh no, sir, that wouldn't do. Protocol must always be observed. There's no telling where things might lead if the Master of the house was to answer his own front door.'

'It's no big deal,' said Will.

'The precise meaning of that phrase alludes me,' said Gammon. 'But I gather the gist. And trust to what I say, sir. One thing leads to another. A decline in standards would lead to chaos. Women being given the vote. The prohibition of opium. Even, God forbid, the decriminalisation of sodomy. Not to mention frotteurism.'

'Frotteurism?' said Will.

'I told you not to mention that.'*

'Answer the door then, Gammon.'

And Gammon went to answer the door.

And once more Will heard the front door open.

But this time he also heard a voice.

He heard the voice of Gammon ask, 'How might I help you, sir?'

And then Will heard another voice, a voice that he recognised, and a voice that he also feared.

It was a deeply-timbred voice of the Germanic persuasion. It said, 'William Starling? Where is William Starling?'

Will who had been seated once more, now leapt up to his feet and drew both his pistols from their holsters.

'No, sir,' came the voice of Gammon from the hall. 'You will have to make an appointment. I cannot allow you admission without a prior appointment. Protocol must always—'

And then there was a thumping sound and Gammon said no more.

Will flattened himself against a bookcase, both pistols raised and cocked. 'Barry,' he whispered. 'Are you awake?'

A gentle purring sound echoed in the rear recess of Will's brain. Barry was still fast asleep.

* God bless you, Spike Milligan.

'Barry!' went Will, more urgently. 'You're supposed to be my Holy Guardian, who warns me when trouble is heading my way.'

'Zzzzzzzzzzz,' went Barry.

'Hopeless,' whispered Will. 'But I can deal with this.'

He peeped around the corner of the bookcase, and found himself staring into the dead black eyes of a terrific figure. It was a terrific figure identical in every detail to the ones that Will had formerly encountered in the future, so to speak. And it smelt equally as bad.

'Ah,' went Will. 'Ah . . . well . . . hello there.'

'William Starling?' The mouth, a cruel hard line, corded with muscle, crooked into an evil leer.

'You, er, just missed him,' said Will. 'He left.'

'Take me to him now.'

'Can't,' said Will. 'Sorry.'

'Then you die.'

'Indeed, I do think not.' And Will fired a pistol at point blank range, right into the chest of the automaton.

And back went he with the force of the blast, and fell onto a Herez carpet, which had been a present to Rune from Shah Jahan for designing the Taj Mahal.

Will blew into the smoking barrel of his gun.

'Job done,' said he.

The terrific figure lay prone upon the carpet. It showed no signs of simulated life.

'However,' said Will, 'I have seen the movies too. And so it would be safer to be sure.' And he stepped forward, over the fallen figure, and emptied the contents of both his pistols into the helpless form.

'And now the job *is* done,' said he. 'And most efficiently too, if I do say myself.'

And then Will called to Gammon. 'Are you all right?' he called.

And then Will was knocked from his feet.

It came in fast, very fast, and through the closed French windows. Amidst a maelstrom of shattered glass and fragmenting timbers, another demonic, black-eyed and evil-smelling figure of terror burst forward and struck Will from behind.

Will tumbled over a William and Mary side table that had been a present to Hugo Rune from William and Mary, and joined the fallen automaton on the carpet.

The second automaton hauled away the table and cast it across the study, bringing down one of the bookcases, smashing priceless artefacts, spoiling precious tomes.

Will was down, but far from out. He leapt to his feet and, as the monstrous figure pressed forward for the kill, somersaulted over its head.

The evil robot turned, snarled at Will.

Will stood amidst the ruination. He thumbed his nose and did a bit of an Ali shuffle. 'In your own time,' said Will and he beckoned his would-be assassin forward.

And forward it came at the hurry up.

It swung a left hand; Will parried it away.

A right; Will parried this also.

And then Will pivoted upon his heel, brought up his other leg in a blurry arc and kicked the thing of dread right in the gob.

The thing of dread paused and readjusted its now lop-sided jaw. 'Dimac,' it said. 'The most deadly of all the martial arts.'

'Best leave now,' advised Will. 'Or I will be forced to punish you further.'

'I have been programmed to destroy you,' said the evil automaton. 'And I have also been programmed with the entire Dimac manual. And also those of Karate, Ninjitsu, Kung Fu and Baritso.'

Will span once more upon his heel and kicked it once more in the face, and the black-eyed monster once more repositioned his jaw.

'And macramé,' it added.

'That's not a martial art,' said Will.

'It's a hobby,' the thing replied. 'I will knit a plant pot holder from your beard, as soon as I have torn your head from your shoulders.'

'Who sent you?' Will asked.

'That is no concern of yours. Prepare to die.'

'I'm prepared,' said Will and he cracked his knuckles and knotted his fingers into fists. 'But come on, before you kill me, what harm can there be in telling me?'

'None,' said the automaton. 'And I will confide this information to you, one second before you die.'

The evil creation flexed its muscular shoulders, pushed out its barrelly chest, took up the martial arts stance known as the prelude to *The Curl of the Curlew's Codpiece.*

Will took up that known as the prelude to *The Peck of the Pigeon's Pecker.*

And then the two engaged in battle.

And it was battle proper.

Fists flew with fearsome rapidity. The study's air boomed as the sound barrier was breached again and again. Furniture splintered, and big chunks of plaster were blasted from the walls and also the ceiling as leaping kicking fighting bodies hurtled here and there and forward and backwards, performing impossible aerobatics and doing all the damn fine stuff that aficionados of martial arts movies (the original Hong Kong dubbed into English versions) know and love, and love some more.

A wonder and a joy to watch, but a blighter to put down in words.

The martial mechanoid tore the marble shelf from the fireplace and swung it at Will. Will kicked it into fragments.

The rampaging robot now flung his right fist at Will, Will caught the fist and tore it free of the arm.

'Bugger,' said the handless horror, and it kicked Will in the stomach.

'Bugger,' croaked Will, doubling up.

And then the evil clockwork creature kneed Will right in the face, and Will went down with a bit of a thump.

The monster came at him.

The fingers of its remaining hand fixed about Will's throat.

Will grabbed at the wrist but was head-butted in the face. Will sank back, half conscious, and the automated fingers closed in about his windpipe.

'You enquired, regarding who sent me,' said Will's erstwhile assassin, applying lethal pressure. 'I am the servant of Count Otto Black, King of all the witches.'

Will gagged and floundered. He flailed at the force that bore down upon him, but his strength was gone.

'See me,' said the voice of Will's doom. 'Look into my eyes and see your nemesis.' And he held Will's face close to its own. Will looked into the eyes of his destroyer, and he saw a face there, in those dead black eyes, as through a camera lens.

A gaunt face with a long hooked nose, dark deep-set eyes, a high forehead and a long black beard. The last face he would ever see; the face of Count Otto Black.

And that face smiled, and that face laughed, exposing a mouthload of crooked yellow teeth. And a voice echoed in Will's ear; the voice of the Count.

'Goodbye to you,' said this voice.

And the fingers closed, and that was that for Will.

39

'And that is that for you.'

Another voice was to be heard in the devastated study. The automaton raised its head and looked around. Above it a scimitar which bore the autograph of Salome hung in the air, motionless and all alone. Hovering. And then it swung down in a vicious sweeping arc and swept the head from the automaton. The robot's single remaining hand left Will's throat and clawed at the empty air that its owner's head had so recently occupied.

And then the automaton collapsed, and that was that for it.

'Wake up now. Come on, William, rouse yourself.'

Will lurched into consciousness, coughing and gagging.

The face of Tim looked down upon him. 'Tim, you saved my life.'

'I'd like to take the credit,' said Tim. 'But it wasn't me. I missed all the excitement.'

'I'm sorry I waited so long before coming to your rescue,' said a voice. 'But I needed, as you did, to know the answer to the question you asked the automaton.'

'Mr Wells,' said Will.

'Pleased to be of service,' said the voice of H.G. Wells.

'And Gammon?' Will did some more coughing and gagging.

'I am in excellent health, sir, a mere concussion, nothing more.' The face of Gammon loomed over Will. 'I telephoned the Flying Swan and had this sent over for you. I thought you might appreciate it.' And a pint of Large now filled Will's vision.

'Let's get him up,' said Tim, and Will was aided into the vertical plane. He clutched at his throat.

'That really hurt,' he said. 'I thought I was finished there.'

'You gave a very good account of yourself,' said Mr Wells. 'All that leaping about and those kicks. Most impressive.'

'The bullets worked somewhat better.'

'Bullets tend to do that.'

Tim righted what was left of the fireside chair Will had recently occupied and helped him onto it. 'There's not much left of our legacy,' he said. 'Couldn't you have been a bit more careful?'

'I was fighting for my life!' Will coughed and gagged some more.

Gammon handed him the pint of Large. 'This will help,' he said. 'Alcohol always does.'

Will sipped and coughed, then gulped, then coughed somewhat less. Then gulped a bit more and a bit more after that.

'Mr Wells,' said he. 'Thank you; thank you for saving my life.'

'My pleasure, I assure you. I received the telegram you sent earlier, asking me to meet you at this address. Came as soon as I could.'

'I unknowingly let Mr Wells in,' said Gammon. 'That first ring at the door. The one I thought was children.'

'I knew it was him,' said Will. 'The second ring, however, I thought was someone else.'

'He's outside,' said Mr Wells. 'He's hungry. He's eating the privet hedge.'

'Eating what?' said Tim.

'The fourth member of our party,' said Will. 'Master Makepiece Scribbens, the Brentford Snail Boy.'

'Eh?' said Tim. 'What's all this?'

Will eased his throat with further Large. 'Allies,' he said. 'In the cause. We're going to need all the help we can get. I telegrammed Mr Wells to meet us here, also Master Scribbens.'

'Why him?' Tim asked.

'Because he helped us at the court house. Remember that it was his idea that we disguise ourselves as him and Miss Poppins in order to escape.'

The doorbell rang.

'That will be him,' said Will. 'Gammon, will you, please?'

'At once, sir.'

Master Makepiece Scribbens peered through the broken doorway at what was left of Hugo Rune's study. He took in the ruinations and slowly shook his bloated head.

'Well,' said he. 'This must have been an incredible party, I'm sorry I missed it.'

'It was *not* a party.' Tim pointed to the two defunct automata.

Master Makepiece Scribbens stared down upon them and then he raised phlegm from his throat and spat it onto the nearest. 'Spawn of Satan,' said he. 'The evil cat's-paws of Count Otto Black.'

'Come in and meet Mr Wells,' said Tim.

'Mr Wells?' said Master Scribbens, peering all around and about.

'Mr Wells,' said Mr Wells.

And all was explained to the Snail Boy, regarding Mr Wells.

Well, not perhaps all, but some.

'And so we are four,' said Master Scribbens and he moved forward into the wreckage of the room. But he didn't walk. His legs and feet didn't move. He slid along. He glided, upon a silky, silvery trail.

'Nice to see you out of your wheelchair,' said Tim, making the kind of face that implies that it wasn't *that* nice, as it happened.

'Miss Poppins had to leave my employ. A more favourable position came up for her, nannying some children in Ludgate Hill.'*

'Well.' Will finished his pint of Large, smacked his lips and drew his knuckle across them. 'I feel fully reinvigorated and I am glad that we are all here. Tim, what did you come up with on Rune's computer?'

'Not much,' said Tim. 'Shortly after you left me the Chiswick Townswomen's Guild website went offline. If I didn't know better, I'd swear that they'd discovered that I'd hacked into it.'

Will sighed.

'Nice sighing, sir,' said Gammon. 'You may not be Dan Leno when it comes to performing the thoughtful face. But when it comes to sighing, your performance is nonpareil.'

Will sighed once more.

'Bravo,' said Gammon and he clapped his wrinkly hands.

'I will explain everything,' said Will, 'to you, Master Scribbens, and to you, Mr Wells, wherever you might be.'

'I'm here,' said Mr Wells.

'And then I will explain my plan. We, together, can win the war against this Count Otto Black and his coven of witches. It can be done, and it will be done, and I know how to do it.'

'Do what, chief?' asked a voice in Will's head.

'Barry,' said Will.

'Barry?' said Master Scribbens.

'Will's Holy Guardian,' said Tim. 'Inside Will's head. It speaks to him.'

Master Scribbens now sighed.

'Not bad,' said Gammon.

* Or wherever it is in the movie.

'You little green sod,' said Will. 'Where were you when I needed you?'

'Sorry, chief. Oh my goodness, Mr Rune's study, what have you done to it?'

'I was in mortal peril and you were sleeping.'

'Time travel, chief. Very exhausting. I needed time to regenerate my awesome powers.'

'I nearly died.'

'You seem fine to me, chief. Although perhaps a bit puffed. Heart rate's up somewhat.'

'Just be quiet,' said Will.

'And Master Scribbens is here,' said Barry. 'What's that slimy schmuck doing here?'

'He's helping me, and so is Mr Wells.'

'Oh dear,' said Barry. 'Oh dear, oh dear, oh dear.'

'Just be quiet. I'm dealing with this.'

'And another *oh dear* for luck.'

'How's Barry?' Tim asked.

'Taking a nap!' said Will. 'Now let's continue. We are here, and we will succeed; the gang of five.'

'Five, sir,' said Gammon. 'Are you thinking to include me?'

'Why not?' Will asked.

'Because I'd rather not, if you don't mind. I have a great deal of cleaning up to do here.'

'All right, the gang of *four.*'

'Five,' said Barry. 'Don't forget *me*, chief.'

'*Four!*' said Will.

'Ungrateful oaf.'

'What was that?'

'I said, "You'll probably want to take a *faithful oath*".'

'Yes,' said Will. 'Something like that,' and he raised his empty glass. 'To success,' said he. 'To the destruction of the witches and to saving the future. We will save the future. We will save history. We are the four.'

'We are the four,' said Master Makepiece Scribbens.

'We are the four,' said Mr H.G. Wells.

'The Fantastic Four,' said Tim.

'That's been done,' said Will.

'The Fab Four, then.'

'That too.'

'The Four Tops?' said Tim. 'The Four Feather Falls Appreciation

Society? The Four Mile Island? The four and twenty blackbirds baked in a pie? The Four Gospels? The Four Horsemen of the—'

'Stop!' said Will.

'How about The Far-Fetched Four?' said Barry. 'That seems about right to me.'

40

Whoa – War! Uh!
Now, what *is* that good for?
In most opinions.
Absolutely nothing!
God Gawd, y'all—

The Far-Fetched Four held a counsel of war, but not in the manse of the late Hugo Rune.

Gammon ushered them out of there amid many apologies regarding pressing cleaning duties and the need for the Four to make good their getaway lest robotic reinforcements arrive.

'I will, as our colonial cousins are want to put it, *muff it out* with them, should they appear,' he said.

'It's *bluff* it out,' said Tim, tittering foolishly.

'You will be needing this, sir,' said Gammon, and he handed Will a slim metal pouch engraved with enigmatic symbols.

'What is it?' Will asked.

'It's a slim metal pouch engraved with enigmatic symbols,' Gammon informed him.

'And what is *in* this pouch?'

'The Scorpion, sir. The Master's Scorpion. To be used against the witches when the moment arises.'

'But what exactly does it do?'

Gammon tapped at his veiny nose.

'And what does *that* mean?' Will asked.

'Shagged if I know,' said Gammon. 'The Master said that I should give it to you when the time was right, and I consider the time to be right. At least it is upon my watch, I don't know about yours. And so, farewell and may God travel with you. And if I might just offer you a piece of advice which is an ultimate truism and guide to life.'

'You might,' said Will. 'If you really want to.'

'It's the best advice I've ever had,' said Gammon. 'I read it on the side of a matchbox. It is, "keep dry and away from children".'

'Well, thank you *very* much,' said Will and he waved goodbye to Gammon.

And now the Far-Fetched Four sat in the Flying Swan, in a corner booth, but close to the door. Tim returned from the saloon bar counter with four pints of Large, skilfully held, and placed them upon the mahogany top of the cast iron Britannia table.

'Cheers, everybody,' he said as he seated himself.

'Cheers,' said Master Makepiece Scribbens, underaged drinker of the borough.

'Cheers,' said Mr William Starling, prospective saviour of the Future.

And, 'Cheers,' said Mr H.G. Wells and his glass rose magically into the air and emptied half its contents into nothingness.

'How does he do that?' Tim asked. 'You'd think you'd be able to see the ale swilling around in his guts.'

'It *has* to be magic, doesn't it?' said Mr Wells. 'Because otherwise, how could I actually see? The light passes through my retinas and travels straight out of the back of my head. Logically I should be blind.'

'Let's not let logic get in the way of anything,' said Will. 'How's the ale, Master Scribbens?'

'Eminently superior to the hog's piss that Count Otto Black used to feed me upon.'

'He treated you badly, then?'

'Not badly, not really, just without care. He is a man without any human conscience. People mean nothing to him.'

'Psychopath,' said Tim.

'I don't know what that word means.'

'It's a person afflicted with a personality disorder, characterised by a tendency to commit antisocial and even homicidal acts without conscience or a sense of guilt,' said Tim. 'Or at least that's what it says in the dictionary.'

'That would be Count Otto.'

'The murderer of Hugo Rune?' Will asked.

Master Scribbens shrugged his shapeless shoulders, replaced his glass onto the tabletop and slid it about in a distracted fashion. The glass's bottom left a silvery trail.

Aware that the eyes of his fellows were upon it, Master Scribbens said, 'Sorry, it happens. I can't help it.'

'Forget it,' said Will. 'I'm glad that you decided to join us upon our quest. You are aware that great danger lies ahead for us?'

'Obviously so. I might be weird, but I'm *not* wyrd, if you understand my meaning.'

'I do,' said Will. 'So let us formulate our plan of campaign.'

Tim put down his glass and rubbed his hands together. 'I just know I'm going to love this,' he said. 'So, what is the plan?'

'Well, the way I see it,' said Barry.

Will shook his head. 'No, Barry,' he said. '*I* will take care of this.'

'But, chief. It's really straightforward. All you have to do is—'

'No!' Will took from his belt the stiletto fashioned from nails and timber reputed to come from the True Cross, pushed the blade into his left ear and rooted all about with it.

'Ow!' went Barry. 'Oooh. Ouch. Stop.'

'Then be still,' said Will.

'It will all end in tears, chief.'

Will applied the blade once more.

'I'm taking another nap,' said Barry. 'Wake me up when things reach crisis point and I'll do my best to get you out of the mess.'

Will wiggled the blade.

'Zzzzzzzz,' went Barry.

'The way I see it is this,' said Will, refreshing his palate with further ale. 'We have fifteen days to locate and destroy the witches' Millennium Bug programme.'

'Plenty of time,' said Tim. 'It should be a breeze.'

'We do have to *find* it first,' said Will.

'Oh yes, we have to find it.'

'So, where do we look?'

'The Headquarters of the Chiswick Townswomen's Guild would seem favourite.'

'I agree.'

'I do not,' said Mr Wells.

'You don't?' said Will.'

'And nor do I,' said Master Makepiece Scribbens.

'Why?' asked Will.

Mr Wells finished his ale. 'I do not go out much at this time of the year,' said he. 'The wind blows right through me. But one of the benefits of being invisible is that you can travel upon public transport without having to pay the fare. Only today I was upon the Clapham omnibus and I overheard a fellow talking. The air was abuzz with rumours and theories of a conspiratorial nature regarding the destruction of the moonship at the Crystal Palace. This fellow believed that the moonship had been sabotaged by Martians.'

Will said nothing.

And nor did Tim.

'An interesting theory,' said Mr Wells, 'although wholly ludicrous in my opinion. However, I do have to say that it gave me an idea. I dabble with literature and have always considered writing a whimsical novel. I thought that I might base a novel upon this. A war between the Martians and men. I have even toyed with a title: *Punch-up of the Planets*. What do you think?'

'*War of the Worlds* sounds better,' said Tim. 'But what has this to do with anything?'

'The man on the Clapham omnibus spoke also of witches. It was his belief that a witch coven existed, dedicated to bringing down society, overthrowing the social order, wiping out technology and installing itself as secret rulers of the world, running the planet through the application of magic.'

'Surely we know all this,' said Will.

'Allow me to continue,' said Mr Wells. 'He suggested that they would do it subtly. Not hurl magical spells about but influence the present rulers of the planet. Kings and Queens have always had astrologers who advise them. They are superstitious enough to take their advice. Prime ministers and potentates, presidents and tyrants all over the world do likewise. Always have done, always will do. Read your history; you will find out that this was ever the case, back to the time of the Pharaohs and the Caesars.'

'Where *is* this leading?' Will asked.

'Towards the future,' said Mr Wells. 'Towards a future controlled by witches in the guise of astrologers who *advise* heads of state. *That* is how they will rule the world once they have swept away all traces of Victorian technology.'

'I understand this,' said Will. 'But what *is* your point?'

'You will find nothing at the headquarters of the Chiswick Townswomen's Guild. Perhaps a computer or two, but not the Doomsday Programme, if I might call it that.'

'You certainly might,' said Tim. 'Millennium Bug was good, but Doomsday Programme – I love it. Brilliant stuff.'

'Her Majesty the Queen—'

'Gawd bless Her,' said Tim.

'Her Majesty the Queen,' Mr Wells continued, 'has her own astrologer.'

'I didn't know this,' said Will.

'But you know the identity of this astrologer. Count Otto Black. The programme will be in his possession.'

'I suppose that's obvious really,' said Will. 'If he is the King of all the witches. So where is he to be found?'

'The Sudan,' said Mr Wells.

'Where?' said Tim.

'His Circus Fantastique is presently playing a season for King Gordon in Khartoum.'

'Right then,' said Will. 'Let's finish up our drinks and head off to Khartoum.'

'A pointless exercise,' said Mr Wells.

'And why?' Will asked.

'Well,' said Mr Wells. 'We might engage an aerial hansom to take us as far as Portsmouth. We would be there before morning. But the next steamer bound for North Africa is in five days' time and will take eight days to reach Khartoum.'

'Still time,' said Will.

'No.' Mr Wells shook his head, although nobody saw it.

'The circus will have left Khartoum by then and be on its way back to England.'

'Then we will intercept it on the way. Take a steamer to Calais and then the Orient Express.'

'And you would miss him once more.'

'Why?' asked Will.

'Because Count Otto Black's Circus Fantastique does not travel by land or sea. It is a flying circus.'

'Like Monty Python's?' said Tim.

'I fail to understand you,' said Mr Wells. 'The circus is airborne. A dirigible, constructed in the shape of a five-pointed star, powered by Tesla turbines. It travels at an altitude of five thousand feet, beyond the range of any aerial hansom. I feel that we must await Count Otto's return to this sceptred isle. According to the posters I have seen all over London . . .'

'The circus will be playing here on the thirty-first of December,' said Will. 'For the celebrations to mark the dawn of the twentieth century.'

'Precisely,' said Mr Wells. 'It has been licensed by Her Majesty—'

'Gawd bless Her,' said Tim.

'Shut up,' said Will.

'– to moor directly above the Whitechapel area.'

'Whitechapel,' said Will, and he said it slowly and meaningfully.

'I'll just bet,' said Tim, 'that this pentagram-shaped flying circus will be hovering directly over the inverted pentagram formed by joining the sites of the Ripper murders. What do you think, Will?'

'Exactly,' said Will.

'Bullshitter,' said Barry.

'Go back to sleep.'

'Sorry?' said Tim.

'Barry,' said Will.

'So,' said Mr Wells. 'We have to await Count Otto's return.'

'I'm good with this,' said Tim. 'Christmas is coming up. I've never enjoyed a Victorian Christmas. Will we have crackers and Christmas pudding and Tamagotchis?'

'Perhaps the first two,' said Will. 'Please get another round in.'

Tim went up to the bar and got in another round.

'This is a particularly splendid ale-house,' said Mr Wells. 'The beer is beyond reproach, the service remarkable, the seating most comfortable.'

Tim returned from the bar. 'There's a big bargee and a small bargee buying drinks up there, said he. 'And they keep looking over at our table.'

'I'll go and have a word with them,' said Will.

'No need,' said Tim. 'I did. The part-time barman is throwing them out.'

Will looked up. And indeed the part-time barman was.

'Top bar,' said Mr Wells.

'You're not wrong there,' said Will. 'So this is the plan.'

'Just one thing,' said Master Scribbens, 'before you outline your plan. I am contracted to appear, "by popular demand". at Count Otto's circus during the New Year celebrations.'

'A man on the inside,' said Tim.

'You really want to do that?' Will asked.

'The money is good and I need it.'

'Mr Wells,' said Will. 'Do you believe that this Doomsday Programme will be on board Otto Black's flying circus?'

'I have no reason to doubt it, do you?'

Will shook his head. 'So we have to do it then. When his circus reaches England and hovers above Whitechapel on the thirty-first of December.'

'And we enjoy Christmas in the meantime,' said Tim. 'Where shall we spend it? Do you know any other posh hotels you can talk your way into, Will?'

'Many,' said Will. 'But that's not how we're going to play this. Action *now* is what is called for. We will dispense with the fifteen days in between and go directly to where the action is.'

'And how do you propose that we do this?' Tim asked.

'Barry,' said Will.

'Zzzz,' went Barry.

'*Barry!*' went Will once again.

'Oh-ah-what, chief?'

'Barry, it is time to rouse yourself and go into action.'

'Have you messed up already, chief? Sorry I missed it.'

'No,' said Will. 'I haven't. But there's something I want you to do for me. Remember when you told me that you could not take me to the exact time and place when the big trouble was going to occur?'

'I do indeed, chief. If it was only known to me and not to you, then I can't do it. Outside my remit. Sorry; that's the way it works.'

'Well, Barry,' said Will. 'Now I *do know* where and when I want to be. Exactly where and when. So you can take me there right?'

'Certainly can,' said Barry.

'So I'd like you to take all of us to—'

'All of you, chief?'

'All of us, Barry.'

'No can do, once more, chief. I can take you and Mr McGregor, but not Mr Wells and Master Scribbens.'

'No matter,' said Will. 'They can meet us there in the future.'

'How far?' Barry asked.

'Not far,' said Will. 'Only fifteen days.'

'Ah,' said Barry.

'Ah,' said Will. 'Take Tim and me to the circus.'

41

It was a wonder.

Even in an age of wonders, it was a wonder.

Count Otto Black's Circus Fantastique hung in the night sky above Whitechapel. The vast star-shaped blimp sparkled with thousands of light bulbs which flashed on and off, the way that some of them do, spelling out Count Otto's name and tracing the outlines of galloping horses, gambolling clowns and dancing bears, high-wire walkers and jugglers, mimes and marmosets too.

It was the thirty-first of December, the year was eighteen ninety-nine, it was half past nine and it wasn't raining.

Will and Tim emerged from the Naughty Pope public house into a thoroughfare that jostled with New Year merrymakers. Almost everyone waved a Union flag and most were already drunk.

Will looked up and whistled. The sheer scale of the flying circus was awesome in the absolute. 'That is big,' was all he could manage for the moment.

Tim shook his head and patted down his wandering hair. 'It's beyond anything,' he said. 'But I just don't get it.'

'What is it that you just don't get?' Will was jostled by revellers. A young ragamuffin called Winston, who had recently failed his interview for the job of curator at the Tate Gallery and decided instead to join the rest of his brothers and pursue a life of crime, deftly relieved Will of his wallet.

'It's technology,' said Tim. 'Astounding technology. Count Otto Black designed the flying circus himself, didn't he?'

'It said so on the flyer we were reading in the pub.'

'So why go to all the trouble and expense, if at the stroke of midnight, his Doomsday Programme kicks in and the whole caboodle goes belly up, ceases to exist, in fact?'

Will shrugged. Winston's brother Wycliff deftly relieved Will of his pocket watch.

'It's a fiendish plot,' said Will. 'And fiendish plots only really make sense to the fiends who plot them, I suppose.'

'Doesn't make sense,' said Tim.

'Curious, that,' Will smiled, 'considering that everything else so far has made such perfect sense.'

'That would be irony, right?'

Will nodded unthoughtfully. Winston's other brother, Elvis, relieved Will of his circus tickets.

'Ah, no,' said Will, taking Elvis by the wrist and hauling him into the air. 'I didn't mind about the watch or the wallet, but I need those tickets.'

'Right you are, guv'nor,' said the dangling Elvis, as Will plucked the tickets from his grubby little mitt.

'Good boy,' said Will, and he set Elvis down.

Winston's other brother, Kylie, deftly relieved Elvis of a digital wristwatch that Kylie had recently swiped from a toff named Burlington Bertie.

Tim reached down and deftly relieved Kylie of a packet of Spangles.

Will, in turn, deftly relieved Tim of his straw hat.

'I wasn't wearing a straw hat,' said Tim.

'That's *mine*!' said a lady, snatching it back.

'Sorry,' said Will. 'I got carried away.'

The lady, once more in her straw hat, kicked Will in the ankle. Winston relieved her of her bundle of *War Crys*.

'Stop it now,' said Will. 'It's all getting out of hand.'

'Who's nicked my boots?' said Wycliff.

'Let's go, Tim,' said Will.

'Do we have to?' Tim asked. 'I've acquired a packet of Spangles. Oh no I haven't, they're gone.'

'We have to go,' said Will. 'It's not clever and it's not funny.'

'What swab's scarpered with me wooden leg?' cried a pirate, collapsing into an ungathered heap of the pure.

Will and Tim buttoned up their coats, thrust their hands into their pockets and pressed forward into the noisy crowd.

Street sellers were out in force, hawking Union flags and roasted chestnuts, centennial souvenirs and pictures of Little Tich.

'Mud on a stick, squire?' asked a young rapscallion.

'Mud on a stick?' asked Tim in ready reply.

'Looks like a toffee apple from a distance, squire.'

'I'll take two then, please,' said Tim.

'No, you won't,' said Will.

'Poo on a stick,' cried another rapscallion. 'Looks like mud from a distance.'

'Press on,' said Will. And Tim pressed on.

'Tell me, Will,' said Tim, as the two pressed on together. 'What of the plan thus far?'

'Thus far,' said Will, 'the plan stands at this. I have here two complimentary tickets dispatched to me by Master Scribbens, who is aloft, probably making himself up even now in preparation for his performance.'

'What *exactly* does he do for a performance?'

Will shrugged. 'I'm not exactly sure. He hinted to me that there was a degree of sliding involved.'

'Hopefully we'll be in time to miss his act, if you know what I mean. And what of Mr Wells?'

'He slipped aboard the flying circus with Master Scribbens this morning. He's had a day to search for the computer programme. Let's hope he's been successful. An aerial hansom awaits us upon the corner of Hobs Lane; I ordered it earlier. It will take us up to the circus. Once there Mr Wells will take you to the computer room, where you will disable the system.'

'Right,' said Tim, somewhat dubiously.

'And I will take care of Count Otto.'

'Bring him to justice?' said Tim. 'How?'

'Kill him,' said Will.

'What?'

'He was responsible for Rune's death. I know I don't have any definite proof, but I believe it all the same. And he is the King of the witches. All of this, everything that I and my other self have been through, is because of him. He has to die.'

'That's savage,' said Tim. 'It will make you a murderer. How can you live with that?'

'I won't be living with that.'

'How so?'

'Because if I thwart Count Otto's plans, our future will cease to exist, Tim. *We* will cease to exist.'

'I'm not at all keen on this plan. Isn't there another we could try?'

'How many times has he tried to kill me?' Will asked. 'And you too. He *did* kill you. One of his clockwork terminators shot you with a General Electric Minigun.'

Tim shivered. 'You do what you have to do,' he said. 'I'll take care of the Doomsday Programme.'

They had reached the aerial taxi. Will turned and took Tim's hand in his. 'It all ends tonight,' he said. 'In a few hours from now. However it ends, I just want to say that you are the best friend I've ever had. And the best half-brother also.'

'Stop it,' said Tim. 'You'll have me getting a crinkly mouth.'

'I'm sorry I got you involved in this.'

'I'm not,' said Tim. 'I've loved every moment.'

'So, shall we go?'

The cabbie swung open a passenger door.

'Slide in, gents,' said he.

The Brentford Snail Boy slid a flabby hand across the table of the 'Lower Rank Performers' dressing room, took up a powder puff and dabbed chalk dust around and about his face. He examined his reflection in the brightly lit mirror and considered it up to passing muster, although not to passing mustard, and certainly not salt.

The Lower Rank Performers dressing room was packed with Lower Rank Performers: conjoined twins, pig-faced ladies, dwarves and midgets, dog-faced boys and alligator girls.

Master Scribbens sighed. These were *his* people. He was a freak and so were they: outsiders, things to be gawped at and laughed at by 'normal' folk.

'A regular dandy,' said a soft lisping voice to the rear of the Snail Boy. 'A regular matinee idol.'

Master Makepiece Scribbens looked up from his own reflection to that of the man who stood behind him.

The man who was partly man.

Mr Joseph Merrick.

Tonight he was maskless and clad in an enormous top hat, white tie and tails. He wore a white kid glove (tanned through a process which demanded extensive use of the pure) upon his serviceable right hand; the other was hidden by a sealskin muff. He leaned upon an ebony cane and grinned in a lopsided fashion that was grotesque to behold.

'Joey,' said Makepiece. 'I didn't know you were on the bill tonight.'

'I'm not.' The Elephant Man took a seat next to the Snail Boy. 'I'm a guest of Her Majesty, Gawd give her one for me. In the Royal Box. I'm sitting next to Princess Alexandra.'

'Lucky you,' said Master Scribbens.

'And she's begging for it,' said Mr Merrick. 'Keeps touching my good knee. I'm in there, I can tell you.'

Master Scribbens sighed. 'I haven't reached puberty yet,' said he.

'But when I do, I hope that I'll be as big a success with the ladies as you are.'

Joseph Merrick made elephantine trumpetings. 'Sorry,' said he. 'I shouldn't laugh. But look at yourself. All you've got going for you is an abundance of natural lubricant. The ladies I pleasure get moist at the very sight of me.'

'You're a very crude man,' said Master Scribbens.

'I'm sorry,' said Mr Merrick. 'I don't wish to offend you. You and I are two of a kind, which is to say that we are not as others. We are neither one thing, nor the other. So what are we truly, tell me that?'

'Alone,' said Master Scribbens and he said it in a most plaintive tone. 'Always alone, no matter whose company we are in. Even among our own kind.'

'Precisely. But things will change. Believe me, they will change.'

'I can't imagine how,' said Master Scribbens.

'Oh they will.' The Elephant Man tapped his pendulous hooter. 'They will change tonight. They will change forever. Be assured of that. I know these things. Trust me, I'm a freak.'

A freak. Someone different; someone apart; someone cursed by their own difference. But let's not get too heavy here. But then, again, let's do.

Mr H.G. Wells was certainly different. You can't get much more different than being invisible. Mr H.G. Wells moved invisibly along a corridor. He had spent the day aboard the flying circus, checking it inch by painstaking inch, and so far had found absolutely nothing. He had entered the great central arena, the big top itself, which occupied the gondola at the centre of the five-pointed dirigible. He had marvelled at its splendour and design: seating for two thousand people, Royal boxes, an orchestra stand, a domed glass ceiling, above which could be seen the star-strung sky; and a mass of gilded ornamentation all around and about, which created the effect of some Rajah's palace.

He had branched out from there, into the numerous offices and sleeping accommodation, and stables, and catering areas and latrines and playrooms and storerooms.

And he had found absolutely nothing.

He had reached the cockpit and the engine rooms.

He had followed upon the polished ivory heels of Count Otto, as he strutted here and strutted there, attending to the minutiae of detail that ensured the Perfect Show.

He'd listened to all that the Count had said, even his whispered words.

And he had learned absolutely nothing, nothing to even suggest that this was anything more than a circus; an incredible circus, albeit, but a circus none the less.

'I am baffled,' said H.G. Wells to himself and he shook his invisible head.

The cabbie shook his head. 'The traffic up here,' he said. 'Chronic it is. Sorry, gents, but we're in for a bit of a wait.'

The aerial cabs were nose to tail, queuing to dispatch their glamorous cargoes of lords, ladies and London glitterati at the circus entrance beneath the central big top.

'We'll be a while,' said the cabbie.

'You'll probably want to switch off your meter, then,' said Will.

'I probably won't,' said the cabbie. 'In fact, I definitely won't.'

'Perhaps there's another way in,' said Tim. 'A back door or something. Perhaps we could slip in unseen.'

'Ain't you got tickets, then?' asked the cabbie.

'Count Otto is a friend of ours,' said Will. 'We'd like to surprise him. Perhaps you might leave the queue and fly around the circus. There might be somewhere else you could drop us off.'

'As you please,' said the cabbie, and he dropped his cab from the queue, then circled it up in a glorious arc and swung about over the dirigible.

'Look at the size of it,' said Tim. 'It looks even bigger up close.'

Will rolled his eyes. 'Fly very slowly around, cabbie,' he said. 'Let's see what we can see.'

'As you please,' said the cabbie once more.

'He's very good,' said Tim. 'A good pilot.'

'Thank you sir,' said the cabbie. 'I got this cab from my brother. It was his you see, but he can't fly it any more. He had a tragic accident.'

'In this cab?' Tim asked.

'Well, actually, yes. He was taking a Colonel William Starling to the launching of the moonship. But the Colonel threw him out of the cab into a pond at Crystal Palace. Broke both his legs. Then the Colonel crashed the cab. Cost me a packet to get it fixed up again. What a bastard that Colonel Starling, eh? I hope they catch him and string him up.'

'Right,' said Tim.

And 'Right,' said Will.

'There,' said the cabbie. 'Down there. See that gantry running the length of the southern star arm, I could drop you off on that, if you like. Then you can fend for yourselves.'

'Do that,' said Will and the cabbie steered the aerial hansom close in to the gantry.

'There you go, gents. That's one and threepence on the clock.'

'Pay him, Tim,' said Will.

Tim patted his pockets. 'I'm penniless,' he said. 'I think someone deftly relieved me of all my money.'

'Me too,' said Will. 'Winston the paperboy lifted my wallet.'

'This is most upsetting,' said the cabbie. 'Generally in such situations, I close my hatch, engage the central locking, then fly the cab round to my other brother, Gentlemen Jim Corbett, barefist champion of Britain, and have him beat the non-payers to a bloody pulp.'

'We don't really have time for that,' said Will. 'But listen, as we're sneaking in, we could let you have our tickets. Numbered seats in the front row. What do you say to that?'

'So where will you be sitting?'

'We'll find somewhere. What do you say?'

'I say, thank you very much. Give me the tickets.'

Will took out the tickets and handed them through the little glass partition to the cabbie.

'Thanks very much to you,' said that man, examining the tickets. 'Seats twelve and thirteen, row A. Careful how you go now.'

'Farewell,' said Will and he and Tim left the hovering cab and clambered onto the gantry.

A bit of a wind was blowing.

'It's chilly up here,' said Tim. 'Like being on a very high rooftop.'

'A rooftop,' said Will and he smiled.

'And why are you smiling about a rooftop?'

'Remember when we were in the cell at the Brentford court house and I told you about the Lazlo Woodbine thrillers I'd read?'

Tim nodded, but his nodding was all but invisible, hidden as it was by his hair, which was wildly blowing all around.

'And how I told you that every Lazlo Woodbine thriller ends with Laz having a final rooftop confrontation with the villain. Who then takes the big fall to oblivion at the end.'

'You did,' said Tim. 'Although I didn't see the relevance at the time. Everything gets explained eventually, doesn't it?'

'It does,' said Will. 'And I'm freezing my privy parts off here, so let's get inside.'

Inside the big top, posh folk were taking their seats. And anyone who was anyone was there.

Wilde was there, sitting upon a swansdown cushion, due to the scalding of his behind which he had received when the moonship exploded. And Beardsley was there, chatting with Richard Dadd about how well his brother Peter was doing playing for Brentford football club and about how a talent scout from Liverpool had recently spotted him. And the Duke of Wellington was there, chatting with Lord Colostomy, who was trying to sell him a bag. And Dame Nellie Melba was there, admiring the boots of Little Tich.

Lord Babbage and Mr Tesla sat next to Her Majesty the Queen (GBH), who sat next to Princess Alexandra, who had her hand once more upon Joseph Merrick's good knee.

And Mr Sherlock Holmes was there, back from Dartmoor with another successfully solved case under his belt. And Dr Watson, who had secretly been shagging the Queen for the last five years, sat with him, sharing a joke about bedpans with the Queen's gynaecologist Sir Frederick Treves.

The Pre-Raphaelites were all there, of course, and these shared a joke with a group of proto-surrealists.

The joke was all about fish.

And there was Montague Summers and Madame Blavatsky, Aleister Crowley and the Pope of Rome.

But they weren't sharing any jokes. They weren't even speaking to each other.

There was an air of expectation breathing all around and about this salubrious crowd, an air of exaltation, of wonder and of hope. For a new century was dawning, and given the advances of the last fifty years, it was a new century that they were all very much looking forward to.

For what would happen next? What great steps would the British Empire be taking? To conquer all the world? And then the stars?

'Definitely the stars,' said The Man on the Clapham Omnibus, who was tonight A Face in the Crowd, albeit a most exclusive crowd.

Exclusive folk filed in and took their seats. Upon a high gantry Tim eased open a door.

'We're in,' said he. 'Follow me.'

'You know where we're going then?' asked Will.

'Not as such,' said Tim.

A buzzer buzzed in the dressing room of the Lower Rank Performers. And a light flashed too. 'Five minutes to curtain up,' came a voice through the public address system.

In the big top, the orchestra took their seats and took to tuning up their instruments. The smell of sawdust from the ring mingled with the perfumes of the wealthy.

'Down this way,' said Will.

'So *you* know where we're going?'

'Not as such.'

The last of the aerial hansoms which had conveyed the rich and famous to the flying circus had now departed. One final cab drew up, this bearing the cabbie Will had passed his tickets to. The cabbie had brought his brother with him, the one with the broken legs. These legs were in plaster. The cabbie helped his injured brother from the cab. 'This will be a real treat for you, bruv,' he said. 'You deserve it.'

'Cheers,' said his brother, supporting himself on crutches.

'I'll just switch off the engine,' said the cabbie, and he leaned inside the cab and did so.

'There,' he said, grinning back at his brother.

The aerial hansom plummeted down towards Whitechapel.

The cabbie's plastered brother said, 'You twat!'

'If we'd thought a little harder about this,' said Tim, as he and Will wandered aimlessly along a service tunnel beneath the dirigible proper, 'we'd have got ourselves a plan of this craft. I'll bet we could have got one from the Patent Office, or somewhere.'

'We'll find our way,' said Will. 'Have a little faith.'

'Oh I do. I have plenty of faith. Listen.'

Will listened.

'What is *that*, do you think?'

Will listened some more. 'Applause,' said he. 'It's applause.'

'The show is beginning,' said Tim.

And Tim was right.

The show was indeed beginning.

42

Applause.

Tumultuous applause.

The big top was plunged in darkness, but for the starlight that twinkled through the vast glass dome. And then a spotlight pierced the black, striking the centre of the ring, and then a figure stepped into the spotlight, and there was deafening applause to greet Count Otto Black.

The Count looked magnificent. He had a huge fur hat upon his narrow head. A gorgeous cloak of gold, its high raised collar trimmed with ermine, swept the sawdust and was secured about the Count's slender throat by a golden brooch, engraved with enigmatic symbols. His great black beard was plaited into numerous colourfully beaded braids. His eyeballs glittered and his mouth was set in a yellow-toothed grin.

The Count threw wide his cloak, to reveal a crimson tunic worked with cloth-of-gold, pantaloons of yellow silk and high top boots of black patent leather. He extended his long and scrawny arms and waggled his twig-like digits. These were weighed heavily with gorgeous rings, many engraved with the inevitable enigmatic symbols.

'Greetings one and greetings all,' cried he.

And the crowd cheered and clapped some more. And the cabbie in Will's seat whistled.

'My lords,' cried the Count. 'My lords, my ladies and gentlemen, your Holiness the Pope, artists, poets, great thinkers of the age, I bid you welcome. And to Her Majesty the Queen, Empress of India, America and the African States, I am your humble servant, Ma'am.'

The Count bowed low, and the Queen giggled foolishly.

'I do believe *he's* knocking her off, too,' Dr Watson whispered to Holmes.

'Tonight,' the Count took to strutting about the circus ring, the spotlight stalking his every step, 'tonight, it is my pleasure to present for you an entertainment such as has never been witnessed before. One surpassing those of ancient Rome, or anything produced before the courts of Russia. You will witness wonders. You will experience thrills that will excite your nerves and stagger your senses. And, as Big Ben tolls midnight and the dawn of the twentieth century—' But then the Count paused and put a long and bony figure to his lips. '—then we shall see what we shall see, and you will bear witness to something that is beyond your wildest imaginings.'

'That's something *I'd* like to see,' whispered the lady in a straw hat to her friend called Doris, 'because *my* imaginings are rather wild.'

'And so,' the Count flung out his arms once more, 'our show begins.'

'We've gone the wrong way,' said Tim. 'Let's try down that staircase there.'

Will scratched at his blondy head. 'Has it occurred to you Tim,' he asked, 'that this flying circus is somewhat bigger on the inside than it is on the outside?'

Tim made his bestest thoughtful face. 'I wasn't going to mention that,' he said.

'Down the staircase, then,' said Will.

The lights went up in the great big top and fifty dwarves upon ostrich-back* trooped into the ring. They steered their mounts through a complex dance routine, to the accompaniment of the orchestra, which played a selection of popular music hall numbers, including 'Don't jump off the roof, Dad, you'll make a hole in the yard', and 'When your grey hair turns to silver, won't you change me half-a-quid?', and 'Get out the meatballs, mother, we've come to a fork in the road', which was always a favourite, but thankfully not the Big Boot Dance.

The crowd sang along with these, for they were the dance anthems of the day. Queen Victoria did the hand jive and Princess Alexandra, the five-knuckle shuffle.

Joseph Merrick simply hummed.

'Not bad, eh?' said the cabbie in Will's seat. 'Enjoying yourself, bruv?'

His plastered brother shook his head. 'I'd be enjoying myself a great deal more, if I didn't know that my aerial hansom was presently embedded in the roof of the Naughty Pope,' said he. 'You big-nosed twat!'

* Not on the back of the same ostrich, obviously.

★

Master Makepiece Scribbens gave his nose another powdering.

'A regular dandy,' whispered a voice at his ear.

Master Scribbens glanced into the mirror. Only his own reflection gazed back at him.

'It is I.' The voice belonged to Mr Wells. 'Remember our rules. Do not acknowledge my presence, other than to nod or shake your head when deemed appropriate. Do you understand me?'

Master Scribbens nodded his wobbly head.

'Did you dispatch the complimentary tickets to William and Timothy?'

Master Scribbens nodded once more.

'Do you know whether they have taken their seats?'

Master Scribbens now shook his wobbly head.

'I have had no success in locating any computers aboard this vessel. Nor have I overheard anything suspicious. I do not know what to make of it.'

Master Scribbens gave his head a nod and then a shake.

'I hope we haven't made a terrible mistake,' said Mr Wells.

'Cavalcade of Curiosities to the ring,' called a voice through the public address system in the Lower Rank Performers dressing room.

'I have to go,' whispered Master Scribbens.

'Break a leg,' said Mr Wells.

Tim tripped down the staircase. 'Damn,' said he, as he picked himself up. 'I thought I'd broken my leg.' His trouser was snagged up on a rivet, Tim yanked it free, ripping a hole in the fabric.

'Try and be careful,' said Will.

'Yes, well, I didn't do it on purpose, you know. And I've ruined my smart trousers now.'

'I'm getting confused here,' said Will. 'Doesn't this corridor look exactly the same to you as the one we've just come from?'

'Do you mean we've been going around in circles?'

'Well, hardly, if we've just come down a staircase.'

'Let's try this direction,' said Tim.

'I'll follow you this time,' said Will.

Mr Wells followed the Brentford Snail Boy as he slid towards the circus ring. Mr Wells was most impressed by all he had seen of Count Otto Black's flying circus and he felt quite certain that he had seen all of it. The symmetry of the corridors, the precision of the engineering. It was all so highly advanced. Even in this age of advancement, it was highly advanced. And he noticed for the first time a curious anomaly; that although the steel-tipped heels of his invisible shoes struck the steely floor of the corridor, they made no sound whatsoever. And yet earlier in the day they certainly had, and he had been forced to creep everywhere upon tiptoe for fear of being heard.

Mr Wells stopped, did a little jump, heard nothing, stroked his invisible chin and continued to follow the Snail Boy.

Will continued to follow Tim.

'Down *this* staircase,' said Tim.

'Fair enough,' said Will. 'Careful you don't trip this time.'

'Yes, as if I would.'

Tim took a step down the staircase, tripped and fell the rest of the way.

'You only did that to amuse me,' said Will, joining Tim at the foor of the stairs and helping him to his feet.

'I can assure you I did *not*.' Tim dusted himself down and gave the staircase a kick. 'That's curious,' said Tim.

'And rather pointless,' said Will. 'Did you hurt your foot?'

'Certainly not.' The expression of pain upon Tim's face made a lie of this statement. 'But the sound.'

'What sound?'

'No sound at all.' Tim kicked the staircase once more.

There was no sound at all.

'Now that *is* curious,' said Will.

'Yes,' Tim agreed, 'and not only that. See there,' and he pointed.

'What is that?' Will asked.

'The piece of my trouser that got torn off when I fell down the other staircase.'

Will looked at Tim.

And Tim looked at Will.

'I think we're in trouble,' said Will.

'You know what the trouble with dwarves is,' said the lady in the straw hat.

Her friend Doris shook her head.

'Nor me,' said the lady. 'But someone must know.'

And the crowd almost rose to its collective feet to greet the entrance of the Brentford Snail Boy and the Cavalcade of Curiosities.

The Dog-Faced Boy juggled pussycats.

The Big Fat Lady sang.
The Man With Two Heads talked to himself.
The Bell-End Baby rang.
The Siamese Twins played saxophones.
The Pig-faced Lady juggled.
And the uniped,
With the pointed head
Bounced up and down and –

'*What?*' Lord Byron asked the Great McGonagall. 'Nothing rhymes with "juggled" and you know it.'

'Smuggled?' the Poet Laureate suggested.

The orchestra in the stand above the artists' entrance played selections from *Joseph and the Technicolor Dreamcoat*, and also *Armageddon: The Musical*, which was having its very first run at a pub in Brentford, but which wasn't going down to great critical acclaim.

'When will the dancing bears be on?' asked Her Majesty the Queen (blessings be upon Her).

Princess Alexandra didn't answer. Her head was in the lap of Joseph Merrick, and it's rude to speak with your mouth full.*

Time goes by very fast when you're having a good time, which might actually mean that there's no such thing as premature ejaculation. But time *does* go by very fast.

And wouldn't you just know it, that after the dwarves on the ostriches doing their dance, and the Cavalcade of Curiosities going through their motions, the high-flyers flying and the jugglers juggling, the wirewalkers walking their wires and Mr Aquaphagus swallowing and regurgitating not only goldfish, but mackerel, salmon, sea bass, hammer-head sharks and an entire school of dolphins; the Cossack Horsemen re-enacting the siege of Leningrad, and Lord Babbage's clockwork ballet and Big Bloke's Little Boot Dance; the dancing bears (who were greatly applauded by Her Majesty the Queen (Da-de-da-de-dah)) and the dancing elephants (which did not amuse her), and countless clowns, many mimes and, of course, Harry the Horse, who was dancing the waltz, the midnight hour approached.

'Are you having a good time?' Count Otto Black was back in the ring.

* Unforgiveable, I know. But hey, we are reaching the end of the story now and how many times is an opportunity like that going to come up in a single lifetime?

The audience applauded.

'Let me hear you say yeah!'

'Yeah!' went the audience.

'Yeah!'

'Yeah!'

'Yeah!'

'Yeah!' said Tim.

'What?' said Will.

'Someone's shouting "Yeah!" Count Otto Black I suppose.'

'Yeah,' Will sighed. He and Tim sat upon the staircase. They'd been up and down that staircase for the last two hours. 'We're stuffed,' said Will. 'We're trapped. We can't even find the door we came in by. We walked into a trap. It's like a möbius strip. No beginning. No end.'

'There has to be a way out,' said Tim.

'There is,' said Will. 'It's just that I'm not too keen to employ it. I mean, I *am* supposed to be doing things *my* way.'

'Don't quite get you,' said Tim.

Will sighed.

'Barry,' said he.

And Will and Tim materialised in the great big top to the rear of the great big crowd.

'You only had to ask, chief,' said Barry. 'It would have spared you a lot of walking around in circles. And look at the time.'

'I can't,' said Will. 'My pocket watch was nicked.'

'Well, it's nearing midnight, chief. Just five minutes to go.'

'What?'

'Always with the "whats?" you schmuck.'

'Yeah!' went the crowd once more, all but deafening Will.

'And now.' Count Otto strutted some more about the circus ring. 'The end is near. And we must face the final curtain.*

'My friends,' he continued, 'I am going to make my case. Of which, as it happens, I am certain. I can tell you that I have lived a life that has been most full. And I have travelled upon each and every highway and more, in fact, a great deal more than this, I have done it all in the service of my Lord Satan.'

'That sort of spoiled the metre, didn't it, chief?'

The audience went 'Ooooooooh,' and 'What?' and 'Eh?' also. Some of the audience even said 'Bless my soul.'

* Careful phrasing, there you notice. No copyright infringement.

'Yes,' Count Otto Black nodded his black bearded head. 'That's what I said, Satan. That's what you heard me say.'

There were shiftings in the audience now. Uncomfortable shiftings, movings from buttocks to buttocks, fans being wafted at increasing speeds, kid gloves being drawn on, top hats being pushed upon Macassar-oiled heads, preparatory to leaves being taken from seats.

'Still yourselves,' commanded Count Otto. 'And do not think of taking leave of your seats. There is no escape for you.'

Grumblings rumbled through the audience, mutterings and utterings of outrage. And into the ring marched automata, many automata, many identical automata, terrific figures all, with the dead black eyes of demon-spawn and armpits reeking of brimstone. They drew out pistols of advanced design and waved these about in a menacing manner.

The crowd stilled to silence. The crowd was no longer such a merry crowd.

To the rear of this crowd, high up and skulking, Tim said to Will, 'Now what do we do?'

'Slip away,' Will whispered back. 'You slip out of the exit. Find the computer room. Sorry, Tim, but this is all fouled up.'

'And what are *you* going to do?'

'Barry,' said Will. 'Take me back in time two minutes, to the centre of the circus ring. I'll shoot Count Otto Black.'

'No can do, chief. Sorry. If you'd listened to me earlier, I could have advised you as to where might have been a good place to hide yourself, but you just wouldn't listen. I can't do what you ask, it's not in my remit. It's *really* cheating. But at least you are in the right place at the right time, which is something, eh? You'll just have to play it by ear now.'

'Thanks a lot,' said Will.

'For what?' Tim asked.

'I was talking to Barry. Slip away, Tim. I'll see if I can shoot Count Otto from here.'

Will drew a pistol from his belt.

And Tim slipped away.

He didn't slip too far however, for Tim found the exit considerably barred.

A terrific figure loomed before this exit. It glared at Tim and fixed him with its dead black eyes. 'Return to your seat,' it said, in a deeply-timbred, rich Germanic accent.

Will took very careful aim.

Way down in the circus ring a red laser dot appeared upon the forehead of Count Otto Black. Will squinted through the telescopic sight and gently squeezed upon the trigger.

And then the gun was struck from his hand.

And Will struck from his feet.

'I know what you must be wondering,' said Count Otto Black. 'You must be wondering what this is all about. Perhaps you are thinking, "Aha Count Otto has some very special marvel in store for us, as a conclusion to his wondrous show. He promised us something extra special, and indeed this must be it". And indeed, to this degree, you are entirely correct, because I promise you something particularly special. I promise you the end of civilisation as you know it.'

'Count Otto,' called Her Majesty (etc.). 'I trust that this special entertainment and end of civilisation as we know it will not take too long. I have to return to Buckingham Palace within a very few minutes to watch the fireworks.'

Count Otto Black shook his head. 'That is neither here, nor there,' he said. 'What you are about to witness, you will have no recollection of tomorrow. You will awaken with memories that you enjoyed the fireworks, and memories too of your entire life, but these will not be true memories, because the past as you remember it and the present as you understand it, will have been erased.'

Queen Victoria made a puzzled face.

'An explanation is necessary, I feel.' Count Otto Black clapped his slender hands together. 'Lords and ladies, one and all, allow me to introduce you to The Chiswick Townswomen's Guild.'

Into the ring marched thirteen pinch-faced women.

They were as alike as those peas that dwell in the pod of metaphor. They wore lavish costumes of black damask embroidered with silk brocade. Their bodies were impossibly slender. The looks upon their tiny pinched-faces were *intent*.

They formed a circle about the Count and joined their hands together. And then they began to sway backwards and forwards, chanting softly and scuffing their heels in the sawdust.

'All ends here,' cried Count Otto Black. 'The future changes, and also the past. Five sacrifices have been made below and now one will be made above.'

The audience did rumblings and mumblings. Most were now very keen indeed to be up and away.

'Be still *now*!' Count Otto raised his hands towards the dome where the stars twinkled on high. 'A demonstration of power is required, I do believe. And why not upon those who have come here to do my master harm. In the twelfth and thirteenth seats of the very first row, I do believe.'

'Eh?' said the cabbie, checking his tickets. 'That's us, isn't it, bruv?'

But sadly he said no more at all, as a bolt of fire shot down from above and reduced both him and his plastered brother to ashes, which really wasn't fair.

The crowd went 'Oooooooh!' and shrank very low in their seats.

Will opened his eyes and said, 'Who hit me?' A terrific figure hauled him to his feet.

'Assassin alert,' said this terrific figure, holding Will in the grip that is known as 'vice-like'.

'Oh,' went Count Otto and he put his finger to his ear, wherein rested a tiny radio receiver that held a Babbage patent. 'I seem to have made an error. Might we have a spotlight shine upon the back row, to the left of the exit?'

A spotlight shone in that very direction.

It lit upon Will Starling. And also upon Tim, both held in the clutches of twin terrific figures.

'Mr Starling,' called Count Otto. 'It is you lurking behind that beard, isn't it? I knew you'd adopt a disguise. Please come down and join me. And your companion too.' He beckoned to the terrific figures. 'Haul them down to me *now*.'

Will's captor had Will's arms pinned to his sides. Will struggled, but to no avail. The automaton hauled him down the aisle towards the ring. The second automaton did likewise with Tim.

'I suppose,' said Count Otto, as Will's terrific captor deftly relieved Will of his weaponry and flung him down to the sawdust, 'that it would be a pity if you missed this, as it does concern you so very personally.'

Will glared up at Count Otto Black. 'You'll get yours,' he said.

'Damn right,' agreed Tim, who now lay beside Will in the sawdust.

'Oh, I don't think so,' Count Otto smiled. 'Not, at least, in the way that you mean. Bring on the sacrificial victim.'

And from beneath the orchestra stand, curtains drew back and two more automata appeared, hauling between them—

'My other self,' whispered Will.

But it was *not* Will's other self.

'Colonel William Starling,' said Count Otto. 'Of the Queen's Own Aerial Cavalry. Your many-times great-grandfather, I believe.'

Will muttered swearings beneath his breath. The automaton pushed his foot down hard on Will's back.

'Get your damned hands off me,' demanded Colonel William. 'Beaten up and thrown into a police cell, then kidnapped from the police cell and dragged up here. Outrageous behaviour. I demand an explanation, sir.'

'Such a task,' said Count Otto ignoring Colonel William's complaints, 'to erase our nemesis. We have tried to kill you both in this time and in the future. Hugo Rune, your most illustrious and annoying ancestor, he was extinguished, but *still* you live. But no more. When the Colonel dies, wifeless and childless, you will definitely cease to exist.'

Will spat sawdust and curled his lip, but that was all he could do.

'My apologies to my audience,' said the Count. 'None of this will mean anything to you. None of you will have the foggiest idea what is going on here.'

The audience did further mumblings and grumblings: the Count, it seemed, was correct on this account.

'You are not entirely correct.' The voice came from the rear of the audience. A spotlight swung in the direction of the voice's location. So to speak, and lit upon . . . Will looked up as best he could.

'Hugo Rune,' said he.

'It is I,' said Hugo Rune.

'Well, well, well,' said Count Otto Black, plucking at his beard. 'The guru's guru himself. And there was I, most certain you were dead.'

'Reports of my death have been greatly exaggerated,'* said Mr Hugo Rune.

'Good line,' said Oscar Wilde, plumping up his cushion. 'I'll use that.'

'Isn't this exciting?' said the lady in the straw hat. 'I've no idea what's going on, but it's very exciting none the less.'

'It's not *that* exciting,' said her friend called Doris. 'It's mostly just talking, apart from the bolts of fire. Those were quite exciting.'

'And the dancing bears,' said Her Majesty (.). 'I really liked those dancing bears.'

'Come on then, Rune,' called Count Otto. 'Join us here in the ring. Witness what is to come. Be here at the beginning of the end.'

Hugo Rune strode down an aisle towards the ring. Tonight he wore

* Rune actually was the first person ever to utter this line. And very well uttered, it was.

his magician's robe; a seamless floor-length white cotton garment, embroidered with the ever-popular enigmatic symbols. His ring of power was upon his nose-picking finger, a jaunty fez perched at a rakish angle on his great bald head. He presented a most striking appearance, especially for a dead man. Hugo Rune stepped down to the circus ring.

Will gazed up at him. The thoughts within Will's head were somewhat confused.

'Time ticks away,' said Hugo Rune, stepping into the circus ring. 'You will shortly run right out of it.'

Count Otto smiled a wicked smile. His yellow crooked teeth all showed themselves. 'There is no more time,' said he. 'As you know it. But pray tell me this, before the new dawn dawns. How is it that you remain alive?'

'A great magician never divulges his secrets,' said Hugo Rune. 'It might lessen his charisma.'

'A cop-out if ever I heard one.' Count Otto spat into the sawdust.

'Then you might put it down to my immortality, coupled with the fact that a dead man has no creditors. It generally pays to fake one's death at least once every century. And upon this occasion it was also necessary in order that young Will here would do the right thing. Which I am proud to see that he has. And, by the by, Count Otto, would it be permissible to allow Mr Starling to his feet? He looks most uncomfortable down there.'

'It is of no consequence.' Count Otto fluttered his twig-like digits. The terrific treader that stood upon Will withdrew its foot and Will climbed to his feet.

'Thank you,' said Will.

'And what about me?' asked Tim.

'Yes, you too.' The Count did further finger flutters. Tim climbed to *his* feet.

'Mr Rune,' said Tim, putting out his hand for a shake. 'I'm so very pleased to meet you. I'm Tim, your real magical heir.'

'Splendid.' Rune raised a hairless eyebrow. 'Then perhaps you'd care to join me later for a cocktail at the Pussycat Club? And Will too.'

'Thanks,' said Will, and shook his head in wonder.

'Enough of this chitchat!' cried Count Otto Black, as the pinch-faced ladies continued to chant all around him.

'Yes,' agreed Rune. 'Enough. Desist from this abominable scheme, Black, or I will be forced to take measures against you.'

'Oh yes?' Count Otto laughed. And then he glanced at his

wristwatch. It was a Babbage digital. 'One minute left before midnight,' said he. 'And all but one of the players in our little drama present and correct. The final countdown begins.'

'Will someone please tell *me* what's going on here?' Colonel William Starling struggled to free himself from his terrific tormentor. 'Who is this fellow who looks just like me, but for his foolish beard and less-splendid sideburns?'

'Strike the idiot down,' said Count Otto.

And Colonel William was duly struck down.

'And guards,' the Count continued. 'Keep these three,' and he pointed to Tim, Will and Rune, 'firmly under control.'

Many guns swung in the threesome's direction.

'Thus and so,' said Count Otto. 'And now I must defer to my master. To he who will perform the sacrifice and seal the future.' Count Otto drew an athame from his belt, put it to his lips and kissed it. 'He comes,' cried he. 'My master comes.'

And lightning flashed above the dome and a terrible chill ran through the air. 'My master,' cried Count Otto Black once more. 'Prostrate yourselves.'

The pinch-faced women ceased their chant and flung themselves to the sawdust. Count Otto Black went down on one knee. Tim, Will and Rune stood defiant, defiant, but not altogether without any fear.

'His master,' whispered Tim. 'Does he mean the devil?'

A shiver ran across the circus ring, rippling the sawdust.

'Stand firm!' ordered Rune. 'Stand behind me if you must.' Tim and Will hastened to stand behind Rune.

A fanfare went up from the orchestra, a limelight spot illuminated the curtained entrance beneath.

'All praise to the Master,' cried Count Otto Black. 'The Prince of Darkness. The Lord of the Flies. He comes, oh yes indeed.'

And the curtain drew back and light flooded through, a dazzling light, a blinding light.

A figure walked slowly from this light, a striking figure, clad all in black but for his blondy hair.

'Evening all,' said Will's other self. 'I'll bet you weren't expecting me.'

43

'Now I know this chap,' the lady in the straw hat whispered to Doris. 'He's the twin brother of the other one.'

'The one who just got knocked unconscious?'

'No, not that one; the one with the beard, hiding behind the big fat bloke.'

'Not so much of the fat,' cried Hugo Rune, whose hearing was acute. 'I am generously proportioned.'

'And you have lovely eyes,' said the lady. 'Perhaps we might go out for a drink later on? The Pussycat Club, did I hear you say?'

'Cease all this,' bawled Will's other self. 'Enough of this stuff and nonsense.'

Will peeped from beyond Hugo Rune's generously proportioned rear quarters, and gawped at his other self.

'You?' was all he could manage to say.

'Me,' said the other Will. 'I am now in control of all this, and you should be upon your knees.'

'Never,' said Will, but was struck from his feet by a nearby terrific figure.

'That's more like it.' The other Will strode forward, stepped into the circle of prostrate pinch-faced women and stood above Count Otto Black.

'Why?' asked Will. 'Why, and how?'

'*Why?*' Will's other self cast Will a withering glance. It withered the rose Will wore in his buttonhole, not that the rose had been mentioned before. 'You ask me why, after all I've been through? Growing up in a future as the Promised One. Doomed from my very birth to die back here. And then, when I arrive here, captured by these.' The other Will booted the nearest pinch-face, who moaned and pressed her face closer to the sawdust. 'Tortured and tormented for a year, made to knit macramé plant pot holders. And fed upon rats, don't forget that.'

'Nasty,' said the lady in the straw hat.

'They're not so bad,' said the Elephant Man, 'if you have them pan-fried with plenty of garlic.'

'Silence!' Will's other self raised his hand, and a heavy silence fell. He cast another withering glance that became a withering stare. 'I have suffered as no man should suffer, but I will suffer no more. I have travelled into the past and into the future. Not the future you came from, nor the one I came from, but another future entirely. The future that *I* will create for myself tonight.'

'How?' Will managed to ask. 'How did you travel through time?'

'I think *I* know,' said Barry. 'I have a very bad feeling about this.'

'In here,' the other Will tapped at his forehead, 'I have communion and conversation with my Holy Guardian. Tonight we will put the world to right. The world that *this man*,' and he pointed at Rune, 'that *this man* has put to wrong.'

'Me?' quoth Rune. 'I mean, *I*? I mean, *one*?'

'You,' said the other Will. 'You are responsible for all of this, the Victorian super technology that should never have existed. You changed the course of history by introducing Mr Babbage to the Queen at the Great Exhibition.'

'It seemed like the right thing to do,' said Rune. 'And it was.'

'So that it should benefit you. You, with your *Book of Rune* that predicted future events, that would find you worshipped in the future I grew up in, as some kind of messiah.'

'That was hardly my intention.' Rune dusted down his raiment. 'But praise where praise is due, I suppose.'

'And yet you still live,' the other Will made fists, 'even though *I* hacked you to pieces.'

'You?' managed Will.

'Me,' said the other Will. 'And those Whitechapel whores. I wasn't lying when the police found me covered in blood. I was a trifle over-excited. But then, being Jack the Ripper was a rather exciting experience.'

'I knew it was him,' said Sherlock Holmes to Dr Watson.

'No shit, Sherlock,' the doctor replied. 'You knew it was him?'

'Everybody knows it was him,' said the lady in the straw hat. 'I was at his trial and it was in all the papers. There's a big reward for his capture, but I don't fancy making a citizen's arrest. Has anyone seen that big bargee?'

'Why?' Will managed once more.

'You really *are* monosyllabic,' said his other self. 'And really stupid, too. But then, if it hadn't been for you getting me drunk for the first time in my life I would never have acquired the knowledge and conversation of my Holy Guardian.'

'It's Larry, chief,' said Barry. 'My wayward brother. This is all his fault.'

'Why?' asked Will once more. 'Why did you murder those women?'

'All part of this.' The other Will threw wide his arms. 'This isn't just any old anti-gravitational flying circus powered through the wireless transmission of electrical energy, you know. This is a very special construction. And it wasn't so much built, as grown, in my *new improved* future, for this very special moment. All of this.' He twirled about upon his heels, and did a bit of a moonwalk. 'Even now it evolves.' He stamped his feet. 'No noise,' said he. 'No sound. Nothing more enters, nothing leaves. A closed system, Will. The past will change and so will the future, but this little system will not. It is immune. Advanced technology, founded upon magical principles, created by myself, with the aid of my Holy Guardian helper, to ensure that mankind gets the future it really deserves. Which is to say, the future *I* deserve.'

'You deserve a smack,' said Will.

'But not from you. Allow me to explain just what is going to happen, what this "Doomsday Programme" is really all about. It has nothing to do with altering the past. That is something which I will deal with personally. The programme will, how shall I put this, spread a little love. In fact it will spread a whole lot of love. Which is why my Holy Guardian is so enthusiastic. It will spread love all around the world.'

'I suspect that it will do a great deal more than that,' seethed Will.

'Well, just a tad.' The other Will placed a hand upon his heart and made an angelic upturned face. 'It will spread the world's love towards me. I have been so unloved, you see. But no more. From the moment that the spell is activated, anyone who meets me will love me. Isn't that wonderful? And so fair, considering all that I've been through. I will be the object of love for everyone. And everyone will want to please me. I shall become the most popular and all-loved leader of all time. The most popular and loved world leader. The first ever world leader. King of the world, ma.'

'Oh dear, oh dear, oh dear,' said Barry. 'Larry's fouled it up big time, this time.'

'You're insane,' Will seethed a little more. 'And if all you want is love, why did you have to murder those women?'

The other Will smiled. 'It's the question that everybody wants to know the answer to, isn't it? Why did Jack the Ripper do what he did? Here, come and let me whisper.'

Will took faltering forward steps. He leaned towards his other self, but not too closely. He hadn't forgotten about what happened to David Warner in *Time Cop*. How two yous must never, upon any account, come into contact, for fear of terrible cosmic consequences.

The other Will whispered words into Will's ear.

'And that's it?' said Will.

The other Will nodded.

'But it's so obvious. Hideous and fiendish, but obvious.'

The other Will shrugged. 'But no one ever figures it out.'

'What did he say?' Barry asked. 'I didn't catch it.'

'Tell you later,' said Will.

'Regretfully not,' said Will's other self. 'Because there will be no later for you. When Colonel William Starling dies, you will cease to exist.'

'You too,' said Will.

'No, not me. I have worked it all out. Only you will cease to exist. One hundred years from now SF enthusiasts will still be debating over exactly how I worked it out. But work it out, I did. And—' He perused his wristwatch. It wasn't a Babbage, it was a Casio. 'Less than a minute to go; time to make the sacrifice and employ the Millennial Love Bug.'

'It's a Centennial Love Bug,' said Tim.

'What?' the other Will glared at Tim.

'Nothing,' said Tim. 'It's just that I haven't had anything to say for a while. Where is your computer, by the way?'

'My computer?' The other Will laughed, loudly, wildly, madly, in the manner that super-criminals so often do. 'I have control here,' he said. 'Control of these,' and he booted another pinch-faced woman. 'Because they fear me. They fear my supernatural powers, that I can be here.' And the other Will was here. 'Or there.' And he was suddenly over there.

'Larry showing off,' said Barry. 'And he's cheating all over the place. The Big Figure is going to be very upset about this. I wouldn't even be surprised if He chose to intervene.'

'A *deus ex machina* ending,' said Will. 'That will do for me.'

'What did you say?' The other Will was now *here* again.

'Nothing,' said Will. 'Pray continue with your most interesting narrative.'

'Nice line,' whispered Holmes to Watson. 'Make a note of it.'

'I know you've had spies looking for the computer system,' said the other Will. 'But they won't have found it, nor the programme that I formulated in my *new, improved* future. The programme is here,' and he plucked a tiny disc from his pocket.

'And the computer?' Tim asked. 'I did ask about the computer.'

'Right here.' Will's other self beckoned Count Otto to his feet, tore off the showman's great fur hat, and then tore off the top of his head.

The crowd did gaspings.

'I still haven't the faintest idea what's going on,' said the lady in the straw hat. 'But that was unexpected.'

'The real Count Otto had to go,' said the other Will. 'There can be only one King of the witches. So I deposed him.'

'You mean, you murdered him.' Will ground his teeth.

'Not all of him.' The other Will grinned. 'I removed his brain and replaced it with a computerised system. The rest of him is all still him, although,' the other Will sniffed at Count Otto, 'he's beginning to hum a bit.'

'You fiend.' Will did further tooth-grindings.

'I know.' Will's other self grinned some more.

Lights flickered from within the open cavity of Count Otto's head, lines of computer language moved across his eyeballs.

'I've been back and forwards in time,' said Will's other self, 'adjusting this, changing that, killing those, failing to kill *him*.' Once more he pointed at Hugo Rune. 'And I have chosen my allegiance. I have taken the King of the Underworld's shilling, signed up to the dark side of the Force. The deal is done, the pact is made, I will rule the world in *my* new future. Much work has gone into this. But now all is complete.' And he slotted the computer disc into Count Otto's open cranium, snapped back the top of his head and gave it a little pat. 'Millennium Love Bug, Centennial Love Bug, Love me Love me Love me Programme engaged,' said he. 'Engaged,' and he tweaked Count Otto's nose. 'Activated. And counting down.'

The other Will did further grinnings. 'And while it's counting down, there is one other important matter that I need to take care of.'

And with that said, he vanished.

44

It was the day before the day before the day before yesterday, and it was raining.

The rain peppered the glass rooftops of the Great Exhibition. The Great Exhibition was in its original location, Hyde Park. The year was eighteen fifty-one.

A horse-drawn hansom moved sedately along the Kew Road towards Brentford. The cabbie turned up the collar of his ulster coat against the rain. His passenger closed an open window and lightly tapped his cane upon the floor. The cane was of ebony with a silver skull-shaped mount.

At length the hansom came to a halt before an elegant Georgian house upon Brentford's historic Butts Estate. The cabbie climbed down from his mount, opened an umbrella and then a passenger door. The passenger emerged, a large and noble-looking gentleman, clad in a fashionable Westbury coat of green Boleskine tweed, with matching double-brimmed topper. He stepped down from the cab and sheltering beneath the umbrella, he addressed the cabbie.

'Put the cost of this journey on my account,' said he.

'But sir,' the cabbie protested. 'Your account now stands at twenty guineas.'

'Due to the generosity of my tipping,' said the gentleman. 'Shelter my person beneath your brolly to yonder doorway and then take your leave without further complaint. Lest I take my business elsewhere in the future.'

The cabbie did as he was bid and returned grumbling to his cab. The gentleman stood in the porch of the elegant Georgian house and perused the brass doorplate. Inscribed upon it were the words

CHARLES BABBAGE
Mathematician and Inventor

The gentleman rapped upon the door with his cane and presently the door was opened.

An attractive young woman looked out at the gentleman. She had a head of glowing auburn hair and a most remarkable pair of Charlies.

The gentleman's eyes strayed towards these Charlies.

'Mr Rune,' said the attractive young woman. 'My husband is away upon business and has not returned home yet. I understood that your appointment with him was at three. You are more than an hour early.'

'A wizard is never early,' quoth Hugo Rune. 'Nor is he ever late. He is always where he should be, when he should be. Time, dear lady, is everything. Time is the name of the game.'

'Quite so, Mr Rune. Then will you come inside?'

'I will, dear lady, I will.'

The rain continued to fall and time continued to pass.

At two-thirty of that rainy afternoon clock, Mr Charles Babbage returned home. He did not knock upon his own front door. He entered by using his key, and he used this key with stealth. And it was also with stealth that he crept up the stairs towards his marital bedroom, and with stealth that he turned the knob on the door, before he flung the door open – to reveal an erotic scene that caused him considerable distress.

'Mary,' cried Mr Charles Babbage. 'Mary, my love, how could you?'

The sexual position that Mr Babbage's wife Mary was presently engaged in with Mr Hugo Rune was, and is still, known as *Taking Tea with the Parson*. You won't find it catalogued in the *Kama Sutra*; it is somewhat too advanced for that.

'It's not what you think,' cried the fragrant Mary, disentangling her limbs with considerable difficulty. 'It's—'

'A Tantric massage to relieve tension,' said Mr Hugo Rune, seeking his undergarments.

'It is what it is.' The face of Mr Babbage was now the colour of a smacked bottom. It matched the colour of his wife's smacked bottom. 'You, you swine!' Mr Babbage addressed Mr Rune, who was now struggling into his trousers. 'You have betrayed me, sir. Betrayed my trust. You promised me an introduction to Her Majesty the Queen, God bless Her, to gain royal patronage for my Analytical Engine. You told me that my computer would change the world as we know it.'

'And it will, sir, it will.' Rune now sought his shirt.

'It was all a trick, so that you could defile my wife.'

'I assure you sir, it was not. Your inventions will change the world.'

'Not through any help of yours, you rogue. Out of my house. I never wish to see your face again.'

'No, I beseech you.' Rune was now in his coat and putting on his hat. 'Your inventions will change the world. Do not let this unfortunate and trifling incident deprive the world of your genius.'

'No more!' Mr Babbage waved his hands about. 'No more work upon calculating engines for me. This is all my fault, leaving my wife alone, whilst I worked upon my machines. My darling, please forgive me.'

'Oh,' said the fragrant Mary. 'Then consider yourself forgiven. But don't let it happen again.'

'No,' cried Rune. 'This must not be.'

'Out of my house, sir. I am done with science. It all ends here.'

'No,' cried Rune once more.

But Mr Babbage ushered him from the house, with no small force and many angry words.

The rain continued to fall and Hugo Rune now stood in it.

'Damned bad luck,' said a voice.

Rune turned to view a lad who lounged in the porch, a tall thin lad, dressed all in black with a blondy head of hair.

'And who are you?' Rune asked.

'Starling,' replied the lad. 'Will Starling.'

'Away about your business, boy.'

'But you are my business,' said the lad. 'Or *were*. You have failed, Mr Rune. Failed in your attempt to introduce Babbage to the Queen, to gain royal patronage for his inventions that would alter the Victorian age and advance it into a technological super future.'

'What?' went Rune.

'Ah, "what", is it? Just like my other self. I have come from the future. I arranged for Mr Babbage to return home early, to catch you doing what comes so naturally to you. You never could resist the ladies, could you, Rune? So simple a downfall. And now I say farewell to you. My work here is done.'

'Why have you done this?' Rune asked.

'You'll know that in forty-nine years, on the eve of the twentieth century. Will it seem like forty-nine years, or simply a second or two?'

And with that said, the blondy haired lad vanished away.

'No,' cried Hugo Rune. 'No and no and no.'

45

And 'No!' once more cried Hugo Rune in the sawdust ring of Count Otto's flying circus.

'But yes,' said Will's other self, all present once again.

'What has happened?' Will asked Rune. 'What did he do?'

'He returned to the past. He changed history. He stopped me from introducing Babbage to Her Majesty the Queen. He's effectively wiped out every piece of Victorian supertechnology as if it never existed.'

And all over London the lights were going out, the electric lights. And one by one the Tesla towers and each and every bit of technology that had come into being through the work of Charles Babbage vanished away and was gone. And then the lights of London returned, the gaslights of London, that is.

'Do something, Barry,' whispered Will.

'Take you home, chief? It's all I can offer you.'

'Take me back in time. Let me put this right.'

'No can do, chief, not in my remit. You know that.'

'Mr Rune,' Will whispered. 'Now would be the time for you to finally demonstrate your magic.'

'Yes,' said Rune. 'Indeed,' and he twiddled his thumbs.

Will's other self took the athame from Count Otto's hand, knelt over the Colonel and cried aloud, 'Great Satan, God of this world, accept the sacrifice and hearken to these words. The future is yours through me. I will be your power on Earth. The Loved One, adored by all. I will cast down every other church but yours. Hearken to these words, these perfected words. Accept the sacrifice and bring the love to me.'

And words spilled from the mouth of Count Otto Black. The words of the Great Spell, the Big Magic Spell, the spell that moulded time and space, the spell that had been brought to absolute perfection through computer technology. And the awful words jarred the air, sending terrible vibrations that rattled the teeth of the rich and famous and knocked the lady's straw hat off.

'Do something!' Will shouted at Rune. 'Employ your magic.'

'It's not quite as simple as that.' Rune's raiment flapped about him now, as an evil wind whipped up from nowhere, blizzarding the sawdust and bringing Rune's generously proportioned belly into startling relief.

'And die that I gain all!' The other Will drove down the athame.

Rune raised high his hands. The athame halted in midswing.

The other Will struggled to push it home but an unseen force held it back.

'Bravo,' said Will.

But a look of puzzlement was to be seen on the face of Hugo Rune. The other Will fought and struggled. Hideous words issued from the mouth of Count Otto Black. Pinch-faced women cowered and fretted. Tim all but vanished beneath his hair. Automata braced themselves against the growing force. The crowd, who'd had more than enough, took to mass panic and took to the exits, screaming and clawing and climbing one upon another.

And then a blinding golden light beamed down through the great glass dome. The blade of the athame, lit by the golden radiance, pressed closer to the chest of Colonel William Starling.

The words that poured from Count Otto Black's mouth, poured forth faster and faster: ancient words of power, the formulae of sorcerers and maguses and warlocks, brought to hideous reality.

The minute hand of Big Ben clunked to the hour of twelve.

And the golden light, the golden light.

'They come,' crowed Joseph Merrick, rising from beneath his seat and making a fist in the air with his one good hand. 'The strike force of the Martian invasion fleet. Right on schedule. Let's get a Mexican wave going.'

'*What?*' went Will, as well he might.

The blade of the athame struck the chest of Colonel William Starling.

'No!' shouted Will, as a maelstrom tore about him.

'Sorry,' came the voice of H.G. Wells, but faintly in the tearing and rending of elements. 'I tried to hold the knife back, but he was too strong.'

The blade pressed into the chest of Colonel Starling.

'No!' Will sprang forward, hurled himself at his other self.

'No!' cried Barry. 'No, chief, don't forget David Warner. You mustn't touch him, you mustn't.'

'No!' cried Will's other self, who had also seen *Time Cop*.

But Will threw himself forward. He knew what it meant for him; it meant certain death. And Will was young and had no wish to die. That it should end like this, so suddenly, after all he had been through, all he had seen and done and experienced, seemed nothing less than absurd. There should have been more, much more: the Lazlo Woodbine final rooftop confrontation, with the villain taking the big fall to oblivion and Will surviving as the hero. And although *this* wasn't original, it would have done for Will.

But it wasn't to be. There would be no eleventh hour reprieve, no twist in the tail, not even a *deus ex machina* ending, with God stepping in and putting the whole thing right. There would be only this. It would end here and end now, with Will and his other self, the meeting of matter and anti-matter, of Will and Anti-Will.

It is a fact well known to those who know it well, although how they know it well remains unclear, that at the very moment of your death, your entire life flashes right before your eyes: like a movie, like a biopic, the director's cut. And as Will plunged forward, he viewed it, as from a plush comfy seat in a private screening cinema.

He saw himself as a child and a youth: the thin lad amongst the fat, the freak, the outsider, like Master Scribbens and Mr Merrick and Mr H.G. Wells. Alone, no matter in whose company he was.

And he saw himself in his orange-walled housing unit in the Brentford sky tower of the twenty-third century, breakfasting with his parents. And at the Tate, discovering the wristwatch on *The Fairy Feller's Masterstroke*. And being attacked by the robots from the past. And travelling into this past, this hidden past with its countless marvels.

And he saw his meeting with Hugo Rune, and the year that he and Rune had spent together wandering over the Victorian world, the sights he had seen in foreign parts and the folk he had met: the Dalai Lama, the Tsar of Russia, the Mandarin and the Pope. And Will knew now why Hugo Rune had taken him upon these travels. Rune had known that Will's time was short. That he was doomed to die, now, at this very moment. Rune had wished to show Will all he could, allowing him to experience all he could, to taste the finest foods and drink the finest wines and stay at the finest hotels there were, and yes, to have had the finest sex also, with many exotic women, in many exotic parts. Which indeed Will *had* done, although he hadn't mentioned it to Tim, because he hadn't wanted Tim to be jealous.

And Will relived his meeting with Sherlock Holmes and with Barry, the time-travelling Holy Guardian sprout, and Joseph Merrick and Will's other self. And he remembered how he had returned to the future and told of his adventures to Tim and brought Tim back to this age; and the courtroom siege and the moonship disaster at Crystal Palace, and all that had led him to this moment, this moment when he would die.

All of this as seen by Will and re-experienced: the wonder, the excitement, the laughter and the pleasure. And there was a sense of satisfaction here, of closure.

He had lived a life, which though short, had been filled with adventure, fantastic adventure, with risk and adventure, with all that he had ever really truly wanted, and if it was to end here and end now, then so be it. Perhaps it wasn't so bad. Perhaps, indeed, this was how it should be, how it was meant to be.

And as Big Ben chimed in the dawn of the twentieth century, Will fell upon his other self. Fell *into* his other self. Matter, anti-matter, Will and Anti-Will. The two merged into one, became one and the same. Which cannot be, because it buggers time and space and sets the cosmic cats amongst the pigeons.

And there was a mighty flash and a mighty crash bang wallop, and the flying circus of Count Otto Black, that evil magical, grown-in-the-future, organic interdimensional transperambulist of pseudo-cosmic tomfoolery which had mostly been Larry's idea, because it really did seem to Larry to have been a good idea at the time, erupted with a force that was nothing less than nuclear.

This force blazed upwards into the midnight sky, engulfing the Martian invasion fleet, much to the surprise and disgust of the captains, crews and onboard troops, who'd been really looking forward to invading planet Earth and getting into all the mass-slaughtering, raping and pillaging that generally went along with interplanetary invasion.

And the force blazed upwards and outwards and onwards, bending space and bending time. And as bath water goes down the plughole, either clockwise or anti-clockwise, depending which hemisphere you're in, the flying circus, the Will and Anti-Will, and the Martian invasion fleet were sucked into a hole in the sky, to vanish, with a pop.

46

'Did you see *that*?' asked Queen Victoria. 'Over there, in the Whitechapel area, above the rooftops? A big bright flash followed by a tiny pop?'

'Probably just fireworks, ma'am.' A courtier bowed his head low. 'And if your Majesty would be so inclined as to wave her handkerchief over balcony, the Centennial fireworks display will begin.'

'Indeed.' Her Majesty fluttered her hankie.

'Gawd bless you, ma'am,' said the courtier.

And down upon the palace lawns, a pyrotechnician lit the blue touch paper and the firework display began.

It was a marvellous firework display and it was greatly enjoyed by the crowds that filled the Mall and waved their Union flags before the Palace gates.

'A new century,' said a lady in a straw hat as a ragamuffin called Winston deftly relieved her of her purse. 'Who knows what wonders it will bring.'

'Electrical lighting,' said The Man in the Street, as Winston's brother, Elvis, deftly relieved him of his clockwork pocket watch. 'And something called the internal combustion engine, which I am told will supersede horse-drawn transportation.'

'Electrical lighting?' The lady in the straw hat laughed. 'That's just a music-hall trick. And nothing will ever supersede the horse. You'll be telling me next that man will be able to fly.' Winston's other brother, Kylie, deftly relieved the lady of her false teeth.

'Fly?' said The Man in the Street. 'I wouldn't go that far. And I think you're right about the horses. But it's my opinion that by the year of nineteen twenty, every street and thoroughfare of this country will be nose to tail with horse-drawn vehicles and London will be thirty-five feet deep in horse manure.'

'Now *that* makes sense,' said the lady, although she lisped somewhat as she said it, due to the lack of her teeth. 'That would be an accurate prediction for the future.'

And fireworks blossomed in the twentieth-century sky.

And Queen Victoria went inside and had a cup of tea.

47

On the first of January, in the year two thousand two hundred, Mrs Starling of number seven Mafeking Avenue, Brentford, gave birth. She gave birth to twin boys and named them William and Timothy. They were not born into the dystopian future of the sky towers and acid rains that our Will had been born to. Nor were they born into the utopian super future that Will's other self had grown up in as the Promised One. Nor indeed any twist or permutation of these two.

William and Timothy were born into *our* future, the future that will be what *we* make it to be, and a future which, if the past and the present are anything to go by, won't be all *that* bad.

It won't be all that good either, of course.

But it won't be all that bad.

It will be somewhere in the middle.

It will just be the future.

Our future, which won't be so bad, will it?

And that, of course, should be that: the end of our tale, and as near to a 'happy ever after' as it's possible to be.

If it wasn't just for a few loose ends.

Five loose ends, in fact, which probably means that it isn't the end, but only the beginning of a great deal more.

And then some.